Isle of Winds

Book One of The Changeling Series

James Fahy

First published by Venture Press, an imprint of Endeavour Press Ltd in 2015.

For Becca

Table of Contents

Prologue – Trouble and Strife

The girl raced through the forest, tumbling through deep drifts of autumn leaves. Moonlight washed down from the starry sky, illuminating her darting figure.

In appearance she was eleven years old. A hunted creature. To judge from her odd clothing of ragged pants, a dirty t-shirt, and a large overcoat patched together from various animal skins, she seemed a homeless orphan. A helpless, young waif.

This, she was not.

Her breath came in gasps as she ran. Her tumbling mass of knotted brown hair snagged on branches, but her eyes were filled not with fear, only fierce determination.

They were also a rather unlikely shade of gold.

Crashes and growls in the surrounding trees told her all she needed to know about her pursuers. They were getting closer. They were much faster than her – they had more legs for a start.

Somewhere in the darkness, a hulking shadow smashed its way through bushes, throwing off clouds of leaves. Four more followed.

The running girl hardly made a sound.

She threw herself down a deep slope, skittering through scree and leaves, her keen eyes scanning the midnight shadows.

If she could make it up the other side, she would be out of the trees. Beyond the rise there was a village. They wouldn't follow her there. They didn't like bright lights.

She stumbled against a tree in the darkness, slapping her hands against it for support. She still had time.

There was a noise behind her.

She whirled, a flurry of animal skins and panic.

Behind her, at the top of the rise, several dark shapes stood beneath the trees. Their outlines indistinct, as though formed of shadow and smoke. She could smell the sweat in their fur, but they were not panting.

She didn't have time after all.

A figure walked calmly from between the beasts. An old man, tall and slender. He was dressed in a rather old-fashioned suit and a long black tailcoat. His face was thin, lined and white as chalk, seeming to float in the darkness like a will o' the wisp. His slick and oiled hair, as immaculately groomed as his clothing, was an unlikely shade of funhouse green. He showed not the slightest sign of having rushed, despite the fact that he had been pursuing her for much of the night.

"Well," he said, his voice as crisp as the cut of his suit. He looked down the slope with cool, calm appraisal.

"Well," the girl said in return, still leaning on the tree, trying not to pant from exhaustion.

The man laid a pale spidery hand on the head of one of the beasts. It made a long guttural growl of pleasure.

"You have led us a merry chase, haven't you?" he called down to her.

"Wouldn't call it merry," the girl replied.

"You know the game is up of course, don't you?" the man said. "I think it is probably a very brave thing you were trying to do, trying to be the first to find him."

"You haven't got a clue what I was trying to do," the girl said. Her voice, strident in her mind, sounded small and annoyingly quavering. She stopped talking and settled for sticking her chin out defiantly instead.

The man on the hill was unmoved. He stared at her with cold eyes. "Oh, I think I have," he said crisply. "I think I have many clues. And I think we both know that you would never have gotten as far as Macclesfield, the way you've torn through. Honestly." He shook his head disapprovingly. "If you had the foresight to come through Janus, the proper way, you could have been much closer. You could have been on the moors by now had you come through at Todmorden. There's a Janus Station there."

The girl snorted. "As if you haven't been watching the stations," she said. "You and your skrikers would have been waiting for me."

The shadowy creatures raised their massive heads at the sound of their name. The ghoulish man on the hill made a soothing gesture toward them.

"Down, Spitak – down, Siaw," he said quietly.

"Enough talk, little one," the man said. "Where is it?"

The girl smirked a little, despite the danger. *He mustn't know. If he was asking, he hadn't guessed.*

"Where is the key?" he said sharply. "Where is the Scion? Tell me now and I may spare your life."

"It's not yours to spare," the girl replied. "We both know Lady Eris is keeping you on strict orders, Mr Strife. Do you really think she'll be happy if you bring me back in pieces?"

"My Lady Eris has not specified the conditions of your return," Mr Strife replied, without the barest hint of a smile on his thin white lips. The cool breeze toyed with his green hair.

"Well..." said the girl. That certainly changed things. "I don't have the key, and neither does the Scion. He doesn't even know it exists yet, so if you kill me he'll never know, and he'll never find it. And you can never take it from him."

Mr Strife's lip curled. His teeth were very straight and white.

She tried to calculate her chances of getting up the hill behind her in one piece. If she could find a quiet spot, a place to tear through, she would be fine. She didn't need a Janus Station. Everyone else did, but she wasn't everyone else. The skrikers were on edge though, waiting for an excuse to pounce. She would have to try and tear through right here. Her fingers gripped the bark of the tree against which she leaned, testing it.

"He will find the key, as has been foretold. He will learn how to wield it and the Lady Eris shall have the use of it."

"No offence," the girl called up. "But if you were him, would *you* trust *you*?"

"Appearances are deceptive, child," Mr Strife said quietly. "He may be relieved to find us guiding him rather than you."

"Let's let him decide, eh? How about that?"

Mr Strife then did something he rarely did. He smiled, like a shark in dark water.

"Oh, I think not," he said.

With a gesture, he turned away and walked back into the trees, leaving her alone with the beasts. On cue, the skrikers descended, charging down the wooded slope. They were nothing more than muscular shadows, almost impossible to pick out in the darkness.

She stared wide-eyed for a second, and screamed a little for good effect. Or, at least, this is what she convinced herself of later. Then she tensed, and, seconds before the skrikers fell upon her, tore through.

There was a wobble in the world.

Had anyone been there to witness the moment, they would have seen something quite impossible. The girl simply sank into the tree. She fell into it as though it were murky water. The bark rippled a little, and then became solid once more, innocently challenging anyone to suggest it had ever been otherwise.

The skrikers collided with the trunk, their teeth clashing off the bole, but it was no use. The child had gone, far beyond their reach … for now.

Eventually they gave up and returned to their master, who was sitting some way off on a damp fallen log. He was looking intently at a large old-fashioned pocket watch. The dial had a large red gemstone which glittered like a droplet of blood.

They slunk up to him, as meekly as possible for a pack of large vicious beasts. One of them made a hesitant rumbling growl.

"It is done?" Mr Strife asked, his voice efficient and clean.

Another low growl.

"I see," said Mr Strife, narrowing his eyes.

He sat quite still for a time. Then, abruptly, he snapped his pocket watch closed and stood, brushing dry leaves smartly from his coat tails.

"My Lady Eris will not be happy to hear about this," he said calmly. He glanced at the assembled creatures. "Follow her scent," he told them. "She cannot have gone far. Tearing is a trick indeed, but you can't stay gone for long. She'll turn up."

He began to walk away, into the deeper shadows of the forest. "When she does, follow her. Let her find him. Once we know where he is, who he is, we can dispose of her and take matters into our own hands."

Another growl, the lowest yet, issued from one of the skrikers.

"Well, try looking like 'dogs' then," Mr Strife said, impatiently. "Must I think of everything? Of course it would not do to let yourselves be seen. What a question!"

There was a shiver in the forest clearing and where there had been five hellish abominations were now five large black dogs. They ran off into the trees, each in a different direction. After a few moments, when he could no longer hear them, Mr Strife sighed. One simply could not get the help these days. After all, she was just a poor girl, alone in a forest, seven miles from Macclesfield. Any number of terrible things could happen to her.

Mr Strife made a mental note to ensure that they did.

A moment later, he too was just another shadow in the dark wood.

Chapter One – Nails and Horseshoes

It had been a very strange month for Robin. But then on reflection, he'd had a very strange life altogether.

Living with Gran had never been what could be called normal. She had some very strange habits and traditions. She liked line dancing for one, which Robin secretly felt was not a suitable pastime for a lady with a blue rinse.

She also insisted on going, every evening, around their bungalow and checking that every window and door was securely locked. Robin would be the first to admit that this in itself was not particularly unusual in little old ladies, but Gran did this three times in succession, without fail. She took care to go on her security rounds clockwise, or 'deosil' as she called it. Robin had looked this habit up on the internet, mildly worried that Gran may be short of a few marbles. Apparently it was called an 'obsessive compulsive disorder' and was reassuringly common. Quite a lot of celebrities had it.

Gran also has an astonishing array of the most inventive curses. "By the breath of the Fates!" … "Snakes and ashes!" … "Neptune's beard!" Robin had gotten used to it over the years.

The bungalow where Robin had lived all his life with his odd Gran was normal. A nice normal bungalow in Manchester. Normal that is, except for two things. Firstly, Gran had hammered nineteen nails into the front step so that you either had to step over it altogether or suffer every morning while forgetfully fetching the milk in. Secondly, she had ensured that every doorway in the house had a horseshoe hanging over it. Every window too.

Most people simply thought that Gran collected horseshoes, in the way that old ladies collect porcelain cats, fluffy toilet roll covers, or holiday-themed tea towels. But Robin knew better. It wasn't just above every door and every window. There were horseshoes on all the cupboard doors in the kitchen as well, on the tiny hatch for the loft in the slanted roof, above the cat flap in the back door. Pretty much everywhere in the house that led from one place to another. Some of them were large and heavy, some were small and delicate. Many of them were merely horseshoe shapes in careful silver paint. But they were everywhere.

She was perfectly normal in every other way. She liked soap operas and strange biscuits like everyone else's Gran. She went to bingo on a Wednesday evening, and Robin went shopping with her every other week. She kept packets of crisps in the fridge, and occasionally bought cat food, though she hadn't owned a cat since Robin was three years old. *Everyone has their funny little ways*, Robin thought. In comparison, he himself felt boringly normal. There was nothing remotely odd about him.

His strange but familiar little life had gotten stranger in the last month. It had all started, if he wanted to put his finger on a moment in time, the night when Gran had died.

Robin had known she was dead. He had known the exact moment, even though he hadn't been with her at the time. It had been 7:15 on a Monday evening. He had been sitting at home alone, eating spaghetti hoops on toast for tea balanced on a cushion on his lap while he watched TV. A skinny, rather pale boy with unruly blonde hair and dark blue eyes. Gran had been at a line dancing lesson at the Over Sixties Social Club two streets over, same as every Monday. He didn't mind being left alone in the bungalow. He was twelve now after all, not a little kid anymore and their neighbour, Mr Burrows, was only next door.

Robin had known the exact second Gran had died, because at 7:15pm every horseshoe in the entire house tumbled from its mooring. They clattered down from the walls, clanking on the carpets and the linoleum in the kitchen. Spinning on the windowsills and banging against the radiators. The one which hung from the bathroom window landed in the bath, where it spun like a large coin for several seconds, making a terrible din. They fell from loose nails and bounced along the hall. Even the magnetic ones on the fridge had tumbled with a clatter to the floor, pinging off the empty cat dish.

The silver-painted, plaster-cast one Gran had brought back from a week in Cyprus, which hung above the fire in pride of place, had cracked into three and fallen down in pieces, scattering on the carpet.

Robin had sat motionless and wide-eyed, a trembling forkful of spaghetti hoops halfway to his mouth, as the brief but deafening cacophony subsided.

The bungalow had fallen utterly silent. Even the TV had muted itself, though Robin hadn't touched the remote. It was so quiet he could hear the soft hum of the fridge. Then he had heard a faint musical jingle, like breaking icicles, at the front door.

His heart pounding, he had put aside his dinner and picked his way along the hall, stepping over the many scattered horseshoes that lay everywhere, and nervously had opened the front door.

There had been no one there. The dark street was deserted. In the distance a dog barked. He had looked down and found the source of the tinkling noise. The nails that had been driven into the front step years ago had been pulled out and each one broken in half.

Robin had stared at them for a while, unsure what to think. Then he had gone back inside and sat down, looking at the phone.

It rang after about ten minutes. He thought about not answering it, but whoever was calling was not giving up. He had eventually picked up, knowing what the police on the other end were going to tell him.

Gran had died. A sudden heart attack at the line dancing class, right in the middle of a Dolly Parton classic two-step.

* * *

In the week that followed, with so many different people rushing in and out of the bungalow, he hadn't had much time to think about the whole business. Little old ladies, friends of Gran, cooed over him and several of them assured him and each other that 'it was how she would have wanted to go.'

Robin had no other family. He had never known his parents. They had died when he was very young, on a safari in Africa. A glider plane had crashed and that had been that. Most of the people coming and going seemed not to know what to do with him. Their neighbour, the rangy old man called Mr Burrows, stayed at the house in the evenings, as everyone agreed a twelve year old boy, no matter how sensible and responsible, could not be alone by himself. Social Services had been to speak with him, a very kind-faced and patient woman whose name he couldn't remember. She had reassured him that they were making investigations as to what would happen to him. *No*, he had told her, *Gran had never mentioned any other family as far as he knew*.

He wondered in a dazed kind of way if he was going to go to an orphanage. He had never been alone before. There were lots of people around him all the time while this was happening, but he realised slowly, none of them were his people. He was alone in the world now.

On the day of the funeral it had rained so hard the cemetery had been waterlogged and Robin, who had fully expected to cry, instead spent most of the graveside ceremony worrying about getting mud on his trousers. He thought that would make Gran very angry if she'd seen. She'd never gone to church but had always dressed well on Sunday.

It was only afterwards, when everyone had gone and Mr Burrows had popped home, that Robin had five minutes alone to lock himself in the bathroom and pull himself together. He got through half a toilet roll, but was dry-eyed and waiting in the lounge when Mr Burrow returned.

The oddness with the horseshoes was forgotten.

* * *

A month later, Robin found himself sitting on a train, with a large suitcase in the rack above his head containing everything he owned, and a letter in his pocket from somebody he had never heard of.

The train rushed through some very pretty countryside. Robin had never really been out of the city much. The countryside, as far as he was concerned, was something that happened to other people. He sat in the softly rocking carriage, listening to the clackety-clack of the train and watching the hills and fields of Lancashire roll by.

He was on his way to a village called Barrowood, somewhere in the middle of nowhere, to meet a woman called Irene who shared his surname, and was apparently his only surviving relative.

He had never heard of her. He had never heard of Barrowood for that matter.

Every time the train pulled into a new station, he strained to see the name. There hadn't been one called Barrowood yet.

He was so intent on finding the right station that when the door to the carriage was suddenly thrown open, he practically jumped out of his skin.

He turned wide-eyed, to see who had entered. It was a small skinny girl with a tangle of long brown hair and a very pale face. She was wearing a large tatty brown coat which was much too big for her and looked like it had been pieced together from bits of other coats. She was about his age, maybe a little younger.

Robin looked at the girl, who stood staring at him with wide and oddly triumphant eyes.

When it became apparent that she was neither going to move or speak, he thought he had better say something.

"Erm…" he began.

She blinked at the noise, as though startled by the scrawny boy's ability to make noises as well as move.

"Erm…" he said again.

"Is this seat taken?" she asked suddenly.

"This seat?" Robin asked, nodding at the seat opposite him, which was clearly not.

"Yes. That one. The empty one there," the girl said eagerly.

They both looked at it.

"No. I don't think so," Robin said eventually. "No one's in here but me."

The girl smiled and slammed the compartment door behind her. She peered through the glass for a second, then pulled down the shade.

Robin was a bit alarmed by this. More so when the girl leaned across him to pull the tasteless orange curtain across the window and plonked herself down opposite him in the now shadowy carriage.

He stared at her in surprise.

"Do you have any idea how much trouble I've had trying to find you?" she started.

"Find me?" Robin replied, deeply confused.

"Well, I knew you were in Manchester, but obviously couldn't get anywhere near you with the wards in place, could I?" she said. "Had to hang around and wait for my chance. Not a very good idea when you've got skrikers on your tail, I can tell you. And then there was all that nasty business with your Grandmother and Mr Strife," she babbled. "There's nothing he won't sink to, that one." She patted his hand a little, making him flinch. "Sorry about your Gran. If we'd known what he was up to, we would have done something, but there was no one to watch you. There's only me who could tear through, and the skrikers have been keeping me on the move. They give a new meaning to the idea of hounding someone…"

"How do you know about my Gran?" Robin interrupted. It was the only thing she had said so far that had made the slightest bit of sense. The young girl completely ignored his question.

"Of course, once the wards were down, there was a right old rush to get at you. I'm surprised Strife wasn't there to jump in the window the minute it happened! You got out just in time, I don't mind telling you! Old Burro can only do so much after all. I don't think he could hold Janus for more than a month. But then no one knew where you'd gone. Off on a train with a suitcase? Who knew? I had to track you through the redcaps." She shuddered. "And they're never fun to deal with… And do you have any idea how difficult it is to tear through on a moving train? From a stationary point over there to a moving point over here?" She shuddered again. "Trust me, the physics involved are horrible."

Robin held up his hands in a desperate bid to stop her babbling. "Wait," he said. "Hold on a second…"

She stopped talking and blinked at him expectantly.

"Who are you? Did you … did you know my Gran?"

The girl seemed genuinely surprised by this. She opened and closed her mouth a few times, staring at him. He noticed that her eyes were a startling shade of gold. He had never seen anyone with eyes that colour before. Was she wearing contact lenses?

"Oh," she said eventually, as realisation dawned. "You don't know … who I am?"

Robin shook his head carefully.

"Your Grandmother never…" she trailed off, frowning with incredulity.

"What do you know about my Gran?" Robin asked. "Do you … I mean, did you know her?"

The girl shook her head absently. "Only by reputation," she muttered, lost in thought. She looked up, golden eyes gleaming. "Well," she said. "This certainly complicates things, doesn't it?"

Robin, who was of the opinion that the conversation was already complicated enough, looked back at the agitated girl helplessly. She had sunk back in the chair. Her small form almost drowned in the tatty coat. She glowered at him moodily, as though he was being difficult on purpose.

"My name's Robin," he said, hoping this might help.

"I know what your name is," the girl replied impatiently. "It's written all over you." She bit her lip in a thoughtful manner. "I was kind of counting on you being up to speed…"

"What's your name?" Robin asked, feeling as though the two of them were speaking different languages.

She looked at him suspiciously. "Can't you tell?"

"How would I tell? You haven't got a nametag on you, have you," he replied. She was beginning to annoy him.

She rolled her eyes. "Ah yes, now I remember. It's different for you lot, isn't it? You have to be told. Sorry, I forget how it works sometimes."

"Us lot?"

The girl held out her hand, very formally. "My name," she said, "… is Karya."

Robin shook her hand a little awkwardly. She had a firm grip. "Okay," he said. "Are you on the train with your parents?"

She dropped his hand unceremoniously. "My what?"

"Your parents?" Robin repeated. "You know, your Mum and Dad?"

"Oh, them…" Karya made a face. "No. I'm here on my own." She glanced at the compartment door with its covered window. "I hope," she added warily.

The train rumbled on for a few seconds. There was nothing but the clack-clack of the tracks and the gentle swaying of the carriage.

"Where are you going, Robin?" Karya asked eventually, seeming to come to some decision.

"Um … Barrowood," Robin replied. "Do you know it?"

"Parts of it," she replied.

"I'm going to meet this woman, she's called Irene. Apparently, she's my great aunt."

"Yes?" Karya pressed.

Robin shrugged. "I think I'm going to live with her," he said, without much enthusiasm. "It's all been arranged with Social Services, but no one really tells me much. It's all a bit mysterious."

"Irene," Karya said in a half whisper. "Well … that's a good move. Good old Burro. Wouldn't have expected her to be up for it…"

"What are you on about now?" Robin asked, frowning at her.

"At least you'll be safe there. She..." Karya noticed that Robin was staring at her in confusion and trailed off.

"Look," she said decisively. "I really can't stay and explain everything to you now. There isn't time. The longer I stay, the easier it is for the skrikers to pinpoint me. I thought things would be easier than this..."

She fumbled in the pocket of her coat.

"Here," she said, drawing out a long slim wooden box and thrusting it into his hands.

"What's this?" Robin asked, staring at it.

"It'll let you find me, later, when things have calmed down a bit. Put it away for now." She flapped her hands at him impatiently.

There was a noise outside the train. It resolved itself into what sounded like a long, mournful howl. It was loud and close by.

Robin stared at the curtained window. "What was that?" he said.

"I've run out of time." The girl jumped to her feet. "If I don't go now, they'll track me. If they find me, they'll find you. Then we're all in trouble."

"Who'll find you?" said Robin. His hand moved toward the curtain on the window.

"Don't open that!" the girl shouted.

Robin jumped. "Why not?"

"Leave it," she snapped.

The howl came again, closer still.

The girl was already at the door. "I have to go," she said. "Keep that safe, Robin. For Tartar's sake, put it away. And don't go talking to strangers."

Robin slipped the thin wooden case into his pocket. "What's that supposed to mean?" he asked. "You're a stranger."

Karya smirked in spite of herself, her golden eyes twinkling. "There are stranger strangers than me," she said. "See you soon, Scion."

She touched the wall of the train compartment.

There was a heavy thud at the window, and a dark shadow filled the small curtained square, blocking out the sunlight. The girl, almost lost in the deepening shadows, muttered something under her breath and seemed to tense.

Then the door to the carriage threw itself open.

Robin jumped and looked from Karya to the figure in the doorway.

"Tickets please," said the conductor. "Hey, it's dark in here!" he exclaimed. His eyes fell on Robin suspiciously. "What are you up to, lad?"

Robin looked back to Karya for help, only to find that she was gone. There was nobody else in the carriage with him. Robin stared dumbfounded at the patch of empty wall against which she had been stood. It seemed, for a split second, to be rippling.

"Hey, I'm talking to you," said the conductor. "You alright, son? You look a bit off."

"I'm fine," said Robin quietly. He looked back at the conductor, wondering if he were going mad.

"Well, if you're feeling sick, open the window," the man said. "It's stuffy in here. Do you no good sitting in the dark."

Robin opened the curtain, filling the carriage with innocent sunlight. There was nothing outside. No howling creature, no shadows. The sunny countryside flew by, as normal as could be.

"Just you in here is it?" said the conductor, reaching for Robin's ticket.

"Apparently," Robin replied absently.

"Eh?"

Robin remembered himself. "Yes," he said. "I mean, yes. Just me … Sorry."

The conductor clipped his ticket and gave him a funny look, as though he wasn't sure if Robin were trying to be cheeky.

"Where you off to then?" he asked.

"Barrowood," Robin replied.

"Nice little village." The conductor nodded as he made his way back out of the door. "Get your bags ready then," he called as the door closed. "It's the next stop."

Chapter Two – Mr Moros and Malcolm Drover

The tiny train station in the village of Barrowood was utterly deserted. Robin stood on the platform with his large battered suitcase beside him. Beyond the quaint stone train station, there was nothing but rising hills covered in a thick carpet of autumnal trees. He assumed that the village lay through the station proper, but for all he could see, he might have been in the middle of nowhere.

Robin pulled out the box the girl had given him. It had a sliding lid, like an old box of dominoes.

Checking first to make sure no one was around, and without really knowing why, Robin slid the lid back and peered inside. It seemed empty. He tilted it a little. Something clunked and fell into view. He pulled it out and frowned at it.

It was a flute, finely carved from a rich golden wood. Small and with only three holes for notes. Robin was sure that it wasn't called a flute. A penny whistle maybe, or a pipe. Whatever you called it, two facts remained: He had no idea what it was for, and he had no idea how to play it.

So for now, he called it a flute, put it back in the box and closed the lid.

His more immediate concern was that he had no idea what to do next. He pulled the crumpled letter from his pocket. It was written in a spidery but firm hand. He read it again for at least the hundredth time:

My Great-Nephew Robin,

It has been brought to my attention that your current housing situation has been somewhat disrupted by the sudden and inconvenient death of your Grandmother.

As your Grandmother made no provision whatsoever for your future in this event (from which I must assume she planned to live forever, a very unwise course indeed), it would appear that it falls to me to offer you sanctuary, so to speak.

No doubt you shall have many questions, as we have never before met and I have as many doubts as you do about the suitability of this arrangement, but we will have to get to these matters when you come to see me.

All has been arranged with the officials through my representatives. Papers have been signed, counter signed and exchanged (I don't presume to understand the bureaucracy of moving a child), and all being well, it will suit me to receive you on the first of September, which is in three weeks' time.

I am aware that boys of your age have schoolwork of some kind to attend to at this juncture in the year. I have secured a tutor for this purpose and lessons have been delayed until after your arrival while we see what is to be done with you.

In short, you are to come to live with me, at Erlking Hall in Barrowood. There is no argument to be brooked.

Please find enclosed with this letter your pre-paid train ticket. Mr Burrows, with whom I have been in contact, will see you onto the train and all of those bothersome details.

I shall expect you at eleven A.M sharp. Please be punctual, as tardiness is not a quality I appreciate, especially in a great-nephew.

Regards,
Ms Fellows

The letter was as weird as it was the first ninety-nine times he had read it. Mr Burrows had assured him that Great Aunt Irene seemed a good enough woman and was merely eccentric. Robin had looked the word up on the internet. It meant, as far as he could interpret, 'rich and senile'.

He did not find this reassuring. He was more surprised by the rich than the senile. Gran had had more than her fair share of oddities, but they had never had enough money to rub together. If Irene Fellows was rich then she had certainly never helped Gran out of a tight spot.

The letter, unfortunately, gave no hint as to how Robin was actually to get to Erlking Hall. He had assumed that she would meet him at the station. Adults were like that usually.

A noise at the station doorway made him look up, snapping him out of his thoughts.

There was a thin old man standing in the arch, leaning against the post with his arms folded casually across his dark suit. He was staring at Robin.

Robin thought the man's suit looked very old fashioned, like that of a Victorian undertaker. He was wearing a bowler hat. The hair underneath, however, was a most unusual shade of orange, not undertaker-ish at all.

"Oh … hello," Robin said, a little awkwardly. It seemed rude not to say something. People ignored each other at train stations in Manchester. It was tradition, unless they were trying to give you a free newspaper. But there were hundreds of people there. Here, there was just Robin and the staring undertaker.

The thin man didn't move. Nor did he reply. He continued to stare at him with bright and eager eyes.

"I didn't see you there," said Robin. "Um…"

The man still did not respond. Robin wondered if he had heard him speak at all.

"Are you from around here?" Robin asked, slipping the letter back into his coat pocket. "I'm not … well, that is … I'm supposed to be meeting someone here, I think. It's absolutely freezing, isn't it? I have to get to Erlking Hall. Do you know it?"

The man with the orange hair ran a finger along the brim of his hat and stopped leaning against the doorpost. "Kind of, not particularly, and yes," he said, in a crisp clear voice.

"I'm sorry?" Robin frowned.

The man stepped away from the door and strolled towards him in neat measured strides.

"There's no need to apologise," he said. "Your questions. Firstly, I am kind of from around here. Secondly, yes, in a manner of speaking, it is freezing. I myself can personally attest to witnessing several instances of frost on bushes, grass and the like on my way here. And thirdly, yes, I am familiar with Erlking Hall, though I have never had the pleasure of visiting." His voice was very eager.

The tall man leaned down and quickly stuck out a hand, making Robin flinch.

"Mr Moros," he announced, rolling the R. "At your service, young man."

Robin, who was fighting the urge to back away, shook hands instead. The man's hand was ridiculously cold, much colder than the chilly air could account for.

"And what, I find myself wondering, for I am, I admit, an unquenchably curious fellow, is such a fine young man as yourself doing in Barrowood?"

"Well…" Robin began, slightly disturbed that the odd man had not yet released his hand.

"Might I know your name, boy?" the man pressed, leaning in over him. "Names tell us so much, don't they? They can indeed reveal a person's true face, one might say."

Robin opened his mouth to speak, but was cut off by another voice from the station door.

"Boy!" the voice roared, as though Robin were in danger of falling in front of a train.

Robin and Mr Moros both jumped at the sound. A very stout and red-cheeked man was hurrying across the platform. He was wrapped in a large coat, scarf and gloves and looked as though he had been hurrying for quite some time. Great gusts of breath went before him in the chilly air, giving him the appearance of a charging, blustering rhino.

"Boy!" the man cried again, with booming theatrical drama.

Mr Moros released Robin's hand suddenly, dropping it as though it was a hot iron. Robin felt inexplicably relieved by this.

The hurrying man closed in on the two. Mr Moros stepped back smoothly out of his path. The two men exchanged a look that Robin could not decipher. The fat red-faced man slowed to a blustering halt in front of them, and looked from one to the other.

"You, boy," he said to Robin, gasping for breath. "Bound for Erlking?"

Robin nodded. He offered his letter by way of confirmation. The man ignored it.

"I'm late," he said loudly. "I'm never late, but today I'm late." He took off the battered flat cap he was wearing, revealing a balding head, and fanned himself angrily with it to cool down.

"I was supposed to be here. To pick you up," he explained. "Miss Fellows, you see? She said eleven sharp. Eleven, she says. And I keep an eye on the clock and one minute it's ten and the next time I look, it's eleven fifteen! Like the time had gone, totally gone, in a second." He shook his head in astonishment. "But I'm here now." He seemed to calm down a little, blowing air out of his cheeks. Robin wished he would stop shouting. "Takes more than clock tricks to keep me off the task, I'll tell you that for nothing." He glanced at Mr Moros again, who stood quite still, saying nothing, looking at the flustered little man coolly.

"My name is Drover," the man said to Robin. "I work for Miss Fellows, look after the place for her, me and my lad, Henry. You'll like him. He's about your age." He grabbed Robin's hand and pumped it with both of his in a warm handshake that nearly dislocated the boy's shoulder.

"I'm—" Robin began, but the man cut in. "Oh, no time for that, no time. We're late as it is and had better get moving. If there's one thing your Great Aunt doesn't like, it's lateness. I should know." He reached past Robin, picking up the boy's case in one hand.

Mr Moros suddenly laid an icy hand on Robin's shoulder. "Excuse me, good sir," he said, finally speaking. "We were barely introduced. This young man was kind enough to pass the time of day with me, most polite you know."

"Is that so?" said Mr Drover, quite rudely, Robin thought.

"It is," replied Mr Moros smoothly, still clamping Robin's shoulder. He could feel a chill seeping through his coat. "It is indeed … so. However, due to your most entertaining and lively entrance, I was unfortunate enough not to catch his name, though he of course has mine."

Robin opened his mouth to speak, but Mr Drover cut in again.

"Catch a name?" he said. "Whoever heard of such a thing?" He laughed gruffly and began to turn away, suitcase in hand. "Come along, boy. Time flies, as I've already noticed once today."

Mr Moros' fingers dug tighter into Robin's shoulder. The boy looked up at him, now quite sure that of the two men, he would rather cast his lot with the short noisy one. Mr Moros' face was very calm and very serious. He was no longer smiling.

"I have a claim here," he said quietly to Mr Drover.

The red-faced man stopped and turned. He looked from Mr Moros to Robin and back again. His eyes were suddenly wary.

"You have no claim here, sir," he replied darkly.

As if suddenly remembering something, he dropped the suitcase and reached into his coat pocket. After a moment's fumbling with his thick gloves he pulled something out and approached Robin. The object in his hand glittered, catching the light.

"Hah!" he said, suddenly loud and cheerful again. "Almost forgot! Never late, but always forgetful." He slipped something over Robin's head. "A welcome gift from your Great Aunt," he proclaimed. "She said I was to give it to you straight away and see you wore it!"

Mr Moros' hand suddenly released his shoulder. It practically flew off him. The white-skinned man hissed, as though he had cut himself on paper.

Robin looked down. Mr Drover had just slipped a slim silver chain around his neck. The centrepiece, to Robin's surprise, was a tiny silver horseshoe.

"A necklace?" he asked, trying not to sound ungrateful. It was more than a bit girly.

Mr Moros took several steps backward and stopped, staring at the two.

Drover waggled his eyebrows, evidently noticing Robin's opinion of the jewellery. "I know, I know," he said. "Well, what do old women know about boys, eh? Best just tuck it in under your shirt? Don't want to hurt her feelings. Keep it on, at least till we get to Erlking."

"Right, no, it's … lovely," Robin lied politely.

"Come on, come on," Mr Drover said good-naturedly. "Best be getting off. No doubt you'll be wanting to see your new home, eh? Get settled in?"

Robin looked back over his shoulder. Mr Moros was standing with his arms folded, as still as a thin white statue, watching them go and looking rather sour.

"Bye," Robin called back, feeling it would be rude not to.

"Until we meet again," the man replied in a smooth clear voice. He touched the brim of his hat in a gentlemanly way, though he did not smile.

Mr Drover didn't look back at all. He hurried Robin along, bristling slightly at the sound of the other man's voice.

On the other side of Barrowood's train station, he bundled Robin into an ancient car. "Careful who you talk to, son," he said. "It's not just your big cities full of dangerous folk, you know." He climbed in and started the engine.

That was the second time that day he had been given that same advice, but Robin didn't say anything. He glanced back at the station as the car pulled away, but from what he could see the platform was now empty.

"You don't want to go throwing your name about to just anyone," Drover continued, though his voice was good-natured. "Did you have a good trip up?"

"Yes," Robin replied, watching the wooded hills and fields pass by as they drove out of the village. He fiddled with the horseshoe charm through the fabric of his t-shirt, wondering vaguely if it was just a coincidence. "… Interesting anyway."

Chapter Three –The Locked Room At Erlking Hall

The village was tiny and they were soon out of it, driving through tiny country lanes. The car slowed as it approached a set of tall iron gates, each mounted by a strange type of gargoyle. Beyond, a long curving avenue climbed a steep slope. The tall trees lining the road were huge and gnarled, the branches interlocking above, making a sun-dappled tunnel of autumn leaves.

At the very top of the hill, the Hall itself.

It was huge.

Robin, who was used to living in a small bungalow, found it hard to believe that anyone could live alone in such a large house. It had four vast floors of leaded glass windows, a steep slate roof dotted with attic windows. An expanse of pedimented wings sprawled to the side. It even had a stubby tower. Columns flanked the dark double doors, in front of which Mr Drover's old car lurched to a halt, wheels crunching gravel.

"There she is, lad," Mr Drover said proprietarily. "Erlking Hall, in all her glory." He gave a gruff chuckle and climbed out of the car. Robin followed, peering up.

"Does all of this belong to Aunt Irene?" he wondered.

"Erlking belongs to itself. But your great aunt watches over, aye."

This had to be some kind of a joke. He couldn't really be coming to live in a stately home like this. Any minute now, Gran was going to jump out of a bush, crying "I got you! Snakes and ashes!", and they would go home again.

But of course, being dead, she didn't do that.

Robin felt bad then, about feeling excited about this place, and guilty as if it was his fault Gran had died, when secretly he knew Dolly Parton was to blame.

Mostly though, he just felt confused.

When he approached the doors though, confusion disappeared. *This is where you belong*, Erlking seemed to say. He shivered as the odd feeling washed over him.

"Well," said Drover, rubbing his hands together. "Let's get you inside, lad. Then, if nothing else, at least you'll be home."

The door knocker was an eagle's talon gripping an egg. Above the huge oak doors was a carved stone circle, where a man's cheerful face sat amidst swirling leaves.

Drover noticed Robin peering up at the sculpture as he looked for his keys.

"That there's the green man," he said, by way of explanation. "Oak king, nice fella."

"Okay," Robin replied, without understanding. "It's … weird."

Drover chuckled.

"Good though," Robin said hastily, in case he'd said the wrong thing. "Weird in a good way."

"Well, he's good enough I suppose, when the mood takes him," Drover shrugged, slotting a large key in the lock. "You wouldn't want to run into t'other one though. Holly king, he's a bugger."

Before Robin could question this, Drover opened the door and stood aside so he could enter. He pointed Robin through a set of double doors to the right.

"Best go in, lad. Don't keep a lady waiting." He patted Robin roughly on the shoulder. "I'll take your stuff up to your room for you. But don't you go getting used to it! I've a lot to do around here, and there's not enough polish in the world to make me into a butler." He laughed gruffly again and set off towards the stairs, lugging Robin's case.

"Thanks," Robin called after him. Then, taking a deep breath, he went through the doors to meet the only living person who claimed him as family.

Inside, there was a large open fireplace crackling away merrily, in front of which sat his Great Aunt Irene.

She didn't look anything like Gran. Gran had been tiny, in typical grandmother tradition. She'd had a tight barnet of curly blue-grey hair and had worn large, old-fashioned cardigans and questionable slippers.

The woman sitting before him was nothing like that. She was, in fact, almost the Anti-Gran.

"Well?" she said imperiously from the chair. "Are you coming in or not, child? Don't stand there in the door. Come in or go out. That's what doors are for."

Robin, feeling a little foolish, shut the door behind him.

Great Aunt Irene was tall and willow thin. She was wearing a long, old-fashioned dress in pale ivory and her silver hair was pulled back from her head in an elaborate bun. Everything about her seemed sharp. She had sharp cheekbones, sharp eyebrows, and her eyes were as sharp as glass. Even her voice cut through the air.

She raised her hands and beckoned him forward. "Well, come forward then and let me have a look at you. If I'm to have you living under my roof and in between my walls and over my floor I want to be able to recognise you."

"Hello, Aunt Irene," Robin said. "Nice to meet you." He had a speech half practised in his head, but it withered like a deflated balloon under her piercing glare.

Tiny dangling earrings glittered in the firelight as she turned her head this way and that. Dark silvery droplets which glittered as she looked him over. Robin thought she must have been very beautiful when she was younger.

"Just Irene will do," she said. "None of this 'Aunt' business, if you please. I have no time for honorifics and I don't wholly approve of familial relations. I have spent a great deal of energy ensuring I have never been a mother or a grandmother or a niece or a sister. I see no reason to start now, even if the Fates have decided it would amuse them to furnish me with a nephew at my time of life, great or not."

She stood gracefully. Her back was very straight. "I shall be Irene," she announced. "And you shall be Robin."

Robin couldn't tell if she was serious or trying to be funny. He settled for a kind of awkward half-smile and nodded. "Sounds good to me."

"Do you like your name?" she asked him in a very direct kind of way, peering at him over her spectacles.

"Um … I suppose. I've never really thought about it before. It's just my name."

She pursed her lips. "You could have another if you wish. Some people can't abide their names, and then they go through life complaining about it, and trying to convince others to call them by some or other tiresome nickname. It's most annoying. I say just change it and have done with it, or like what you've been given."

This made a kind of sense to Robin. He nodded in agreement.

She narrowed her eyes at him. "You are certain, then? There will be no 'Robby' in a few months, no 'Rob' or 'Bob' or 'Bobby?' I have neither time nor the inclination to go chasing a hatful of names all over this house. My duties keep me busier than you can imagine and young boys are notorious for having minds as whole as broken mirrors."

"No, really," Robin insisted, unable to suppress a smile. "Robin's good. I like Robin."

She peered at him a moment longer, and then smiled herself, ever so slightly. It was gone as soon as it had appeared.

"Good. Then we are of one mind and are well met, Robin."

He had the terrible fear that she was going to hug him then as old ladies are wont to do, but instead, she shook his hand firmly, her hand warm and dry.

She looked him over curiously. "Hmm, blonde hair, I see. Rather unkempt as well. Blue eyes, eh? Well that's something of a relief at least. Could be green, then you'd be a handful," she muttered dismissively.

She looked him up and down

"You are very thin, Robin," she said, rather challengingly.

"Sorry," said Robin. He didn't really know what else to say.

"Hmm," she said again. "Well, again … it could be worse. You don't have a tail, do you? No horns?"

Robin knew she was being silly now. He grinned lopsidedly. "No, not that I've noticed."

She peered at him with her cool blue eyes.

A moment of silence passed between them, while the old lady seemed to consider him on the whole. A small golden clock on the mantelpiece ticked loudly in the opulent room.

Eventually she seemed to reach some silent decision. She nodded, ever so slightly, as though reluctantly approving of him.

"Welcome to Erlking Hall," she said. "This is your home, for as long as you wish it. It is old and rambling and draughty, but then so am I, and the two of us go well together. You'll have to get used to my ways, Robin. I am too old and too stubborn to start changing now."

"I won't be any trouble," he insisted.

She raised an eyebrow, smiling her tiny smile again. "You are a twelve year old boy," she told him. "Trouble is your nature."

She waved a hand, dismissing her own comment. "And I am an old woman, and complaining is mine." She turned again in a swish of silks. "I think the best thing for you to do now is to find your room, which I believe Mr Drover should have made ready for you. Wash, unpack, find your feet, and then … we shall have lunch I think."

Robin thought this was a very good idea. He hadn't eaten all day.

She sat down again. "You'll find your room on the top floor, in the east wing, at the back of the house. You can't miss it. It's the tower room."

Robin's eyes widened.

"Don't panic," she said, catching his expression. "You're not nearly pretty enough to be Rapunzel, and there are stairs in and out."

Robin grinned and made for the door.

"Off with you. Be down here in an hour," she called after him. "And be punctual this time."

Robin got as far as the doors to the hallway before he remembered. He turned and looked back at his Great-Aunt. "Oh, thank you for the chain. The lucky charm," he said.

She nodded at him from the fireplace. "You don't have to wear it now. It's a hideous old thing. Pop it in a drawer or something."

"No … I think it's really nice," Robin lied politely.

Irene raised one eyebrow again. "Then you have terrible taste," she remarked. "Do what you will with it, it's served its purpose now. You don't need it in here."

Robin was halfway up the stairs before he even wondered why she thought he needed it outside.

* * *

Robin had a hard time finding his room. The house seemed somehow larger on the inside. There were corridors and stairs. And then more corridors with doors leading onto seemingly countless rooms filled with old furniture and books. There were statues of continental marble people wearing next to nothing and looking very unhappy about the British weather. Robin found a room with a dusty grand piano which looked as though it had never been played. Other rooms were completely empty with nothing but bare floorboards and sunny windows, where a faint smell of turpentine hung in the air. He found another room with a large harp and a lot of ancient-looking sofas. Next, a chamber large enough to hold a ball in. And of course there were rooms with beds, quite a few of these, but none of them seemed to be in a tower.

Robin was lost in an endless labyrinth of corridors. Some had windows, or little steps up and down. Some with rugs and runners, some without. There were busts of old emperors and statues of strange figures everywhere. Paintings adorned the walls, as well as tapestries and clocks of every size and shape.

Consequently, it was quite some time later that Robin finally arrived at a door on the third floor near the back of the house which opened onto a tight spiral stone staircase.

This at last seemed promising. At the top of the curling stairwell lay a good sized circular room, with a high-peaked roof and windows set in four places around the wall at the compass points.

This was definitely the tower. The room was sparsely furnished. A large king-sized bed, covered in many white sheets, an ottoman of dark oak, an old-fashioned writing bureau and a huge looming wardrobe, all in dark wood. His battered old suitcase was laid at the foot of the bed.

Robin crossed quickly to the wardrobe and opened it. Things had been so odd lately it wouldn't have surprised him to have seen a lamppost lurking behind fur coats. He threw his own coat inside and opened all the windows, peering out in every direction at the rolling green landscape.

He was above the roofs here in the tower and the views were excellent. Behind the house, the land sloped off, disappearing into dense forest. There was a faint twinkle amongst the trees, sunlight on water.

He was hanging out of the window, enjoying the cold air on his face, when he heard a noise behind him.

He pulled his head back in and looked around.

There was a scruffy-looking boy leaning in the doorframe. He was taller than Robin and looked a little older, with longish messy brown hair that looked as though it would defy any attempts to comb it. He was smiling in a friendly way and wearing old jeans and a brown jumper. It was possibly the most unremarkable sight Robin had seen all day.

"Hello," Robin said.

"Alright?" the boy replied in greeting, coming into the room. "Robin, is it?"

"Yeah," said Robin.

"I'm Henry," the boy said amiably. He sat on Robin's bed, which squeaked alarmingly, running his fingers through his unruly hair. "My dad said you were coming today. He picked you up from the train station in our rubbish old banger, didn't he?" He was looking around the room with unashamed curiosity. "I've never been in here before. Been nearly everywhere else in Erlking. Always figured Irene must keep all her dead husbands up here or something like that."

Robin suddenly realised who this was. "You're Mr Drover's son, aren't you?"

Henry nodded. "Yep. My dad looks after the place. We live down in the village." He grinned lopsidedly. "We're hardly ever there really. We're up here more." He smiled. "Big place, don't you know. Takes a lot of looking after. Do you play football?"

Robin shook his head. "No, not really. I'm pretty rubbish at sports to be honest. Do you go to school in the village?"

Henry nodded. "Yeah, more's the pity. Are you going to be coming? It's rubbish. Tiny too. We got a pool put in last year though, finally. It smells like feet. You're from Manchester, aren't you? Is it good living in a big city?"

Robin shrugged. "It's alright," he replied. "Living in the city, I mean. That is … it was alright. Busy, noisy, you know."

Henry looked a little uncomfortable. "I feel like a country mouse." He seemed to remember something and suddenly looked a little awkward. "Oh, sorry. I heard about your Gran from Dad. That must have been awful. You know, what happened to her. Bad business." He swung his legs, banging his heels against the bedpost.

Robin didn't really want to talk about it. Especially with someone he'd only just met. "Yeah," he said bluntly, effectively cutting off that line of conversation. Silence hung between the two boys for a moment.

"But you'll like it here," Henry brightened up. "Erlking's great, I wish I lived here. I mean, I'm here all the time, like I said, but it's not the same is it?" He lowered his voice to a whisper. "Though I reckon someone should give you the heads up. Irene's a nutter. Totally off her rocker."

Robin laughed. "I just met her," he said. "She is a bit … weird I suppose."

Henry grinned. "She's not weird, lad, she's a nutter, I'm telling you. A proper, howl at the moon type, if you know what I mean." He pushed himself up off the bed. "One time, right, my dad broke a statue. One of those little ones that's just head and shoulders, and she chased him clean out of the house with a fireside poker. You'd never know she could move so fast on those old lady pins, but she was off like a crack. She's a wild one, no mistake."

Robin laughed again, though he found this hard to believe.

"It's true," the other boy grinned.

Henry ambled over to Robin. He leaned out of the window next to him, peering down at the treetops beyond the grounds. He was a good head taller than Robin. "She's a good enough one though," he conceded gracefully. "A straight arrow … if you don't mind her temper."

"My Gran was a nutter too," said Robin affectionately. "So I don't think it'll be a problem." He sighed a little. "It's a lot of change though. Feels weird not knowing anyone here."

Henry idly flicked a bit of dried bird poo off the windowsill. "Well, that's one problem solved already, isn't it? You know me."

His brow furrowed. "Are you sure you don't play football?"

Robin, who had never had the slightest interest in sport, shook his head. "Sorry, no."

Henry looked a little disappointed.

"I can show you how rubbish I am, if you want."

They spend the remainder of the hour kicked a ball around outside, feeling oddly as though they'd known each other forever.

* * *

At lunch, which was taken at a ridiculously long table in a grand dining room, Great Aunt Irene didn't display any signs of being 'off her nut'. She seemed, in fact, to be quite on it, asking Robin all manner of normal and polite questions. Mr Drover and Henry had joined them for lunch. The four of them sat up at one end of the table, sharing a mix of pancakes and scones with jam and cream.

She had announced that their first meal together should not be a time for discussing all those troublesome things that no doubt they would need to discuss eventually. They would have a proper talk later, just the two of them. For now, they were to eat, as she had read somewhere that boys have to eat at least every two hours or they die. Mr Drover had found this very funny. After lunch, Robin would be put under the charge of young Henry, who could show him around and make sure he knew all the places not to go and the things not to mess with. This would save time later, she reasoned, when he was looking for trouble.

Henry grinned at this, under Great Aunt Irene's raised eyebrows, but he had the good sense to look slightly abashed as well.

The boys wandered through the house. Henry showed Robin around proudly. He showed him how the planesphere worked, a large brass model of the universe in a first floor study. Robin pointed out that the planets were all wrong. There were too many of them and they didn't rotate in the right way. Henry just shrugged at this in his casual, disinterested way.

Robin learned where the main stairs were, how to get from the tower to the ground floor without a fifteen minute search, and the important fact that sliding on the banisters, whilst incredibly tempting, would result in a severe poker chase.

"It seems like such a massive house for just one old woman," Robin remarked as they made their way along a long corridor. "All these rooms ... I bet she doesn't use most of them."

"Well, there's me and my dad too," Henry shrugged. "We stay here overnight sometimes, if dad's working late. Or if it's the holidays. We've got a set of rooms in the east wing." He led Robin up a set of four steps, seemingly set into the middle of the long corridor for no other reason than to liven things up a bit. "And then there's the housekeeper, Hestia. She lives here too. She's got rooms on the second floor, though she's usually poking about in the kitchen. She's the cook too." He rolled his eyes at Robin. "You haven't met her yet, lucky you. She's an absolute battleaxe."

"Really?" Robin asked.

"Whatever you do, don't make the mistake I made and call her Esther." Henry held up a finger in warning. "It's Hestia 'with a haitch'. She's a bit of a snob. Calls me Master Drover." He made a face. "Hate that."

"She sounds like a barrel of laughs," Robin said doubtfully.

"She's very house-proud," Henry explained. "Likes everything and everyone in its place. You can't miss her. Face like a spade."

They had reached the end of this particular corridor. A red wooden door blocked their way. Henry grabbed the handle and went to walk through, carrying on his charming tirade. The door didn't budge and he stumbled straight into it.

"It's locked," Robin said, trying not to laugh.

Henry frowned. "Huh … that's weird," he said.

"What?"

"That it's locked. The doors are never locked. Trust me, I get about. Idle hands and all that." He frowned at the large black iron keyhole. It peered innocently back at him. "In fact," the boy continued. "I don't think I've ever even seen this door before." He looked back down the corridor.

"Third floor, bathroom corridor," he muttered to himself. He looked at the row of closed doors which punctuated the corridor behind them. "There's the spare bedroom with the blue wallpaper and the rug that smells like dogs. There's the music room with the windows painted shut. Round the corner's the study with the planesphere and the hatboxes…"

Robin looked from the boy to the red door.

"This door's never been here before, I'm sure," Henry said.

"It must have," replied Robin. "Doors don't just appear. You must have missed it."

The door looked very old. It had a bit of carving on it, but it had faded away over time. The round doorknob had a small letter 'J' and some curly leaves carved into it.

Henry looked at him sarcastically. "Listen, mate, I've crawled all over this house since I was born. Thirteen years of exploring." He shook his head.

He dropped down and put his eye to the keyhole.

"See anything?" Robin asked.

Henry shook his head. "It's all dark," he said. "Maybe the old bird used to have something in front of it. A grandfather clock or a painting, something like that."

"Why don't we go ask her?" he suggested.

Henry stood up. "Nah. I've got a better idea. We'll get the keys off Hestia. She must have keys for every room."

"I thought you said no other rooms had locks?" Robin argued.

"Well … she must have one for this at least."

"You reckon she'd let us have it?" he asked. "The key, I mean?"

Henry laughed. “Hestia? No way. Are you kidding? Not a chance. She won’t give me the time o’ day, never mind lending me her keys.”

“But you just said…”

“I said we’ll get the keys,” Henry grinned. “I didn’t say we’d ask.”

Chapter Four – Woad at the Fountain

The plan to get the housekeeper's keys would have to wait until morning, as they discovered that the formidable Hestia was away in town for the day.

The back-up plan of football also had to be rethought due to a sudden change in weather. The rain came out of nowhere, gusting in great sheets and turning the blue sky to slate.

Robin, though, was not about to be put off by a bit of wet. He'd been dying to get out into the gardens all morning. He looked at the forest beyond the lawns, lost in a rainy mist. Between, there was a small fountain down there in a neat herb-garden.

"What's that statue?" he asked.

Henry appeared at his side, looking with a bored half-hearted expression. "It's one of those goat men with pipes, you know, they have little beards and go prancing about the show."

"Fauns," Robin supplied.

"Something like that. The water comes out of the pipes."

"Fancy going and having a look?" Robin asked.

Henry made a disdainful face. "It's lashing down! Are you out of your mind?"

"So?" Robin was about to turn and look away from the fountain, when something caught his eye in the bushes behind the statue. If there's one colour that really stands out against green, it's blue. That's what he now saw. A blue face and blue shoulders, blue chest and blue arms. The legs he saw weren't blue, they were browny-green – but that was because they were in browny-green pants. The feet at the end of them, however, were blue.

It was in short, a small blue boy, standing by the statue. He saw Robin looking and, quick as a cat, he darted into the bushes and was gone.

"Did you see that?" Robin asked, staring.

Henry looked down. "Look, I know it's pretty, but it's only a fountain, Robin."

"Not the fountain. There was a kid, a boy like us. Only he was blue. Just in pants, no shoes or shirt, he was right there, by the bushes!"

"Well, I'd be blue with no shirt on in this rain."

"Not cold blue, properly blue. As in blue skin."

Henry snorted. "Oh. Alright then. Because that makes much more sense."

"I'm not kidding, will you look?" Robin said. Henry sighed and peered down at the fountain and its ring of bushes.

"So," he said after a minute, his breath fogging the glass. "Where's the smurf?"

Robin elbowed him. "Very funny. He must be hiding in the bushes."

"Why?" Henry asked.

"Because I saw him, obviously," Robin replied, scanning the area like a hawk. "I don't think he expected anyone to."

"No, I mean why would some random boy come all the way up here from the village covered in blue face paint and prance about in the rain freezing to death?"

"Maybe he's not from the village?" Robin countered.

"Well, there's nowhere else to be from, not for miles," Henry noted. "We don't get many visitors here in Barrowood."

"You ever seen a man dressed like an undertaker on Halloween?" Robin asked. "Old dusty coat-tails, white face. Bright orange hair like a pumpkin?"

Henry was looking at Robin with an even stranger expression now. "No. I think I'd remember him."

"Well then, you've got at least one visitor in the village," said Robin. "'Cause I saw him this morning. He was the creepiest thing I've ever seen."

"Maybe this freaky man and your blue boy are part of a travelling circus," Henry offered with a snigger.

Robin shot him a very serious look. "Listen, lots of weird things have been happening to me. Ever since Gran died. Only little things, but if you add them up, they equal big weird."

"Are you always like this?" Henry asked after a moment. "'Cause it could get exhausting."

"So if I say there's a blue boy spying on us, then there is, right?"

"Alright … alright! Stranger things have happened, I suppose," Henry replied. "What do I know eh?"

"Let's go out and have a look," Robin said.

Henry sighed, peering out grudgingly at the rain.

It took them so long to find boots and coats that Robin began to fear that the blue boy would be gone. When they got outside, it seemed he was right.

Henry stood sulkily by the fountain, which was a great deal larger and more impressive up close, hood up and hands thrust deep into his pockets. Rain splattered off his shoulders hard enough to make new rain of its very own. "I'm so very glad we decided to leave the warm, dry indoors to have this ripping adventure," he muttered dryly.

Robin ignored him. The breeze drove the water under his hood, plastering his blonde hair to his forehead. He peered into the bushes, hoping to see a blue face hiding behind the leaves.

There was no one to be found.

"There was someone here," Robin said determinedly. "I saw him."

Henry diplomatically said nothing.

"Hello?" Robin called into the bushes. "It's okay, I just want to talk to you … whoever you are."

The bushes showed no signs of replying. Robin thought about getting a sharp stick and poking them, but that would probably give the wrong impression.

"Can we go in now?" Henry asked patiently. "Not that it's not a laugh, chatting to topiary, but I reckon I'm growing gills."

Robin sighed down his nose, frustrated. He wondered briefly if he was going mad. "There's nothing out here but us and the goat man," he agreed gloomily. "Let's go back."

"Come on," Henry smiled. "I'll thrash you at cards instead."

* * *

Nothing further of an unusual nature happened until later that evening. Mr Drover had finished for the day and gone home, taking Henry with him. Robin, at a loose end with nothing else to occupy him, went in search of his aunt.

He found her in a study. Floor to ceiling bookcases lined the walls, crammed with every kind of book, map and even scrolls. She was at a sitting at a desk in the corner, papers arrayed all about her, wearing half-moon spectacles and seeming very intent on her business, so much so that Robin was loath to disturb her. But after a few moments, she seemed to sense him at the door.

"I thought I made it clear earlier, Robin, that I am not fond of those who lurk in doorways," Irene said mildly, without looking up. "There are plenty of dark corners in this house which are much better suited for lurking, if that is your wont. Doorways are for using."

Robin came into the study, closing the doors behind him.

"I can come back later if you're busy," he said.

She laid down her pen and shuffled some papers. "I shall still be busy then," she said simply. "Now is as good a time as any."

Robin crossed the room, floorboards creaking under his feet. It was very quiet in the house. The rain had finally stopped and the sun had gone down an hour ago. It was strange not to have a TV or radio blaring. Gran had always disliked things being too quiet.

"Have a seat," Irene waved him towards a chair by the fire, which was popping away merrily. "Tell me how you are finding your first day here at Erlking."

Robin flopped into the high-backed chair as Irene tided her papers away and turned to face him.

"It's a nice house. I like it," Robin said. "It's massive. I keep getting lost. My room's great by the way, thanks."

Irene looked at him for a long moment, and then removed her glasses, folding them away.

"I'm sorry, Robin, about all the upheaval in your life at the moment. We haven't had time to get you settled in the right way, have we? There has been so much to do today. I feel I have been a most ungracious host so far."

Robin shook his head. "No, it's fine. I don't want to be any trouble."

"Well," she replied. "It's a little too late for that. You're here now, though, for better or worse."

Robin wasn't sure what to say to that, so he didn't say anything.

"Your grandmother, she never mentioned me, did she?" Irene asked.

"No. She never said I had any aunts, or uncles or anything. I just thought it was the two of us," Robin replied. "Until … after…"

"The reason she never mentioned me, Robin, is that she never knew I existed. We thought that would be for the best."

Robin was confused. "We?" he asked.

"Your parents and I," Irene said simply. "They thought it best if you were kept away from all this … complicated way of things."

Robin looked around the study, not sure if she was talking about the books, or the house or what. He didn't understand how Gran could not have known his new guardian. If she was his Great Aunt, then surely they would have been sisters? Or maybe they were from different sides of the family. Gran had never been much for family history, but Robin thought she had been his mother's mother. Perhaps Great Aunt Irene had been his father's mother's sister. His head hurt trying to work it out, so instead he said, "You knew my mum and dad?"

"Once," Aunt Irene nodded. "Though it seems like an awfully long time ago that I had any dealings with any of your family."

"I don't remember them at all," he said. He looked at his hands. Light from the fire flickered over them. "Gran hardly ever talked about them. Not really, she didn't even have any photos, said she didn't trust cameras, and I was only just born when they…"

Irene made a noise in her nose. "Well, all you need to know about your parents is this: they died. They left you as the last of your line. No brothers or sisters … and they also left a very complicated situation for the rest of us."

Robin was about to ask who 'the rest of us' were. Did he have more family he had never heard of? But as he opened his mouth to speak there was a noise outside the window, a scrape on the dark glass.

Both of them turned and peered at the window, but it was fully dark now and all they could see was the room reflected.

"Go and close the curtains, boy, and come straight back," Irene said quietly.

Robin did as he was told. He looked out onto the dark grounds, but could see nothing but trees and grass. It was odd, not having the world outside lit up with orange streetlamps. It made the night seem much bigger out here than it had ever had back in the city.

"Probably just a fox," Irene said. "But some things are not for eavesdroppers, don't you agree?"

She jabbed at the fire a little with a black poker. Quite effectively, Robin noted.

"Perhaps there are things which should be left unsaid until later. Dark is a terrible time for this kind of thing." She put down the poker and looked at him.

"Have you noticed anything … odd lately?" she asked him lightly.

Robin almost burst out laughing. Odd? He thought. Well, only the girl on the train disappearing, the weird old man at the station, the horseshoes committing suicide, the blue boy spying on him, and discovering he had a mad aunt who lived in a mansion where doors appeared out of nowhere…

He didn't say any of this, of course. He said, "Odd?"

Great Aunt Irene peered sharply at him, with her hawk-like eyes.

"Well…" Robin began haltingly. "I met a strange man at the train station…"

Irene cut in. "Yes, a man by the name of Moros. Thin gangling chap, yes? Mr Drover told me about that." She leaned forward towards him. "Now, listen to me, Robin. You don't want to go speaking to him. He's a bad sort."

"You know him?" asked Robin.

"That I do. Him and his … family," Irene nodded. "If you see any of them, and you'll know them if you do, don't go near them or speak to them. Is that understood?"

Robin nodded. "Henry's dad … I mean Mr Drover, he didn't seem to like him either."

"No," Irene replied. "Don't you worry. They won't bother you here, but just keep your eyes open, that's all I'm saying."

"Why would they bother me?" Robin wanted to know.

Irene pursed her lips. "It's … complicated," she said eventually. "Your parents," she began. "When they died, they left you an inheritance of sorts. Mr Moros and his kin would like very much to get their hands on it."

Robin frowned at this. "An inheritance? Money, you mean? Am I related to Mr Moros as well?"

Irene shook her head. "No, not in the least. You're no kind of that sort." She sighed. "It would have been much simpler if your guardian had explained things to you. She probably thought you were too young. I'm quite sure she wasn't planning to die."

"I don't understand," Robin insisted. "Did Gran know?"

"Yes, of course she did," Irene replied. "It's not money, Robin. It's … something they left for you, and only for you. The reason you've never heard about it is because your parents were very clever people. They knew there would be those, like the charmless Mr Moros, who would want to claim it for themselves. So they made sure that no one would be able to find it."

"My inheritance is hidden?" Robin asked, confused.

Irene shook her head. "Parts of it, I suppose, although circumstance has decreed you to be the only one who could ever really 'find' it, so to speak. Think of it as a lock somewhere, and only you can open it," Irene tried to explain. "Even if someone else had the key, they couldn't open it. Only you can. It was made for you."

"Okay. I see," said Robin, who honestly didn't. "But what am I supposed to unlock? This inheritance, what is it?"

Irene looked thoughtful. "The answer to all our problems, I hope," she said. "Or the cause. It remains to be seen."

Robin didn't think this was a very good answer.

"All you need to understand for now is this," she said. "You are very young, Robin, and through no particular fault of your own, you are very important to a lot of people. Your grandmother knew this, though she never told you. She was a very clever woman, no matter what a lot of people thought. She was able to keep you … safe. For twelve long years, which is no mean feat. I can do the same here, at Erlking. That is within my remit. That will have to do for now."

She patted his knee, which seemed, from a lady such as herself, quite a forced and unnatural show of affection. "No more questions about all that now though. You have enough on your mind settling in here."

Robin wanted to protest. He wanted to know about Mr Moros, and all this lock and key business, and most importantly why Aunt Irene thought he needed to be kept safe.

"You seem to have been taken under young Henry's wing," she said, abruptly changing the subject. "He's a good sort. A complete dunderhead, and he doesn't always act too bright, but it is probably good for you to have someone close to your own age to knock about with."

Robin nodded.

"In the morning, you shall meet the rest of us. Hestia, my housekeeper, who will no doubt be brimming with excitement to give you the rules of the house. And of course, your tutor." She leaned back, and rubbed at the bridge of her nose tiredly.

"Hopefully, when he arrives, things will begin to make more sense to you, Robin. He should have been here by now, though I gather he was delayed. I do so abhor tardiness. But I am sure he will clear most things up."

Robin was not sure he was looking forward to meeting a tutor. He was uneasy with the idea of being taught at home, with just him and a teacher breathing down his neck all the time.

"Couldn't I just go to the village school?" he asked. "Henry goes there, so I'd already know someone."

Irene looked at him. "No, no. That would never do," she said dismissively. "They don't teach the right kind of things there."

"Am I going to be taught here in the house then?" he asked.

"In a manner of speaking," she replied. She smiled a little. "Don't worry about it. I think you may enjoy your lessons."

* * *

Later that night, after a hearty supper, he spent a few hours musing around the large study, looking in old books filled with strange maps and pictures. Robin was feeling a little odd about his first night in a new house. It didn't feel like home at all.

It was only when he was getting undressed for bed and into his pyjamas that he noticed he was still wearing the little horseshoe on the silver chain. He slipped it over his head and dropped it in his top drawer.

A faint howl floated in from the open window. It was long and mournful. It reminded Robin of the noise he had heard outside the train. It gave him goose bumps, so he crossed the room and shut the window.

Or at least he tried to, but the window pane jammed on a set of fingers and wouldn't close, and a short yelp of pain came up from the darkness outside.

Robin looked down at the fingers on the sill. They were blue. He opened the window again and looked out. There was a small boy clinging to the ledge, hanging in thin air, legs flailing wildly beneath him.

"What are you trying to do?" the boy said angrily. "Kill me?"

Robin stepped back in alarm as the blue-skinned boy vaulted up with a strange, graceful ease. He flipped in through the window and landed softly with a catlike crouch on the floorboards in front of Robin.

He stared wide-eyed at the intruder. The boy stood up and sucked at his recently trapped fingers, glowering angrily at Robin with narrowed yellow eyes. Around his neck, on a black leather lace, hung a small smooth gem, like a misty opal. It was half the size of a chicken egg and glittered in the light from Robin's bedside lamp.

"Wha—what..." Robin tried. This didn't make much sense, so he tried again.

"Who ... are you?" he asked shakily.

The blue-skinned boy blinked at him.

"How did you get up here?" Robin asked. The house itself was four tall stories high, and the tower higher still.

The blue boy's tail swished a little. "It was easy," he said testily. "An idiot could have done it. A moron, a pixie."

"I saw you before," Robin accused him. "You were spying on me. I saw you in the bushes! Why are you dressed like that?"

The boy looked down at his makeshift clothing. "What have my pants got to do with it?" he asked snappily.

"Not that!" Robin said exasperated. "The paint. Why are you painted blue? Why have you got a thing stuck in the back to look like a tail? And..."

"I'm not painted blue," the small boy interrupted. "This is just me."

Robin snorted. "No it isn't! That's ridiculous!"

"Yes it is!" the boy snapped back. "I should know." He pointed a finger at Robin, who looked far less intimidating in his striped pyjamas. Robin noticed that the nails on the end of the boy's fingers were quite long and sharp. "What about you? Why are you painted pink?"

"Don't be stupid!" Robin said.

They stared at one another for a moment.

The boy sighed, and then suddenly dropped into a crouch and sprung into the air. He landed on one of the bedposts of Robin's bed, perching there impossibly on the balls of his bare feet. His tail switched back and forth, helping him balance.

"You weren't supposed to see me," he said grumpily. "I'm going to be in a right load of trouble now."

Robin sat down, very slowly. All the blood seemed to have drained out of his head. Of all the things that had happened recently, this was the strangest. There was no point trying to explain it away – whatever this boy was, it wasn't paint and false tails.

"This," Robin said finally, "... is too bizarre for words."

"Well, I would have come to see you sooner," the boy said sulkily. "But I couldn't get close 'cause of the ward. I've been skulking around in the grounds all night, waiting for you to get rid of it."

"What?" Robin asked.

"The ward," the boy said short-temperedly. "The thing you were wearing round your neck."

Robin looked at the drawer with the horseshoe pendant in it. He looked back at the animal-like child, then back at the drawer.

"Maybe," he said slowly, "… we should start again." He took a deep breath. "I'm Robin."

The boy grinned, showing his white teeth. "I know. I knew it. I'm good at finding people. Much better than she is anyway, she couldn't find her backside with both hands … Don't tell her I said that though. Boss says she's the best tracker but I'm better."

"What's your name?" Robin asked, trying to stop the creature talking. "And what … are you?"

"Forgot my manners," he said. "Forget my tail if it wasn't attached." He grinned impishly. "I'm Woad, and though I'd expect any reasonable person to be able to tell instantly, I'm a faun."

"A faun?" he asked. "But fauns aren't blue. And they have goat's legs and beards. There's a statue of one in the garden."

Woad rolled his eyes in a tired fashion. "Honestly, what imaginations you have." He raised his eyebrows at Robin. "I mean, how many people do you know who've ever seen one of us?"

"Well … none," Robin had to admit. "Because fauns aren't real. They're make-believe, like … like fairies and centaurs and … and dragons."

"Ohhhh," Woad nodded sagely. "That explains that then. I met a centaur once. Nearly gored me to death. Evil creatures. No wonder they work for Lady E."

Robin counted to five in his head. It was all too strange. Lady *who*? He looked at the blue boy scratching his stomach. "Aren't you cold?"

"No. I can never be bothered," Woad replied dismissively. "Too busy, spying on you, making sure you got to Erlking safely, which you did." He looked pleased with himself. "Mission accomplished." He put his hands behind his head and lay back on the floor, contented.

Robin peered over the edge of the bed.

“What’s going on?” he asked. “Why is everyone so careful to make sure I’m safe? And who are you people?!”

“Hasn’t your tutor told you yet?” Woad asked lazily, looking up.

“Told me what?” asked Robin angrily. He was tired of being given the run around.

“Oh…” Woad said quietly. “I guess not.” He sat up, cross-legged. “Told you,” he said, peering intently at Robin. “About whom … you … are.”

Robin was not impressed.

“What’s that supposed to mean?” he asked, irritated. “I know whom I am – I mean, who I am.”

“Do not,” Woad argued petulantly.

“Yes I do!” Robin said angrily.

“Don’t,” Woad said playfully.

“Yes I damn well do!” Robin said.

“Who then? Who are you, Robin?” Woad demanded, suddenly challenging. “Tell me if you think you know, ‘cause I bet you don’t, and then you’ll look stupid. Dumb as a pixie.”

“I’m … I’m just … Robin. I’m no one. Just me!” Robin almost yelled.

Woad cackled. “You haven’t got a clue,” he taunted. “You don’t know what you’re talking about, you brontosaurus.”

“Well, what am I then?” Robin was beginning to find the young blue boy very irritating. “If you’re so clever, you little blue … thing! You tell me.”

“You’re the Scion,” Woad said gleefully.

Robin blinked. “The what?”

Woad rolled his eyes again. “Oh, this is useless,” he said. “I’ll come back after you’ve had your first lesson. Then at least it won’t be like trying to have a conversation with a head of lettuce.” He sprang to his feet energetically.

“Wait,” Robin said with alarm. “You’re not going anywhere until I get some answers!” He made a grab for Woad, but the blue creature was far too fast and darted out of reach.

“Wrong again!” Woad said merrily. “See you later, if you wise up and don’t get yourself eaten by skrikers that is.”

Woad jumped onto the window ledge.

"Go to sleep, Robin," he called back. "Things will make sense in the morning."

He flicked his hand, the milky orb around his neck flashed, and Robin, who was just about to let forth a string of extremely angry swear words, found himself sinking to the floor. He was asleep before his head hit the floorboards, which it did with a very final and deep thud.

Chapter Five – Phorbas' First Lesson

Robin didn't mention Woad at breakfast the following morning. Partly because he suspected that he'd be carted off to an insane asylum if he did, but chiefly because there was no one at breakfast to mention it to. He had awoken on the floor of his bedroom, with his pyjama top twisted round his throat and one of his buttocks completely numb. He made his way downstairs after washing and dressing, only to find that there was apparently no one in the vast house but him.

In the dining room, there was a place set for one at the end of the long table. A cooked breakfast had been laid out. The plate was still hot.

A note had been tucked under the knife and fork beside the plate. It read:

Robin,

I have been called away on business. I shall be back at precisely 1pm this afternoon. My housekeeper, Hestia, is back, should you require anything in the house.

Your tutor is due to arrive at 11am. I will not be there to greet him, so the onus is upon you. I trust you to make a good impression. And try not to act too surprised, as he is easily offended.

Until then, you have, as always, free rein of the house. Do not get stuck in any chimneys. Do not fall out of any windows. Do not leave the grounds of Erlking Hall for any reason whatsoever!

Irene.

Robin thought this was quite an odd note. He checked his watch as he wolfed down his mysteriously cook-free breakfast. It was already almost ten. He had slept very late and his tutor was due in an hour. He supposed that meeting make-believe creatures, especially extremely annoying blue ones, took up a lot of energy.

After breakfast, he went outside, where the stone fountain was babbling merrily. It must be old, he thought. One of the satyrs horns was missing, broken off long ago. It looked rather sad and dejected.

With his hands thrust deep into his coat pockets to ward off the cold, he looked around for a while, but could see nothing out of the ordinary. He wasn't really sure what he was expecting. Robin scanned the tree-line at the edge of the forest, but if Woad was hiding in the trees, he was hiding very well.

He circled Erlking Hall completely, discovering a large vegetable plot and a walled rose garden. There was an extremely large and old-fashioned looking conservatory, filled with lots of large leafy plants. There was a vast lone oak tree and a sundial in a shadowy nook. There was a well, covered with a large and, as Robin discovered, utterly immovable stone. But there was no blue faun.

Robin wished that Mr Drover and Henry would show up. He didn't know whether to tell Henry about his encounter last night or not. He probably thought Robin was half-cracked anyway. But it would be better to have someone to talk to while he waited for his tutor.

His wish was granted in a way. He circled around the great hall to the front door and its tall, imposing columns. A person stood there.

Unfortunately, it was not Henry, or Woad, or anyone he knew. It was a woman, short and dumpy with a pinched, humourless face. Her black hair was scraped back off her face and she had her arms folded tightly across the front of her black dress.

She stared at Robin with such clear disapproval that he almost checked his shoes to see if he had stepped in something.

"Master Robin is it?" she snapped.

"Er ... yes," said Robin, not too sure about the 'master' part. "Hello."

"Well, what are you doing out on the wet grass, you foolish little boy? Do you think you are going to come now and spread mud all through this hall?"

"No ... I..."

"Well, you can think again!" she spat. "As if I don't have enough to do in this place, without clearing up after another mucky, thoughtless little child! Perhaps you think I get bored, is that it? Cleaning windows and hoovering the stairs and washing the dishes?" Her beady little eyes glared at him in barely suppressed fury. "Maybe you think you are doing me a favour? Keeping me busy?"

"No ... I don't think..."

The woman threw her hands up dramatically. “You think this house cleans itself? Do you!? No. I do it! All of it, on my own. And what would happen if I didn’t? Eh? Does anyone ever stop to think about that? No, they do not!”

Robin gave up trying to join in the conversation. She seemed to be getting along fine without him.

“I’ll tell you what would happen!” She pointed a finger at him portentously. “This place would fall apart without me! Then there would be trouble! Yes there would!” There was a strange gleam of manic triumph in her eyes. “They don’t notice when it’s done, do they? No. But they’d notice quick enough if it wasn’t! Quick as a flash!” She snapped her fingers, presumably to show Robin how quick a flash was.

“Are you the housekeeper?” Robin asked, coming up the steps, as she paused to take a breath.

Her eyes flew wide. “I have JUST washed those steps!” she cried. “Look at them. Look what you have done, you horrible, horrible child!”

Robin had indeed traipsed a fair amount of mud up the steps. He looked at the horrified woman, his eyes widening with panic at her expression.

“I’m sorry,” he said quickly. “I didn’t mean to … I’ll clean it up…”

“You’ll clean it up, will you?” she snapped. “Oh yes? And what do you think you know about cleaning steps? Have you cleaned steps in this house for the last hundred years? Think you know so much better than stupid old Hestia?”

Robin looked up horrified. The frantic woman looked halfway between bursting into tears and screaming with rage.

“I didn’t mean…” he began.

She flapped her arms at him like a furious chicken. “You never *mean*! None of you ever *mean*! But you still *do*!”

Robin backed down a step in the face of her outrage.

“You will take off your shoes! That is what you will do! Thoughtless child! Take them off right now and carry them to the kitchen and leave them on newspaper on the table! Then you will go straight to your room, and make no fingerprints in the polishing on the way! You will wash and clean and try to look more like a human child and less like a savage. Your tutor is due any minute! Think I want him coming here and seeing my steps all covered with mud? Are you trying to shame me?”

Robin dropped down and frantically unlaced his scruffy old trainers, while the woman ranted above him. He ran up the last two steps in his socks.

"Gone with you!" she cried after him as he slipped inside, mumbling sorrys. "And leave no footprints!"

Robin thought Henry was right. Hestia the housekeeper was a battleaxe, and she did have a face like a spade. He wondered briefly if anyone in this house apart from him was sane. Then he considered that he had spent the previous evening talking to a blue creature with a long tail, and shrugged it off.

He deposited the offending trainers in the large and austere kitchen, but didn't bother going to his room to clean up. It was only his shoes that were dirty and he didn't have a spare pair. By the time he had dawdled back to the lobby again, the front steps were gleaming and clear, Hestia gone. He was just wondering where he was supposed to be meeting his tutor when the large grandfather clock chimed eleven.

At the last melodic and genteel 'bong', there was a polite cough behind him.

"You must be the young master of the house," a voice said.

Robin stopped in mid-step. He turned to face the owner of the sudden and unexpected voice, only to find that there was no one behind him. He blinked in confusion.

"You'll have to do better than that, young Master Robin," the voice came again genially. Robin spun in confusion.

The hallway was empty. There was no one on the stairs or the distant shadowy landing.

"Who's there?" Robin called, searching the room. There was no one in sight.

"Your first lesson," the voice said, so close to his ear it made him jump, "… is to learn to see."

Robin found himself turning in a circle. "Where are you?" he asked, slipping slightly on the polished floor in just his socks.

"You have to learn to look at things and be prepared for what is actually there," the dislocated voice said again. "If you think you know what you are going to see, then all you will see is what you will expect … and that would be terribly dull."

The voice seemed to be coming from above him. Robin looked up, but there was nothing but the chandelier, glittering in the shadows above.

"Close your eyes, young Master Robin," said the voice.

Robin was at a loss. If this was a trick, he didn't know how it was managed.

With no other more sensible option at hand, he did as he was told and closed his eyes.

"Now," the voice said. "What do you see?"

"Nothing," Robin replied, thinking that this was a very stupid question.

Something moved right in front of him. "What do you expect to see? When you open your eyes?" the voice asked, very close to him.

"Erm … my tutor?" Robin guessed. He couldn't think who else it could be.

"Correct," the voice said, sounding very pleased by this answer. "Now of course, when you open your eyes, you will no doubt expect to see a tutor of general disposition. A man of middling age perhaps, with a sour expression and maybe a jacket with tweed involved and leather patches at the elbows, yes?"

"Erm … I haven't really thought about it."

"Nonsense," the voice replied. "It is impossible to hear of a thing without seeing it in your mind. Your Plato had the right of it there. And as I have said, once your mind has made its mind up, you will only see what it expects to see. And that will never do."

"O-kay…" Robin said. He had to admit, he did have a vague impression of a dusty, bad-tempered old schoolteacher in mind. "So…?"

"So get rid of that image," the voice said. "Allow it no quarter in your mind, or we will be off to a very poor start indeed."

Robin nodded. "Okay … I think," he said uncertainly.

He felt a fleeting pressure on his eyelids, as quick and light as the brush of a moth's wing, then it was gone.

"Now you can open your eyes."

Robin did so.

There was a man standing in front of him. Or at least, that was Robin's first thought. He was concentrating on not having any image in his mind, and for a moment, his vision wavered, a trick of his confused brain, and then there was something else standing in front of him instead.

It looked fairly like a man, thinnish with wild tufty brown hair and a pointy beard. Robin noticed was that the man was not wearing tweed of any kind. He was in fact wearing nothing at all. His skin was very darkly tanned, nut coloured, and his arms and chest were decorated with swirling tattoos in berry-coloured ink.

Fascinating though this was, Robin's attention couldn't help but be drawn to the fact that the man's legs were covered in sleek fur the same colour as his hair and, ending in ivory-coloured hooves which stood innocently and quite firmly on the well-polished floor.

The final thing Robin noticed, when he dragged his eyes away from the goat legs, was that sticking out of the man's thatch of curly brown hair there were two small, stubby horns, like large acorns.

The man smiled at him. His eyes were very bright and alert. His teeth were alarmingly white.

Robin stared.

"Very good," the man said, sounding genuinely pleased. "That is very impressive on a first try." He held out his hand in greeting. "I, Master Robin, am Phorbas, and I am to be your tutor in the arts of the Arcania."

Robin stared at the offered hand for a while, feeling a little stunned.

"It is customary," Phorbas said politely after a moment, "to shake it."

Robin shook the hand, suddenly feeling very impolite. His was numb with shock. "Sorry," he mumbled.

The silence dragged out. Phorbas politely waited for Robin to get to grips with things. "You're a … you're a … faun," he said eventually.

Phorbas raised his eyebrows. "A faun indeed! Do I look blue to you? Have I displayed an irritating urge to do acrobatics? No. I am a son of Pan. A satyr. The two are quite, *quite* distinct. It's the humans who clump us all together."

Robin said nothing. He stared at the satyr. This wasn't really happening.

"Aunt Irene … hired you?" he asked, trying not to stare at the goat legs. Phorbas had released his hand and was walking in a slow circle around him, his ivory hooves clacking neatly on the floorboards.

"Oh yes," Phorbas said. "I come with excellent credentials."

"And she knows … she knows that you're a … a…?"

"Satyr?" Phorbas supplied. "Yes, of course. She's very bright you see. She would never have the temerity to confuse satyrs and fauns."

"I think maybe I should sit down," Robin said weakly. His feet suddenly felt a very long way away at the end of his legs.

Phorbas snapped his fingers under Robin's nose. "No time for that, Master Robin. Your education has already begun. Your aunt informs me that due to a terrible series of mishaps and misunderstandings, you have no idea who you are, where you are from, or of what you are capable. You have been living in the human world far too long." He shuddered slightly at this. "Which is most unfair on you. But all can be put right."

"I thought you were coming to teach me schoolwork," Robin asked weakly.

Phorbas made a distasteful face. "There's time enough for frivolities like that when you are older," he said. "A child like you needs to be tutored in the Arcania."

"The what?"

"The arts of casting," Phorbas said, with an extravagant gesture of his arms.

Robin looked at him blankly.

"Magic," the satyr explained, grinning. "Fire, water, earth, wind, light, darkness and spirit! The seven towers of the Arcania! The seven fields of magical expertise. All of our kind learn these. Some specialise, some are hopeless. We will not know your limits, Master Robin, until we test them." He smiled. "And test them we shall."

The satyr walked towards the staircase. "Come, the Netherworlde awaits us!"

"The what?" Robin asked, following the quick stepping goat man.

"The Netherworlde," Phorbas repeated. "I thought perhaps your aunt had exaggerated when she said you knew nothing, but I see she was, as ever, most carefully accurate with her descriptions. The Netherworlde, Master Robin, the flip side to what you know as the human world."

Robin didn't really know how to process this. He settled for the simplest question. "How will we get there?"

"Through Erlking of course," Phorbas replied. "Erlking is a station." He noticed the confused look on Robin's face. Robin was remembering the small blue boy from the previous night. He had mentioned stations too. "There are permanent pathways between here, the human world, and the Netherworlde," Phorbas explained, leading Robin on at a quick pace up to the third floor. "These passing places are called stations, and are governed mainly by Janus, which is our doorkeeper."

He turned a corner and set off down a long corridor, trailing Robin behind him.

"There are a few..." he continued, "... a very select few, independent stations, ungoverned, unmonitored by the peacekeepers, Eris' people. Erlking is one of these."

"Why's that?" Robin asked.

"Erlking is a law unto itself, and cannot be governed." He glanced at Robin. "You would do well to bear that in mind, Master Robin. While your aunt holds mastery of Erlking, while she watches over, no harm can come to you within its walls. It is a fact most irksome to her enemies."

They ascended a couple of steps and turned a corner. Robin was trying desperately to take all this on board.

"Why have I never heard of any of this before?" he wanted to know, still struggling with the fact he was following half a goat upstairs.

Phorbas laughed. "Very few humans know of the Netherworlde. We would never get any peace if they did."

"So why me? Why tell me all this?" Robin asked.

Phorbas gave him a sidelong glance. "Because you, Master Robin, though I appreciate it may come as something of a shock, are not altogether human. You are the last of a long, long line."

He stopped at the end of the corridor abruptly and turned to face the shocked boy. Robin's eyes were very wide.

They had arrived at the locked red door. The same door which he and Henry had found the previous day. The door that according to the other boy, had never previously been there.

"You," Phorbas said, leaning down and peering into Robin's face intensely. "You, my young Master Robin, are the world's last changeling."

Before Robin could query him, the satyr slipped a slim silver key from the pocket of his waistcoat. It turned with a polite click and the door opened.

Robin peered within.

The room beyond was bizarrely out of place with the rest of the corridor and house. The walls and floor were rough stone, like an old castle. There was another door on the opposite wall, very old fashioned with huge black hinges and a ring of iron for a doorknocker.

What struck Robin was that the room looked so old and partly ruined. There were large green bushes here and there, growing through the cracks. Ivy covered much of the dark walls. There were even a couple of wizened trees pushing up through the flagstones, their leafy canopies hiding much of the ceiling.

There was a large stone table at the centre of the room, covered in odd paraphernalia and scrolls, and a lantern casting a golden glow over the odd room.

The strangest thing, however, in an ever-growing list of exceedingly strange things, was that through the window in the room, the sky outside was dark and dotted with bright stars.

Considering that on this side of the door it was eleven o'clock in the morning and quite sunny, Robin found this quite hard to take in.

"Come on through," Phorbas said. "Take your first steps in the Netherworlde."

Robin followed the satyr into the room. The air shimmered a little in the doorway as he passed through, as though in a heat haze. He couldn't help but feel a little self-conscious that he took his first steps in the Netherworlde, apparently the world's last changeling, in his socks.

Chapter Six – Magics and Mana-stones

Phorbas followed Robin into the large, ruined room. A cool midnight breeze rolled in through the windows, carrying with it the sweet smell of night-time grass and odd flowers. Was this really happening, he wondered? He breathed deeply. There was a faint smell, like jasmine, autumn and burning wood, beneath the breeze. It smelled … familiar. Stepping through the locked door felt inexplicably like coming home.

"Ah," said Phorbas, noticing Robin breathing the sweet dark air. "Nothing quite like it is there, Master Robin? The night blooming scents of the Netherworlde. No fresher air anywhere else you care to look, I would wager my beard upon it, and a beard is a very serious thing for a satyr to wager, I don't mind telling you."

Robin didn't reply; he was still taking it all in. A small and slightly frantic voice kept jabbering in the back of his mind. He felt slightly dazed, drunk on the unremitting weirdness of it all.

Phorbas turned and looked at the door which led back to the side of Erlking Hall which reached into the human world. The corridor stretched away unassumingly. In the distance, very faintly, Robin could hear Hestia grumbling to herself as she hoovered. The normal, everyday sound seemed ridiculous in context. To be standing in a ruined castle in the middle of the night in one world and be able to hear someone vacuuming noisily in the sunshine in another. The satyr frowned, as though he wished to shut the door, cutting off anything mundane that might detract from the experience, but he gave a rueful look and thought better of it. "Your aunt has granted us use of Erlking's doorway so that I might show you this. A small slice of our world," he said. "She thought you might be more easily convinced by this than my merely telling you about it, but perhaps she is wise in forbidding us to close this door while we are on the Netherworlde side. It is not the … safest place at the moment, for you to linger."

Robin had to admit, seeing was believing. He doubted he would have swallowed Phorbas' revelation about a hidden world whole if they were sitting downstairs sipping tea. He looked back at the goat man. "Not safe?" he asked with raised eyebrows, as his new tutor's words sunk in.

Phorbas ushered him further into the room with a flap of his hands. "Oh, worry not, young sir," he said lightly. "You are still in Erlking, even if the Netherworlde side of it is rather larger than the mortal world's. No harm can come to any in Erlking as long as your aunt watches over the place. And she is watching over the place, even if she isn't in it. As long as her eyes are working, and no one has sharper eyes than she."

He noticed Robin glancing toward the window. "Go then," he chuckled indulgently. "Take a look at the Netherworlde for the first time, why don't you?"

Robin made his way across the room, rustling against a large bush covered in tiny flowers which looked like small golden trumpets. He startled a little as they turned silently to follow his progress. One or two of them seemed to sniff in his direction.

"Try not to brush against those," Phorbas said conversationally, as he made his own way across to the paraphernalia-covered table. "They're Snapping Foxgloves. They won't kill you but they can give a heck of a nip."

Robin gave the bush a wide berth as he made his way past, staring at it with wide eyes. He was sure he heard some of the tiny flowers growling quietly as they shuddered like angry Chihuahuas.

He reached the window and leaned out into the night.

On this side, he was more than four stories up. Much more. The wall fell away beneath him, many stories down into the darkness, studded everywhere with windows, turrets, balconies and a good smattering of ivy. In the darkness, low hills rolled lazily away, rippling in the breeze like a dark ocean. There was a tangled-looking forest beyond, the trees made an impenetrable black wall in the darkness.

Robin's gaze travelled upwards to the sky. There was a fat moon hanging in the darkness. It looked three times bigger than the moon had ever looked back in what Robin couldn't help thinking of as 'the real world'. The rest of the sky was dotted with countless unfamiliar stars, winking in and out of view behind grey-silver clouds as large as full-sailed ships.

Robin tore himself away from the view of this strange land and turned back to the room. Phorbas was leaning against the table patiently.

"This place, you said it's called the Netherworlde?" he asked Phorbas, aware that his own voice sounded a little shaky. "And it's really real? A whole other world? I mean, I haven't just gone mad or anything? I'm not really sitting in some hospital somewhere dribbling cornflakes down my pyjamas?"

"Does it seem real to you?" his new tutor asked, his head cocked to one side.

One of the biting foxgloves near Robin's elbow growled quietly, and then abruptly sneezed, dislodging several leaves. The flagstones, cold under his socks. They felt real.

"Yeah, it does," he said wonderingly. "It's hard to explain, but it feels … realer … than anywhere else I've ever been."

The satyr nodded sagely. "And so it should, young Master Robin. You were, after all, born here. You are the world's last changeling."

"You said that before," Robin said, trying to step over some vines. The idea that he had come from such a place as this, to be raised in the human world, seemed outlandish. Ridiculous. "I don't really understand…"

"Aha!" said Phorbas, holding up a finger. "And that is the crux! That is why I have brought you here. To explain to you about the Netherworlde, and of course, about who, and indeed what, you are." He indicated a battered old three-legged stool next to the table. "Sit!" he commanded.

"Your first lesson, under my tutelage, is a history lesson." He removed from his belt a slender, ornately-carved dagger of shining silver which he fiddled with as he spoke, twirling it on its point absently on the table top. There was a bright orange garnet gemstone set in the pommel, which flashed as it caught the light.

"The Netherworlde has existed, side by side, as long as there has been the mortal world," Phorbas began. "The mortal world is the realm of humans, of mankind. The Netherworlde is the realm of your people, Robin. Of the Fae."

"The Fae?" Robin asked helplessly.

"Don't interrupt," Phorbas said, waggling his knife at Robin in a bizarrely unthreatening manner.

"Sorry," Robin mumbled.

"The Fae," Phorbas continued, looking off into middle distance. "A race as proud as they are wild, as pure as they are varied. Humans have always known, even if only in dreams, of the existence of the Fae. They called them faeries, or goblins, or elves, or any number of strange fairytale names. But they were not make-believe tales. They were real. They still are … what's left of them." He glanced sharply at Robin. "For there are fewer Fae than there were. Far, far fewer, and those that do remain are hidden and secret even here in the Netherworlde. And with good reason," he said darkly.

Robin opened his mouth to question this, but then remembered he was not meant to interrupt.

"It is essential that you understand, Master Robin, that the Fae have ruled the Netherworlde for time immemorial," Phorbas explained. "Led by the noble King Oberon and the fierce Queen Titania, they have watched over the provinces of this land for as long as there have been mortals in your world." His face grew serious. "All of that began to change one hundred years ago." He paused, peering at Robin oddly. "For even timeless peoples must face change, young Master Robin. Even the noble and undying must submit to the whim of the Fates." His eyes narrowed thoughtfully, as though he were thinking of times long past. "You see, something happened in the Netherworlde a century ago. Another race of beings appeared at that time, a people distinct entirely from the Fae. These were the Panthea, and they were every bit as wise and old and varied as Oberon's people. Their own history is muddled, and forgotten even to them. They were, in effect, refugees. A lost race."

Robin nodded to show he understood.

"The Fae accepted these new people into their homeland," Phorbas continued. "Into the Netherworlde, and for many, many years, the two races lived alongside one another, the Fae and the Panthea, in relative harmony. The Netherworlde is a large place, young Robin, there is more space on this side that in your mortal world."

He sighed ruefully. "But although they lived together … they did not share power. The Fae ruled supreme, the sovereignty of Oberon and Titania was unquestionable, and they held power over the fair land by wielding the ultimate magic. This was, and still is, known as the Arcania."

He spoke the word reverently, and a little greedily, as though he were speaking of some great treasure. Robin could not hold his tongue this time.

"What's that?" he asked.

Phorbas tilted his head to one side, making a lazy circle in the air with his knife, "What is the Arcania?" he said. "A weapon, some would say, of a kind. Or perhaps the ultimate source of magic. Used for good or for ill as the wielder sees fit." He looked directly at Robin. "The Arcania, my pupil, is the source of all the magic in the Netherworlde. It is the strength and raw energy of Oberon and Titania, and they were without equal while they possessed it."

"So … what happened?" Robin asked. "What changed?"

"The peace between the two peoples, alas, was fated not to last," Phorbas said sadly. "There are always those who will seek power. There will always be those unsatisfied with their lot, and they will always seek to rule. A group of Panthea, jealous of the Fae, resentful of the king and queen who had once given them sanctuary, plotted against them. They were tired of being ruled. They wanted to seize power for themselves. They were led by a very powerful and dangerous Panthea named Eris."

As he spoke this last word, Robin felt the breeze which drifted in the window cool a little. It rustled the leaves on the trees in the room, making them whisper. All of the Snapping Foxgloves closed their petals, retreating into themselves and growling quietly.

"Lady Eris," Phorbas continued. "Majestic. Charismatic. Manipulative. Calculating. Ruthless. She waged a war against the ruling Fae. She was determined to wield the Arcania for herself, and to make the Panthea the new rulers of the Netherworlde."

He shook his head forlornly. "The war was terrible, Master Robin. As all wars are. Many lives were lost. Much blood was spilled, and the Netherworlde became a darker, more dangerous place for us all. Lady Eris was fierce and unrelenting. The numbers of her followers swelled and swelled, but though they were powerful, still they could not hope to overcome the Fae king and queen. Not, at least, while they held the power of the Arcania. The war raged across the whole Netherworlde for almost a hundred years. And then…" His eyes widened. "… Something unexplainable happened."

Robin, who was now perched on the edge of his wobbly stool, looked up into the satyr's eyes. "What happened?" he asked eagerly.

"The two sides were so equally matched, they were at loggerheads, stalemate," Phorbas explained. "And then, one day, King Oberon and

Queen Titania simply…" He spread his hands, like birds taking flight. "… disappeared."

Robin frowned. "Disappeared?" he asked incredulously.

"No one could explain it," Phorbas continued. "They vanished completely." He narrowed his eyes. "There are many who believe they were betrayed by one of their own. Without King Oberon and Lady Titania, the Fae could not stand against the rebelling Panthea. Their loyal commanders, known as the Fae Guard, were decimated. Lady Eris was victorious. The Panthea ruled the Netherworlde." He sighed and stabbed his dagger into the table-top, where it lodged in a crack in the stone. "There was much confusion as to what happened. As it is said, when war is declared, truth is often the first casualty. Many said that Eris had managed to have the Fae king and queen assassinated. Others said they had fled, deserting their people. In the end, no one knew the truth. But the facts remained: the Panthea were, and are now, the true rulers of the Netherworlde, and under Eris' cruel rule, they persecuted the Fae. Enslaving many, imprisoning some, killing more. Eventually, those few Fae who remained free went underground. Hidden, on the run. Outlaws in what was once their own land."

"That's terrible," Robin said.

"One would think," Phorbas said, "… that Lady Eris would be happy. She now rules the Netherworlde supreme. She is the Empress of all she surveys. But her fury is terrible to behold, because she does not yet wield the ultimate power."

Robin was confused. "You mean this Arcania thingy?"

The goat man nodded, pleased Robin was keeping up. "Indeed. It had vanished along with the king and queen. Rumour said that, rather than let the ultimate power of the Netherworlde fall into Lady Eris' murderous hands, the King and Queen of the Fae shattered the Arcania. They split it into seven pieces, and then they scattered these pieces throughout the Netherworlde. Even the loyal members of the Fae Guard did not know where. Hidden forever from Eris' eyes." Phorbas looked deeply troubled.

"Without the power of the Arcania, Lady Eris can never crush the remaining Fae. Those who have formed a secret resistance against her." He held up a long finger to Robin. "And … without the power of the Arcania, the Fae can never hope to overcome Lady Eris, and claim back rulership of their homeland."

Phorbas stood and walked through the foxgloves to stare out of the window. "The Netherworlde under Eris' rule is a dangerous place, young Master Robin, especially for a changeling such as yourself. It is a shame you could not have seen it before the war."

"You said before…" Robin began, hardly believing what he was about to say. "About me being a changeling, about me not being … human?"

Phorbas turned back to him. "A shock, I'm sure. But yes, the truth. You are not human, Robin. You are of Fae blood. Your parents were both Fae. You were born in the Netherworlde as the war reached its bloody conclusion. Twelve years ago, Lady Eris rose to ultimate power, the Arcania shattered and the Fae rulers disappeared. You were born, as they say … in interesting times." He gave Robin a sympathetic look. "You have to understand, it was chaotic and dangerous for all Fae when Eris took over. Your parents feared for your life, Robin. A newborn Fae in such a world? You could not hope to survive. So they arranged to have you brought secretly to the mortal realm and placed you in the care of a human friend. A woman who you have always called grandmother."

"My parents … gave me away?" Robin stammered.

"You were to be raised as a human, Robin," Phorbas said beseechingly "Far from the Netherworlde, away from the war, from danger. You would not remember your home, your family, even what you were. But you would be safe. You would live. Your parents…" He halted, looking at Robin from the window. "… I'm sorry to tell you, they were lost in the war, Robin, soon after they sent you here. As were so many of your people. They could never come back for you. Everyone thought it best you know nothing."

Robin felt an angry lump rising in his chest. "And now that whole plan is out of the window, eh? Is that it?" he asked hotly. "Now Gran's dead, all of you people from another world are suddenly dropping out of the woodwork?"

Phorbas returned to the scarred table. "All that was done, was done for your own safety, Master Robin. It is dangerous to be the world's last changeling. Eris and her people would like very much to get their hands on you."

"Why?"

Phorbas' eyes were unfathomable. "We will come to that in time," he said maddeningly. "For today, I wish not to give you so much information that your brain explodes. That would never do. It would be horribly messy."

Robin stared down at his hands. They looked very normal to him. Utterly unremarkable. Not in the least like the hands of a magical creature from another world. His nails were a little dirty.

Phorbas rapped his knuckles on the table, bringing the boy back to himself.

"Enough history for today," he said, clearly noticing Robin's shell-shocked expression. "Revelations aside, we have other matters to attend, and our time here in the Netherworlde is limited. On to other, more interesting things."

He walked to the table and gestured expansively with his arms at the odd mish-mash of clutter on it.

There was a small bowl filled with loose earth, a jug of water, a closed lantern, and a black pouch tied with a silver drawstring.

"I am to teach you the Towers of the Arcania, the seven disciplines of magic," the satyr said.

"The what?" Robin looked up, confused.

"There are seven areas of magic," Phorbas explained. "They are known as Towers of the Arcania." He counted them off on his fingers. "Earth, air, fire, water, darkness, light and mana." He raised his eyebrows. "Every Netherworlde child begins learning these disciplines from a very early age, so I'm afraid we have a lot of catching up to do."

"We're talking about real magic, right?" Robin said.

Phorbas nodded. "Allow me to demonstrate."

He waved a hand over the water jug. "Water."

The contents of the jug sloshed a little, and then to Robin's astonishment, rose up out of the container and floated across the table, a slow wobbly bubble. It hovered, a translucent globe, just above the pot of earth.

Phorbas made a complicated looking hand gesture, and, as Robin stared, the blob of suspended water began to rain, like a small cloud, watering the pot of earth, until there was none left hanging in the air at all.

The satyr passed his hand over the pot. "Earth."

There was a creaking noise, and a green shoot sprang out of the wet earth. Robin watched as it twisted and sprouted, growing at alarming speed, until a miniature tree stood there, tiny leaves unfurling slowly.

Phorbas flicked his hand towards the tiny quivering tree.

"Air." A tiny, localised whirlwind sprung up out of nowhere, making the pot totter on the tabletop. It shook the tiny branches, tearing the miniscule leaves away and sending them spiralling up into the air, so much green confetti.

Phorbas raised his hand again. "Fire."

The leafless tree burst into flames, making Robin jump. It blackened and shrivelled under the heat, until it was nothing but a lifeless wizened stump. When the flames died away, the satyr put the pot to one side. He smiled at Robin's rapt attention, and indicated the closed lantern.

"Darkness," he whispered. The flame inside extinguished immediately, plunging the entire room into near blackness. The only light was that of the moon, filtering in softly through the tall window.

Though he could not see his tutor's face, Robin heard him say. "Light."

A small orb, like a tiny watery sun appeared in the palm of Phorbas' hand, illuminating the room again. He opened the lantern and tossed the orb inside, where it stuck to the wick like a shining marshmallow.

"There you have it," he said happily. "A small demonstration of each of the Towers of the Arcania. I have not demonstrated the seventh tower, spirit, or mana as we sometimes call it, as that is very advanced casting indeed. We need not come to that yet. I shall be tutoring you in the first Tower, Air, and we shall go on from there."

"And you're going to teach me how to do this?" Robin asked, incredulous. "I mean, I can really do all this stuff?"

"Yes. You have the inherent skills. I am here to help you discover and control them."

Robin looked confused. "So how come I've never done anything magical before? Even by accident?"

"Aha, I was coming to that!" Phorbas said happily. He picked up the black pouch, shaking it in his hands.

"You see, Master Robin," he explained. "Back when the Arcania was whole, anyone could do magic at the drop of a hat. But with the Arcania lost, the energies are now harder to harness. Where once the magic flowed like music and we were able to pick up the tune with ease, with the Arcania lost and fragmented it is as though the radio is untuned. There is only static, and to pick up even the faintest signal one must have an antenna."

"It is almost impossible for any of us to channel our energies into casting without using a mana stone."

"What are manner stones?" Robin asked.

"Not manner, *mana*," his tutor said. "Mana is raw magic that has been refined and put to an object, tied in to a physical body that is. Every single one of us, Fae or Panthea, has a mana stone. And they are each different. We have found in the last twelve years that mana is best channelled through gemstones. You will note that mine…" He indicated the large sparkling gem in the hilt of his dagger, "… is an orange garnet. You must now choose yours." He held out the pouch for Robin.

"How do I know what kind to choose?" the boy asked doubtfully, placing his hand in the bag.

"Every mana stone is unique," Phorbas said slowly. "Each has different properties, different strengths. It is less of a choice and more of a discovery. This is a great rite of passage for anyone from the Netherworlde, Master Robin. This is the key to unlocking your magical potential."

Robin could feel cold hard objects inside the bag, clattering and rolling over his fingers. The pouch from the outside only seemed large enough to hold three or four stones, but there seemed to be many, many more inside. Robin made a few grabs, but the stones seemed to roll and slip out of his grip.

"Stop trying so hard," Phorbas said, a hint of amusement in his tone. "Let your stone come to you."

Robin relaxed his hand. The stones in the bag rolled around of their own accord, and then something slammed into his palm. His hand was pushed out of the pouch by some unseen force, and the drawstrings closed themselves tightly with a faint *swoosh.*

Robin turned over his hand and opened his fist.

He was holding a smooth gemstone, roughly the size of a flattened egg, oval and slightly narrower at one end. Cloudy, grey-green and shot through with flecks of silver which caught the light from Phorbas' lantern, it looked like a thunderstorm frozen in a rock.

His tutor took a small, quick breath, frowning. Robin looked up. "Did I do it wrong? Is that bad?" he asked a little nervously.

"No," Phorbas said quietly, peering intently at the mana stone. "No, there is nothing wrong. But your stone. It is very, very rare you see. It is seraphinite. Hardly ever found." He stroked his beard, looking at Robin wonderingly. "Very curious indeed." He noticed Robin staring wide-eyed at him and seemed to gather his thoughts. "But it is the stone you have chosen, and it is the stone that has chosen you. Welcome to the world of magic, young sir."

The seraphinite stone felt very warm in Robin's palm. It made his fingertips tingle.

"Now that I have this, I will be able to do magic?" he asked, looking up at Phorbas. He held out his hand to pass the stone to his tutor, and was surprised when the goat man flinched away.

"No, no, you keep it, my young student. It is yours and yours alone. It is very bad etiquette to touch the mana stone of another. It is a very personal object." He looked a little abashed. "Your aunt will show you how to bind it so it can hang around your neck. While you are learning, it will do to keep it close to you at all times. The two of you need to get to know one another."

Robin slipped the stone into his pocket. He felt an odd tingle as it left his hand.

"To answer your other question," Phorbas said brightly, gathering up the objects on the table. "No, it does not mean you can do magic now. A mana stone works a little like a focus. But merely possessing one is not sufficient for casting. The Towers of the Arcania must be learned, like any other skill. Your first lesson will take place tomorrow morning." He tucked his knife into his belt, and passed a list to Robin, his manner suddenly brisk and cheerful.

"Until then, I have a few books you will need for your studies. I'm sure your aunt will be able to show you where in Erlking you can procure them."

He looked toward the window. The moon had disappeared behind a low cloud. "And now, I think you should run along," Phorbas said distractedly. "Your aunt specified you were only to remain here, on the lip of the Netherworlde, long enough for me to tell you what I have. It is not … safe … for you here." He guided Robin by the shoulders back to the door. Robin looked half-longingly over his shoulder past the trees and biting foxgloves at the slim window and the world beyond it. Phorbas noticed Robin's gaze, and frowned at him most seriously.

"Your aunt has asked me to tell you in no uncertain terms that the Netherworlde is strictly off limits. You are never to come here alone. You are not to enter the Netherworlde through this or any other station. Lady Eris is dangerous, and there are many things involved here which you do not yet understand."

Robin almost laughed a little at that. He barely understood any of this. It was madness, all of it. They passed through the doorway, swapping cool moonlit cobbles for warm, sunlit carpeting. Robin felt inexplicably smaller on this side of the doorway.

"Off with you then," Phorbas flapped his hands. "Your first real lesson will be tomorrow morning. I shall instruct your aunt as to the details."

Robin turned and stared at the corridor, at the bright morning of Erlking Hall stretching before him innocently as if the last half hour had never happened. As though his entire world had not just been turned upside down. For a moment, he hadn't a clue what to do next. What on earth did you do when given information like this?

He frowned. His parents hadn't died in a glider plane accident. They had been killed in a war in a world he had never known about. Gran had known all this. She hadn't told him anything. She had kept such huge secrets from him. She hadn't even been his real grandmother.

He couldn't confront her now. That was one of the problems with being dead. But he could confront Aunt Irene.

Chapter Seven – Newly Nonhuman

The conservatory at Erlking was immense, a giant greenhouse fashioned from three storeys of shimmering, cool glass, each pane so old its surface was filled with frozen ripples. Black wrought iron made the space into a pretty cage. It was here, among the giant tropical plants and hairy banana trees, that he finally located Great Aunt Irene. It was hard to remain as angry and confrontational as he had felt earlier, distracted as he was fighting off huge leafy fronds and grasses.

She was sitting on a stone bench at the intersection of one of the many winding avenues between the plants, leafing through a pile of old papers in a cardboard folder. She looked as though she were balancing her chequebook – although some of the papers looked even older than she did, discoloured scrolls with large lumps of ancient-looking wax seals. Other documents seemed not to be paper at all, but vellum and papyrus, and Robin was sure that he glanced a sheet which appeared to be a tax return printed on animal hide.

Aunt Irene was wearing half-moon spectacles and a harassed expression.

Robin stood beneath the leafy bowers of a nearby tree for as long as seemed polite, dappled in the bright autumn sunshine, waiting for her to look up. It was very quiet in the conservatory, with nothing but the distant tinkle of hidden fountains and the occasional burst of birdsong. His was still reeling from all that he had been told. He couldn't think how to begin.

Eventually she looked up, after placing all of the papers slowly back into the box in careful order.

"Good afternoon, Robin." Her blue eyes regarded him sharply.

"I'm not human," he said, rather more angrily than he had intended.

She removed her glasses, letting them rest around her pale neck on a fine silver string.

"Is that so?" she said levelly.

"You know," Robin said, feeling his face go hot. "You knew already. You hired my tutor. Did you know he was a faun?"

"He is a satyr," Irene corrected him politely. "Fauns are blue, troublesome and leave thumbprints in the butter. Satyrs are altogether more civilised."

"So you do know," Robin said, feeling a strange combination of relief and horror.

She smiled her brief smile at him. "I see you have had a most illuminating morning. Forgive my seeming cowardice, Robin. I thought it best if I let your new tutor tell you some of the history of our world, the Netherworlde, before we spoke together properly. I thought he might explain better than I could that—"

"You know … what I am?" Robin cut across her.

Irene nodded, not unkindly. "Yes, Robin. I know all about you. I didn't know your grandmother, as I told you, but I knew your parents. They were good people. Long before the troubles with Lady Eris and her followers threw the Netherworlde into turmoil. Long before they sent you here." She waved a hand around her. "To the human world I mean, not to Erlking obviously. You have never been here before."

Robin nodded and swallowed hard. "You're … not exactly … human either, are you?"

"That is correct. I am not human. I am Panthea," Irene confirmed. "We are not truly related, you and I. I have taken your surname and the role of your great aunt in order to be able to have you live here with me. Human laws are quite fiddly about these things. I thought it simplest. I take it your tutor has instructed you on such. He, as I'm sure you have already noticed, is also Panthea, one of my people."

"Eris' people," Robin blurted, regretting it immediately.

Irene gave him a long thoughtful look. "It is very important that you understand this, Robin," she said patiently and firmly. "Not all panthea are the enemy of the fae. You are amongst friends here, I can assure you. We all, fae and panthea, lived in peace together for a very long time before the war." She stood, placing aside her paperwork. She was much taller than he was. "There are those amongst the panthea, many of us, who still oppose Lady Eris and her wicked rule. We wish an end to the persecution and a restoration of the balance. We are the strong and the foolish. I am one of those, though I would not readily say which." She smiled oddly. "I suppose we are 'rebels', or so Eris would call us. I am afraid you are unwittingly a conspirator to a company of outlaws."

"I … I didn't mean…" Robin began.

She waved her hand airily. "Erlking was once the most powerful bastion of faeriekind. The very home of King Oberon and Queen Titania themselves." She fixed Robin with a stare. "It was entrusted to me by them, before their disappearance. I am the steward of the fae court, if you will, keeping Erlking from Eris' hands until…" Her blue eyes glittered as she looked over him. "… Well, until hope arrives. If the King and Queen of the Fae trusted me, please believe me when I say that you can trust me."

"Lady Eris wants this place?" Robin mused, looking around at the sunny arboretum. "I don't understand. I mean, don't get me wrong, it's nice and all, but why would she care about one house when she rules all the Netherworlde?"

"Erlking was once the seat of the fae court and holds many, many secrets. There is knowledge here and much power, which she would pay dearly to get her hands on."

"Why has she never tried to take it from you, if she wants it so badly?" he asked.

"Oberon and Titania set *me* as the guardian of Erlking for a reason," she replied, which didn't really help clear things up.

"May I ask," she continued, a hint of curiosity in her voice. "I assume you have now chosen a mana stone. What is its nature?"

Robin fumbled in his pocket and brought out the large, egg-shaped stone. It swirled and glittered with light. Just holding it seemed to calm him. "Phorbas said it was called…"

"Seraphinite," breathed Irene, her eyes widening a little. "Why, I have not seen such a stone in years." Her eyes flicked to Robin, and he thought he sensed a veiled approval, maybe even pride, from the old woman. "You are as full of surprises as we are, Robin," she said.

"How come…" he began hesitantly, but trailed off.

She inclined her head. "What is it? Speak freely, Robin."

"I was just wondering … Most of my life, I've had the truth hidden from me, no sign of magic. How come all of a sudden I'm learning it? Why all this now?" He slipped the mana stone back into his pocket. "Because Gran died?"

Aunt Irene regarded him inscrutably for an eternity before answering. Eventually, to Robin's surprise, she placed a thin, warm and firm hand on his shoulder.

"Because things have changed of late, in both worlds," she said sadly. "Lady Eris has discovered you exist. It is impossible to impress upon you the gravity of what this means. You cannot know what Eris is capable of." Irene's eyes roamed Robin's face, and he thought, for a second, he detected a look of pity. "She has heard whispers of a changeling, and she would like very much to get her hands on you."

Robin resisted the urge to shift uncomfortably under the old woman's hand and her steady stare.

"This is to do with my inheritance, isn't it?" he said. "What you said last night."

Irene nodded. "It is best to arm yourself with the skills of the Towers of the Arcania and begin your lessons. It is no longer … prudent … to leave you without defences."

She gave another of her fleeting half smiles.

"After all," she added, in a lighter tone. "It is magic, you know; you may even enjoy it."

* * *

Aunt Irene was right. If nothing else, Robin had to admit, deep down, that he was excited. He wanted nothing more than to find Henry and tell him what had happened. But how was he going to go about explaining everything? Would the older boy even believe him? He didn't want to lose the only friend he had left.

As it happened, he had plenty of time to worry about this, as Henry didn't come up to Erlking until after school. He arrived at around half four, still in his school uniform, with his tie messily undone and his shirt hanging out of his pants. Robin was sitting on the front steps, passing his new mana-stone from hand to hand, alternating between excitement and worry.

Henry waved at him idly as he crunched across the gravel. "What are you doing out on the front steps, then?" he called out. "Shouldn't you be down at the bottom of the garden under a toadstool? That's more the style for your lot, right?"

Robin's mouth fell open. "W-what?"

Henry grinned. "That's where you're supposed to find fairies, isn't it? Or is that racist? I don't want to be accused of stereotyping, after all."

"F … f…" Robin said uselessly. Henry grinned at the his dumbfounded expression.

"You … know?" Robin asked incredulously.

"Yeah," Henry said sheepishly. "Look Rob, I'm really sorry; I wasn't allowed to talk to you about it until today."

Robin was still staring at him.

"I wanted to, really I did, but I wasn't allowed," Henry said urgently. "I hate sneakiness, me." He looked at Robin critically. "I have to admit, you don't look very magical to me."

"Are you fae as well? Or panthea?" Robin spluttered. "Are you from the Netherworlde?"

Henry laughed out loud. "Me? Not likely, I'm from Yorkshire." He grinned at Robin's wide-eyed stare. "Thoroughbred Human through and through. Same as my dad. Not a drop of magic in either of us."

"Then how do you know about…"

"Drovers have always worked for Erlking. My dad's been in the service of your aunt since he was my age. Trust me, grow up around here and you kind of notice it's not exactly normal. We had a pixie stuck in the chimney last Christmas, stupid bloody thing." He grinned. "And the old man had a right to-do with a couple of redcaps last summer. Pilfering his cabbages. Vicious lot. Bite your knees off if you let them, or so I'm told. I've never actually met one. Dad had to get your aunt to put horseshoe wards up all round the allotment to drive them off."

Robin sat down heavily on the steps. His head was spinning.

"My dad's told me all about the Netherworlde," Henry said, sounding fascinated, "when I was younger. I thought it was all just fairy tales, you know? Then I discovered it's not. It's about as real as it gets." He looked a little embarrassed "I'd give my right arm to go there. I know my dad's been once, ages ago. I've never even seen it though, not a glimpse. Never met a real faerie either … Well, not until yesterday, I mean." He punched Robin in the arm affectionately.

"This place is going to drive me absolutely mental," Robin said quietly to himself.

"Well, you'll fit it perfectly then, won't you? Fantastic," Henry replied bracingly, in his matter-of-fact way.

They walked around the grounds for a while, Henry pumping Robin for every detail of his day. He was amazed to hear that Robin's new teacher was a satyr, and was beside himself with jealousy that Robin had been through the red door to the Netherworlde. "We've got to obtain the key from Hestia now," he said, walking idly around the lip of an ornate fishpond. "I mean … I've been dreaming of a way to get a foot in the Netherworlde since I was a nipper. Just ten minutes … in another world, can you imagine? It'd be ace."

Robin pointed out he was not allowed in the Netherworlde, about everyone there wanting to grab him, and, you know, possibly kill him, but this didn't seem to deter Henry much. He spent much of the afternoon hatching elaborate plots to get the keys off the old housekeeper.

It was only later that Robin remembered his reading list. "Does this place have a library?"

"Yeah, sure. I think…" Henry pulled a face. "Not exactly the biggest draw of the place, y'know. Not with all the other stuff to mess about with. Like, there's this staircase from the kitchen which leads up to the cellar and down to the attic. And I found one room somewhere in the west wing once where the wallpaper changes pattern depending on your mood."

"Yeah, well, I'm supposed to find the library and get some books before my first lesson tomorrow."

"Bloody hell! Your tutor doesn't waste time, does he? What are they for?"

"Magic lessons," Robin said, and couldn't help but grin. The excitement bubbled up inside him again.

"Oh man…" Henry screwed his face up. "That's so much cooler than trigonometry."

"I'll never find the library," Robin said, rolling up the list again. "It took me long enough to find my bedroom last night. I need a trail of breadcrumbs in this place."

"Come on then, I'll go with you. I'm starving anyway. We'll grab some food from the kitchens on the way." Henry pulled the other boy to his feet and they set off inside the cool building, intrepid adventurers in search of arcane knowledge and sausage rolls.

Chapter Eight – Faeology

At the end of a corridor on the second floor were the old oak doors of the library, above which, etched in stone was the Latin motto:

Studio sapientia crescit

And beneath, this:

IGNOTUM PER IGNOTIUS

The library itself, they discovered, was old and dusty, and very large, with a wall of tall stained glass windows letting in the late afternoon air. Shelves covered every wall, filled with books arranged in no particular order. Whoever had stocked the room had clearly run out of space before they had run out of books, as there were tottering piles everywhere. Some of the larger tomes served as table tops, upon which were yet further piles of books. In the few gaps between the books were scrolls and parchments, tucked away as though to prevent draughts.

Robin looked around the chaotic room in utter hopelessness. "We're never going to find anything in all this mess. It'll take forever!"

Henry thrust his hands into his pockets and turned full circle, looking up at the towering shelves.

"Don't ask me," he said unhelpfully. "I've never even opened a book in here. I always say that if it's worth reading, sooner or later there'll be a movie about it." He puffed out his cheeks. "What's the first one called?"

Robin glanced back at the parchment. "Nine White Winds," he read aloud. "By Zephyr Muldoon."

Both boys jumped in surprise as, almost immediately, there was an audible thump from an old lectern in front of them. A large green leather-bound book had just thrown itself from one of the highest shelves. It now lay innocent-looking in a small cloud of dust.

"O-kay," Robin said speculatively after a moment.

"Nine White winds by Zephyr whatsisname," Henry read from the looping title page. An elaborate engraving of a cherub's face, cheeks puffed out as it blew golden cartoon curls of winds across the cover. After a few seconds, it began again, like a loop of animation.

"Well," he grinned at Robin. "This should make things a little easier."

Soon the two were taking turns to shout out titles from Robin's list, watching happily as books large and small sailed through the air, their pages purring in the breeze, to land on the old lectern in a most satisfying way.

Before long, they had a respectably tottering pile, which they divvied up and carried back into the winding corridors of Erlking Hall.

"You're never going to get through all of these by tomorrow," Henry said sympathetically in a muffled voice from behind his armload. They were hauling them back up to Robin's room, and the spiral staircase was proving quite a challenge with no clear vision.

Robin nodded, peering around his stack to try and navigate the tight turns.

"Tell me about it," he muttered.

"Almost makes me glad that I'm only a lowly human," said Henry cheerfully. "Not goblin or pixie or…" He paused uncertainly. "Whatever you are," he finished.

"Fae," Robin supplied, reaching the top of the stairs and kicking open the door to his room unceremoniously.

"That's like a fairy, right?" Henry smirked, following Robin into the room. "So where are your wings then?"

Robin said something very rude before dropping the heavy stack of books onto the bed.

"Well … no offence, mate," Henry grinned, setting his pile down carefully. "But you're the ugliest fairy I've ever seen. If I found you at the bottom of my garden, I'd fetch the weed killer." He chuckled.

Robin grinned back, though it was an unsettling thought. He still knew so very little about what it meant to be fae. Henry could be right. He could very well end up sprouting wings, or growing horns, or maybe turn bright blue like a faun.

Slightly disturbed by this train of thought, he resolved to question Phorbas about this tomorrow.

* * *

Robin spent the remaining evening poring over the books. They were dense and confusing, filled with complicated diagrams and glyphs. None of them were printed, but written in a variety of handwritten styles – from cramped and dense to spidery and elaborate. They didn't make much sense to Robin, who felt intimidated after only a few minutes of reading.

Henry had stuck around for a while, out of loyalty, but had wandered off after an hour or so to do his chores after failing to convince Robin to take a break.

Sighing, he lay back on the bed, turning on the bedside lamp. He picked up volume one of 'Ethercraft' and read aloud:

"'…The Tower of Air, to many a novice, is an erstwhile and trickstorious art to master. Notwithstanding the Borgic issues of moulding simple zephyrs, the manipulation of spaces Swedenborgian and the various rites and incantations required to gird the boas of the aurora and the daughters of Aeolus, there are also the matters to consider both of relative motionionic energy displacement, and the control of resultant extremis spedralis, a stumbling block which had left many a novice weak and exhausted after nothing more exerting than a simple wind charm…'."

Robin took a deep breath. He closed the book abruptly with a clap. He hadn't understood a word of that. He regarded the messy sprawl of books all over the bed. He decided it would be better to wait until after his first practical lesson before trying to decipher any more of this gibberish. Besides, he could smell supper wafting up through the large house enticingly. He didn't know what they were having, but to the newly nonhuman boy it smelled a lot tastier than Swedenborgian space.

Chapter Nine – Air and Silver

The first lesson in the Tower of Air took place, quite appropriately, in a large domed room on the top floor of Erlking Hall called the Atrium. The chill September air, and numerous rogue leaves, blew in through the open apertures which circled the room. It looked to have been at one time home to many birds. Rusty and elaborate coops and cages, many still with odd feathers caught in the bars, hung from long chains from the ceiling, swaying gently in the constant breeze.

Robin entered, noticing the composed figure of Phorbas, standing by one of the many windows, staring at a wintry-looking crow which seemed to be considering coming in out of the cold.

The satyr clapped his hands together once, quite sharply, making the boy jump and the bird take flight.

"Good!" he said brightly, stepping away from the window. "Here at last. Come, come!" Phorbas gestured enthusiastically at a table. "Let the learning begin!"

Robin noticed that there were several items arranged on the table. A large gold coin, a slip of blank parchment, a heavy glass paperweight and Phorbas' oddly decorated silver knife.

"As you will know from 'Nine White Winds'," Phorbas began, rather presumptuously referring to one of the books Robin had utterly failed to digest the night before. "Air is often overlooked as one of the more powerful Towers of the Arcania. Fire is flashy and fun, yes. Darkness is mysterious, there is no doubt. But Air? Air is not to be dismissed. Without it, we would die. Air can be a gentle breeze or a hurricane! Air can lift and pull, carry and support, repel or restrain!"

"It can chill as well," Robin said quietly, rubbing his arms. His hair was rippling constantly in the harsh wind blowing in from the many glassless windows.

"A fine point indeed!" Phorbas said. He waved a hand in a sweeping gesture at the circular walls. There was an odd pop, and suddenly the wind fell completely, leaving the room as still and utterly silent as a hushed tomb.

Robin stared out of the nearest window. He could see the treetops outside still whipping about in the wind.

"A simple cantrip," Phorbas said by way of explanation. "Breezeblock, by name." He smiled. "It creates a barrier through which no air can pass. Useful if ever stranded on a windy mountain top at night, let me tell you." He shrugged. "Although, of course, not a long term solution, as the air within the barrier, if people are inconsiderate enough to breathe it, will eventually run out."

Robin raised his eyebrows.

"Not to worry, young Master," Phorbas smiled. "There is air enough in this large room to keep us both with hearty lungfuls for the duration of the lesson."

"Am I going to be able to do stuff like that?" Robin asked.

"That depends entirely upon you, Master Robin."

Considering that Robin felt as magical as, say, a cheese sandwich, this didn't inspire much confidence.

"Air…" Phorbas continued loftily, "… can be used for good or ill. What better way to kill your enemy than to pull the very air from his lungs?" He stared at Robin fiercely, his green eyes brilliant. A moment of uncomfortable silence passed.

"We will, of course, not be teaching that particular spell."

He swept a hand over the various objects on the table.

"No death today. We begin with a simple spell from 'Ethercraft Vol I', known as 'Featherbreath'. As I am sure you know from your reading, this spell floats an object on an invisible bed of air."

Robin had a moment of panic but Phorbas continued without stopping.

"Observe," said the satyr.

He pointed at the scrap of parchment and puffed out a tiny mouthful of air.

The parchment fluttered once and then rose smoothly a foot above the table, the air beneath it churning slowly.

"The difficulty lies in keeping the shape of the cushion of air, and matching its strength to the size and weight of the object. Too little and it will fall, too much and you will blast it to shreds."

Phorbas gestured to the large gold coin and again blew out a tiny puff of air. The coin leapt into mid-air beside the parchment and began to spin slowly, its smooth yellow faces glinting as they caught the light.

"And again," Phorbas said. The satyr pointed at the large glass paperweight and blew.

This too rose steadily into the air beside the paper and the coin, spinning slowly, a translucent moon.

Robin looked at the three floating objects with awe.

"As I'm sure you can imagine," Phorbas said, with no small hint of pride, "applying Featherbreath to these three objects of different weight and dimension all at once takes considerable effort and a great deal of mana focus. For your very first lesson, we will be sticking to the parchment only."

"Could you make me float?" Robin asked.

"With Featherbreath? Alas, no," the tutor explained. "Long ago, when the Arcania was still whole and magics were stronger, there were those who could lift almost anything. These days there is not much record of holding aloft anything larger than your average squirrel."

The satyr looked a little wistful. "There is a place in the Netherworlde, a city long deserted, where once those who were dedicated to the study of the Tower of Air practised their art. They were strong and powerful indeed." His face darkened. "But when the trouble began, when Lady Eris rose to power, they made a bold move against the growing war, and performed perhaps the greatest feat of air magic ever."

"What did they do?" asked Robin.

"Legend tells that they took the entire city, mountain and all, and lifted it high into the sky, far beyond the reach of the coming war."

"They floated a city away?" asked Robin incredulously.

Phorbas nodded. "So it is told. A floating island it became, shrouded and hidden forever in the highest clouds. The Isle of Aeolus, the island of winds. It is nothing but a myth now, as sadly are all great feats of magic performed before the shattering of the Arcania."

He shook his horned head, bringing himself back to the present. "But that was long ago, before the Arcania was broken and lost. Such magics, such power, is unknown to us now. Like I said…" He smiled sadly. "…Squirrels."

Robin nodded.

"If you would like to know more about our myths and legends, young Master Robin, there are several chapters on the floating island, and other stories of interest, in 'Hammerhand's Netherworlde Compendium'. I believe there is a copy in the library." He tapped the tabletop. "But for now," he said, pointing to the parchment. "Make this float."

* * *

By the time Henry called in after school, Robin was too tired to do much of anything. Magic, it seemed, really did take it out of you. Or perhaps, as Henry pointed out, he was just out of practise. "You've got flabby mana, mate," he joked.

The afternoon was fine and surprisingly warm for autumn. Henry had dragged Robin down to the large and austere kitchen and somehow managed to convince Hestia to make them both something to eat. The woman complained at length about the hundreds of other things she had to do, but she made them both hearty ham and cheese sandwiches anyway, grumbling all the while.

Henry seemed unfazed by this, so Robin assumed it was the housekeeper's general behaviour and felt slightly less guilty about the incident on the steps. Henry merely rolled his eyes and muttered to Robin that if she had a heart attack, at least they could get the keys off her and go exploring through the forbidden locked room into the Netherworlde.

They took their colossal sandwiches and bottles of pink lemonade outside into the autumn sun and found a large shady tree to lounge under.

Robin amused Henry with anecdotes from his lesson. His attempts to float the parchment had been paltry at best. The only time he had managed it successfully was when he had blown too hard after getting frustrated. After that, he had lost his temper completely, and proceeded to blow each piece of parchment to smithereens. He had saved some of this confetti for Henry to look at because, after all, it was his first act of magic and he felt bizarrely proud. Henry had snorted lemonade down his nose when Robin recounted how he had finally managed to levitate a piece of parchment right up to the ceiling, where it was still pasted for all he knew, as no amount of coaxing from Phorbas had managed to dislodge it.

Still, thanks to his mana-stone, he had performed actual magic.

Henry was leaning against the bole of the tree, idly picking his teeth with a tough bit of long grass, while Robin lay on his stomach, propped up on his elbows in the grass. He was frowning over the schedule of study which Phorbas had put together.

"It says here I've got Practical Casting on Mondays and Wednesdays up in the atrium; Tuesdays and Thursdays are Physical Manoeuvres in the grounds." He raised his eyebrows. "Whatever that means."

"Maybe he's going to teach you to dance," Henry joked.

"Fridays I've got Mana Management in the blue parlour on the third floor," Robin read on, frowning. "Wow … he's even split my evenings up here, lists what books I should be reading every evening. Monday to Friday, I've got three hours every day in the library after classes. 'Follow reading plan A'…"

He flipped a few pages to a sheet marked with an intimidatingly large list of books.

"… Followed by 'free study' in my room, learning Netherworlde History from Hammerhand's Compendium."

"Tough ride, Rob," Henry looked at Robin, his face full of sympathy. "Has he pencilled in when you're allowed to go to the loo as well?"

Robin couldn't help but agree. He supposed though he had a lot of catching up to do.

"Hey, at least I've got the weekends off though," he conceded.

"Shame you're not allowed to leave the grounds really," Henry mused. "I could take you round the village, show you Barrowood. Not that there's much to see really."

Robin looked at the expansive grounds around them. He was remembering the strange, orange-haired cadaverous man at the train station. With people like Mr Moros around, he wasn't sure he wanted to go wandering around the village right now anyway.

"I bet there's loads to see here on Erlking's turf though anyway," he said.

Henry nodded, looking back at the looming house. "Yeah, there is at that," he grinned. "And no one knows this place like I do. Let's go to the woods and find a squirrel for you to float."

Chapter Ten – The Faun's Warning

Robin found himself that night back in his room in the tower, leaning on the windowsill and looking out over the night-shrouded grounds.

He was enjoying the silence and thinking how pleasant it was to be able to see the blue-tinged ground below him and the stars above. Back when he had lived in the city, there was so much light from the streetlamps, it was hardly possible to see the stars at all. Robin let his gaze roll over the hillsides, thinking how strange his new life here was, and whether he was ever going to get used to it. He wondered about what had become of the strange girl on the train. He was lost in thought, fiddling idly with his mana-stone, when suddenly, something at the tree line moved, catching his eye.

He scanned the trees below, hoping to see a wild boar, or even a deer. But the creature which had ruffled the undergrowth was neither of these. It was blue and boy-shaped.

Robin blinked in surprised recognition. He had almost forgotten about the strange, excitable faun who had invaded his bedroom. Now here he was, skulking around the bushes, as blue as the shadows, tail swishing back and forth.

Robin almost called out to him, leaning out of the window, but then remembered the time. It must be almost midnight. Probably not the best time to bellow down four stories in greeting.

The small faun scampered across the lawns and stood by the hedge, staring up at him. As he caught Robin's eye he waved briefly, then motioned for Robin to come down.

Robin shook his head and gestured for Woad to come up. This resulted in the small creature shaking his head a lot and pointing at the ground at his feet. He held up what looked to be a tightly-rolled scroll and shook it pointedly. Robin considered for a moment. There was no way he could scale down the walls. That way lay splattered doom. He would have to make his way through the house and out.

He held up his hand to Woad, indicating 'five minutes' in improvised mime. The creature nodded his head and, folding his arms, leaned against the bushes, tail swishing impatiently like a furry whip.

Robin quickly ducked back into his room. He found his trainers and put them on, not bothering with socks. They felt odd coupled with his pyjamas. He walked to his door as quietly as possible, thankful that the floorboards didn't squeak. The spiral staircase and corridor below were in total darkness.

Making his way downstairs, feeling rather like a thief in the silent hall, Robin wondered where everyone else was. Mr Drover and Henry were at home in their little cottage of course, but what of Phorbas and Aunt Irene? He didn't encounter his tutor outside of lessons, so wasn't sure if the goat-man had rooms in Erlking Hall or whether he came and went through the locked door to the Netherworlde. Aunt Irene was likewise difficult to pin down, frequently out and about on urgent business. He asked her once what she was working on. She muttered something distractedly about Trojans and Achaeans having a dispute, and a treaty in Versailles, which didn't really clarify things for Robin.

He decided not to try and get out of the main doors at the front of the house. Woad was waiting around the back after all, so instead he stole through the labyrinthine passageways deeper into Erlking.

He was brought up short when he turned a shadowy corner and came face-to-face with the kitchen door. There was a bright band of lamplight coming from beneath the dark doorjamb, and he could hear voices murmuring from inside.

Hestia! He had forgotten all about the bad-tempered housekeeper. He shuddered to think what she would have to say if she found he was out of bed at such a late hour.

"Very decent of you to be so accommodating," came a muffled voice through the wood, and Robin, who had been in the process of slinking away down a side corridor, paused despite himself, recognising his tutor's crisp voice.

Curiosity overcoming caution, he crept back to the kitchen door to listen.

"Don't be ridiculous!" came Hestia's tremulous voice in reply. "It is no trouble at all. Don't even think on it a moment!" There were sounds of drawers opening and closing.

Robin thought Hestia's voice sounded a little fluttery. Frowning, he closed in on the door, noticing it was open a crack. He spied into the cosily lit kitchen, peering closely.

Phorbas was sitting on a chair by the open back door, smoking a long curving pipe and drinking a cup of tea. Hestia was busy at one of the chopping boards, dicing vegetables.

"I realise it's late," Phorbas said apologetically to her. "We satyrs keep odd hours you see, and when you are hungry, I'm afraid … are you certain you won't let me make it myself?"

Hestia flapped her hands at the goat-man, looking a little flushed. "I wouldn't hear of it! The very idea! A guest in Erlking Hall, going hungry? And Hestia here with two good hands attached! I am only too happy to help. Now where did I put that Glam-glam jam?" She rooted through the cupboards.

Robin had never imagined Hestia saying 'no trouble at all' or 'happy to help' before. He made a face, half-amused and half-revolted. Did she fancy his teacher? There was definitely more of a titter in her voice than he had ever heard before.

Hestia patted her black hair fussily as she brought further ingredients back to the worktop. "Now let me see. Glam-glam jam, beetroot, Mobotom mushrooms … Would you like anything else on your sandwich?"

"I don't suppose you have any crumbly Lancashire cheese about the place? I do so get a hankering and it's so very hard to get these days in the Netherworlde."

"Of course, of course. Nothing but the best here."

"I would expect nothing less from so accomplished a host as yourself."

She flushed, bringing him his sandwich, which he scooped up eagerly. Robin made a mental note to tell Henry he had heard Hestia titter. He would never believe it.

"So, tell me, dear lady," Phorbas said, pouring her more tea from the steaming pot. "However did you come to work here at Erlking? It's a fascinating place. Have you been in the service of Lady Irene long?"

Robin decided that the two of them were settling in for a good long chat. He didn't have the slightest interest in hearing Hestia's autobiography. Not when there was a mysterious faun waiting for him outside. He left them to it and continued outside.

The night had turned cold, making him shiver as he approached the hedges that lay beneath the tower of his bedroom. He was disappointed when he reached the tinkling fountain only to discover that Woad was nowhere to be seen. He called the blue boy's name several times, hissing it as loudly as he dared into the night, but got no response. He walked in circles around the dark hedges, peering into the gloom and scanning the dark, distant tree-line at the edge of the lawns. There was not a speck of blue anywhere. Robin cursed himself for being distracted by the scene in the kitchen. Woad had clearly tired of waiting and disappeared.

Shivering in his pyjamas, he decided to give up and sneak back inside. It had been a wasted trip after all. The wind was picking up. Fingering the silver horseshoe ward in his pocket and looking at the dark trees again, he reminded himself nervously that Irene had said no harm could come to anyone at Erlking. He resisted putting the horseshoe chain on. He knew Woad didn't like it, and he didn't want to give up on the hope the creature might make a sudden reappearance. Turning to go, he glanced up at the fountain. As he did so, he saw, wedged between the statue's broken horns, the tightly-rolled scroll he had seen Woad waving frantically at him from his bedroom window.

Reaching up on tiptoe, he was able to retrieve it. It was too dark out here to read, so he turned and, as quickly and quietly as possible, stole back across the lawns and inside.

He crept back through the house, having removed his soaked trainers, and did not stop until he had safely reached the top of the spiral staircase.

Rubbing his arms to warm up, he dropped his trainers carelessly by the door, took one last look out of the window to see if Woad had reappeared and then closed the window and curtains.

Sitting on the bed he unfurled the scroll.

Scrawled hastily across the top, in what Robin could only assume was Woad's handwriting, was:

You took more than five fingers Brontosaur! Too slow. Have to run. Skrikers can smell me. Back in month!

Robin shook his head in bewilderment. The rest of the letter, spattered here and there with messy ink, was in a different hand entirely. It was addressed to him, and read:

Robin,

I have very little time in which to write this letter. The Peacekeepers are everywhere and I don't have much in way of shelter, so I will keep it brief. Woad informs me you have arrived at Erlking in one piece and for that at least I am thankful. And also surprised! I would come, but I'm not convinced your aunt would approve and there is no tearing allowed at Erlking unless she's out of it!

Until I find a way around that, you will have to stay out of trouble. Strife is on my trail, so I should be grateful he is off yours! Be wary of the others, I do not know where they are. Woad tells me Moros was in Barrowood but he has now gone missing and might be skulking around in the mortal realm or in the Netherworlde, though I don't know why and that makes me nervous! These two are VERY DANGEROUS! Stay away from them.

Irene is a good sort but stuck in her ways. I will need to talk to you soon. She doesn't know everything I know!

If the visions are true, you may be the last chance we have, so don't let them get their hands on you. Stay put until I can work out how to get there. There are three skrikers after me, and I know Strife has five, so I don't know where the other two are. They may be tracking you! Don't go out alone. They are vicious! Spitak and Siaw are the oldest. They are afraid of nothing except themselves. Be wary of them.

Do not get killed! Not even a little bit killed. I will be very cross!
K

Underneath the signature, in Woad's scrawled hand, was:

Don't show this to the big ones! It is a secret!

Robin re-read the letter several times. If anything, it made less sense with each reading. Exasperated, he finally rolled it up and put it away in his drawer, lying back on his bed amongst his books. 'Don't show it to the big ones?' He wasn't sure what to think about that. Irene was his guardian now. Shouldn't she be told if he was getting secret letters from mysterious strangers? Especially ones who admitted they could not get in Erlking while she was there.

And what were skrikers anyway?

The most disturbing news was the letter's claim that Mr Moros had vanished. The creepy man from the train station was out there somewhere right now? Maybe hiding in the woods at Erlking's borders? Watching Robin? Waiting for his chance to … to … what?

Robin didn't know.

Before he went to bed that evening, Robin slipped the silver horseshoe chain over his neck. It didn't make him feel any safer, but it reminded him of his Gran.

Chapter Eleven – Galestrikes at Dawn

Robin didn't mention the letter to Aunt Irene at breakfast next morning. He couldn't think of a very convincing reason not to, but it was just a letter after all – hardly a death-threat. He ended up trying not to examine his motives too deeply. His aunt was clearly a good woman, but she felt distant and austere, and he could picture the piercing stare he might receive were she to discover he had been receiving mysterious notes from stranger. And so, feeling rather guilty, he said nothing.

The two of them sat munching toast and marmalade in amiable silence while his aunt read half a dozen morning papers over her half-moon spectacles. They were spread out all over her end of the table. Hestia fussed around the breakfast room like a disgruntled hedgehog, swapping plates when appropriate with much clatter. Robin almost lost a finger as she snatched his half-finished bacon and eggs away, tutting under her breath at the toast crumbs on her spotless tablecloth. Her good mood of the previous night was apparently reserved solely for handsome and hungry satyrs. Robin finished his orange juice as quickly as possible, fearing it too would be snatched away before he had a chance to drink it.

"How did your first lesson yesterday progress?" Irene asked, watching Robin wryly. "Were any sticks of chalk thrown at you? Were you made to sit in the corner of the classroom with a dunce's hat on?"

"No," Robin smiled at his aunt's inquisitively raised eyebrows. "It went … okay I think. I was learning the Featherbreath cantrip."

She nodded, setting her newspaper down. "Featherbreath. I see. And how did you do? I do hope squirrels were not involved in any way."

"I…" Now that he came to think of it, his performance, of which he had been very proud at the time, didn't seem too impressive in hindsight. "I managed to … stick a piece of paper to the ceiling," he said, rather lamely.

Irene nodded appreciatively. "Well," she declared brightly after a moment's pause. "If we cannot make a Master of the Arcania out of you, I suppose you could always make your name in the world of interior decorating."

Robin squirmed uncomfortably. Irene smiled her tiny smile. "Give things time, Robin. Your inherent skills have lain dormant for twelve long years. They just need to be jolted awake. Even a small and quivering shoot may become, in time, an oak."

Robin tried to look cheered by the encouragement, whilst also trying not to feel small or quivery.

She turned her attention back to her newspapers. "Off you go then."

* * *

By lunchtime, Robin was covered in bruises and grass stains. His first lesson in Physical Manoeuvres and Phorbas had been teaching him the Galestrike cantrip, a concentrated spear of air thrown like a javelin. Somehow though, he couldn't bring himself to care about his aches, fixating instead on the fact that he had failed spectacularly. He could only form the most basic and tiny strikes which hardly had the power to flutter the satyr's beard.

His offensive skills would come on with time, Phorbas had assured him, but his defensive skills had improved greatly with just one lesson. His progress at repelling attacks was, in his tutor's words, phenomenal. By the time they finally broke for lunch, Robin had gained much control over this trick and had managed to deflect Galestrikes thrown at him singly, in quick succession, and two at once. He had parried strikes shaped like spears and discs, diamond-shaped strikes, even air moulded into the shape of a fist. It was tiring work, but he felt elated.

When Phorbas was apparently satisfied that there was not a single inch of Robin's body that was not bruised, smarting or aching, and his manastone felt like a heavy lump of coal around his neck, he declared the lesson ended and the two retreated inside out of the chilly air.

* * *

It was just after lunch. Henry had a free afternoon and they spent much of it devising further plans to liberate the key to the locked door from Hestia.

Robin had given up trying to dissuade Henry from this ambition. He knew what lay beyond the red door, and though he had been told it was forbidden and dangerous even for him to enter the Netherworlde, he had to admit, he was as curious as his friend.

"We'd never get the keys off her though," Robin said later that day, applying a pack of crushed ice to a particularly sore graze on his elbow. "She's got the eyes of a hawk that woman."

The two boys were sitting in the large sunlit library, reading 'Mana Management – channelling your potential,' by Spurious Sveldinger. Or at least Robin was supposed to be reading it in preparation for further lessons in the blue parlour on Friday, but the morning's combat training had left him exhausted, and it was all he could do to resist Henry's insistent and 'fool-proof' plans to obtain the fabled key.

"What we need," Henry said, blithely ignoring Robin's reservations. "Is some kind of distraction." He turned a book over and over in his hands while he mused.

"Like what though?" Robin asked, rolling his sleeve back down and wincing. "I could make her earlobes flutter with my hugely powerful Galestrike skills if you like?" he said wryly.

"Well," Henry leaned back in the stiff library chair and put his feet on the table. "I've been doing some reading." He nodded vaguely at the bookshelves. "On mystical monsters and their weaknesses."

"There's a book on that?" Robin asked, raising his eyebrows. His face became suspicious. "I thought you hated reading anyway?"

"There's a whole section on that!" Henry said, picking up a book with a wicked-looking imp on it. "You can learn loads of useful stuff. Chimeras can't stand blank verse for instance, and Gorgons are very susceptible to flattery." He nodded sagely. "And I don't mind reading. Not if it's research for a good cause." He smirked. "There are lots of mystical monsters with lots of weaknesses. Apparently the Bodmin bog-hag has a weakness for sugared almonds and romantic fiction." He waved Robin's weary glance away. "Anyway, I found out there are these creatures, right, who look after places, houses and homes and things. They're called hobgoblins, and apparently they're absolutely obsessed with tidiness … sound familiar?"

"Hestia's definitely obsessed," Robin was forced to agree. "But…"

"So if, say, you empty a sack of rice onto the floor," Henry butted in. "They can't do anything else until they pick up every last piece."

He twirled the book in his hands gleefully. "Or even better, you could mix together a bag of sugar and a bag of salt, and they have to sort out all the different grains before they could do anything else. Pure genius. Think of the distraction potential!"

Robin considered this. "I'm pretty sure Hestia's not a hobgoblin though," he said.

Henry frowned. "Sure fairy-face?" he asked. "I thought she was one of your Netherworldey people?"

"She's not fae, if that's what you mean," Robin replied, still unused to referring to creatures and people from another world as 'his people'. "Aunt Irene told me that Hestia's one of the panthea, same as her. Hobgoblins are creatures all on their own, aren't they, like lantern-claws or pixies?" His night-time reading of 'Hammerhand's Netherworlde Compendium' was useful.

"Bugger," said Henry, looking glum. "Ruined a perfectly good plan that did."

"And stop twirling that book will you," Robin said. "You're making the imp dizzy."

Henry tossed the book onto the desk glumly, where the imp staggered queasily for a while, clinging to the gold-leaf border. Robin continued studying, secretly thankful that the plan had come to nothing.

Chapter Twelve – A Most Unwelcome Caller

Life at Erlking soon settled into a natural rhythm. Robin continued his casting lessons in the atrium and his largely disastrous combat training on the grassy knoll. His spare time was spent either in the library or his bedroom poring over books. Only Henry managed to keep him sane playing top-trumps and devising ever more outlandish plans to sneak into the Netherworlde. Time passed without Robin really noticing, and slowly Erlking became his home, his school and his sanctuary from the nebulous forces beyond its boundaries.

Robin's lessons on Fridays with Phorbas on focussing and controlling his mana were met with dubious results. They took place in the aptly-named blue parlour, a small snug room filled with overstuffed furniture, all upholstered in blue. Thick blue curtains, blue patterned wallpaper and blue carpet underfoot. Even the candles on the tables burned with blue flames. Phorbas talked him through the arts of meditation and channelling during these lessons, explaining how learning to control his mana would improve his casting in practical and combat situations. But the cosy, dimly-lit room was so snug that most Fridays were spent drowsing when he should have been contemplating his navel. He didn't think Phorbas seemed to mind too much. His tutor merely smoked his pipe in peace while Robin snored his way to a higher plane of consciousness.

Weeks passed, and the weather turned steadily colder. Days full of rain and wind arrived, rattling the windows in their old frames and whistling down the chimneys.

Over time, Robin progressed with Featherbreath so that he could float the paper with ease. He could just about levitate the golden coin, though it made him feel like he was going to burst a vein in his head every time he did it. The heavy glass paperweight, on the other hand, had become his nemesis. It stubbornly refused to budge, no matter how hard he tried. It merely sat on the table, unmoved by his efforts.

Combat training continued twice weekly in the grounds until the constant rain churned the grass into slippery mud. They abandoned outside in favour of the large, empty ballroom. Its vast polished floor was scattered with mats and many large cushions for when Robin was inevitably sent flying through the air. Henry often joined them there when his own schoolwork permitted, sitting on the sidelines and acting as cheerleader and critic alike. Robin still couldn't knock Phorbas off his hooves, he did manage once to part the satyr's beard neatly in two, which had Henry in fits of laughter.

Between lessons, the two boys were often to be found up in the tower. Henry had brought his Nintendo DS round once but it stopped working as soon as he passed through the gargoyled gates. They played cards or a game Henry called 'clackers'. It was a lot like draughts, only much noisier and Robin secretly suspected Henry may have invented it, as the rules changed every time they played, especially whenever Henry was losing.

Though Robin kept a daily eye out for Woad, the blue faun didn't reappear. Things seemed to have quietened down. This bored Henry deeply, and he resumed with gusto his plan to steal the key to the Netherworlde from Hestia's keeping. While the older boy elaborated on his cunning and complicated stratagems, Robin focussed on floating his socks across the room to the laundry basket with Featherbreath instead.

They were often confined to the house due to the poor weather. Robin took the opportunity to explore the great hall with its endless rooms. Aunt Irene, unexpectedly, positively encouraged him to do so.

He discovered the odd staircase in the kitchen, which Henry had mentioned once. It led up two flights and brought you out into the dark and dusty wine cellar, and when you retraced your steps, you ended up inexplicably in the large airy attic. It made him feel quite dizzy. He ran up and down them for some time, until Hestia eventually chased him out of the kitchen.

Robin avoided Hestia's domain after that.

One unusually sunny Sunday some time later, when the rains had finally stopped, he and Henry found a wrought iron spiral staircase that led up to a small observatory. There was a large brass telescope, taller than either of the boys, through which Henry was able to show Robin his house down in the village. Robin felt a pang of longing to go and explore the small collection of houses. The tiny cottage looked snug and inviting, with ivy climbing its sides and grey smoke curling out of the chimney.

At times like this, he envied Henry his freedom to come and go, which the older boy seemed, quite naturally, to take for granted.

Robin began to spend a lot of his free time alone in the observatory, watching the village through the telescope, or picking out sheep on distant hills as the great shadows of autumn clouds rolled across the grass below.

* * *

A few days later, answering a knock at the front door, Robin had something of a shock. He was confronted with the spectacle of Henry dressed in black pyjamas, upon which had been painted the bones of a skeleton in green paint. His dark hair was sticking up wildly, and his face painted to resemble a skull, with sunken black eyes and hollowed cheeks. He grinned at Robin's wide-eyed stare.

"Trick or treat?" he said merrily.

"Eh?" Robin replied, utterly confused. Henry looked Robin up and down, disappointed to see the blonde boy wearing jeans and a very unremarkable grey hoodie. "Don't you know what day it is?" Henry said. "Don't tell me you've had your head stuck in your books so much you don't know! It's Halloween!"

"It is?" Robin asked. He'd had no idea whatsoever.

"Yes, I'm trick or treating. Good laugh I thought. Also thought I might make a bit of cash."

"It's ten o' clock in the morning," Robin said dubiously, glancing at his watch. "Aren't ghosts and goblins supposed to come out after dark?"

"Yeah, well … just getting a head start on all those kids from the village, aren't I?"

He looked past Robin into Erlking's hallway, disappointed. "Aren't you doing Halloween here, then?" he said, "Dad's covered our cottage in fake cobwebs, paper skeletons and everything. We've got a massive pumpkin in the window. Looks good, wish you could … come and see." He looked at Robin a little awkwardly as his brain seemed to catch up with his mouth.

"Yeah, me too," Robin replied, shrugging and thrusting his hands into his pockets. "I don't think Aunt Irene's the sort to go for Halloween though."

"Shame really, spooky old house on a hill and all," Henry said. "It's classic Halloween gold!" He shook his head sadly. "You'll get some kids coming up here later, guaranteed. They come up every year, trick or treating, you know. They dare each other to. Everyone reckons it's haunted anyway."

Robin grinned. "Maybe we should have Phorbas answer the door if they do. But Aunt Irene isn't going to do anything, I don't think. She's pretty busy."

"Is that so?" said a cool voice behind them. Irene has just emerged from a side room, her arms today filled with odd hourglasses of dark green glass. "Too busy to indulge my young ward on this night?"

She glanced at Henry appraisingly. "Your father is not feeding you enough, young Henry." Her blue eyes flicked to Robin. "We have never celebrated this holiday you call Halloween before. It is a mortal thing … But this is your house now. I shall speak to Phorbas and see if we cannot arrange something." She glanced back at Henry. "Run along, Robin has a mana management lesson to attend to right now and your clumsy bones are cluttering up my hallway. Come back tonight, let us say … after the moon is up and darkness falls?" She arched an eyebrow. "And bring your father."

* * *

That evening, Erlking Hall seemed to undergo a strange kind of transformation. Up in his room, Robin found a pile of clothing folded on his bed, and a note atop in Irene's handwriting.

My dear nephew,

I have done some research into the mortal traditions of this night you call Halloween, and as both your tutor and I feel you have been putting every effort into your studies with little reward, I see no reason why this night should not be one of festivity. I have of course had limited time to prepare, but I hope you will find this costume agreeable.

Irene

Robin unfolded the clothing with raised eyebrows and a lopsided grin. It looked like an extremely ornate and gothic tuxedo, exactly his size. There was a black cape attached, with a deep red velvet lining and a blood red gem in the clasp.

Robin changed out of his clothes and put the suit on, feeling a strange sensation as he fastened the collar, a small ripple of goose bumps flowing down his body. Frowning he looked down at his hands. Beyond the frayed cuffs of the outfit, they were suddenly longer and white, and the nails very sharp.

Surprised, he passed to the wardrobe and opened the door, the inside of which was covered with a full-length mirror. His face was deathly white. His blonde hair had slicked itself back and somehow he seemed to have acquired a widow's peak. Grinning with delight, he saw his whiter than white teeth, his long fangs.

"Brilliant!" he said, and spent a few minutes making faces at himself. When he eventually went down to the house proper, he found it lit with an eerie green glow. Cobwebs and dust, which had certainly not been there fifteen minutes earlier, covered everything. The curtains at each window floated in an unseen breeze. There were carved pumpkins dotted everywhere, each filled with a guttering green flame. How there had been time to decorate the hallways like this Robin had no idea, but they looked impressive.

Aunt Irene, Phorbas and Hestia were all waiting for him in the entrance hallway. It was newly gloom-shrouded, cobwebbed and spooky-looking. The chandelier swayed tinklingly of its own accord, and from deep in the house, mournful wailing could be heard.

Irene smiled briefly up at him as he descended vampirically from the upper landing.

"This meets with your approval?" she inquired, gesturing at the haunted entrance hallway.

"It's fantastic! How did you…"

"The Hall? Just a few rather advanced glamours, they will not last the night," she glanced around. "Fairly effective though, if I do say so myself."

Hestia was staring around at the dusty cobwebbed hallway with tight-lipped, mute horror. Her fingers twitched involuntarily, searching unconsciously for a duster.

"But this costume?" Robin said. "I'm a vampire!"

Phorbas smiled, looking rather alarming in the sickly green light. "Ah yes. That would be my doing," he said. "And, to clarify, you only appear to be a vampire, Master Robin. The stone clasp around your neck has been treated with a paste made from Mobotom mushrooms and Glam-glam jam, a very powerful illusion-maker indeed. The stone itself once belonged to a vampire. Its old mana-stone actually. Luckily we had it here. While you wear it, you take on something of its old appearance. A crude glamour, but effective nonetheless."

"Again, it will not last," Irene said, smiling. "But long enough for you to enjoy yourself a little."

Before Robin could comment or question on what he considered to be the rather large bombshell of vampires being 'real', the doorbell rang and Phorbas crossed to answer it, his goatish shadow leaping like a demon on the haunted walls. It was Henry and Mr Drover, who made their way inside, Henry still dressed as a skeleton. Mr Drover chuckled to himself appreciatively as he looked around the crypt-like room.

"Do you have any idea how spooky this place looks coming up the hill?" Henry said breathlessly. "All the green windows and pumpkins? And there's fog rolling over the grass everywhere outside? It's brilliant! It … Bloody Nora, Robin!" he exclaimed, catching sight of the short blonde vampire in the foyer.

Mr Drover laughed heartily. "I understand there is to be a feast?" he said to the room in general, patting his stomach happily as mournful wails and distant wicked laughter echoed through from the inner reaches of the house.

* * *

There was indeed a feast to be had. The dining room, like the rest of Erlking, had been transformed into a haunted castle. Robin saw bats flitting around the rafters, ghostly green fire crackling in the hearth, and the many portraits which normally lined the walls of the room had been replaced with cobwebby images of shadowy creatures and ghostly shapes, some of which scuttled around in their frames or made threatening faces at the diners. One painting was dripping blood in long gloopy lines out of its frame down the walls to pool on the floor. Hestia kept staring at it, her lips tight.

There was enough food to feed fifty people. Some of it was quite normal, like sausage rolls and jacket potatoes. But there were also plates of twitching pastries shaped to look like severed hands, a large spiderweb trifle complete with struggling raisin flies, a platter of wriggling green spaghetti, the sight of which made Henry heave, and an enormous bowl containing numerous eyeballs. Robin steered clear of these, unsure of quite how seriously Aunt Irene had researched Halloween, although throughout the meal Phorbas took great delight in crunching them down like gobstoppers. Hestia, who seemed unused to sitting for a grand dinner, kept trying to get up and serve everyone and had to be almost physically restrained. Robin and the satyr floated the plates to each other in a suitably spooky way, and Mr Drover entertained them all as they ate by telling several hokey ghost stories.

Some of the village's braver children did indeed come trick or treating as the night drew on. Phorbas, munching on a mouthful of eyeballs as he answered the door, scared most of them away, screaming before they could claim their treats.

Robin, though hugely impressed with the authenticity of his costume, found it quite difficult both to eat and to speak with long fangs. To everyone's amusement he kept biting his bottom lip, so as they eventually moved onto dessert he took off the vampire's old mana stone, feeling the glamour lift. Henry had been attacking the food with such gusto that his own painted skeleton face was smudged beyond recognition, and he now looked rather un-spookily like a dishevelled panda.

After they had all eaten, Phorbas led everybody outside into the grounds where a large bonfire waiting, its crackling orange flames warming them all on the chilly October night. There were clear skies overhead, dotted with many stars, and they sat around the fire on hewn logs, although a garden chair had been fetched from the conservatory for Aunt Irene.

It was, Robin thought, extremely pleasant sitting by the crackling bonfire under the stars. He had enjoyed a wonderful night. Their stomachs were all straining contentedly from so much food and Phorbas produced a set of pan-pipes. He played a wild and merry tune, which chased the white and orange sparks of the bonfire high into the night.

"This has got to be the best Halloween ever," Robin said happily to Henry.

"Couldn't agree more. I'm stuffed," Henry said happily, stretching the elastic of his waistband away from his stomach. "We never did this before you came here. I never thought your Aunt would go in for something like this. Perhaps it'll be a new tradition? Do it every year."

Robin grinned. He sometimes forgot that he would be here for years – that Erlking Hall was his home now. He only wished Gran could be here with them as well.

They sat and talked until their faces were toasty from the flames and their feet frozen from the ground, the bonfire crackling against the cold and the merry babble of Phorbas' music floating into the clear dark sky.

Hestia had gone inside after an hour or so from the kitchen door. Robin and Henry watched her reappear, making her way across the lawns. She crossed to Aunt Irene, bending to speak low in her ear. Irene rose and followed the housekeeper back to the Hall without a further word to anyone. It was approaching midnight now, and the macabre glamour at last seemed to be fading. The sickly green light in the windows was slowly bleeding back to a warm orange-yellow and the creeping tendrils of mist were almost completely gone.

Robin, momentarily at a loose end, looked around. He was idly scanning the gorse bushes beyond the rose gardens, when from the corner of his eye he glimpsed something moving. A swish of activity beneath the trees. He blinked. No one else had seen anything. Mr Drover and Henry were talking and Phorbas was engrossed in cleaning out the bowl of his pipe.

Robin stared back towards the trees, just in time to see a bush rustle and a small arm frantically waving. It was gone as soon as he saw it.

Robin rose slowly from his log and stepped slowly out of the circle of firelight and off into the shadows of the grounds. Robin made his way across the dark lawns. The ground was hard and almost frozen solid, making it lumpy and uneven, and once or twice he almost stumbled, his night vision ruined after sitting in the glare of the fire for so long.

"Woad?" he hissed as he leaned forward into the trees, squinting to make out anything in the cold darkness.

He listened for a reply, but none was forthcoming. So after a moment's hesitation, and wishing dearly that he was wearing something warm and woolly instead of a mini-tuxedo, he stepped between the trees, hands out before him in the blackness to ward off eye-poking branches.

"Psst!" came a whisper from the darkness between the trees. Robin squinted into the gloom.

"Stop saying 'psst!'," Robin said quite loudly. "Nobody actually says 'psst'."

A small shadow detached itself from the deeper darkness, mere inches in front of his face. Robin took a faltering step backwards in surprise, but as he stumbled, losing his balance, an arm shot out of the shadows and small blue fingers caught around his wrist, pulling him upright with surprising strength.

"Jumpy little pterosaur, aren't you?" a familiar voice piped up, and Robin saw a flash of white teeth beneath the eyes. "Jumpier than a trampoline full of fleas."

"What are you doing here?" Robin hissed, once he had gotten over the initial surprise.

"Spying," Woad replied, hunkering down on his haunches and looking sternly over Robin's shoulder back at the house. "Keeping an eye out. Someone has to watch what goes on around here. You and the other pink one might as well have your eyes closed!"

"The other one?" Robin blinked. "You mean Henry? I haven't seen you in weeks. Where have you been?"

Woad stood up straight again, sniffing the air suspiciously. "I'm good at not being seen," he said. "I'm the best. I can not be seen for ages if I want to. No one's better at it than me. That's why she's got me watching your back. And your front and sides, of course," he added conscientiously.

Robin opened his mouth to question further but Woad held up a hand impatiently. "No time, Pinky," he snapped. "I've come to warn you. I never thought he'd get in the grounds. But that old woman let him in. I could feel him nearby. I'm very clever at that." He made a face. "He feels like ants."

"Woad, what are you talking about?"

The faun's eyes flicked to Robin, and he saw for the first time with some alarm that the small creature looked very worried indeed. "Eris' man. Aren't you listening? He's come to Erlking. I saw him come up the path while you were all at your big fire. I've got the sharpest eyes in the Netherworlde. They're so sharp you could whittle wood with them."

"Eris' man?" Robin asked, confused.

Woad nodded. "He had to leave the skrikers at the gates, of course. Even mad as she is, the old woman wouldn't let them on the grounds. But he's here all right. I saw him striding up here in his old suit looking like a scarecrow."

Robin's heart seemed to pound against his ribs. "You mean Mr Moros? He's here at Erlking?" A chill had begun to crawl up Robin's back as he followed the faun back through the trees.

Woad shook his head impatiently. "No, no, no. Not him. No one's seen him in ages. Don't you read your letters? Honestly, you're as dim as a trilobite sometimes. The other one. The dangerous one! Mr Strife. They're like brothers, I suppose. Only Strife's nastier. Makes your Moros look like a puppy in a basket of flowers."

Woad led the way across the dark grass, away from the bonfire, towards the front of the house.

"How can he be here?" Robin asked, as they half loped, half ran in a crouch. "I thought nothing bad could get into this place?"

"There's nothing stopping him turning up if he wants to. He just can't do any harm while he's here." Woad considered for a second. "Which is probably really going to annoy him. It's his favourite thing, doing harm." He vaulted a small sundial, the seat of his trousers barely clearing the gnomon. Robin wisely decided to circumnavigate it instead. "My guess is that he has asked to come and speak to her, and she said yes."

"Why would she do that?" Robin whispered, stumbling over pot plants in the darkness. His night vision was not as good as Woad's.

"Rules, rules, rules," Woad explained in a sing-song voice. "She has to say yes, if he's only come to talk. It's only proper. It's hospitality, isn't it? Parley and whatnot. She probably wants to know what he's after anyway. She's a nosy old bird if you ask me."

They had reached a ground floor window at the front of the house. Light spilled out onto the frost-glittered grass. Woad stopped so suddenly that Robin almost stumbled over him.

"In here," Woad said. "I can feel him."

Robin held his breath and listened. From within the room, he could hear the low murmuring of voices, muffled through the thick, wobbly glass.

"Open the window, so we can hear," Woad said in a quiet hiss. Robin looked up at the window. It was latched from the inside, and for a moment he blinked at the small blue boy in confusion. Woad rolled his eyes and tapped at the pearly stone which hung at his throat.

Of course, Robin realised. He fumbled through the tuxedo shirt for his own mana-stone. He wrapped his fingers around it, reassured by the sudden warmth, and concentrated. Weeks of practise came in handy as he focussed his mana and with featherbreath lifted the latch until the window swung open half an inch. The voices within came out clearly.

"… do not know why you insist on this exile, my lady?" a man was saying. His voice rasped like a cutthroat razor down a leather strap. Where Mr Moros had sounded rather brittle and giddy, his brother Mr Strife sounded much more grim.

"I am not your lady, Mr Strife," Aunt Irene replied. Robin had never heard her sound so unfriendly. "And my presence here in the mortal realm is not of your concern, I am sure."

"The ruined palace of a defeated people," Strife interrupted rudely.

"Hardly a defeated people, as I hear," Aunt Irene replied. "And as for exile, you know as well as I that there is no place for me in the Netherworlde while your mistress rules. We can no more coexist there than oil and water can mix."

"Be reasonable," Strife said. "There can never be an end to our war without your help."

"Is this why you have come here? To beg me in your mistress' name to return to the fold? Surely even such a simple creature as yourself can understand, there can never be peace where chaos reigns."

"It is a shame," he said in a low voice. "My Lady Eris is not without mercy. She wishes it to be known that she is offering forgiveness and pardon to all panthea who renounce this mindless warmongering, recant their sins and swear fealty to their own people, to her."

"How convenient," Irene replied. "And I suppose the fact that Erlking would then fall under her control would have nothing to do with this offer?" She scoffed humourlessly. "Lady Eris is, as we both know, utterly without mercy. It is a concept as beyond her as are the pleas of a ship to the ears of the tempest which beats it against the rocks. Do not insult my intelligence. I agreed to your request for an audience, did I not? If this is all you have to say I shall replace the wards at once and—"

"Without mercy?" Mr Strife interjected angrily. "You say this, though you know full well that the very captain of the peacekeepers was once—"

"I have no time for your history lessons," Irene snapped, furiously angry.

"We shall not speak of him then…" he said toadily.

"Is this all you came for?" she asked. "I rather think not. Do not insult my hospitality, Mr Strife. We both know you are really here about the boy."

"It is true … he is the Scion," Strife hissed, and his eager tone made Robin feel queasy. "A valuable tool to any who know how to wield it. The seers in the sacred grove have lately whispered of his coming."

"He is not a 'tool'. He is a boy, and I am well aware of his potential. It is lucky we got him here to safety before you got your claws into him. You and your skrikers are not the hunters you once were, perhaps? Or is it more than you are merely losing your edge? Some kind of problem with one of the seers, I understand, was involved in your … sloppy timing?"

Strife hissed furiously. "Everywhere we are betrayed by our own kind, yes. The oracle spoke in the wind, and the seers, as always, heard the future. But one of the Seven has … uprooted." he spat the word out like poison.

"You have lost part of your prophecy?" Irene mused. "How frustrating for you, when you cannot even trust your own soothsayers. Unprecedented, I believe."

"It will be dealt with," Strife said, his voice dangerous. "It matters not. We found the boy at last. We know you are holding him here, keeping him from his destiny!"

"Keeping him safe you mean," Irene corrected. "Until he can defend himself against you and your mistress. What you want him to do…"

"*Debetis velle quae velimus*!" Strife spat. A chair scraped on the floor.

"But I do not," she replied calmly after a moment. "I wish only for peace, as you know. Not domination. Your dark desires are not mine. They are not even your own. You have no desires other than those of your mistress. You are nothing but echoes of her mind."

"So," Strife glowered. "You will not release this boy, this faechild, this traitor to the realm?"

"No sooner than I would throw a fox to a pack of wild hounds, no," she replied levelly.

Strife hissed at her like an angry snake. "If he is truly the Scion, if the seers speak true, you know what he is capable of, what he can do. The source can yet be reunited!"

"*Hoc fonte derivata clades in patriam populumque fluxit,*" she whispered quietly. "Perhaps it is best that what is lost remains lost."

"You are not worthy to use the high tongue any longer, my lady," he snarled. "Exile that you have chosen to become. Conspirator of the fae. Traitor to the panthea. You hold the Netherworlde's only hope from his true purpose. With the source reunited, the Netherworlde could be reconciled with the mortal world."

"Or torn utterly from it," Irene replied. "You have had a wasted journey, Mr Strife. And you have outstayed your welcome."

"You presume to dismiss me?" Strife hissed, but Irene cut him off.

"I am the custodian of Erlking, and yes, you are dismissed. I revoke my hospitality to you. Do not enter Erlking's grounds again."

Silence reigned in the room. Finally, there came the sound of footsteps and a door opening and closing. Robin looked to Woad.

"What the hell was that all about?" he whispered.

Woad made a face. "Who knows? Come on, if we're quick, we can get to the doors before Strife, make sure he leaves like he's supposed to." He set off through the darkness, leaving Robin to follow him once more, too slow to argue.

They reached the front door at a run, almost tripping over one another as they were flung open and the tall and willowy figure of Mr Strife appeared, stalking down the steps. There was a horrible, terrifying moment when everything seemed to freeze. Robin and Woad, caught in the light spilling from the entrance hall, stared up at the silhouetted figure, just as Strife himself stopped mid-stride, looking down in surprise at the two boys.

"Well," he said icily after a moment, his eyes boring into Robin. "Here we have the man of the moment." A smile appeared on his face, like a slit in old parchment. It reached nowhere near his eyes. "How … very … interesting."

He descended the last few steps, his pointed black shoes crunching lightly on the gravel, the tails of his frock-coat floating out behind him. He looked remarkably like his brother, Moros. But where he had had orange hair, Strife's was a vivid green.

"We have not had the pleasure of being introduced, young fae," he said. His eyes flicked for a second to Woad. "And look here, you have a pet. How nice."

"My Aunt told you to leave," Robin said defiantly.

Strife took a step towards the two boys. "Yes, she did," he acknowledged with a courtly nod. "And I must. Rules are rules, after all." He smoothed the front of his waistcoat. "But we shall meet again, young one. Of that, have no doubt. You cannot stay in Erlking forever." He looked at Robin, and the boy could not help but notice that his eyes looked like those of a shark. Dead and black and predatory. "It will be most … interesting to find you, out in the world." Small sharp teeth appeared between the thin lips. "Yes, that will be a most educative day for both of us."

Robin refused to back up a step, though his skin felt like crawling away. "Maybe you should try looking for your brother instead," he said sarcastically, trying to sound braver than he felt. "I hear you've lost him. Shame, really. You make such a handsome couple."

Strife's smile widened into a humourless grin. "You are not one to be lecturing me about family, young faechild. Look to your own relations first."

Robin felt his face grow hot. "My parents are dead because of your stupid war!" Woad grabbed his shoulder. He had not noticed that he had taken an angry step towards Strife, who had not backed away.

Strife's eyes narrowed. "I wasn't talking about your parents, child," he hissed.

"Oi! Get out of it, you!" a voice suddenly bellowed, making Robin jump. Mr Drover had come around the corner of the house, trailing both Henry and Phorbas behind him. He looked furiously at the looming Mr Strife. "You ain't welcome here! You get off before I throw you off."

Strife curled a lip at the hurrying man in total disregard. He glanced once more at Robin.

"Good day to you, young master," he said, bowing slightly. "When you come to my Lady's court, you will find more hospitality than I have found here."

He turned and strode off down the gravel path, Mr Drover and Phorbas following after him.

Henry joined Robin and Woad at the steps, the three of them watched as Mr Strife made his way towards the gates.

"What happened?" Henry asked, wide-eyed. "You just upped and disappeared, and then Hestia comes out to get dad, saying there's some man come to see your aunt who shouldn't have, and that she told him to go away and he didn't, and no one knew where you were and … bloody hell is that a faun?" Henry blinked, having just noticed Woad.

Robin, who stared after Mr Strife until he was out of sight, looked back at Henry at last. "What? Oh. Yes." He flicked a thumb at Woad distractedly, still mulling over his confrontation. "Henry, this is Woad. Woad, this is Henry."

Henry nodded in approval. Robin was always faintly amazed how unsurprised the boy seemed by all things otherworldly.

"Good to meet you," He said. "Nice tail. I'm Robin's friend, Henry."

Woad eyed this newcomer suspiciously for a second or two, his tail swishing back and forth for effect. Then he said, quite challengingly, "I can hold my breath for eleven minutes. I bet that's longer than you."

Chapter Thirteen – The Lady of Dannae

Woad stayed at Erlking after that night.

It was all very strange how things happened. Hestia jostled the boys inside as usual. She had given Woad a horrified double-take, and then tried to shoo him away like a stray dog, casting about the hall for her broom.

Before anything dreadful could happen, Aunt Irene appeared in the hallway, looking rather harassed and peering at them all archly.

"What is the commotion?" she asked quietly and crisply. "Is the house on fire? I cannot imagine what else would cause such a furore when I am trying to have two different conversations at once."

"A faun!" Hestia cried, near hysterical. "A faun on my steps, my lady! As blue as an arctic fish and as bold as brass! I shall expel it at once!"

Irene waved her into silence and peered at the three figures standing in the doorway.

"Is this your faun?" she asked Robin simply.

Robin stuttered in confusion. "Mine? No … he … I mean, we…"

"It is a rogue faun!" Hestia shrilled, her thin hands fluttering about her apron. "Come to stick the windows and loosen the floorboards! My poor heart! It will take the leading from the windowpanes and hide the soap!" She waved a furious finger at Woad. "I will not have soap hidden in this house!"

"Is it a strange faun?" Irene asked Robin calmly, ignoring the housemaid's histrionics. "In so far as there has ever been a faun that was not."

"He's not a stranger, exactly…" Robin floundered. "He's called Woad. We've … met … before."

Irene nodded as though not remotely surprised by this. "So he is your faun after all then," she said. "Very well, upstairs all of you. I want to speak with your father, Henry, and your tutor, Robin, and I cannot do that with any degree of concentration with a hissing faun and a shrieking housekeeper rattling around the foyer."

All the blood drained out of Hestia's face and she began shaking slightly with mute indignation.

Henry grinned in triumph and clapped Woad on his back, ushering him over the threshold. “Fantastic!” he said, “Welcome to Erlking, little ‘un.”

The three boys went to Robin’s room. Woad, who had apparently lost all interest in the events of the evening, was rifling nosily and unashamedly through Robin’s sock drawer with all the curiosity of an archaeologist.

“You can stay if you want, I think,” Robin told Woad. “Unless you’ve got somewhere to be. Where’ve you been staying anyway?”

“Under a bush in the woods,” Woad replied, sniffing cautiously at a can of coke.

“A bush?!”

“It’s a very good bush!”

Woad looked at the window. The wind was howling around outside. There was frost forming on the glass. “Although … I suppose I can keep a better eye on you if I do stay here.”

“Why though? Who told you to?”

“You’d have to ask *her* that,” Woad said.

“Ask who?” Robin pressed.

“You’d have to ask her that too.” He seemed to reach a decision. “I will stay. For your own sake…”

Robin couldn’t help but grin. “Well if you’re sure. I know you might miss your nice bush out in the forest.”

Woad made a put-upon face, jutting his small chin out bravely. “I’ll make the best of it here.”

Woad declined to use the bottom end of Robin’s bed and instead elected to curl up on the windowsill, tucking his blue tail around him. Before Robin was into his pyjamas, the faun was already fast asleep snoring like a chainsaw.

* * *

Aunt Irene had left Erlking by the following day. She did not, in fact, return for the entirety of the week, during which the weather turned colder still and the sky over the hills filled with snow that refused to fall. Robin asked where his aunt had gone, but Phorbas, far too intent on giving Robin ever more reading and homework, didn’t seem too interested.

Aunt Irene returned at Saturday lunchtime, and much to Robin's delight and Hestia's exasperation, did not immediately expel the faun from Erlking.

Robin was called to her study that evening. Hestia stood beside his aunt with her arms folded and a look of determination on her face. Woad tagged along and both of them filed quietly into the study.

"Robin," Irene began. "I must thank you for your patience in my absence. There were matters I needed to attend. Hestia informs me that your faun has been staying with us since Halloween."

"Yes, that's right," Robin replied, with a glance at the tight-lipped maid. "He's not 'my' faun though. He's his own faun."

"I have also heard reports that he has been making quite an impression here," said Irene. "Hestia has memorised a rather impressively list of infractions."

Robin opened his mouth to protest but Hestia jumped in first. "I have not had one wink of sleep! I have so much to do in this house. And now I turn around and always there is the little blue animal trailing footprints through the hallways, hiding my dusters, shouting at the soufflés!" She took a deep, shuddery breath. "It is out of control. It brings disorder and chaos wherever—"

"Enough, Hestia," Irene raised a hand to silence the trembling woman.

"Soufflés are a cursed food," Woad muttered quietly. "They cause insanity and lycanthropy."

"He's not that bad!" Robin argued. "He is noisy, okay, and I suppose he gets underfoot, but he's just got a lot of energy, that's all."

Woad grinned white teeth at Irene innocently.

"You must keep your faun under better control if he is to stay here, Robin," Irene said sternly. "I will have peace in this house. It is not in my nature to go running after boys, blue or pink, and I cannot abide a swishing tail at the breakfast table. It is not considered decorous."

Robin's hopes rose. "So, he *can* stay?"

"Stay?!" Hestia shrieked.

Irene glanced at her, then back to Robin. She laced her long fingers in her lap. "I do not know why you have befriended this creature, my nephew. And I have many questions as to what it is doing here, and why it has been watching you." She peered momentarily at Woad. "I could, of course, ask you, but I am not your gaoler, Robin. Erlking is yours now as much as it has ever been mine and your associations are your own." Robin opened his mouth to speak but she silenced him with a gesture. "I would not expect you to question me on my comings and goings, and so to you I extend that same courtesy ... within the boundaries of reason. The faun may stay. I shall arrange rooms for it."

Hestia made a choking noise. "Madam, I must protest! The creature is a thief!"

Irene peered at the housekeeper. "That is a very serious accusation, Hestia," she said mildly.

"Woad hasn't stolen anything!" Robin protested angrily.

"He has been in my larder!" Hestia shook an accusing finger. "I had a whole winter's supply of Mobotom mushrooms and nearly half have gone! Little by little! He is stealing them from under my nose!"

"You are mistaken, Hestia," Irene said. "Fauns only eat meat."

"This one..." Hestia insisted with narrowed eyes, "... is greedy!"

Irene looked to Woad, who said nothing.

"I shall not place any accusations at the faun's feet," Irene decided. "But Hestia, I shall arrange for Mr Drover to place a lock on your larder door. That way, only you will have access to the foodstuffs. This, I hope, will not hamper you in your midnight snacks with the estimable Mr Phorbas." A tiny smile flickered at the corner of the old woman's lips as the housekeeper flustered, turning crimson.

* * *

The house was busy almost every day from then on. After one of Robin's extremely boring mana-management lessons, Henry announced that he and his father would be moving up to Erlking until the New Year.

Irene also spent more time there as November wore on. She seemed busier than ever and spent most evenings locked away in her study with only the scratching of her pen and the tick of the clock for company.

Woad did his level best to balance out this serenity, however. Though Robin explained that a little more restraint was required inside the house, Woad seemed to interpret this as moderating his sprint through the corridors to a fast trot, now just barely making the vases wobble on their plinths.

To Robin's relief, within a few weeks the faun had finally been convinced to use the inside toilets instead of escaping outside whenever nature called, although he burst into hysterical laughter when Robin patiently explained how the loo worked. Indeed he spent the remainder of that particular day flushing toilets on every floor until Hestia caught up with him and chased him outside with a broom.

Aside from this, Robin's studies with his tutor carried on as normal during the ever-shortening days. His progress in practical casting was coming along well. He had got the basics of Whitewind now, a healing cantrip, but he was still rubbish at offensive magic. Friday's mana-management were also troublesome. In an effort to stop Robin nodding off, Phorbas tried to liven up these sessions by bringing artefacts from the Netherworlde, a kind of supernatural show-and-tell. Each week there was something new and bizarre to see. A potted version of snapping foxgloves, which Robin learned grew best on a diet of chicken eggs, and a large glass jar of what looked like very old pickles, until Phorbas laughingly explained that they were Gorgon's eyes in bile. One Friday, Phorbas brought a carved pipe, which his tutor grimly explained was carved from fae-horn. It was important, Phorbas explained, that Robin have no illusions as to how his people were now regarded in the Netherworlde.

As November wore on, the last autumn leaves fled from the grounds. Mr Strife made no further appearances and there were no strange howls at night. It seemed that when Aunt Irene had told the cadaverous man to stay away, her word had been law. Robin began, against all odds, to relax.

* * *

"Your aunt would like to see you, boy," Hestia announced one evening, bursting into Robin's room without knocking. Henry had mutteringly suggested that she did this in her endless quest to find them doing something wrong. Instead, Henry and Robin were lying on their stomachs playing draughts, while Woad rummaged through Robin's sock drawer, trying on every pair methodically before casting them aside.

"What does Aunt Irene want me for?" Robin asked, puzzled.

Hestia's eyebrows swooped up haughtily. "'What does she want', he asks! Does the child think Hestia hasn't enough work without being a secretary as well?"

"It can't be anything bad," Henry said, noticing Robin's worried expression. "I mean, it's not like we've done anything wrong since…" He sighed wistfully. "Well, since forever."

Robin found his aunt in the red sitting room. "Come in, boy, and close the door. This house is full of draughts. It makes the old wood warp and does my bones no favours either."

"You need not be concerned, Robin" she said, noticing his expression. "You have done nothing wrong." She paused, thoughtfully. "Or at least nothing that has yet reached my ears."

Robin smiled with relief.

"I am, as you know, unaccustomed to many traditions of the human world," Irene continued. "However, I have been doing some reading and Mr Drover has also informed me that during the following month, it is Christmas, and that usually … presents are involved."

Robin now gave his aunt his full attention.

Irene reached over to the desk and picked something up. "In view of this…" She held out a gift. "You may open it tonight." She seemed to falter for a moment, as though trying to remember something. "Ah yes … and, well, greetings of the season."

Robin looked up at her. "I can open it now? Really?" There were still four weeks to Christmas.

Irene nodded. "I see no reason why not. There will doubtless be other gifts on the day itself, but this…" She tapped the package with a fingertip, "… This is something I feel you might find enlightening now." She smiled briefly. "Open it in your room. One-oh-seven," she added cryptically.

Robin frowned, but she shooed him out of the room, turning her attention back to her desk.

Later, alone in his room, he threw himself onto his bed, package in hand. Tearing off the wrapping, he found a large, ancient-looking book, bound in cracked brown leather and covered in traceries of gold. Robin's face fell. A book … More homework?

The embossed lettering declared the haughty old work as:

'A CONCISE AND INCOMPLETE GENEOLOGY OF THE HOUSES OF THE FAE'
BY DAMSON, HAWTHORN AND THISTLEDOWN

Etched on the frontispiece was a large, multi-branched tree. Its boughs swaying silently in some unfelt breeze.

Robin flipped through the pages at random. The old, mottled parchment felt stiff and waxy between his fingers. Each page was filled with tiny handwriting, squeezed in around the pictures. Some of the sketches were nothing more than faint pencil lines. Others were inked, coloured with dark pigments.

He flicked back and forth through the many pages, reading the titles.

House of Coltsfoot: including Baron Coltsfoot and the Battle of Briar Hill.

House of Buckthorn: with ref. to Lady Buckthorn's silver mirror.

House of Wormwood: descrying the medical genius of the Marquis of Wormwood.

The entries were almost endless.

This is a book of fae families, Robin realised.

His heart stuttered as realisation dawned.

One-oh-seven…

Robin flipped to the page:

The House of Fellows: Inc. Lord Wolfsbane, favoured of King Oberon, and Lady Dannae.

There was a picture, an ink sketch, nothing more, but it was well-rendered. It showed two figures in profile. A tall male fae with straight pale hair falling past his shoulders. He looked proud and assured. His ears were long, pointed and rose through his hair. He had four horns. They swept up, close to his skull, and curled back around his ears in twists like barley sugar.

Standing in front of him, and a head shorter, was a woman. Her hair was dark and curly, bouncing down her shoulders in wild waves. She had two horns, twisted coils playing upwards around her hairline.

My parents, Robin thought numbly, seeing them for the first time.

Mum and dad.

Robin stared at the picture, scrutinising the figures. He could see echoes of himself here and there, the shape of his mother's eyes, his father's nose and chin. Like distant reflections of himself, though he supposed it was the other way around. His father's hair, Robin felt sure, would have matched his own perfectly.

After a while, the page became blurred. Gran obviously had no photos of his parents. He had never seen these faces before. Now they called out to him silently from across a sheet of inked vellum which felt as wide and impassable as an ocean.

His mother had an arm raised and a slim hand placed on his father's chest. Around her throat hung a pendant…

Robin blinked several times and looked closer, holding the book up for inspection. It was her mana-stone no doubt. A large greyish teardrop, and shockingly familiar. His free hand went to his own. The seraphinite beat softly against his chest. It was the same. He was sure of it.

Around the picture, like every other page in the book, dense script crowded. Squinting, he read:

The House of Fellows is amongst the most esteemed of the ancient houses of fae. The lineology can be traced back almost to the First Song, and counts amongst its family such great and noted personages as Turin Oddfellow, the infamous smuggler turned philanthropist who founded the first school of the Arcania; Mulberry Truefellow, who led the fae into battle alongside Lord Oberon against the forces of the Whitefolk; Gossamer Merryfellow the noted master of the Tower of Air, with whose inventive direction, the guardians of the Air Shrine developed the now famous Aurora-craft, and Hemlock Slyfellow, the much praised double agent in the Redcap Wars, about whom many popular ballads are still sung today.

On this page: Wolfsbane Truefellow, the last in the line of Fellows and youngest son of his father Robbin. Wolfsbane is a favoured and most trusted advisor to Lord Oberon and a great general in the Shide army. Also his wife, Lady Dannae Truefellow, lineage unknown, whose kindness won the trust and confidence of Lady Titania, and who is now a healer and master of the Tower of Water currently residing with her husband at Erlking.

Robin stopped. This had been written back when his parents were still alive. Before Eris' war … before he was born.

He read it again twice. His parents had names: Lord Wolfsbane and Lady Dannae. And he, it would appear, was named after his grandfather. He smiled, pleased at the thought.

He propped the book open on his parents' page like a photo-frame. It was while doing so that he noticed that the following page was missing. Confused, Robin examined the book closer. The page had been cut out. Whoever had once occupied page 108 had been removed. The following entry went onto The House of Mudthistle and showed a rather long-faced fae with a goatish beard. Who was missing?

He sighed. Like everything else, it seemed that each answer brought new questions. He ran his finger along the coarse nub of parchment where the missing page had been.

He curled up in bed and that night, as November slid silently into December and snow began to whisper against the windowpane, Robin, for the first time in memory, fell asleep with his parents watching over him.

Chapter Fourteen – The Broken Horn

It was a week before Christmas and tempers at Erlking were fraying. Hestia had been complaining even more than usual lately, mainly about the decorations.

Mr Drover had felled an enormous pine the previous week, which now stood at the bottom of the main stairs, glistening with baubles. In Woad's bedroom, it was inexplicably snowing, and the meltwater was constantly seeping out from under his door. Confined as they were to the house, the children were constantly under Hestia's feet, the last place they wanted to be.

Phorbas had clearly noticed the rising tensions, and so to avoid a full mutiny, had devised a field trip, a sort of herbal treasure hunt. Robin, understandably, leapt at the chance.

Henry had no such luck, as the covered well had overflowed, flooding the kitchens, and he had been drafted in to help clean up by his father, deaf to pleas and protestations.

And so, armed with a scrap of parchment containing a list of odd sounding herbs, berries and plants to gather, Robin and Woad enjoyed a breath of relative freedom, tramping happily through snowy woods. Robin was fairly certain he had gathered everything on the list, though it had taken all afternoon. Woad had been good company but not much help, running off constantly to search trees for hibernating squirrels. It was late afternoon when they finally made their way back toward the hall, tired and content.

Robin's feet crunched satisfyingly in the snow and he wondered vaguely what was for dinner. He hoped it would be something hot. Roast beef and Yorkshire pudding would be just the ticket.

His culinary daydreaming was cut off when Woad stopped sharply and Robin ran into the back of him.

"Woad," he said, muffled behind his scarf. "What are you…?"

Woad carelessly dropped the many gifts he was carrying into the snow and tore the mask from his head.

"What's up?" Robin asked.

"Something is wrong," Woad whispered urgently. "Something is very wrong, Pinky."

Robin peered up the avenue of trees. The house was still out of sight.

"What? How do you…?"

"Come!" Woad set off without warning, tearing off his cumbersome jacket as he hared off up the hill. "Hurry, there's trouble! Bad!"

Robin started after him, all thoughts of dinner forgotten. Fear rose in his chest as he ran. What was it? Was someone ill? Had there been an accident while they'd been away? Was Erlking on fire? Woad disappeared ahead, a fleet blue smudge in the white, his obvious panic infectious.

When he finally reached the top of the hill and the great sprawling mass of Erlking Hall came into view, Robin's heart froze.

Dusk had almost completely fallen and the snow seemed to glow in the twilight. Against it, Erlking stood utterly dark. There was not a single lighted window.

Ahead of him, Woad had stopped in the doorway, framed by the darkness.

Robin forced his legs to move, abandoning his own presents and parcels. It seemed to take forever to cross the lawn. The main doors were wide, hanging off their hinges. Snow had been falling heavily for some time and had spilled into the darkness of the foyer on Hestia's usually spotless floors.

Robin skittered up the slippery steps. "Henry?! Phorbas?!" he yelled. In the hallway he collided blindly with a statue, knocking him off his feet.

"Aunt Irene?" he called hoarsely, scrambling back to his feet and staring around, willing his eyes to adjust to the darkness. "Is anyone here?!"

There was a terrible smell in the air, pungent and bestial. Instinctively he froze, the hairs on the back of his neck standing on end.

"Robin! Be careful!" Woad's piping voice floated urgently through the gloom. Robin glanced back. The faun was silhouetted in the doorway, nothing but a small tense shadow. Only the opal on its chain around his neck was visible, glowing brightly like a tiny moon.

"Skrikers," Woad whispered in a shaky voice.

From the blackness of Erlking's interior came a low growl, slow and deep. Robin turned slowly, making out the shadowy outline of the curling staircase. The smell flowed over him again and in the shadows he saw, to his horror, two pairs of shining yellow eyes.

The creature from the train, he thought as his heart stuttered. Two of them. Inside Erlking.

Robin didn't have time to think as, with one wild howl of pleasure, they sprang forward, swift and deadly.

He raised his arms instinctively in useless defence, but the creatures barrelled past him, huge jaws snapping inches from his face. Woad leapt aside as the skrikers burst out of the front door and disappeared howling into the night, vanishing with astonishing speed.

"Woad!" Robin picked himself up and ran back to the door, but the faun had already reappeared unharmed, stepping inside.

"They've gone," he said. "Stinking skrikers."

"What … happened here?" Robin asked, looking around, his heart still pounding in his ears. "Where is everyone?"

"Skrikers like the darkness," Woad said, stumbling into a small table by the door, making the vase atop it wobble loudly. "Find the light-switch."

Robin fumbled along the wall, forcing himself to calm down. His nostrils were still full of the rank skriker smell. His numb fingers eventually found the light-switch.

"Ohh," Woad whispered after a moment. "This is bad."

Robin could not believe his eyes. Tables were overturned, ornaments smashed, and a large tapestry now dangled in shreds from its moorings. The Christmas tree was on its side in a sea of pine needles and shattered baubles.

In the middle of the room were two statues. Robin had paid them little heed when he'd run into one. Now, in the bright light, he couldn't tear his eyes from them.

Aunt Irene and Mr Drover stood before them, carved from dark stone. Both wore looks of frozen shock upon their faces. Mr Drover's arms were thrown up before him as though to ward off a blow. Aunt Irene's stone hands were by her sides, the creases in her long dress carved ripples, as though she had been half-turning.

"Aunt … Irene?" Robin's voice was a shaky whisper.

Woad approached the statues cautiously, walking around them in a slow circle, sniffing.

"They've been calcified," he said in a low voice. Robin looked at him blankly. "Turned to stone," Woad explained. "Magic from the Tower of Earth – very powerful, very difficult. Strong mana."

Robin stared up into his aunt's frozen face, with its blank unseeing eyes. The statue looked lifelike but … was this really his aunt?

A muffled banging came from deeper in the house, making both boys jump.

They managed to tear their eyes from the horrifying statues and together, cautiously, they went in further.

They found the source of the noise coming from the larder in the large kitchen. It was locked from the outside.

"Someone's in there," Robin whispered. There was another muffled thump and what sounded like sniffling. He turned the key and forced the stiff door open, bracing himself for another lunging skriker.

Instead, the door swung inward, revealing a near-hysterical Hestia, sitting alone in tears amongst the sacks of potatoes.

* * *

For several minutes, the housekeeper cried too hard to make any sense at all. Robin and Woad managed to confirm that she was alone, and to coax her into coming out of the safety of the larder. She allowed herself to be led back through the house to the statue-filled hall, clutching at Robin's arm the entire way as she sniffled and sobbed. When they reached the entrance and she caught sight of the calcified figures of Mr Drover and Aunt Irene, she dissolved into hysterics again.

They helped her into a chair at the foot of the stairs. She was so distraught she didn't even seem to mind Woad's presence.

"Hestia, can you tell us what happened?" Robin asked, as patiently as he could. "Where is everyone else?"

She looked at him with red-rimmed eyes and he couldn't help but feel sorry for her. For some reason, worrying about Hestia was helping him to feel a bit calmer.

"I … it … it was all so confusing," she sobbed eventually. "… So horrible!"

"Just … try to calm down," Robin said soothingly. "Tell us what happened."

Hestia nodded bravely, her hand fluttering on her chest.

She explained how she had been in the kitchen, watching Mr Drover and Henry trying to clear up the flooding water when they had all heard the howling.

Mr Drover had left, telling her and Henry to stay put, but Henry wouldn't have it. "He is always such a disobedient boy," she sobbed. "Never doing as he is told. He does not listen to me and leaves me alone! Then the kitchen door, it bursts open." She sniffed breathlessly, hiccupping. "Mr Phorbas is there and he has blood down one side of his face. He is always kind to me, always a gentleman, and so he hides me." Her lip quivered uncontrollably "And then … and then I hear terrible fighting and horrible noises."

She looked up at Robin, who was staring down at her with wide eyes. "Then all is quiet … for such a long time." She wiped at her eyes. Her watery eyes wandered over to the statues and her lip began to tremble again at the sight. "And now all is stone and sorrow, and what has happened … what are we to do?"

Robin, patting her shoulder awkwardly, looked over at the horrible statues too, and felt his own heart sink again. "But what about Henry and Phorbas?" he asked.

"Pinky, I have found something," Woad announced from the front door.

"I do not know where they are," Hestia said pitifully.

"Robin," Woad said again, more sharply this time. "You need to see this."

The faun had closed the broken doors against the night and the cold, and Robin now saw, pinned to one of them was a yellowish sheet of parchment.

"They've been taken," Woad said. "Both of them."

Abandoning Hestia, Robin ran across the hallway, broken decorations from the tree crunching underfoot.

The parchment had been pinned to the door with Phorbas' silver knife, the satyr's prized possession, with its garnet mana-stone in the hilt.

"There are traces of blood on the knife," Woad said grimly, keeping his voice low so as not to set Hestia off again.

With trembling hands, Robin reached up and ripped the parchment from the door.

He read it aloud:

To the Scion of the Arcania,
I have taken the human child and the traitor.
This is the price for rebellion and resistance.
The glorious rule of Lady Eris WILL NOT BE CHALLENGED.
Yours in service,
Mr Strife

"What does it say?" Hestia asked, peering at the two boys from across the hall.

"It's Mr Strife," he said hoarsely. "He's … kidnapped them. He's taken them both into the Netherworlde."

Hestia crumbled in sobs. Woad looked at Robin with wide, horrified eyes. Robin merely stood with the parchment in his hand, feeling numb. Cold air whistled in through the broken doors.

His eyes wandered across the floor to a chip of stone. Only he saw it wasn't a stone at all. It was one of Phorbas' acorn-nubbin horns, and it had been snapped off at the root.

Chapter Fifteen – Advoco Cantus

Robin's first instinct was to call the police. Woad scoffed at the idea. Robin had never actually heard anyone scoff before, and was quietly impressed at the accompanying toss-of-the-head. It was still irritating however.

"What?" Robin barked. "They've been kidnapped! We've got to do something! We've got to tell someone!"

Woad stood with his small arms folded. "And what would your city men do exactly, brontosaur brain? Think about it. This is no time or place for the people of the human world. What would we tell them?"

Robin started to stutter a reply, but faltered. What would he possibly tell the police?

"Okay," he reasoned, pacing back and forth, running his fingers through his hair. "No human police. Okay. What about in the Netherworlde? Surely they have police there, or something like them?"

Woad sneered and spat on the floor. Even Hestia took a break from sobbing to look up and stare at Robin as though he had just swore.

"'Course they do, dimwit," Woad said. "They're called peacekeepers … and they work for Eris." His face darkened, as serious as Robin had ever seen it. "You don't want their attention on you." He shivered his narrow shoulders. "You forget, Pinky, the panthea here at Erlking, we're all outlaws. None of us are very popular in the Netherworlde. The peacekeepers would love you going to them for help. Oh yeah, I reckon they'd had a great old laugh about that. Right before they served you up to Eris with an apple in your mouth and a sprig of parsley up your—"

"Enough talk about the peacekeepers if you please!" Hestia quivered. "I don't think I can take any more horror!"

Robin sat on the steps, looking from the statues to the crumpled parchment. He could almost hear Mr Strife's cold voice rising from the scrawled words.

He balled the note tightly in his fist. "How could this happen?" he asked. "I thought no harm could come to anyone at Erlking?"

"As long as Mistress watched over," Hestia affirmed gloomily.

"She's not watching much of anything at the moment," Woad observed.

This is all because of me, Robin thought bleakly. I'm the one they're after. If I hadn't come here, Henry and Mr Drover would be fine. Phorbas and Irene—

"I have to go after them," he said out loud, surprising himself. "It's because of me they've been taken." He took a shuddering breath. "It's my fault."

To his surprise, no one argued. He had expected there to be an uproar, even if only from Hestia. Cries of "don't be ridiculous" and "you're not going anywhere!" but she only stared at him, her expression unreadable.

"Very noble," Woad said, flatly. "Only … how? How are you going to get there? Strife has taken them to the Netherworlde, remember? Not down the road."

"The locked room upstairs," Robin answered. "Phorbas took me through it when I first got here, back in September." He looked over to Hestia. "It's a station, a pathway between the worlds. You've got the key right?"

The housekeeper stared at him. "I have no such key," she stammered, confused. "I … I am just a housekeeper. I polish the floors, I count the silver. I've no business with the station!"

Robin gaped at her helplessly. All Henry's plans. Every plot and scheme. And Hestia didn't even have the key?

"It won't work anyway, brainiac. The door won't be there. She controls it," Woad said, nodding at the statue of Aunt Irene. "It only opens when she says."

"So we're stuck here then?" Robin said. "I have no idea how to get to the Netherworlde apart from through this door."

Woad looked at him. "There is another way," he said.

Robin stared at the faun.

"Well, how do you think I got here from the Netherworlde?" Woad continued. "I certainly didn't come through a station."

"How did you get here then?"

"She brought me, didn't she," the faun said. "I told you before. She's good at tearing through. She doesn't need Janus."

"'She' who?" Robin asked, confused. The mysterious letter writer?

Woad nodded, bobbing his spiky head. "She can help us. She's good at finding people. She found you before Mr Strife knew who you were."

"Who is 'she' though?" Robin asked. "Is she one of the fae? Panthea?"

Woad raised an eyebrow "Neither. There are lots of types in the Netherworlde. More than you could count on your little pink fingers."

"Can you get in touch with her?"

The faun shook his head. "Not being found is another thing she's good at," he said. "Strife and Moros and the rest of Eris' brood have been after her for a long time. She's on the run. She's always the one to find me when she needs me to do something for her."

Robin's heart sank. What good was she then? "So we have no way of contacting this fabulously useful person of yours then?" He threw his hands up in exasperation.

"Honestly…" Woad scratched at the back of his neck absently. "You really are a diplodocus sometimes. Are you sure you're the Scion?"

Robin looked at him blankly. Mentally, he was counting to ten.

"I can't contact her," the small boy said slowly, as though speaking to an idiot. "But you can."

Robin wouldn't have considered it possible but his confusion actually deepened.

"I … don't … even … know … who … she … is!" he grated. "I've never even met her!"

"Count to five and twenty, Robbiecorum," Woad said reproachfully. "You have met her, she told me. She found you on that long noisy thing that brought you here, and she gave you her calling card."

Long noisy thing? Robin thought for a moment. The grandfather clock ticked patiently in the background. The train? Surely not that odd little waif? He had forgotten all about her. What had she said her name was? Carla? Cora…? No, Karya. With a K.

The letter writer of foreboding doom, the employer of Woad, this mysterious and enigmatic figure … was a small girl?

"You must be joking," Robin said. "She's the one who can get us to the Netherworlde?"

Woad nodded grinning. "Yep."

"But … but, she's just a little girl!"

"So?" Woad frowned. "You're just a little boy."

"I'm taller than you!" Robin said hotly. He shook his head in disbelief. Well, why not? It was no stranger than anything else around here. But she hadn't given him a calling card…

'If you need to contact me…' The memory of her sharp voice echoed in his mind. Of course! Not a card, but she had given him something.

Minutes later, Robin and Woad were up in the tower, the faun watching with interest as Robin rummaged through the large trunk at the bottom of his bed. His fingers closed at last around a long slim wooden box.

He pulled it out, slid back the lid, and emptied the contents into his hands.

"Ooh, a Summoning Beacon. Nice," Woad said appreciatively, looking over Robin's shoulder.

"I thought it was a flute," Robin said, peering at it.

"Well yes … that too," Woad conceded. "Come on, let's take it outside."

"Outside?" Robin asked, getting to his feet.

"Well, there are no living trees inside are there, brain-freeze," Woad said, dragging him hurriedly down the spiral staircase by the front of his sweater.

Robin felt very foolish. He was standing outside on the dark snowy lawn with Woad by his side and a flute in his hands. Hestia stood shivering in the doorway, holding a tea-tray covered with far too many cups, looking worried and confused.

"So … what now?" Robin asked Woad.

"Play it. It should call to her. If she's got her ears open, that is."

"But I can't play the flute," Robin said, his teeth chattering in the cold.

"You can play this one," Woad assured him. He had changed back into his old brown trousers, his freed tail swishing behind him with impatience. Snow was settling on his blue shoulders, but if he felt the cold at all he didn't show it.

Reluctantly, Robin raised the flute to his lips in the darkness. Then an odd thing happened. As the flute touched his lips, a strange feeling flowed through him, that he knew how to do this. It felt like remembering.

His eyes closed and he blew, his fingers moving over the holes of their own accord. A simple, haunting tune rose up through the dark air, spiralling over and around them. Robin no longer felt cold. The music sounded somehow ancient. It made him think of forests, deep and old, where no one had ever walked, of rustling leaves in the wind, hidden birds.

Almost as suddenly as it had begun, the feeling passed. The music ended and Robin opened his eyes, lowering the flute from his lips and staring at his hands as though he had never seen them before.

"Not bad," Woad said with reluctant admiration.

For a moment, there was silence and stillness. The wind whispered softly across the snow and the snowflakes seemed to hang motionless in the air. Then there was a loud CRACK! and against all sense and reason, a small girl in a large ragged fur coat appeared out of thin air in the branches of a nearby tree. She stood for a moment, silhouetted dramatically against the snow clouds, her tangled hair whipping about her shoulders. And then she slipped on the wet branch and with an 'oof' fell out of the tree to land with a muffled thud in the deep snowdrift at its base.

"Boss!" Woad cried in alarm, running over the lawn to help her, but the girl was already getting unsteadily to her feet, shaking snow out of her hair.

"Yes, not my most graceful entrance, that," she muttered. She took Woad's hand and heaved herself free of the snow, blinking her golden eyes and looking over at Robin.

"Hello, Scion," she said. "It's colder on this side, isn't it?" She looked past the dumbfounded boy at Hestia, and the statues of Irene and Mr Drover beyond her, taking the scene in quickly and quietly.

"Strife?" she asked Woad succinctly.

"With skrikers, yeah, boss," Woad nodded.

"Right then." She made her way across the lawn towards the house. "Looks like the fat's well and truly in the fire now then. Good job you called me." The girl clapped her hands together decisively. She nodded to Hestia. "Is that tea?" she asked. "Good. I could murder a cuppa. Then you three had better tell me what's going on."

* * *

Hestia made a fire in the parlour, and Robin and Woad sat with the strange girl, drinking tea while they explained their plan to go after them.

"You do realise, don't you," she said darkly, "... this is a clearly a trap? Strife wants you in the Netherworlde where you won't be protected. Little horseshoes don't cut the mustard over there, Scion."

"I don't care!" Robin said hotly, irritated by this strange girl's bluntness. "I can't just leave them! Woad says you can get me to the Netherworlde. Just get me there. I'll figure out the rest."

"What? All on your own, eh?" Karya scoffed. "You wouldn't last two minutes."

"I'm going!" Robin said determinedly. He was finding this girl quite annoying.

"Fair enough." She shrugged. "If you're that hard-headed ... I can get you there, but I mean what I said. You wouldn't last a day alone." She narrowed her golden eyes at him. "There's only one option. I'll come with you."

"I don't need a babysitter," Robin frowned.

"You need a tracker," she argued. "I'm the best you've got. We'll go together."

"And me," Woad piped up. Robin and Karya both peered at the faun.

"Henryboy is my friend too," he said defiantly.

Karya nodded. "That's settled then." She shook her head in disbelief. "Honestly, I try my best to keep the Scion of the Arcania out of the Netherworlde and here I am now, giving him a guided tour. Maybe the prophecies cannot be denied after all."

She left the room to go and speak with Hestia, mumbling about supplies. Robin went back to his room to pack a few things. He had no idea what he would need. He threw some socks and a sweater into his bag, and defiantly picked up the horseshoe pendant. As an afterthought, he grabbed a couple of books from his shelf: 'Hammerhand's Netherworlde Compendium', as well as the book of fae lineology.

Back downstairs, he found everyone waiting. Hestia gibbered something about foolish children getting themselves killed, but she thrust a large package at the three of them, a mass of sandwiches and cured meat wrapped in greaseproof paper, along with jars of preserves and drinks. They gratefully packed these away. Karya had picked up Phorbas' silver dagger and handed it to Robin wordlessly. He took it reluctantly, remembering how the satyr hated anyone else to touch it.

"This is no time to be sentimental, Scion," Karya said firmly, noting his expression. "Better to have a weapon if you need one. There's plenty of danger in the Netherworlde beside Strife, you know. Hey, you can give it back to your tutor if we find them, eh?"

"*When*," Robin said thickly. "*When* we find them."

He slid the dagger into his belt, hoisted his pack and followed the others outside into the night.

Karya led them to the nearest tree and laid her small palm against the cold bark. With her other hand she grabbed Woad by the wrist, who in turn wrapped his fingers around Robin's free arm.

"So … how does this work?" Robin asked nervously. "You can really tear, or whatever you call it, between the worlds? Without a Janus station I mean?" He was nervous at the thought of following Strife into the unknown but, despite himself, also quite excited. He was about to step into another world after all, away from everything he had ever known. This was something he and Henry had been daydreaming about for months. He paused. Just thinking about Henry gave Robin a sick feeling in his stomach.

He glanced back at the dark house. Hestia stood in the hallway between the statues looking lost and forlorn. She was clutching the snapped off nubbin of Phorbas' horn. Robin looked away, across the wintry landscape. Down in the quiet valley below, warm lights twinkled cozily in the windows of the village. Normal people were settling down right now to their dinners or watching soap operas.

Robin felt an odd pang of envy.

"You want to know how it works, Scion?" Karya said, looking back at him over her shoulder. Her golden eyes twinkled and Robin saw a bracelet of amber flash at her wrist. "You hold on tight, that's how. And bend your knees when we hit the other side, my aim's a bit off sometimes."

Woad gave a mischievous chuckle at this, flashing his small white teeth alarmingly.

"Here we go!" Karya grinned darkly. Her hand moved on the tree trunk. There was a loud cracking noise like ripping wood. A great wind came out of nowhere, the world folded swiftly away and Robin was pulled forward off his feet into a howling blackness, Woad's giddy laughter still ringing in his ears.

Chapter Sixteen – Through the Barrow Wood

Robin lay on his back, wheezing as though he had just been punched in the stomach, his eyes screwed shut as he fought the dizziness in his head. He felt as though he had just rolled down a huge hill, tumbling over and over.

From somewhere nearby came Woad's piping voice. "Pinky! You okay? Anything broken?"

"Is he dead?" came Karya's voice from somewhere nearby, sounding equally winded but also quite business-like.

"Ugh…" Robin managed, opening his eyes as the nausea subsided.

"He's not dead … just clumsy," Woad called.

"Oh. Good," Karya muttered. "I did tell him to bend his knees. You heard me tell him."

Robin ignored their chatter, staring up at the sky above him. All snow clouds had vanished. The sky was filled with more stars than he had ever seen, and the blackness behind them wasn't black at all, but the deepest most velvety blue. He didn't recognize a single constellation.

Sitting up woozily, the second thing he noticed was that there was no snow. He was lying in a large field, the grass so tall he was almost hidden in it. A breeze rippled softly around him.

"It's … warm," he said in disbelief. "We're really here?"

"Nothing broken then?" Karya came into view, ploughing through the sea of grass like a small determined ship.

Robin glanced up at her and saw, at the top of the hill he had just tumbled down, Erlking Hall.

He stared, his mouth hanging open. Here, in the Netherworlde, it wasn't just a grand stately home. It was transformed.

Atop the hill a castle loomed, massive and dark. Countless towers and turrets, roofs and bridges crowded together like a small town. It looked black and glossy in the moonlight, as though carved from shining obsidian. Every single window was dark. The place looked deserted. Haunted.

It was only when Robin got over the initial shock of seeing it so transformed that he noticed it was largely a ruin. Crumbling in places and half-covered with straggling ivy.

Karya heaved him to his feet with a grunt. She followed his gaze.

“Big, isn’t it?” she understated.

Robin didn’t answer. He was scanning the castle, wondering which of its countless windows he had peered from in the locked room with Phorbas.

“Yep, the Erl King’s Hill.” Karya clapped him on the back. “Seen better days, of course. And that’s where we have come from, not where we are going.” She turned him around by the shoulders.

Beyond the grassy slopes, where Robin’s mind insisted the village should be, there was nothing but rolling silvery hills bereft of any sign of habitation, and a distant smudge of a shadowy forest.

“Ah, it’s good to be back,” Woad said, turning a few cartwheels around them, sending up sprays of pollen. “I’ve been stuck in the human world for far too long! Smell that Netherworlde air!”

Karya ignored him, scanning the hills and woods. Robin assumed she was searching for signs of Mr Strife or his skrikers.

“Where are we going?” he asked. “Can you tell where Henry and Phorbas were taken? Are there any signs? Tracks?”

Karya shook her head, though in Robin’s opinion she hadn’t looked very closely.

“There won’t be any tracks,” she said flatly. “Strife’s too sharp a knife for that. There are other ways to find them, though. Come on.”

She led the way further down the hill, away from the crumbling ruin of Erlking. At the very bottom there was a wide river. Karya knelt by the sandy bank, grabbed a nearby twig and began scratching strange shapes and symbols in the dirt.

“What are you doing?” Robin asked.

“It’s a finding spell,” she replied distractedly, laying the twig flat in the centre of the symbols. “It should point to wherever they are. Wherever they are standing, the ground beneath them will echo here, and then … well, we’ll know where to go.”

“So it works like a compass then?”

Karya ignored him completely. She waved her hand above the stick. The chunky amber bracelet she wore flashed yellow as she released her mana.

The twig rose slightly from the ground and hovered in mid-air. As they watched it began to spin slowly.

"Here we go," Woad said, sounding pleased. "We'll have them back before breakfast."

No sooner had the faun spoken, there was a loud crack. The tiny spinning twig, rotating faster and faster until it was nothing but a blurred disc, had snapped into countless tiny splinters and fallen uselessly to the ground. There was a faint smell of burned wood as the shower of sawdust fell to the sandy riverbank.

"Hmm," said Karya quietly, looking irritated.

"Um … what does that mean?" Robin asked.

"Apparently … wherever they are, they're nowhere on Netherworlde soil," she mused. Woad and Robin exchanged confused looks.

"But they are in the Netherworlde, which means…" Karya continued, getting to her feet, "… that the spell didn't work. I don't know why. I'm very good at the Tower of Earth. I'm in my element." She folded her arms. "I don't suppose you are proficient?"

Robin held his hands up sheepishly. "Sorry, I've only started on the Tower of Air, and I'm not too great at that yet."

"Wonderful," she muttered. She looked around at the horizon with narrowed eyes, biting her bottom lip as she considered. On the far bank of the river, the forest closed in, dark and shadowy. "Strife must have come this way. I can still smell the skrikers." She glanced at Robin. "I've gotten very good at recognizing their scent. They've been hunting me all year."

"Why?" Robin asked.

She ignored him scuffing at the symbols on the dirt with the toe of her boot, obliterating them. "There's nothing else for it … we'll have to go through the Barrow Wood," she said, unenthusiastically.

"The village?" Robin looked around at the empty landscape in case he'd missed something.

"Boss means the forest," Woad supplied, looking anxious. "That's what it's called."

Karya looked to Woad. “We need help tracking. I’m good, but I’m not so good that I can find someone even a finding spell can’t even pin down. We’re going to have to go and see them.”

“Who’s them?” Robin asked, seeing Woad’s eyes widen and feeling rather out of the loop.

“The redcaps,” Karya replied. “They live in old barrows, deep in the forest. But nothing escapes their notice. If Strife or his lackeys came this way, the redcaps will know. They don’t miss a trick.”

Woad put on his bravest face, which Robin found worrying. He had never seen the faun look ruffled.

The forest, however, was on the other side of the river. Robin wondered how on earth they were going to get across but Karya merely told them to stand back and, after muttering a few words, a great writhing tree root, pale and snake-like, erupted from the wet earth in front of them. While the girl muttered under her breath, the root grew tall, creaking like a ship in a storm. With an immense groan it bowed over, spanning the river and dug into the far bank, burrowing deeply into the earth.

Karya lowered her hands. Beads of sweat stood out on her brow. Her amber bracelet looked dark and smoky, its brightness gone. They now had a crude but perfectly serviceable footbridge in front of them.

“That was amazing,” Robin said, deeply impressed, as Woad scampered fearlessly over the wide root. “You’re really good at this earth magic stuff.”

“I should be,” Karya replied in a brisk tone, but Robin noticed a tiny smile on the girl’s face.

When they had made their way across the bridge and all were on the far bank, Karya turned and clapped her hands. The dark root immediately began to whiten, crumbling like chalk and, falling into the river, was quickly washed away.

“We have to be careful, Scion,” Karya explained in a quiet, stern voice as they reached the borders of the forest. “The redcap’s burrow is quite some distance through the wood. We’ll be lucky to reach it before morning. But there are other things in the wood to be wary of. This isn’t one of your human forests.”

“Bog hags,” Woad said grimly.

“And lantern-jacks,” Karya nodded.

"Not to mention Creeping Dread," Woad added.

Seeing the look of confusion on Robin's face, Karya explained as she led the way under the night-darkness of the trees. "It's a plant," she said. "Looks like black vines, but sneaks up on you. It gets you tangled so you can't move and its poisons seep into your mind, filling it with hopelessness until you stop struggling. And then you just … well, eventually you become part of the forest."

"Ah," Robin said anxiously, pushing aside tree branches.

"Then there are the mireflies," Woad said. "Nasty little creatures. Snapping Foxgloves too. They don't look dangerous but they can give a nasty nip. Once, I was absolutely desperate for a pee and didn't notice that…"

"That's enough, Woad!" Karya snapped. She smiled hastily at Robin. "Don't want to scare the Scion off now, do we?" She patted his arm, a gesture Robin didn't find very reassuring coming from a girl a head shorter than him. Woad muttered on to himself quietly.

"Don't worry, Scion," Karya said. "The worst thing we're likely to run into is redcaps, and we mean to find them, so at least it's not a nasty surprise, eh?"

"And that…" muttered Woad grimly to himself, as the three of them disappeared into the woodland gloom, "… is when I decided to start wearing trousers."

* * *

All night, they walked through thick woods. Karya led the way, frowning as she followed a path Robin couldn't see. Woad darted back and forth constantly as they went, dashing off ahead like an excitable dog. The faun made almost no sound as he scampered about. Robin on the other hand, made plenty of noise, stumbling along in the darkness. There was a full moon over the forest, much larger than he had ever seen back in the human world, but its light was caught in the canopy. It only reached the leafy floor in dappled shafts of sieved moonbeams. Robin lost count of the times he caught his foot on a root. Compared to the swift-moving and silent pair ahead of him, he felt like an elephant crashing through the wood.

"Where are we going?" he asked breathlessly. "Did Strife come this way? Are you tracking their … um … tracks?"

Karya didn't look back at him, but plunged ahead, stepping lightly over a stream and forging up a leaf-strewn hill. "Strife left no tracks, I told you earlier," she said. "He would know better than to try and lose me of all people in a forest."

Robin attempted to leap the stream, slipping and plunging an already soggy trainer into the dark icy water. From somewhere in a dark bush, Woad sniggered.

"Then how do we know we're going the right way?" Robin asked, hurrying to catch up.

"We're not following Strife. Please try and pay attention. We need information. That's why we're going this way," Karya replied. "This is the Barrow Wood. You know what a barrow is?"

"Erm … a kind of grave?"

"A burial mound." Karya nodded, glancing back at him. "There was a great battle here. This forest is full of barrows. We're going to see the redcaps, like I said. They like battlegrounds. They make their homes in the graves of the dead."

"They sound lovely," Robin said weakly.

Karya snorted. "Hardly. But they have eyes everywhere. Strife can't simply have entered the Netherworlde and then vanished into thin air. The redcaps will know what happened."

"Will they help us?" Robin wanted to know, as she led them on through the tangled undergrowth.

"Hmm," Karya replied, which he found a tad evasive.

"Redcaps are bad news, Pinky." Woad's voice came from somewhere in the darkness above him. He looked up to see that the faun was keeping pace with them up in the canopy. "They want, want, want, all the time. Greedy, they are. They'd take the shine out of your eyes if you let them."

"Hush, Woad," Karya hissed. "It's not wise to speak so freely here."

Woad gave a muted raspberry and disappeared ahead in a flurry of leaves.

"We have a long walk ahead," Karya said to Robin. "I doubt we'll reach the barrow until close to dawn, so save your questions for now."

Robin nodded. "Sorry, I just don't know anything about this place. Or about you. Who are you anyway?"

"Didn't I just say no questions?" the girl replied bad-temperedly.

"But…"

"I'm on your side alright? I'm certainly not in league with Strife, if that's what you're worried about. He's been chasing me as well as you."

Robin opened his mouth to ask why, but thought better of it.

Hours passed before they stopped to rest. The Barrow Wood was hilly and dense and Robin's legs were aching from trudging through the darkness. He was grateful when Karya called a halt. "Are we here?"

Karya shook her head, dropping to the floor to clear a patch free of leaves. "No, but we'll rest for a while. You look like you can barely stand and you've been wheezing like a village elder for the last few miles."

"We can't stop!" Robin said indignantly. He was indeed tired, but there were more important things right now. "Strife already has a head start on us. If we stop for a breather they're only going to get further ahead!"

Karya looked up at him. "Well, you're not going to be any use if all you can do is cough and wheeze with exhaustion, are you? Sit down."

Woad appeared out of the foliage, carrying an armload of branches. He bounded over and dropped it into the patch of bare earth Karya had cleared.

"Campfire!" the faun said brightly, and without further ado, hawked and spat into the wood, which flashed and promptly burst into merry crackling flames.

Robin stared, astonished. "I didn't know you could do that," he said wonderingly at Woad, who puffed his skinny chest out proudly and grinned.

"The things you don't know would fill five of those books you've got in your bag," he teased. "Trilobites know more than you."

"Woad has a little skill in each of the towers of the Arcania," Karya explained, warming her hands on the crackling fire. "He's too undisciplined to focus on one in particular, as most panthea do, but his skills come in handy."

"Can you do that as well?" Robin asked, flopping down on the ground on the other side of the flames.

"I have no skill for fire," the small girl muttered. "But I'm the best tracker around, and I have other talents elsewhere."

"Boss has strange memories sometimes," Woad began proudly, but the girl gave him such a murderous look that he snapped his mouth shut.

They ate a little of the food Hestia had packed for them. Woad sniffed it suspiciously but decided against risking a meal from the human world. After a while he wandered off to find a squirrel. When he had gone, the silence at the tiny campfire became uncomfortable. Robin cleared his throat. "So … um … how do you and Woad know each other then? He called you 'boss'. Does he work for you?"

"He is bound to me," she replied with a shrug. She gave a weary half smile. "He's more like a tiring pet, I suppose, in some ways."

"But it was you who sent him to spy on me at Erlking, wasn't it? And it was you who sent me that letter?"

"Yes and yes. Someone had to keep an eye on you, didn't they?"

"Well, Henry and Phorbas didn't leave the grounds and they still got kidnapped, didn't they? I thought no one was supposed to be able to get hurt there?"

Karya stared into the fire, eyes narrowed. "Yes, I've been thinking about that. Very puzzling. I don't suppose the old girl can watch over much with eyes made of stone. Clever little loophole. Strife has a mind like a corkscrew."

Robin poked the fire with a stick for a while, looking around at the alien shapes of the ancient forest.

"So, Woad is bound to you? What does that even mean?"

"I saved his hide," Karya explained. "We met earlier this year. I was … well … let's just say I had just left home and I was – still am – trying very hard not to be found. I was travelling and I came across an extremely loud faun stuck in a bog. He was sinking quickly – his own stupid fault for not looking where you're going, but that's beside the point. The short version of the story is, I helped him get free and since then he says he owes his life to me."

She glanced up at Robin, one eyebrow raised, "I can't seem to shake him," she said. He thought she was joking, but it was hard to tell.

Robin grinned. "He seems alright to me," he said. "He certainly likes living with us at Erlking, I mean."

"Well, he's got no one else but us," Karya said. "He's an outcast from his tribe."

Robin looked up at her through the crackling ashes of the flames. "Why?"

She shrugged. "That's for him to tell you, not me. Point is, he's all on his own … same as me."

"And me," Robin reflected.

Karya snorted with what might have been amusement, muffled as she was in her huge coat. "That's three of us alone," she muttered.

"Well then," he said. "Perhaps we call all be alone together then … and that won't be so bad."

* * *

Robin had evidently dropped off at some point as he was abruptly awoken by Woad kicking at his legs. The sky seemed lighter, the promise of dawn not far off.

"Come on. We have to get going. They won't open up in full daylight," he said.

Robin struggled to his feet, aching everywhere. He had never slept outside before; Gran had never really been big on camping. The closest she had ever come to the great outdoors had been a cup of tea at the local garden centre. "What time is it?" he mumbled, shouldering his pack and checking that Phorbas' dagger was still tucked into the belt of his jeans.

"Time to go," replied Karya bluntly, shouldering her own knapsack. She turned and swept out of the clearing, followed by Woad.

Robin sighed, and set off after them.

The sky, glimpsed through the interlocking branches above, was turning a scarlet-gold when they eventually came to a stop.

"Finally," Karya breathed. Robin noticed, with some small satisfaction, that the girl was as out of breath as he was. "And not a moment too soon." She looked at the burning sky. "The sun will be up any minute."

Robin came up beside her. They'd reached a large clearing, empty of trees. In the centre rose a towering grassy mound. It looked as though someone had buried a giant in the woods and the grass had grown, lush and green, over the fallen form. An archway was set in the side, sealed with a round slab of old stone, and several small towers poked out of the huge mound at odd angles, some issuing wisps of blackish smoke. It was a moment or two before Robin realized that these were chimneys.

Frankly it looked like the creepiest, most uninviting Hobbit-hole he could imagine. "This is where the redcaps live?" he asked, staring.

"Underground," Woad replied. "In the dark with the grit and the worms. This is just the entrance."

"Let me do the talking," Karya said. "In fact, you two wait here by the trees until I call for you."

She walked off without waiting for a reply. At the door, she placed her small hand in the centre of stone and muttered something Robin couldn't hear. For a moment, nothing happened. Then he heard a chittering noise deep in the earth, growing louder.

He was just considering how much he really didn't want to meet these redcaps, when the large slab rolled aside with a gravelly roar and, over Karya's shoulder, he saw one for himself.

The creature was small, smaller than Woad even, and skeletally thin. Its head was much too large for its body and wrinkled like old fruit. The fingers were very long and ended in sharp claws. The redcap's ears were tall, pointing straight up above its head, and it had blood-red skin, making it look like an evil lobster.

He watched the redcap peer at Karya with tiny black eyes. It chattered something harshly, too quiet for him to hear, and Karya replied.

"That's a redcap?" Robin hissed to Woad, who nodded, scowling. "It's hideous."

"So would you be if you lived your whole miserable life deep underground with dead bones," the faun muttered. "It's not really red. They paint themselves that colour. They're as white as fish bellies naturally."

Karya was gesturing back at Robin and Woad. He felt the redcap's flinty eyes fall upon them from across the clearing. Then the creature was gone.

Karya waved them over encouragingly.

"What's happening?" Robin asked as they approached.

"He's gone to tell the Chieftain we're here. We're going inside," she replied.

"Into the big grave full of monsters?" Robin said as cheerfully as he could. "Sounds great."

"They're … interested in you, I think," Karya mused. From the sound of her tone, this didn't seem very reassuring. "Put that knife away, though. If they see it, they'll want it. They always want something."

Before he could say anything, the demonic-looking creature reappeared, a spluttering torch grasped in his bony hand.

"In," it snapped. "Big feast today. You come at good time, soft ones. You are guests of Chieftain today. Hurry though, sun up soon, light too much for open doors."

It turned and disappeared into the darkness.

"Watch your step," Karya said and followed it inside.

Inside the mound, a low, dark corridor of musty-smelling earth led deep into the hill. It went down forever and ever, or so it seemed to Robin, corkscrewing into the earth.

Eventually, the passageway opened into a gigantic, vaulted chamber. An echoing underground crypt the size of a train station. Twisting stone columns supported the roof and countless chambers led off here, there and everywhere. Steps went up and down from every conceivable opening. From the ceiling, bridges connected the upper levels in a mad cat's cradle of flying traceries.

And everywhere Robin looked, there were redcaps – hundreds of them, all hurrying about their business like alien red ants. The place was like a maze.

No, not a maze, Robin thought. *It's a hive.*

Their guide hurried them on to the far end of the subterranean hall where, upon a raised stone dais, sat a particularly wizened and ancient-looking creature. Unlike the other redcaps whose skin was as scarlet as blood, this one's was the deep purple of an old bruise. It wore a filthy-looking robe of gold and black, and a tall black rimless hat. All of its teeth were gone, giving its face a caved-in, mushy look. It looked fast asleep. *Or worse*, Robin thought.

As they approached, Karya gave a deep and graceful bow, gesturing at Robin and Woad to follow her lead.

Their redcap guide scurried up to the stone throne and chattered something into the ancient one's ears in its strange clicks and pops. The old creature's eyes snapped open and peered at the three children, lingering on Robin as if he were a particularly tasty morsel. Its eyes were wide and yellow.

"A strange selection of creatures here in our barrow," the redcap chieftain said, its voice a dry whisper. "Two outcasts we see here … and a fae from the human world. A fae indeed. It has been an age since we have seen your kind abroad in the Netherworlde, child." It beckoned with a long and trembling finger. "Come closer, Faechild, so that we can see you clearer."

Robin looked sidelong at Karya, who nodded almost imperceptibly. He warily approached the stone, uncomfortably aware that countless redcaps had stopped what they were doing and hundreds of gimlet black eyes were now trained on him.

The redcap chieftain grabbed him by the chin as soon as he was within reach.

"A fae … with no horns … and blue eyes?" it rasped in a wondering whisper. "Rumours had come to our barrow that such a creature was abroad in the Netherworlde. News travels fast for our kind, but we would never have believed it, had we not seen it with our own eyes."

It turned Robin's head from side to side, beady eyes studying every inch of the boy's face as though considering buying him at a cattle market.

"Umm…" Robin said uncertainly, wishing that Karya would say something. He didn't want to seem rude by wrenching his head free. He had no idea what customs he might be offending, but he didn't like the feel of the creature's leathery fingers on his face. Its grip was surprisingly strong.

"What mana does it possess, we wonder?" the redcap hissed to itself. "What stonework?"

"He carries Seraphinite," Karya said conversationally.

The chieftain gave a quick inhalation of sour breath, releasing Robin's face so suddenly that he almost toppled backwards. The redcap's eyes flicked to the mana-stone strung about Robin's neck.

"Seraphinite…" it mused. "Well, we are most surprised. Many years has it been since such a stone was seen anywhere west of the Whispering Sea."

Robin's hand came up to cover his mana-stone reflexively. The redcap did not seem to notice. It held up its gnarled old hand, displaying a heavyset and very ornate gold ring. It was set with a large black stone, glittering in the torchlight.

"Jet we have," it declared. "Jet is strong and wise, good for Earth Tower. Good for tunnelling. You surface folk, your mana stones are weakened by the sun. Seraphinite? Good for ghosts, no good down here." He sounded smugly self-satisfied.

Karya stepped up onto the dais beside Robin, gripping his elbow companionably. "We need information, Deepdweller," she said, in her most respectful tone. "You see and hear much. We have lost our friends and think they may have passed through the Barrow Wood. Have your people heard anything?"

The chieftain sat back slowly on its stone throne, gathering its dusty robes around itself.

"Our people hear everything," it said. "Every footstep echoes into the earth, every shadow falls upon the ground, and we are under it, and we listen well." It looked from Robin to Karya in a calculating manner.

"What will you trade for the information you seek? We do not work for renegade panthea or outlawed fae, or for your kind girl. Not without…," it spread its long fingers like purple twigs, "… compensation."

"I have a little money," Karya replied. "Not much, but it's brass and unmarked, and I can get more, maybe silver? It will depend how useful your information is."

The chieftain sneered. "Brass, silver, what use are shiny metals to us? They run through the body of the earth, and so do the redcaps. We can find our own metals." It snorted dismissively.

"What is your price then, Deepdweller?" Karya asked, her voice straining to remain polite.

"Surface things. Things we can trade." Its eyes flicked momentarily to Woad. "Things we can eat."

"We have some food and drink," Robin suddenly remembered. "Hestia made us some, I think she put some kinds of herbs in our packs too." He began to unshoulder his rucksack.

"The pelt of your faun would fetch a pretty price in the Agora market-town," the redcap chieftain said, ignoring Robin, his voice greedy. Several of the redcaps around them were eyeing Woad's bare blue skin with hungry calculating eyes. "Soft and supple, especially from one so young. It would be a fine hide for any redcap to possess."

Woad made a low growling noise in the back of his throat, flexing his small claws slowly.

"Unfortunately," Karya said as politely as she could manage, "our companion is currently using his skin and cannot spare it. He would be awfully inconvenienced by its loss. Perhaps there is something else we could trade?"

"There must be something else," Robin said, trying to draw the chieftain's glossy eyes away from the faun. "I mean, we don't have much, but we really do need to find our friends. They were kidnapped, you see. We can't track them. If you know anything, anything at all, we'd really owe you one."

Karya and Woad both gasped. The redcap chieftain snapped its eyes back to the boy.

Utter silence had fallen throughout the hall.

"Owe us?" it hissed slowly.

Robin had the horrible feeling that he had just said something very wrong indeed. Karya was staring at him in mute horror.

"Yes … yes that will be a most agreeable arrangement to us," the chieftain replied, smiling its toothless grin. It seemed very amused. "A good turn … to be repaid. Too long has it been since the trading of favours has passed between the redcaps and the fae. Truly you are an unusual specimen of your people, hornless boy." A murmur of whispering passed through the hive in a chittering wave.

"Here are the terms of our accord." The creature leaned forward on its throne. "The redcaps will discover if your companions have indeed passed this way, and if so, to where they were headed. We will share with you what information we have, and in return, we will hold a favour in trust, to be recalled at a later date."

"What favour?" Robin said carefully.

"We do not know yet," the chieftain replied. "There is nothing we want from you … at present." It looked at its own hands, examining the ring's jet stone. "But there will come a time for a debt to be repaid."

Robin could feel Karya and Woad both watching him, but neither of them spoke up. He got the feeling that this was his responsibility alone. But what choice did he have? In his mind he saw the stone faces of Aunt Irene and Mr Drover. He remembered Hestia describing Henry yelling and the finding of Phorbas' broken horn. He had to find them, no matter what the cost.

"Okay," he said, swallowing. "That sounds fair." He held out a hand to shake. The redcap gripped it in both his strong claws, grinning toothlessly. Robin's skin felt as though it wanted to crawl off.

"An addendum to this deal of yours," Karya suddenly said, "is the safe release of all three of us from this barrow."

The redcap's eyes flickered with annoyance, but it nodded in acceptance. "Very well, little girl. None amongst us will prevent you from leaving this barrow." It held up a long finger. "At nightfall." He looked to Karya. "The sun is up now. The sky is bright. The doors remain fast until the shadows return.

Karya nodded. Woad shivered at her side, tail twitching, clearly uncomfortable with having to spend the whole day down here. Robin was frustrated. Every moment they wasted was time for Strife to get further away from them.

"Agreed then." The chieftain released Robin's hand. He resisted the urge to wipe it on the leg of his jeans.

A smaller, scarlet-skinned redcap appeared at the old creature's side. There was an exchange of chittering commands, then the drone scuttled away across the hall to a large carved stone. Intricate spirals and whorls made a dizzying pattern there. The redcap picked up a pair of small sticks and began to beat a complicated tattoo on the stone. It echoed strangely through the cavern.

"We are spreading the word," the chieftain said. "The gong is connected to our next barrow, and from there to many others. They in turn will spread the message. If your friends are to be found, we will find them."

Karya nodded and bowed again.

"Hospitality has laws," the redcap continued. "We shall feed and entertain you while we wait."

* * *

It was something of a relief when Karya, Woad and Robin were ushered out of the chieftain's presence and taken to another shadowy cavern. Robin's stomach had been growling all night and the supplies Hestia had provided were meagre enough that he was already considering rationing. They were seated at one of many long low tables on a soft cushion. Redcaps swarmed around them, chattering and piling food high on the tables. Robin had half-expected the meal to consist of bugs and grubs, but in fact there were platters of sausages, mashed potato, roast chickens, sliced hot hams, and goblets filled with a strange wine. Karya ate sparingly, trying to look relaxed and aloof. Woad on the other hand, showed no such restraint, piling his plate high over and over again. Food, Robin was coming to realise, was clearly a faun's weak spot. As long as none of it had been cooked in the human world.

"I can't believe you did that!" Karya hissed at Robin quietly.

"Did what?" Robin replied out of the corner of his mouth.

"You put yourself in the redcaps' debt! It's one thing to trade with a redcap but to offer your services? You really shouldn't have done that ... It's simpler to bargain with a demon than a redcap!"

"Well, what was I supposed to do? We don't have anything else to go on. We need their help, don't we? That's why you brought us here in the first place."

"I'd rather have given them Woad's skin that agreed to some ill-defined future 'favour' like you did." Karya shook her head in bewilderment.

"Oy!" Woad mumbled indignantly, his mouth full of sausages.

Karya narrowed her eyes at him "Oh hush, Woad, you know what I mean. The Scion has put himself in the debt of the redcaps!"

Woad only glanced at Robin and rolled his eyes.

"Well, I don't know what else we could have done," Robin snapped. He was getting fed up of this strange girl bossing him around. "They said they'll help us at least. All I care about is finding Henry and Phorbas. We'll worry about the rest later."

Karya sipped her wine sullenly, sinking into her huge fur coat. "I just don't like this," she said to no one in particular. "Sitting here, waiting for news. What's taking so long, anyway? That's what I'd like to know. It's been hours now since Deepdweller sent his message to the other barrows. And all this feasting. It's like he's trying to distract us, keep us here. Something smells wrong."

"I think it's the sausages," Woad sniffed at the banger on the end of his fork, then shrugged and bit it in half anyway.

* * *

It was hours later, much to Karya's increasingly evident impatience, that a slender, wide-eyed redcap approached and informed them that the chieftain wished to have their presence again.

The three companions were led, not back to the throne room as they had expected, but back up the long spiralling corridor to the entrance of the barrow.

The doors to the outside world were closed fast, but the chieftain was waiting for them, his black and gold robes bulky around him.

"You have some information?" Karya asked as they approached.

"We will keep our end of the bargain," the creature replied. "Redcaps always do. We will tell you what we have heard. That is what was agreed between your people and mine."

"Do you know where they are?" Robin asked eagerly.

The chieftain peered at Robin in the gloom. "We have heard that a servant of Lady Eris did indeed pass across the Barrowood, and that those who you seek to find were present. They travelled east, beyond the borders of the forest and far over the moors, but they did not walk. They left no track which you can follow."

"Then how will we ever find them?" Robin asked.

"You would do well to seek guidance from the Phythian perhaps," the redcap murmured. "Or at least, that would have availed you, if you had had more time."

"What do you mean?" Karya demanded.

The redcap's mouth split into an ugly smile. Behind it, the vast circular stone which barred the door to the forest outside slowly opened.

"Redcaps hear much … see much. All know this to be true. You three are not the first to come to us of late looking for information."

Karya narrowed her eyes. "What are you talking about?"

The door was open fully now, the fresh forest air rushed in to greet them. The blood-red light of the setting sun washed through the trees outside and, on the other side of the clearing Robin could make out several shapes.

Woad's nose twitched. "Skrikers!" he yelped in alarm.

The redcap grinned toothlessly. "A deal is a deal."

Karya's eyes were wide with shock. "You tricked us! You kept us here all day. That message you sent through the stone, it wasn't asking after our friends at all, you were sending a message to…"

"Mr Strife!" Robin cried out in alarm.

"We have given you the information we had on your friends," Deepdweller replied, unabashed. "We have kept our end of the bargain. We also had a bargain with Eris' man, and now that too is fulfilled. This has been a good day for business." It chittered to itself. "A good day indeed. Farewell, surface dwellers."

It turned and crept off slowly down the tunnel.

"That two-faced, double-crossing…" Robin spat angrily.

Woad glared. "Well, what did we expect? He's a redcap. You can't trust them at the best of times."

"Shut up, both of you!" Karya snapped as the barrow's door-stone clunked shut behind them with a very final thud.

Across the clearing, two skrikers growled low in their throats, making Robin's skin crawl.

"Here we all are," Mr Strife said smoothly, stepping out from between the trees. "How … nice." He smiled at them, a horrible rictus filled with small even teeth. His green, slicked hair shone in the light of the setting sun.

Karya pushed Robin behind her. "Stay away from him!" she warned.

"Ah … Karya," Strife said smoothly, as though greeting an old friend. He looked at her with his head cocked. "I've been looking for you for quite some time now. How fortuitous to find you here with the Scion. One might call it chance, but I prefer to think of it as fate; a concept I'm certain one with your nature would understand. Two of my Lady Eris' most wanted personages here in the palm of my hand together." His eyes narrowed. "Two birds, one stone. Tell me, girl. If a tree falls in the forest and no one is around to hear, does it make a sound?"

"Where's Henry?" Robin said, cutting her off. "And Phorbas? What have you done with them?" Woad grabbed his arm, holding him back.

Mr Strife's cold eyes fell on Robin. "I have them," he said softly. "And now I have you."

Karya turned to Robin. "We have to run," she hissed in a whisper. "Get ready."

"But Henry…" Robin protested.

"Can't help Henryboy if we're dead," Woad growled. "Skrikers make us into dog food, then what?"

"Robin Fellows, all of the Netherworlde is very interested in your potential," Mr Strife said, stalking across the clearing toward them. The skrikers padded at his side, their dark shapes wavering as though seen through a heat haze.

"My inheritance, you mean?" Robin spat. "Yeah, so I've heard."

"I am sure that my friends here, Spitak and Siaw, will be most persuasive in convincing you that your cooperation is for the best," Mr

Strife said in his oily voice. The dense carpet of autumnal leaves crunched under their paws as the skrikers advanced.

"We have to get to the trees," Karya whispered urgently. "Behind the barrow."

"We'll never make it, boss," Woad said. "Skrikers too fast; we run, they run."

Karya looked about hopelessly. Mr Strife produced a long, slim-bladed knife from the depths of his frock coat.

"Scion … the leaves," Karya said, her eyes lighting up.

"What?" Robin stammered, distracted by the approaching beasts and knife.

"We need a diversion," Karya snapped, "A smokescreen. The leaves on the floor, Scion. Hide us!"

"I … I don't know if I can. I'm still learning…"

"Learn faster," Woad suggested urgently.

Mr Strife lunged towards them, arm outstretched as though to seize Robin from afar. The skrikers growled, leaping forward, and Karya and Woad stumbled back in shock.

Robin didn't stumble. He stood his ground, his hand flying to his mana stone. Gripping its solid warmth, he closed his eyes tightly and pointed his hand, fingers outstretched, at the forest floor before him. He had time to think briefly, 'this had better work!' and then, with all of his strength, he cast Featherbreath on the leaves beneath them.

Only this wasn't floating a sheet of paper in a classroom. This was fighting for his life in the lonely wilderness.

All over the clearing, the countless leaves exploded upwards, rustling and roaring in the wind, a tremendous wave of solid red and gold spiralling between them and their attackers. Mr Strife disappeared from view, crying out in surprise as he was lost in the sudden maelstrom. The skrikers, invisible in the storm, howled in alarm, disoriented.

Robin stood shocked, his pale hair whipping about his face as leaves battered him like angry moths. His mana stone felt as hot as blood against his chest.

Karya grabbed his arm and dragged him back.

"Now! Don't just stand like an idiot! Run!"

He clambered the barrow's sloping wall and crossed the top of the grassy cairn, darting between the makeshift chimneys. He half-ran, half-slid down the steep slope of the far side. The others were almost at the trees on the far side of the clearing already. Robin pounded after them, his bag slamming painfully against his back, heart thudding in his ears.

He heard a shriek of inhuman fury behind him and risked a look over his shoulder. Mr Strife had clambered to the top of the barrow and stood, his face contorted in fury. Leaves were still falling from his shoulders and sticking haphazardly in his garish hair.

The skrikers were already bounding down the slope, headed straight for him at terrible speed.

Karya and Woad had stopped running. They had reached the edge of the trees and were standing, breathless and white-faced waiting for him. Karya had her hand splayed on the tree bark and Woad's skinny blue arms laced around her waist. They were both shouting at him to hurry.

His legs burning as he ran, he suddenly saw that Karya's hand wasn't on the tree at all – it was somehow *in* it. She held out her other hand, reaching for him. He heard a growl close behind and was suddenly sure that he could feel the skrikers' breath on the back of his neck.

Robin threw himself forwards, arm outstretched.

Behind him, a blood-freezing howl. Karya's fingers closed around his, jaws snapped inches from his head, and before he could form another coherent thought, he was being pulled forwards into a sudden rushing darkness, leaving far behind the fading howls and dying red sun.

Chapter Seventeen – The Ghost Stone

Robin floundered blindly in darkness, panic clutching at his throat. His jumper snagged, dragging him backwards. Flailing, he tore free with a loud rip, falling to the snow-covered ground. He blinked in the darkness, looking back over his shoulder. It hadn't been skrikers tearing at him. He'd been half-buried in a thick and prickly hedgerow. Wherever they were now, it was not the Barrow Wood. Here it was full night, and bitterly cold.

"Woad? Karya?" he called, his voice still hitching in panic. He was answered not by his companions, but by a roaring, bright yellow light bearing down upon him. He froze, as helpless as a frightened rabbit as it barrelled towards him in the darkness. It was almost upon him when a firm blue hand grabbed the back of his collar and dragged him back off his feet.

"Is your brain jellified, Pinky?" Woad gasped irritably. Robin stared after the light, confused, as it disappeared into the darkness. A red winking light disappeared around a bend and was gone.

"A … a … motorbike?" he stuttered. "We're back in the real world?" He struggled out of the ditch, wobbly on his feet. "The human world, I mean?"

"Will you two please get out of the mud?" Karya's voice came from the darkness. "Strife won't be far behind." She glanced around, taking in their surroundings. "I think I put some distance between us but I don't quite know where we are yet. Somewhere far from Barrowood village at least."

Robin scanned the views. It was hard to believe that mere moments earlier they had been running for their lives in another world. His teeth chattered in the cold and he hugged himself against the wind, his heavy book bag shielding his back a little. All around them was dark, snow-covered moorland. They were high up somewhere, wherever they were.

In the distance, Robin saw the lights of a city, sprawling and twinkling, oblivious in the darkness. Closer by was the odd isolated speck of light from a farmhouse nestled in the hills, these pinpricks of light both lonely and cosy.

"Where are we?" he asked.

"I think I may have outdone myself," Karya replied, hands on her hips. "I meant to put as much distance between us and Strife as I could, but I'll be a chalpie's aunt if I haven't only gone and moved us fairly close to where we're going anyway." She sounded quite pleased with herself.

"Where we're going? Robin asked. "You mean we're heading towards somewhere? I thought the main plan was just to be heading … you know … away?"

"Don't you ever pay attention, Pinky?" Woad asked. "We need to see Pythian Lady. That's what the redcaps said."

"Redcaps?" Robin spluttered incredulously. "We can't trust anything they say!"

"Trust? No, of course not." Karya shook her head. "But believe? Certainly."

"But…"

"Look, Scion, redcaps can't be trusted," Karya said flatly, cutting him off. "That's just their nature. Don't take it personally. But they don't lie outright. Deepdweller may have had an earlier arrangement with Strife, but he was also honour-bound to keep his deal with us. He told us to go and see the Pythian. She's an Oracle of the Netherworlde, so that's where we'll go." She peered up at the dark moors around them. "And as I said, we're closer to our goal than I expected."

She pointed down the snowy country road. A lonely pub sat some way off, a kindly grandmother smiling down from its swinging sign, cosy windows filled with welcoming light.

Robin fervently hoped this was where they were headed. He had to admit though, it might be difficult to explain what three unkempt children, one of them blue, were doing out in the middle of nowhere in late December.

Karya however, wasn't pointing at the pub, but at the snowy hills beyond. The landscape rose up and up, rugged and huge. Robin's legs ached just looking at it.

"That hill, you see," Karya said. "It's called Knowl Hill. If I remember rightly, there's a Janus station right on top. Good job really, as I used all my mana on that last tear. I'll be good for nothing for a while."

"I don't like the look of all the dead people between us and it though, boss," Woad said darkly, squinting into the darkness at the looming hill.

Robin stared at the faun, confused. "Sorry? Dead people?"

"There's nothing to worry about," Karya reassured him briskly, setting off towards the hills behind the pub without further ado. "Dead people can't hurt you."

"Zombies can," Woad argued, scampering after her. "Ghouls can, revenants too…"

"Yes, yes, alright!" Karya replied irritably. "But not regular dead people. Ghosts are just ghosts."

"Seriously … what are you both talking about?" Robin said. "I don't see any ghosts anywhere."

"You will. Up on the moors," Karya said without looking back.

* * *

The snow deepened as they trudged onwards, the slopes becoming steeper. Soon, Robin and his companions were wading through thigh-deep drifts. Even Woad struggled.

"Ghosts, which are not really dead people at all, but more like memories of people…" Karya explained as they forged ahead, "… are attracted to specific places to haunt. Funny really that you're learning the Tower of Air at the moment, cause they seem to have a thing about air and wind."

"What do you mean?" Robin asked breathlessly.

"Well," Karya went on. "It's always draughty cliff tops and windswept castle battlements with ghosts, isn't it? Occasionally the crow's nests of shipwrecks, places like that. But these days there's one kind of place in the human world where ghosts seem to show up more than ever." She pointed ahead.

For a moment, his heart jumped. Robin could make out shapes ahead in the darkness, huge and slender, looming over the hills. It took a moment for his eyes to adjust to what he was seeing.

"Windmills?" he said. "There's a wind-farm here?"

"Oh, they're everywhere these days in your human world," Karya said. Robin watched the vast blade-like sails turn slowly, slicing the night sky in almost complete silence. He had never realised how immense the structures were.

"Ghosts seem to love them," Karya said. "I think they get caught up in all the churning air energy here." She shrugged inside her furs. "Or maybe they just like it, who knows. Look, there's one now."

Robin followed her pointing arm. High ahead, at the top of the nearest windmill was a greenish-grey translucent shape, tangled in the blades.

"That's a ghost?"

"Yes. They're everywhere if you look for them."

Robin glanced around. Scattered liberally throughout the dark hillside, dotted over the moors and under the watchful care of the towering windmills, there were hundreds of misty ghosts.

Robin stopped walking, taken aback by the sight. Karya and Woad turned around.

"What's wrong?" the girl asked.

"There are … so many of them," Robin replied, stunned. He stared at a distant shimmering figure. It looked like a woman in a long old-fashioned dress. She passed between the shadow of a tower and, as he watched, her barely substantial form caught in the updraft. Her form stretched out upwards, growing thinner until she was pulled up into the blades above, losing form altogether. Robin couldn't be certain, but he thought he heard a distant 'whee!', although it could have been a mournful wail. The spinning ghost was flung free and shot out across the sky. It hit a distant hillside and slowly reformed back into the shape of the woman in the old fashioned dress, who then continued her mournful walking as though nothing had happened.

"They're much easier to see than they usually would be," Karya told him, looking out over the snow at the gathered masses milling around. "It must be your mana stone," she reasoned. "It calls out to them."

Robin's hand went to his mana stone. He automatically expected it to feel cold and lifeless after all the mana he had channelled back in the forest, but it was warm and light. "My mana stone?" he asked, confused. "What would that have to do with it?"

"Seraphinite is an excellent mana-stone for channelling the seventh and most difficult Tower of the Arcania."

"The seventh tower?" Robin replied distractedly. His attention was focussed on the ghost of a young street urchin, who was running along in the snow with a spectral hoop and stick. As he watched the boy ran headlong into a tall snowdrift and disappeared, his form blown apart like smoke.

"What are the Towers of the Arcania?" Karya asked impatiently, "Honestly, hasn't your tutor been through all this with you?" She counted them off on her fingers. "Earth, air, fire, water, light, darkness and…?"

"Spirit!" chirped Woad helpfully.

"But I don't know how to do any spirit magic," Robin argued.

"Of course you don't, you dolt," Karya scoffed. "The seventh Tower is the most difficult of all. What I'm saying is that certain mana stones are good for certain Towers. My mana stone is amber." She rattled her bracelet. "Good for Earth. Woad's stone is a fire-opal. Seraphinite," she pointed at Robin's chest, "… is good for spirit."

"My mother had Seraphinite," Robin said, remembering her portrait. And now she's as good as a ghost herself, he thought. He didn't say this out loud.

"It's incredibly rare," Karya nodded. "But it's certainly why the spirits are so clear around us now. You're boosting their signal."

"Dead ones don't normally notice the living. Don't worry, Pinky. They're not going to eat your brains; that's just zombies," Woad said, in an attempt to be reassuring.

"Really?" Robin said, with raised eyebrows.

Karya grunted in assent. "It's true, the dead ignore the living. They're normally too wrapped up in being dead, or living the same few moments over and over again. They have little time for breathing people."

"Um … perhaps someone should tell *them* that," Robin said hesitantly, pointing to the nearest windmill.

They followed his gaze. A group of ghosts had gathered at the base of the windmill, six or seven of them – it was hard to tell for sure as some of them kept breaking apart.

They were all staring at the three living children quietly.

"Those ones seem to have noticed us," Robin pointed out worriedly.

As he spoke, one of the ghosts floated forwards. An old man, leaning on a walking stick. This ambassador from the other side made its way across the hill slowly, drifting toward them like a human-shaped fog.

"Hmm, that's … interesting," Karya said quietly, in a not very reassuring way. Her stance was suddenly tense. Robin tore his eyes from the advancing spectre and glanced her way. Her eyes were bright gold in the dark.

As it approached, they could make out more details. The old man was dressed in simple clothes. Though his feet didn't quite touch the ground, indeed sometimes they passed through it, he leaned heavily on his knobbly stick for support. His face was lined and his head bald. He seemed to have no teeth.

"What should we do?" Robin asked urgently.

Before they could decide, the ghost jittering forward in a sudden flickering blur, until he was suddenly standing right in front of them.

Woad let out an involuntary yelp of surprise.

The old man seemed not to notice Robin's companions at all. His moon-like eyes were fixed on Robin alone. The seraphinite stone under the boy's jumper was beating like an excited heart.

The ghost opened its gummy mouth to speak. Robin felt his whole body tense.

"Well, I'll be blown," he said. "It's only a bloody honest-to-goodness faerie, isn't it?"

He turned back and waved its walking stick over its head, a signal to the other ghosts, who were waiting apprehensively in the slowly moving shadows of the windmill.

"I was right!" the old man called in his wavering voice. "It's a bloody faerie, it is! I said it was! Right here on our hill!"

The other ghosts began drifting over slowly. The old man turned back to Robin.

"Well I never!" he said, as though surprised to see him all over again.

"Um … hello," Robin said, not sure what else to do.

The ghost grinned a broad gummy smile. "Hullo indeed! You know, I lived eighty six years long, and I never thought I'd see another one of you again, not in all my life." He seemed to consider this for a moment. "Well, I suppose I was right about that really, but you know what I mean. I saw one of your kind when I was a lad – long, long time ago. Used to live on a farm up over there." He gestured with his ghostly walking stick vaguely at the hills behind him. "With me mam and dad. There were none of these big metal things around then though. It was all just earth and sky back in those days. Less machines." He sighed wistfully "Saw a faerie I did. Dressed right fine he were, like a lord or something, very swish, all black cape and white furs, carryin' his lockbox. Figured he were some rich bugger from the city, passin' by on his horse. But when I saw the horns, then I said to myself, 'Hob, that's no man there, that's somethin' else'."

The old man looked wistful. "Spoke to me, he did. Great amber eyes, bright as fire, and horns like a ram in the wildest mop of black hair you ever did see. Face for the ladies, if you get my meaning. Been in the wars though," he said. "Had a scar on his temple, right across his eyebrow. Didn't expect me. Gave me a gold coin for my silence, not to tell no one I'd seen him. I didn't stop starin' at those horns, I can tell you." He flicked his cane up at Robin's head, almost taking the boy's eye out. Robin flinched back in surprise. "That's how as I knew what you were."

"But … but I don't have any horns," Robin said.

"Eh? What's that?" the old man squinted. "Don't have horns? Hah! Clear as day, lad! There's no hiding what you are. You got the same look about you. Could have been your father I suppose … if it weren't so long ago, but then, I don't know how long your kind live, as a rule."

"My dad had blonde hair," Robin stammered.

The old man shrugged. "Ah well. One of my best memories, that's all. And a pleasure to see another one of you, even after all this time. Don't get many of you about no more."

"There aren't many of us left…" Robin explained, a little awkwardly.

A loud harsh caw suddenly startled him. On a snow-dusted rock near to the closest windmill, a fat black crow had settled, like a sooty smear against the white powder.

Robin and the others stared at it. It stared back, head tilted to one side, then let out another caw. It took off into the air, shedding feathers messily.

"That's not good," Karya said, watching it go.

"Just a crow," Robin said, dragging his eyes back to the translucent old man who was ushering his ghostly friends closer. A real life ghost was more interesting, in his opinion, than a noisy bird.

"That's not a crow," Karya insisted. "That's a grimgull trying very hard to look like a crow. We're being tracked."

Woad clambered atop a small clump of rocks, scattering a couple of nervous ghosts. He pointed into the sky, back the way they had come. "It is a grimgull, and it's not alone, boss."

Robin peered up into the sky. There were several more crows fluttering around in the darkness. They were slowly getting closer as they circled in the air high above.

"They're Mr Moros' spies," Karya said under her breath. "They must know we're nearby. The skrikers won't be far behind them, you can bet on that."

Robin found himself wishing desperately that it wasn't so snowy. They would have blended in easily against the dark ground, but here against the white backdrop, they stood out like three sore thumbs.

"We'll never make it up the hill," Woad said. "Too exposed. Bad birds will spot us."

Karya hissed in frustration, biting her bottom lip. "There is no other plan," she growled, "I can't tear us through, not so soon. The only way out of here is through the Janus Station, and the only way to get to it is up this hill."

"What we need is a distraction," Robin said. "Maybe I could cast a few Galestrikes if they get too close? Blow them off course perhaps?"

"That won't work, Pinky," Woad said, jumping down from his pile of rocks. "It'll just draw attention to us. Plus you're rubbish at Galestrikes."

The ghost of Hob cleared his throat politely. All three companions looked at his happy, slightly transparent face.

"Sorry to eavesdrop, it ain't usually my way, but I couldn't help overhearing … Looks like you and your funny little friends are in some kind of trouble here, eh?"

"Funny little friends?" Karya growled dangerously through her teeth.

"Um, yes, a bit," Robin said quickly, ignoring Karya's irritation. "Long story really."

"Secret faerie business no doubt," the old man cackled happily, tapping the side of his insubstantial nose in a conspiratorial manner. "Just like that other one all those years ago. You lot and your capers. Well, it's none of our business, I'm sure, but Master Faerie, it would be an honour if old Hob and his friends can help in any way."

"I don't see what you can do," Karya said flatly. "No offence, but you're dead."

Robin winced, wishing she had a little more tact. He pointed at the whirling birds, circling ever closer. "We need those birds distracting. We have to get to the top of Knowl Hill, without being seen by them. Can you help us?"

The old man turned away, falling into a ghostly huddle with his fellow spirits.

Karya, Woad and Robin exchanged speculative glances. The distant croaky voices of the flock of grimgulls echoed toward them through the night. Somewhere, distantly, there came a long, mournful and all too familiar howl.

The ghost of the old man turned back to Robin.

"We will cover you, don't go worrin' about a thing. Don't know how long we'll be able to hold them, though. Some of us are getting a bit long in the tooth, so to speak, so you better go now, young sir."

Robin grinned with relief. "Thanks for this," he said. "I'm only sorry I don't have a gold coin to give you."

The old man cackled happily. "It's a pleasure to serve the faerie folk. In life or in death."

He doffed his flat-cap at the children, and then the ghostly group turned as one and floated away, their forms disintegrating as they rolled down the hillside, becoming nothing more than vaporous trails of ectoplasmic smoke. Individual ghosts began merging into groups, flowing in swift streams across the dark snow, forming a mass of roiling ground-mist which grew as it collected more and more ghosts.

Robin stared as the ghosts combined into a sea of shimmering fog, spread out across the hills like a cold blanket. A skriker howled again, far off in the darkness. As they watched, the fog quested upwards, coiling around the windmills, threading up through the vast turning blades until the seething mist was gathered up from the hillside and dispersed into the air above them. In a matter of minutes, the sky was blotted out with a wispy cloud of swirling, sentient ghost-smoke.

Robin heard the startled and disoriented cries of the now invisible grimgulls. Somewhere in the rolling shape above, ghostly hands and arms formed at random, pushing and shoving at the wildly flapping creatures, slapping them off their courses.

Karya tugged Robin's jumper at the elbow, dragging his attention from the spectacle above. "Impressive to look at and all," she said. "But we have to go, Scion. Now."

Woad had already forged ahead, dashing between the colossal windmills. Karya and Robin blundered after the faun, ploughing through the snowdrifts, panting as they fought their way upwards as fast as they could. Skriker howls and growls came again, closer.

"Hurry, hurry!" Woad cried. He had already reached the summit of the hill and was literally jumping on the spot with impatience as he waited for Karya and Robin to catch up.

They crested the vast hill eventually, exhausted and sweating, despite the cold night air. Snow clung heavily to the legs of Robin's jeans and caked the tattered hem of Karya's coat.

Gasping for breath, he glanced around. He wasn't sure what he had been expecting a Janus station to look like, but there seemed to be nothing on top of the wide flattened hilltop apart from snow and a broken, unimpressive circle of stones.

"What … what's this?" he panted, nursing a stitch.

"Janus … station," Karya gasped, staggering. "No time … to explain."

She and Woad rushed around the circle, touching the squat blackened standing stones seemingly at random, like a ridiculous game of tag. Robin peered at them, at their hands slapping stone after stone in some odd sequence which made no sense to him.

He glancing nervously back the way they had come. The ghostly cloud was beginning to thin now that Robin's seraphinite stone was no longer in the midst of it. The ghosts were running out of energy. It couldn't hold much longer.

"Setting coordinates," Karya explained, hitting a small stone twice with a sharp slap of her palm before moving on to another diagonally across from it. Robin noticed now that each stone carried a crude carved glyph, a symbol of some kind. "There are hundreds of stations to choose from and you have to make sure you pick the right one or you could end up … well … anywhere."

"Anywhere's better than here," Robin offered, stamping his feet in the snow.

"Wrong again, Pinky," Woad said. "There's a Janus station in Eris' court. You fancy being spat out into right her throne room?"

"Nearly there," Karya said, darting a warning glance at Woad. "This should take us through to the equivalent of 'here' in the Netherworlde. A straight and simple flip."

A sudden raspy caw drew their attention skyward. One of the horrible fat crows had broken through the cloud and was wheeling erratically around in the sky, trying to get a fix on them.

"Hurry!" Robin urged.

"We're done!" Karya replied with triumph. "Get over here, in the middle with me and Woad."

When they were all gathered together, Karya made a hand signal in the air. "Here we go," she said.

Robin braced himself for the same rushing, tumbling sensation of flying head over heels through darkness. It didn't come. Instead, the inside of the circle filled suddenly with a soft golden glow. Then the snow stopped falling, the ugly cries of the grimgulls ceased, and the cold wind dropped utterly, leaving them in silence.

Chapter Eighteen – The Oracle

For a moment, Robin was blind in the golden light, conscious only that Karya gripped his wrist and that Woad's small hand was on his other shoulder.

"Hello again, Netherworlde," came Woad's voice happily.

"We're here?" Robin asked incredulously. "I mean … that's it? That was a hell of a lot smoother than…"

"Well, you try tearing through without using a Janus station and see if you can do it any easier," snapped Karya. "You certainly weren't complaining when I pulled you out of the Barrow Wood just before a skriker had your arm off!"

"I didn't mean…" Robin spluttered. "No, you were great, I just…"

"Janus is slightly smoother," Karya said loftily. "Easiest way to get around the Netherworlde. It's a big place after all." She stamped the remaining snow off her feet. "Anyway, we made it through … that's the point. Skrikers and grimgulls are smarter than I'd like, but last time I checked they can't operate a Janus station, so that's bought us some time."

"No opposable thumbs, see?" Woad said happily, waggling his own. "Can't plot a course with paws."

"Welcome to the Temple of the Oracle, Scion," Karya announced.

Robin followed Karya's nod and turned on the spot. Behind the circle, where in the human world there had been nothing but snow and moss, there now stood an imposing temple. It loomed over them, warm yellow lamplight pouring from the windows. The tall brass doors were flanked by man-high braziers filled with flickering blue flames.

"Wow," Robin breathed, taking in the sight.

"The Temple of the Oracle, secret keeper of the kept secrets," Woad said reverently. "… Or something like that."

"Secret keeper of the hidden knowledge," Karya corrected him patiently. "Come on, you two."

They reached the large doors of the temple. There were long crimson swathes of cloth decorating the doorway, emblazoned with a golden eye in a triangle sat between two clasped hands, as though shielding a candle from the wind. A star glimmered in the pupil of the stylised eye.

Above the door, carved into the stone itself:

Temet Nosce

"Do you really think this oracle of yours is going to be able to help us?" Robin asked, as Karya raised a fist and banged rather unceremoniously on the large brass doors. "We thought the redcaps would be helpful too, remember."

"The redcaps were helpful," Karya replied matter-of-factly. "They led us here."

Before Robin could reply, the great doors swung open, enveloping the three in a large cloud of escaping incense. The smell of poppies, sandalwood and something darker washed over them, a sharp coppery smell like old pennies or blood.

There was a small woman standing in the doorway. She was very old and very round, wearing a long dusty-looking robe of a scarlet so dark it was like black dreaming of red. She had a mane of wild white hair on which rested a crown of golden laurel leaves. Her eyes, sharp and dark, seemed to peer through them right to their bones.

The overall effect was somewhat ruined by the flowery pinny she was wearing over her robe. She was carrying a tray of freshly baked cookies with novelty green oven mitts designed to look like happy frogs.

"Yes?" she snapped irritably, after a moment of silence.

"Um, we are here seeking wisdom from the Oracle," Karya said uncertainly. At her shoulder, Woad was sniffing the tray of cookies discreetly, his tail swishing back and forth. "Are you the Pythian?" Karya asked.

The old woman gave a one shoulder shrug. "Some of her, yes," she croaked. Her eyes flicked over each of them briefly. "I suppose you're on some sort of quest, then? Or fleeing terrible danger? It's always one of the two. In the middle of the bloody night, honestly."

"It's both actually," Karya said, a little awkwardly. "We're searching for a couple of friends who have been kidnapped, and yes, we are also fleeing danger."

"Terrible danger?" the old woman clarified, pointing an enquiring oven mitt.

"Is there any other kind?" the small girl replied levelly.

"Hmm." The woman frowned, her ancient face a mass of deep wrinkles. "You'd better come in and meet the rest of me then. But I warn you, some of me is in a bit of a mood this night."

She led them through corridors of polished marble, flickering firelight dancing on statues and columns. Their footsteps echoed in the grand silence.

The old shuffling Oracle brought them to an enclosed circular courtyard filled with delicate trees and tinkling fountains. The moon shone down through an oculus in the domed ceiling. There was a sunken pool directly below, around which two other figures lounged. One was a young girl. She looked about five years old and had a shock of wild golden curls. She was wearing a shortened version of the old woman's robe, an almost pink shade of red. The girl was sitting at the pool's edge, swinging her legs and looking bored. The other was a tall willowy woman, who smiled at them as they approached, showing not the slightest sign of surprise at their arrival. Like her two companions she wore a red robe, although hers was the brightest scarlet. Her hair was a mass of perfect golden ringlets, crowned with a golden laurel. She was, in Robin's opinion at least, stunningly beautiful.

"Found these three at the door," the old woman muttered unceremoniously, sounding none too happy as she crossed the room.

The young girl jumped up, scooping cookies from the tray greedily. She glared at Woad, who was eyeing her suspiciously, stuck her tongue out and ran off without a word.

"Yes," the beautiful woman said. "You three arrive here, now. This is how it happens." She cocked her head to one side, like an enquiring bird. She seemed oddly distant, as though daydreaming.

"Sorry," Karya said, looking around. "I'm a little confused. We came to see the Oracle. Which one of you is that?"

"We are the Oracle," the women replied in unison. The dreamy looking one took a cookie from the proffered tray. "Cookies … I really wanted some earlier."

"So I see," the old woman replied, glancing off into the distant edges of the room, where the young girl was sitting, half hidden by the foliage and guzzling down cookie after cookie. The old woman burped and made a face. "I'll regret it later, though; they give me terrible indigestion."

Robin glanced confused at Karya, his eyebrows raised. "There are three Oracles?" he asked.

"No, young fae," the old woman replied. "There's only one of me."

"It's a lot of work for just one person, believe me," the other woman nodded, daintily nibbling on a biscuit. "I find it much easier this way. Dividing my labours so to speak."

"I haven't introduced myself, have I?" the old one said, setting the tray aside on a small pedestal and fussing with her apron strings. "I am the Oracle, and so is the me over here, and the me over there."

"You can call me Praesto," the pretty woman said, holding out a hand which Robin shook, faintly bemused. "This is Posterus." She nodded at her elderly companion. "And the greedy bad-tempered one eating all the cookies is Preteritus."

"You're one person … in three bodies," Karya exclaimed wonderingly. "Past, present and future?"

"I've never been a person, what a stupid thing to say," came a high piping voice around a mouthful of cookies.

"You'll have to excuse my manners," the old woman said grumpily. "It's way past part of my bedtime."

Robin just stared. Things in the Netherworlde just seemed to get stranger and stranger.

"I'm afraid I shall have to ask you to surrender your weapons while you are here," Praesto said. "This is a place of sanctuary. Precious few such places remain in the Netherworlde. The dark empress has seen to that. You may leave them on the tray, don't mind the cookie crumbs."

"Weapons?" Robin said confused. Then he remembered. He had completely forgotten he was carrying Phorbas' silver dagger.

He pulled it out of his belt, feeling the odd tingle in his fingers from the satyr's mana stone.

The Oracle watched with interest as he placed it on the tray.

"How very interesting," the younger one said, in a lilting, dreamy voice. "If steel could talk … this would have a tale to tell."

"It belongs to my friend, the one we're looking for," Robin explained. "Well, one of them. I don't think it would have many stories to tell. He told me it's never seen any more action than opening letters."

"A secret lies buried in silver and steel," Preteritus sang out from the undergrowth. She giggled to herself.

"Hush my mouth," the old woman said. "Sorry, sometimes I see things in the past clearest. It's always easier to look backwards than forwards, isn't it. I find if you do it too often though, you tend to trip over your own feet. Look to the future, that's what I say."

"Live for the moment is a good motto," her dreamy-eyed companion said helpfully.

Posterus snorted in derision, crinkling her withered old face in a scowl. "I won't think that in the future," she scoffed. "Any other weapons? Other than the faun, I mean? He wouldn't fit on the tray anyway I think." She looked to Karya. "How about you, love?"

"I'm unarmed," Karya replied simply.

"Liar," the crone replied with a sly smirk. "Knowledge is power they say, eh? Your kind is never unarmed and not all weapons are carried in the hand." She tapped her head a few times, looking quite demented.

"She's practically one of me anyway," the other, distant-looking woman said. "One of seven, always one of seven. But the whole is not always greater than the sum of its parts, it would seem. Eris should not have meddled in the order of such things."

"You're talking in riddles," Robin said, getting rather annoyed.

"'Course they are," Woad said. "What did you expect? She's the Oracle. If you wanted the shipping forecast you're in the wrong place, Pinky."

"Look, we need help," Robin said. "We were told you might know where my friends have been taken. We did a finding spell but they're nowhere."

"Everything's somewhere," Preteritus trilled, skipping over to the pool.

"I used a cantrip to locate them," Karya explained. "It failed. We think Strife is taking them to Lady Eris, but there are no tracks."

"They are not headed to Dis. They are nowhere your feet will take you," Praesto said, looking into middle distance.

"Can you help us?" Karya asked.

"We will and do," Posterus cackled. "I remember it all."

They positioned themselves around the placid pool, each version of the Oracle kneeling and peering into the water. As one, they reached out their hands and began tracing strange patterns in the liquid, making it eddy and swirl. The flames in the braziers seemed to dim and gutter.

"What are they doing?" Robin whispered after watching the three figures sway for a few minutes. The light was growing dimmer until the only illumination came from the moon high above.

Karya shushed him. "Looking," she said quietly.

The Oracles' eyes rolled back in her heads, until only slivers of white showed. There was an odd feeling of growing pressure in the air.

"What are they doing now?" Robin persisted in a hushed whisper

"Seeing," Woad replied. "They are seers after all. Now hush!"

They watched in silence as the misty waters rolled back and forth hypnotically until, just as the motion was making Robin feel drowsy, there was an almighty crash. The water in the pool jumped as though a giant hand had slapped its surface, and for a second Robin thought he glimpsed shapes in the mist.

The images were gone as soon as they had appeared and the pool clearing, settling back into its innocent state. The feeling of pressure lifted and the braziers flared back to life, filling the temple once again with bright, cosy light. Wisps of steam coiled from the pool's surface.

The Oracle stood up, all three of her opening their eyes. "Well," said Praesto. "I have looked and I have seen. I can tell you three things."

"Your friends have indeed been attacked by Eris' men, Moros and Strife," little Preteritus said in her piping voice. "Both Phorbas the satyr and Henry the human boy have been used for the sole purpose of bringing you here to the Netherworlde."

"No place for a human," Praesto said, her pretty face a perfect composition of elegant concern. "Your Henry does not belong here. He is in terrible danger. He is being held nowhere on Netherworlde soil. But he is indeed in the Netherworlde."

"What? That doesn't make sense!" Robin cried, frustrated. "Are they here or not? They can't be both."

Posterus raised her arms to the sky. "Hidden in the clouds he is … on the isle in the sky." She looked back at them, dropping her arms and regarding them shrewdly. "Far beyond the reach of any down below."

Robin was about to exclaim that he didn't understand, but the Oracle held all six of her arms up to silence him.

"Three things I can tell you," she said with three voices, speaking in unison. "And three things I have. To ask more than is offered is to ask a boon … which requires sacrifice."

Their faces had darkened as though the shadows were gathering around them. The smell of incense seemed to fade until only blood remained.

"But…" Robin began.

Karya gripped his shoulder "Don't, Scion," she warned. "We've got what we came for. Trust me, we have to tread carefully here. There are rules with the Oracle. Very old rules."

"Very wise," the old woman nodded, suddenly rather normal-looking again.

"I hope this information helps you in your quest." She passed a hand across the small pedestal which held Phorbas' blade, an oddly business-like gesture. "Now then, don't forget to take your weapons with you when you go. It would be a terrible thing to find your friend the satyr and to have lost his mana stone. They cannot be replaced."

"Please feel free to take a cookie on your way out," Praesto said cheerfully, her head cocked on one side like a bird again, smiling wanly. "It's a long road ahead."

* * *

They recovered the dagger and filled their pockets with cookies before leaving. The eldest version of the Oracle shuffled them back to the door in her brusque manner, and before long, they were sitting outside in the warm night air.

"Hidden in the clouds," Woad mused, stroking his chin in what he seemed to hope looked like a thoughtful way.

"On the isle in the sky…" Karya added. "I've never heard of any such place." She sighed, picking stray hairs from the lapel of her tatty coat. "Well, perhaps coming to see the Oracle wasn't as good a plan as I thought. You never get a straight answer … I should know."

Robin ignored them. He was busy rummaging in his backpack.

She glanced over at him curiously. "What are you looking for, Scion?"

Robin heaved a large book from his pack.

"'Hammerhand's Netherworlde Compendium'," he said triumphantly, heaving it onto his lap. "It's a kind of encyclopaedia." He cracked open the cover and began flipping through the index.

"And … you think now is the best time to be catching up on your homework?" Karya asked curiously as Robin tilted the book to catch the light from the braziers.

"No," he said, giving her a sidelong look. "I'm sure there's something in here about an island in the sky. I'm certain of it. Back when I was learning Featherbreath, Phorbas mentioned it. It's like a Netherworlde myth or something."

"A myth?" Woad asked questioningly.

"A lie that tells the truth," Karya explained to the faun.

"Here it is!" Robin pointed at the page. "'The Isle of Aeolus'." There was a sketchy illustration showing a massive mountain floating in mid-air. Near the peak of the mountain there seemed to be some kind of town. Karya and Woad peered over Robin's shoulder, watching the inked clouds swirl silently on the yellowed page.

Robin's eyes roamed over the dense script. "It says here that, before the Arcania was shattered, the Tower of Air was a powerful field of magic. The people who lived in this city despaired for the other members of the Netherworlde. When Eris' war began, as a protest against the bloodshed, they uprooted their city from the earth. They lifted the mountain into the sky, creating the Isle of Winds."

"So, where is it?" Karya asked.

"No one ever saw the island again," he reported despondently, reading ahead. "Apparently it was lost in mists and clouds and retreated over time into legend. There's no indication of where it might be, and no real proof that it ever existed."

"Well, apparently Strife and Moros have found it," Karya said. "Though, why would they take Henry and Phorbas there? It doesn't make any sense."

"Perfect place to hide them, isn't it?" Woad said. "Where do you hide something you don't want to be found? Somewhere so secret everyone thinks it's a myth. Clever." He narrowed his blue eyes. "Clever like velociraptors."

Robin and Karya had to admit this was sound logic. Robin searched through the compendium for more information.

He flattened the page as it rustled in the breeze. "It says here … '*Ad augusta per angusta*'." Robin made a face, "… Whatever that means."

"It means 'to high places by narrow roads'." Karya said. "No idea why though. Anything else?"

"'*Alta alatis patent*'," Robin read aloud carefully. "Seems these words were on a map, somewhere near the Singing Fens, wherever they are."

"North-east from here," Woad said. "A week's solid travel just to get to the Fens, or two weeks on lazy non-faun feet."

"'*Alta alatis patent*' … 'The sky is open to those who have wings'?" Karya translated. She threw her hands up. "Well, we don't have wings, so that's a fairly useless clue. I suppose we're expected to tame some harpies, are we?"

Robin ignored her, reading on. "There isn't much more. Lots of pretty dry explanations about how technically difficult and impressive it must be to float a mountain … blah, blah, blah … nothing useful." He flicked to the final page in the section. "Only… here at the end the legend says 'the path of wind is open at dawn. Look to the goddess to find your road'."

He snapped the book closed in frustration. "More riddles," he said. "Doesn't anyone ever just say what they mean here?" He ran his hands through his hair, making it stick up all over his head in blonde spikes.

Karya pursed her lips. "Well … it's something to go on at least. We know that your tutor and the human boy are being hidden on the Isle of Aeolus, which would suggest that it's not a myth. And we know that to get there we need to take a high, narrow road somewhere near the Singing Fens, and that apparently we need wings. Hmm."

"And we need to get there at dawn. Or ask some goddess. Don't forget that bit," Woad said, scratching his ear absently.

"Look, the only lead we have is to go north, to the Singing Fens," Karya said. "We can try and figure things out along the way. Like Woad says, it's about two weeks' travel, and it's best for us to keep moving. We need to gain some ground."

She set off down the winding steps which led down to the moorland below.

"We don't have time for this," Robin argued, shouldering his backpack and hurrying after her. "Anything could be happening to Henry and Phorbas. We can't just trudge across the moors for weeks on end."

"Well, if you have any better ideas, let me know on the way, eh?" Karya huffed.

Chapter Nineteen – Hawthorn's Way

By the time the sun rose over the craggy moorland, they had put some miles between themselves and the hill of knowledge. It was now nothing more than a vague misty shape on the horizon behind them. Karya insisted they keep going, wanting to put as much distance between them and their pursuers. Woad didn't seem remotely affected by the long march, but Robin was growing weary from the constant travel. However, Henry and Phorbas needed him, so on he went.

They walked through the morning. There was a nip in the air, but the sky above was clear and sheeny-blue. Robin was immensely grateful that it was warmer here than back in the human world. They never would have made it this far over deep snow.

Robin and Woad were bickering about how many miles they had travelled by the time they crossed the moors and came down into gentle rolling hills beyond. To Robin's inexperienced legs, it felt about fifty miles. Woad, however, was certain they had done exactly nine and a half. Karya ignored them both, lost in thought.

Woad began to say something rude, but stopped, open-mouthed, staring ahead.

Atop of the next before them, a tall figure stood. A man was leaning rather nonchalantly against the tree-trunk. He wore a tatty kind of leather skirt and sandals, like a gladiator. His chest and arms were bare and the three companions could see that he mustn't have eaten a full meal in a long time.

What shocked Robin most, though, was the sight of large curling horns spiralling out from the man's mop of curly brown hair.

"That's a … that's a … fae," Woad sputtered.

"What do we do?" Robin whispered urgently to Karya.

"I don't know!" Karya whispered back. "I've never actually met one of the fae before … Apart from you, of course. You never see them. Your kind are supposed to be in hiding!"

"We are in hiding," the man said, his voice deep and resonant, at odds with his half-starved body. His long oval eyes regarded them with a curious mixture of amusement and suspicion. A brief smile flicked across his hollowed cheekbones. "No better place to hide than plain sight … sometimes."

His attention flicked lazily from Karya to Woad before finally settling on Robin.

"I know what she is," he said slowly. "And anyone can see that that thing there is a faun. But what in all the Netherworlde are you?"

Robin felt himself wilting a little under the scrutiny. He was trying not to stare at the horns.

"It's polite to introduce yourself first!" he said, sounding much more defiant than he felt.

"Names have power," Karya said, sticking her chin out proudly, seemingly bolstered by Robin's example. "They shouldn't just be given away because someone happens to have a bow and arrow."

The fae flicked his eyes to her momentarily, as if she was a bothersome distraction, then drifted back to Robin. "I didn't ask what you were called," he said. "I asked what you were. And I find that these are hardly the times for proper etiquette, more's the pity."

"You are a fae, aren't you?" Robin asked, cutting off Karya. "A real one. You're the first one I've ever seen. I've seen pictures and sculptures, but never a living, breathing fae."

The man eyed him carefully. "You don't own a mirror then, little hornless one?" he said, not unkindly. He smiled again as Robin's eyes widened with surprise. "Yes, I can put two and two together. You're a fae who seems human, which probably fools most people, but you can't fool your own kind, boy. You don't know where you belong, which can only mean one thing. You're a changeling." He straightened up, adopting a more relaxed pose. "I haven't heard of such a thing in an age. Since before the war even, and that was long ago."

"He is the last," Karya said solemnly. "You seem so interested, and you have us alone out here in the wild, so I have decided to trust you, in so far as I trust anyone." She folded her arms, regarding him appraisingly. "If you were up to mischief you could have dropped all three of us with your arrows before we even spotted you." She sighed. "My name is Karya. My companions' names, however, are not mine to give."

"They call me Woad, bighorns," Woad said, suddenly at ease with the fae now that Karya had capitulated.

"My name is Robin," Robin said. "Robin Fellows."

The fae's eyes widened in surprise. "Fellows? There are no Fellows any more. Eris ended that line most definitely. Strigoi saw to that personally." His lip curled in distaste. "Certainly no children remain."

"There's one," Robin said thickly. "My parents hid me in the human world. Before Eris ended them…"

A look of sympathy crossed the fae's face. He looked very grim. Robin wondered how long this creature had been living in the wild. Whoever he had been before the war, clearly his time on the run had worn him down.

"I am called Hawthorn," he said, bowing his head in deference. "And if you speak truly, and are indeed the last of the line of Fellows, let us hope you are a good one, like your grandfather before you."

"He is the Scion," Karya said with great gravitas.

Hawthorn stared at the three. "Old stories and tales," he said eventually, with an air of dismissal. "I stopped believing in prophecies long ago. Stories don't keep you warm at night, or put food in your stomach." He narrowed his eyes at Karya. "Not all that is broken can be fixed, little twig."

"Hope is never broken," Karya replied, levelly meeting his stare.

Hawthorn smiled again. Wearily, Robin thought. "Spoken like a child," he said.

He looked to Robin. "So, last changeling, great Scion, saviour of the Arcania … What are you doing blundering around in the Netherworlde?"

The three companions exchanged glances.

Hawthorn raised his arched eyebrows loftily. "Ah … a long story?" he surmised. "No doubt filled with high adventure, intrigue and drama." He sighed. "Then you had better come with me. It's best not to linger out in the open." He turned away. "Come," he commanded. "I know a more secluded spot nearby. We will talk there."

* * *

Hawthorn's secluded spot turned out to be a good half hour's march away, off over the hills and down into a steep rocky valley. A crude cave was formed at the base of a natural quarry. He ushered them inside. The floor was strewn with rough animal hides and even a few books and candles were scattered around.

"Don't make such serious faces, little ones. You have nothing to fear from me," he assured them, lighting a candle. "But perhaps you should be more cautious of strangers in the future. Not everyone you meet will be handsome and helpful fae-folk." He shook out the match. "Some smiles are all teeth."

They sat down amidst the furs and hides.

"You live here?" Robin asked.

"Of course not. This is just a hiding hole. I'm a scout. Sometimes I'm out looking for supplies for days. I can't exactly sleep out under the stars, can I? Not unless I want to wake up on the end of a Peacekeeper's sword, that is. Now … I believe you had a long story to tell me."

It took quite some time for Robin, Karya and Woad to explain everything that had happened. The fae Hawthorn sat cross-legged and silent as their tale unfurled, nodding occasionally, his horns casting leaping shadows on the walls.

Karya relayed the confusing advice they had received from the Oracle, and their subsequent search for the Isle of the Winds.

"I can help you I think, in a small way," Hawthorn announced when they were up to date with events. "Not to find the Isle of Aeolus, I don't even know whether such a place exists. But your riddles … Look to the goddess? … Hmm, well, everyone knows that the goddess of dawn is called Aurora, but I don't really see how that helps…" He stroked his chin. "But high roads to narrow places? Beyond the Singing Fens is a mountain range and I believe I know the pass to which this information refers."

"Really?" Robin asked hopefully.

"You will need to get to the path of the Gorgons," Hawthorn said. "It will take you a long time to make your way across the Singing Fens, though, a trackless mire with little cover for you. You will be sitting ducks for skrikers, not to mention bog hags and sloe."

"Well, we have to cross through the fens to get to the mountains beyond," Karya said, "So there's no point complaining about it."

"This is where I think I can help," Hawthorn said, holding up a finger to silence her. "There is another way to the mountains." He smirked. "Why cross over the fens when you can cross under them?"

Robin was deeply confused. "Um … because we'd drown?" he suggested.

"Not if you are deep enough under them, under the rock." Hawthorn narrowed his eyes secretively.

He stood and walked to the back of the dark cave. "How do you think I travel around and manage to avoid capture? Admittedly, unlike yourselves, I only have Peacekeepers on my trail, not the rather alarmingly dangerous Mr Strife, but still, I find it is always best to go by secret paths and to tread quietly."

He placed a hand against the rock wall at the back of the cave. The bow on his back flashed with red gems, causing a secret door to open in the stone. A long black tunnel stretched away, sloping steeply down into darkness.

Karya stood up, clearly impressed. "Is that a redcap tunnel?" she asked, her voice full of curiosity.

"A very old one," Hawthorn replied, nodding his tousled head. "Disused for centuries. These tunnels lead to many places, but I believe you could use them to cross under these hills and all the way across the Singing Fens without once having to come up for air. That at least will keep you out of sight and off Strife's radar."

Robin thanked the fae for his help. "I mean, you don't even know us, why would you help us?"

Hawthorn gave the three of them an odd, unreadable look. He must have been handsome once and noble to behold. Here in the cave, he looked hungry and bedraggled, but his eyes were still full of burning energy.

"Because, while I might not believe in old prophecies," he said, "… there are many who do. If you are indeed the Scion of the Arcania, last of the Fellows, then perhaps hope is not broken after all – merely battered."

Without further discussion he led them into the tunnel until they were far beneath the hillside. Eventually, the ground levelled out. A rusted mine-cart track ran off into the darkness. Sitting atop the tracks was a large flat stone.

At Hawthorn's insistence, the three companions clambered atop. There was just enough room for them all.

"This," he explained, "… is a cantrip of my own invention. The flat stone you rest upon is my magic carpet, of sorts. It sits atop a horde of many small stones. A little Earth mana and it rolls along at quite some speed." He seemed quite proud. "I should warn you, keep your hands away from the walls or you may lose a finger. And try not to fall off, as it gathers quite some speed and the stone won't stop until it reaches the Holly and Ivy doors on the far side of the Fens."

"Before we go, is it true?" Robin asked. "Is there a real rebellion? Or are the remaining fae all just hiding and surviving? Doing their best not to be captured?"

Hawthorn smiled. "There will always be a resistance against Eris, as long as one fae stands. But yes, Robin Fellows, our people have gathered. We meet and plan and plot. Our leader is brave and fierce. One day, we will have our world back. Perhaps you will live to see it. I will send news of your existence to the leader, our greatest fae, Peaseblossom. He will be most heartened to hear you are real." He grinned. Robin could not tell whether with sarcasm or genuine amusement.

Chapter Twenty – Holly and Oak

They bid farewell to Hawthorn, thanking him for his help. The horned man nodded his farewells and promised their paths would no doubt cross again in the future. He wished them luck in finding help from the goddess Aurora, and with a complicated hand movement, made their stone carriage rumble into life.

With an initial jerk, it began to roll down the large dark tunnel – slowly at first, but quickly gaining speed. Robin watched the silhouetted figure of the slender fae grow smaller and smaller in the distance until the tracks turned a corner and he was lost to sight.

Robin felt an odd pang at leaving the fae. He was, after all, the only one of his kind he had ever seen, and he had seemed so sad and strange, and so very alone.

Soon, the stone was racing along underground, the wind caused by their passage ruffling Robin's hair wildly. The three gripped the edges of the stone when it banked alarmingly at the corners or swooped unexpectedly as the ground fell away from beneath them. It was a little like being on an underground rollercoaster, only with no safety harnesses. The only light they had to go by was a small, unshakable flame which Woad had conjured up and affixed to the front like a headlight.

Karya and Robin found that travelling in this odd way took quite some getting used to, but Woad found the whole thing wildly fun and giggled merrily for a long time, grinning from ear to ear.

They went on in this manner for a long time, their small flickering flame only illuminating a few feet of rocky tunnel ahead of them. Whenever Robin glanced behind them, there was nothing but blackness.

At times, they passed other tunnels branching off from their own, leading off to who knew where. Many of these had similar rails affixed to the floor. Robin tried to glimpse down these, but the stone was moving so quickly that they went past in a blur. Other mine cart rails criss-crossed their own, but the travelling stone seemed to somehow know its own path and veered onward implacably.

Sometimes the tunnels they passed through closed in around them, growing narrow, the walls close enough to scrape alarmingly along either side of the stone. At others, the tunnels spat the mine tracks out into underground caverns; huge, dark and echoing, sprawling chambers the size of cathedrals. The tracks often crossed deep chasms, supported only by rickety stilts and struts of banded wood and steel, jutting out haphazardly like a huge scaffold. Robin did his best not to glance down over the sides of the stone. Hurtling through these large high spaces on their slaloming ride was alarming enough without a dizzying drop around them.

Odd clusters of luminescent crystal sprouted here and there in some of the chambers, glowing in the distant walls or hanging from the pitted cavern roofs in glimmering stalactites. Robin could appreciate that their unearthly radiance would have been beautiful in different circumstances, but he was secretly relieved each time the tunnels closed in again swapping deadly drops for suffocating darkness.

Eventually, the novelty of careering through the darkness began to wear off, and the constant rocking of the travelling stone began to lull the three of them to sleep.

Woad curled up in a semicircle like a blue cat, fast asleep despite the noise. Karya was trying to stifle a yawn herself, flicking idly through Robin's copy of 'Hammerhand's Netherworlde Compendium'. Robin on the other hand was occupied with Phorbas' dagger, oddly comforted by the weapon he held. The garnet stone flashed in the light from Woad's fiery lamp. As they tore through the tunnels on the speeding rock he mulled over Hawthorn's words. There was something which the fae had said on parting which had struck a chord with him, but he couldn't think what. A distant memory, something he had heard before…

"What's troubling you, Scion?" Karya asked eventually, peering at him over the top of her book, her hair whipping about her head. "You should try and get some rest while we can. We might be clipping along at a fair speed but there's still a long way to go until we cross under the Fens."

Robin slipped Phorbas' dagger back into his belt. "It's just something Hawthorn said. It rang a bell in my head and I can't put my finger on it," he explained, frustrated.

Karya raised an eyebrow. "Why would you want to put your finger on a bell in your head?" she asked flatly.

Robin glowered at her. "You don't have to be so difficult, you know. It would be nice to be able to have a regular conversation sometimes." He sighed. "And I wish you'd call me Robin, not 'Scion' all the time."

The small girl looked genuinely puzzled. "But you are the Scion."

Robin snorted down his nose derisively. "I don't even know what that means," he said. "I'm sick of hearing about it to be honest, and sick of everyone we meet giving me boggle-eyed stares because of it. I know next to nothing about this secret inheritance I supposedly have, and I know even less about you, while we're at it," he grunted. "Mr Strife has been chasing you longer than he's been chasing me and I still don't know why. I don't know why you're so full of secrets, but I can tell you this … it's very annoying." He looked directly at her. "I'm supposed to be trusting you and your good intentions, but it's not easy when you're all cloak and dagger about everything."

Karya pursed her lips.

"Fine," she sighed resignedly. "If you want to know why I'm on the run, why Strife is chasing me and why my life is pretty much hell these days, I'll tell you. It's because of you."

"Because of me?!" Robin replied, shocked. "I didn't even know you existed before I came to Erlking!"

Karya glared at him harshly with her golden eyes, snapping the book closed. "You may not have known I existed, but I knew you did," she said gruffly, her cheeks red with temper. "That's the trouble. That's what got me into this mess in the first place."

She ran her fingers through her hair. "I was the only one who knew about you. It's a long story and now is not the time. So please, don't argue. Just know this, seeing as you're so desperate for answers about everything: Eris discovered I knew things she didn't. Which is why she suddenly became interested in me. And trust me…" she said with widened eyes, "… no one wants Eris interested in them."

"Tell me about it," Robin muttered.

"So that's why I ran, and that's why Strife is after me. And that's why I have done my level best to keep you safe and out of the bloody Netherworlde since then."

"I can't just leave Henry and Phorbas to rot," Robin began hotly.

"Of course you can't," Karya said, exasperated. "You're one of those good types, aren't you? And they know that – Strife and Moros and Eris.

They're counting on it. So now you're here in the Netherworlde, which is the last place you should be, and we're on the run, and we barely know where we're going, and I'm doing my level best to keep you out of trouble. But what with redcaps and skrikers and grimgulls, not to mention you attracting ghosts and rubbing shoulders with renegade fae, it's hardly the most relaxing job. And yes, if you must know, sometimes I wish I'd just kept my mouth shut and stayed at home with my sisters!"

"Well, sometimes I do too," Robin snapped back. "I didn't ask to be thrown into all this, you know. You're the one who sent Woad to look over me, and gave me that funny flute to call you. I never asked for your help. I never asked for Gran to die and start all this!"

"Some things," Karya said, through gritted teeth, "… are bigger than what you want!" She made a visible effort to calm herself down. Her cheeks were flushed. "Or what I want. Some things are just bigger," she finished quietly.

She sighed and looked ahead. Faint phosphorescence glowed in the darkness indicated they were coming up to another open space. They rolled into the open, hundreds of tall purple-blue crystals dotted the ceiling, casting a wan light over their rumbling progress below. Robin didn't know quite what to say. He had never heard her say so much all at once before.

After a long, uncomfortable silence, Karya looked back at Robin.

"Have you remembered yet?" she asked politely as though they had not been arguing a moment ago. Her face was carefully calm and composed.

"Remembered what?" Robin asked.

"The thing you almost remembered when the fae was talking to us? If it's important you should be focusing on that, not on me."

Robin fumed quietly. She was the most difficult person he had ever met.

"It was something he said about the mountain pass," he said, figuring that if she had decided to call a truce, so would he. "Or perhaps something the goddess mentioned in the clue. What was her name again?"

"Aurora," Karya supplied, as the travelling rock left the vast glittering cave and darted once again into a tight tunnel of stone. "What about her?"

"I've heard it somewhere," Robin said, frustrated.

"Well, it's certainly not in this book," the girl replied sniffily. "I've been over everything about the Isle of Winds and there's no mention of the either the dawn or the goddess." She glanced at Robin, who stared back, a grin forming. "What? What is it? You have epiphany-face."

Robin rummaged in his backpack, pretending not to have heard her. She eyed him with interest as he pulled out the other volume he had brought with him. It was the book on fae lineage.

"Aunt Irene gave me this for Christmas," he told her. "It a who's who, from before the war obviously. It … it has my parents in it," he finished awkwardly. He opened the book and began flipping through the entries, skipping past names and portraits.

"And what? Are you telling me the goddess Aurora was one of the fae?" Karya said. "Was she your great old auntie or something?"

Robin gave her a sarcastic scowl. "No, not a fae, but connected with one of the Fellows, someone in my family, I'm sure of it. Just let me find the right entry … Here!"

His finger stabbed the page.

"The noble House of Fellows," he read aloud by the flickering candlelight. "Listen to this: 'Gossamer Merryfellow, the noted master of the Tower of Air, with whose inventive direction, the guardians of the Air Shrine developed the now famous Auroracraft'!"

"What in all the Netherworlde is the 'Auroracraft'?" Karya asked, leaning forward with interest to stare at the page.

"It says here, 'Gossamer Merryfellow was one of the most celebrated scientists and inventors in all the court of Oberon and Titania. During his lifetime he invented such marvels of the Netherworlde as the mechanical nightingale. Also attributed to him are spider-repellent wallpaper, the non-stinging blowing bubble, and everlasting candles. Perhaps most famously is the Auroracraft, widely considered to be both his magnum opus and greatest folly'."

The travelling stone crested a hill and plunged them down a steep slope in the narrow tunnels as Robin continued.

"'Originally designed as a present for the great Lord Oberon and Lady Titania themselves and due to be presented to them on their midsummer anniversary, the Auroracraft was sadly never unveiled, due to the tragic and untimely death of Merryfellow from an infestation of Bograt Malaise. The craft's original purpose was, according to Merryfellow's own notes, "a carriage to the clouds, and would allow faekind to explore the lofty heights and walk amongst the very stars themselves". The project, like all of Merryfellow's inventions was shrouded in the greatest secrecy, and after his untimely demise, lay largely abandoned. The incomplete model was put on view in the grounds of Erl King's Hill for many years in his honour, and many later fae scholars have attempted to recreate his efforts working from his surviving sketches, although sadly with no success. It is rumoured that Merryfellow may have already completed a smaller working test model at his private home high in the Caelumvesica mountains'."

"That's where we're headed," Karya exclaimed. "To the Gorgon's Pass. The Caelumvesica Mountains are the mountains beyond the Singing Fens. I wonder if this working model is still there … and still a working model." she added.

"It can't just be a coincidence," Robin said, shutting the book. "The clue said 'the path of wind is open at dawn. Look to the goddess to find your road'. The goddess of dawn is Aurora, and this Auroracraft sounds like some kind of flying machine to me. Maybe a hot air balloon or something, who knows?" He grinned, warming to the idea. "What better way to get to a flying mountain?"

She was quiet and thoughtful for a while. Eventually she said. "Good work, Sci…" She stopped herself, "… Robin. Not bad detective work I suppose … for a hornless wonder."

* * *

There was nothing further to be done until they arrived wherever they were going. Robin finally nodded off. He lay curled on his side beside Woad, careful to keep his hands and feet away from the edges.

He slept fitfully, just below the surface of consciousness. It seemed many long and disjointed hours later that he roused from sleep, looking around blearily, trying to orient himself. They were cruising through a large empty space, another epic underground hole, along one great wall of which there was, against all odds, a wide roaring waterfall, rushing and dark, falling a great distance into the blackness below.

"We are beneath the Singing Fens," Karya said, without preamble. "We have been for a long time now. I've never known anyone sleep as long as you. I think we may have crossed almost to the far borders, the speed this thing is going."

Robin stared ahead, grabbing for his water bottle to parch his thirst. The long stone viaduct they rolled along stretched on into the empty darkness ahead, seemingly forever. It was an impossibly long drop either side.

"So, we're nearly there?" he asked.

"I hope so," Karya replied. "I think we're being followed."

Robin peered back, but could see almost nothing in the darkness. "What?" he asked worriedly. "Do you think it's Strife?"

"No, not Strife," Karya shook her head.

Robin looked from Karya to Woad for an explanation, fully awake now. His hand had unconsciously moved to his belt, close to Phorbas' knife.

"Harpies," Woad muttered, spitting the word as though it tasted bad. "Foul critters."

"Harpies?" Robin said, his eyebrows climbing his forehead. "Are you serious? As in flying ladies with wings and birds legs?"

Woad made a face. "Don't know what you're talking about, Pinky. Nothing ladylike about harpies. They're all teeth and claws, wings and flappy tentacles. Eyeballs and suckers."

"Harpies look nothing like people," Karya said. "They're the scavengers of the Netherworlde. Picture a very large leathery bat with a whole lot of teeth, a bit of squid thrown in for good measure, and more arms and legs than you'd like. Run the whole thing through a cheese-grater and you'd be getting close to how they look."

"But … we're underground!" Robin said, searching the darkness urgently for any sign of leathery, be-tentacled harpies and finding nothing but gloom and darkness. "There's a distinct lack of sky down here. Flying things tend to be in the sky right?"

"Harpies roost in dark caves, brainwave," Woad explained. "Like bats … only they eat bats." He made a face. "They like the dark. I'd like the dark too if I was that ugly." He shrugged his blue shoulders. "They eat anything. They only go up to the surface to feed, when they can't find food down here…"

"I don't know how many there are," Karya said. "I'm sure I've seen a few clusters of eyes now. If they grow in numbers enough, they'll get the courage up to attack."

Robin could still see nothing behind them but blackness. He briefly worried about the fact that harpies apparently had clusters of eyes, but decided to add that to the ever-growing list of thing not to dwell on.

"Look!" Woad said, staring upwards. The other followed his gaze. Far above, countless red eyes stared down at them from the shadows. It was like looking up at the night sky, only all the stars were red. They were everywhere.

"There must be hundreds..." Robin said quietly. "Hawthorn never mentioned harpies, did he? Did I miss the part where he mentioned harpies?"

"He probably didn't think it was worth mentioning," Karya replied dryly. "You fae-folk are like that, as a rule. Always leaving out small and inconsequential details like the likelihood of gibbering death. I wouldn't be surprised if this track eventually just ended and spat us into an abyss and he forgot to mention that too."

"I don't think this is the time, boss," Woad said in a small voice.

"We should be okay..." Karya said, rather unconvincingly. "As long as we have light. They're not fond of light."

All three of them looked at the tiny flame. It flickered and wobbled in the wind. Suddenly it looked very small indeed.

"Um ... Woad?" Robin asked quietly. "How long has your little magic fire been burning now?"

Woad seemed to calculate this carefully. "Hours and hours ... and hours," he concluded.

"And how long can you keep it burning for?"

Woad touched his moonstone pendant. The usually shiny trinket looked quite dull and lifeless.

"Um ... minutes and minutes?" he offered. "Not much mana left. Even astonishing fauns have their limits."

"I can't conjure fire or light," Karya said. "I'm only proficient in the Earth Tower." They looked at Robin expectantly.

"Well, don't look at me!" Robin held up his hands. "I can barely perform simple air cantrips. My Galestrikes probably couldn't even blow that flame out."

They finally reached the other side of the cavern and the tracks plunged them back into a narrow tunnel, the walls closing in. The stone lurched on an angle and began a very steep descent, making Robin's stomach lurch. They gripped the stone and held each other to steady themselves as they plunged on into deeper darkness. From the cavern they had just left, there came a great whooshing noise, like a hundred umbrellas being opened at once.

"How deep do these tunnels go?" Robin wondered aloud as they plummeted along on the track.

"To the bottom I would imagine," Karya answered distractedly. "They're following us … all of them."

There were jostling flashes of red in the tunnel behind them. In some ways, it was worse not being able to see them, no matter how horrible they might look. It couldn't possibly be worse than what Robin was imagining.

The travelling rock levelled out, banked around a corner sharply, so that they momentarily lost sight of their pursuers' shining eyes. The tracks began to climb again steeply. Moments later, the flickering red eyes appeared in the blackness behind them again as the harpies gained ground.

They must have eyes like spiders, Robin thought. He tried to picture what the creatures' faces might look like, and forcibly stopped himself. A vivid imagination could be a curse…

"How much further can it be until we get to the end of this thing?" he asked. Karya gave a noncommittal shrug with one shoulder.

"We may need to burn your books if Woad's light goes out," Karya said thoughtfully. "That would give us a few extra minutes, at least."

Robin, horrified at the idea of burning a book which contained the only know picture of his parents, balked at the idea.

"What good will a few minutes do us?" he said. "There could be hours more travelling for all we know. What do we do when the books are gone? Burn our clothes?"

Woad sniggered inappropriately at this. Karya and Robin both shot him a hard look.

"Sorry," he said, withering under their glares. "Nerves. If it helps, there's something up ahead, something new – I can smell it. Doesn't smell of stone or earth or water."

This was promising, although the skittering mass of unseen harpies seemed to be gaining ground on them.

"Not soon enough. We need to try and hold them off until we get there," Karya said determinedly.

"Hawthorn mentioned something about the doors of oak and holly?" Robin said. "He said the stone would take us that far. I didn't think to ask him what that meant."

"Holly and oak won't stop harpies," Woad said. "They'll tear right through."

The tiny flame affixed to the front of the travelling stone flickered and spluttered. They stared at it in desperate silence. It wavered and re-asserted itself.

"I hope you're good at fighting in the dark," Karya said to Robin.

"I've never fought in the dark," he replied urgently. "I've never even been in a fistfight … in daylight…!"

"We need to think of some way to keep this flame alight," Karya said, a hint of panic bleeding into her usually stoic manner. "It mustn't go out!"

The tiny flamed wavered, and then, with a small pop, as though in sheer defiance of her words, it went out.

They were plunged into darkness.

Not the darkness of a night sky, but utter, crushing blackness. The smothering dark which only exists deep down under the world.

Woad yelped in alarm, and Robin, utterly disoriented, almost lost his balance. He groped wildly in the inky void with unseen hands until Karya caught him by the shoulders.

A chorus of screeches erupted in the blackness, amplified by the narrow tunnel. Hungry animal voices raised in joy, as the unseen harpies, emboldened by the darkness, lurched forward to claim their prize.

The wind rushed past Robin's face in the darkness. He hunkered down, his heart beating wildly as he ducked, trying unconsciously to make himself a smaller target. With rising panic he tensed and awaited the inevitable brush of jagged razor claws across his back.

"Light!" Woad cried in the darkness. Robin thought at first that the faun was casting a cantrip, trying to make another flame, but then he realised that he could somehow just make out the dark outline of the faun, leaning out at the front of the stone like a masthead.

"Tunnel ends ahead!" Woad cried.

Something brushed Robin's shoulder, leathery and heavy. He batted it away in panic, revulsion making him shudder. Another scraped across his flailing arm, and an unseen claw closed tightly around his wrist in a cold and clammy vice. Robin struggled against it desperately. There was foul breath in his face and with peaking terror he felt himself being jerked upwards, lifted from the stone.

There was a sudden flash of amber, blinding in the darkness, as Karya's arm beat fiercely at the unseen grappler, wrenching Robin free of its grip. There was a screech of fury and pain, though it was too dark to see exactly what she had done to the harpy.

"Stay away from us!" Karya shouted to the flurrying maelstrom surrounding them.

Her bracelet flashed again and again, silent golden gunfire. Yowls and yelps reverberated through the blackness. In the flashes, Robin saw frozen images of the small girl surrounded by a whirlwind of wings, claws and long black glossy limbs.

The light was growing imperceptibly around them as they barrelled onwards. Robin, trying to keep low beyond reach of the grasping harpies, could now clearly make out Karya's silhouette. She seemed to have somehow rooted her feet into the stone to keep her balance. He could see the harpies moving in a seething, maddening mass. It was impossible to separate one from the crowd; they were everywhere.

A claw reached down and tangled in Karya's hair. She yelled, crying out in pain as it tried to tear her from the rock.

"Boss!" Woad shouted in alarm.

Robin stood, fury and fear rushing through him, and with all his concentration, focussing on every lesson he had ever had with Phorbas, he threw a Galestrike at the cloud of monsters above.

It was poor, by anyone's standards, but he must have clipped a wing with the blast of air, as there was a screech of surprise and Karya was released, the harpy spinning off from the flock, glancing off the rock wall and taking several of its fellows with it.

"Good shot, Pinky!" Woad said, his voice filled with astonishment.

"Lucky, not good," Robin gasped. He risked a glance forward. The light ahead was brighter, growing with every second, but it was still agonisingly far away.

"I can't keep throwing rocks at them!" Karya shouted over the din. "There're too many!"

An idea suddenly came to Robin. A flash of inspiration as he remembered his very first lesson at Erlking. The piece of parchment stuck flapping to the ceiling. The large windowless room and the cantrip Phorbas had cast to block the wind from the room.

"Breezeblock!" he shouted.

"What?" Karya replied bellowing to be heard.

"Flying creatures! They can't fly through the air if there isn't any!" Robin yelled back.

He pushed his way past Karya to face the mass of harpies head on. He held his hands out in front of him, palms outward. Closing his eyes, he forced himself to focus. His mana stone flashed with heat and light, and he felt the cantrip leave his palms like a vast shuddering breath, throwing up an invisible wall.

The flying mass of claws and wings hit the unseen barrier, suddenly finding their wings useless in the lack of air. They fell like a cascading wave, tumbling over each other, blocking the thin tunnel with their interlocked bodies.

Unencumbered, the travelling rock carried the three children onwards, swiftly putting distance between them and their disabled attackers, the light around them growing brighter and brighter with every passing second.

Woad whooped with triumph. Even Karya gave Robin a brief look of astonishment.

"Not bad for a hornless wonder, eh?" he said, panting with relief. His hands were shaking, his bones vibrating. He had put every ounce of his mana into the cantrip, and now expelled, he was light headed and dizzy, his legs like water.

"That won't hold them for long," Karya said in her usual flat manner. She looked ahead toward the light at the end of the tunnel. "We're slowing down … have you noticed?"

Robin hadn't, but now that she mentioned it, the travelling stone was indeed finally losing speed. "I suppose we're about to arrive, wherever we are."

The track levelled out as they finally reached the top of the long slope, the cries of the harpies distant now. With a clatter, the rolling stone emerged from the tunnel, delivering them into another large cave, the floor of which was dotted with dozens of shimmering pools of water. The source of the bright light was evident now. The walls and ceiling were covered, every glittering inch, with crystals. The violet and blue light was dazzling after so much darkness.

The travelling stone chugged to a jerky halt in the very centre of the cave, where the rusted mine cart tracks ended rather unceremoniously. It stopped with a clatter, the sudden lack of motion after so long making them all lose their balance.

"Look at this place," Robin said in wonder, weaving slightly on his feet. It was like being inside a geode.

Unlike the astonished boy, Karya leapt off the stone, wasting no time and barely giving the glittering cave a second glance. After wobbling slightly, she rushed back to the tunnel and stared down into the gloom. Viewed from the top, the tunnel stretched away like a long dark coal shaft. Echoes of angry struggling harpies floated up distantly.

"Your idea was good, Scion, I'll give you that. We were nearly mincemeat back there, and that breezeblock stopped them in their tracks, but unless you can do that again in about two minutes, all we've done is make them angry as well as hungry."

Robin took a step and had to stop and steady himself against a stalagmite. Dizziness washed over him. He wouldn't be using any mana for a while. He shook his head, trying to clear it.

"They won't come into the light," Woad said. "Will they? Bright and shiny's no good for slimy monsters."

"They will if they have to," Karya said darkly. "We have to get out of here, and quick."

"I'm guessing," Robin said, "… that this over here would be the way out then."

Beyond the pools, amidst the translucent stalactites, stood two vast stone doors, placed side by side. Both doors were tall and wide, towering over the children like ancient city gates, each covered entirely by a vast carved face.

The right hand door was carved to resemble an old man, but in place of hair and a beard, there were twirling oak leaves, fat and broad, growing straight out of the carving's head.

The other door was identical in design, but the enormous face was framed with a mane and beard of spiky stone holly. It looked far sterner.

"The doors of Holly and Oak," Karya said. "I think that's a fair assumption."

They stared up at the vast stone features.

"Which one do we take?" Robin asked. "Which one leads out of this place?"

"I've no idea which one to choose," Karya admitted, glancing over her shoulder at the dark tunnel on the other side of the cave. "Another thing Hawthorn completely forgot to mention. As long as the door closes firmly behind us, at the moment I'm not too fussy to be honest."

"Unless one of them leads into a bigger harpy nest," Woad pointed out conscientiously. "Then it's pretty darn important which one we choose…"

"**Choose? Choose! Why Would We Let You Choose?!**"

The voice had boomed out of nowhere, startling all three of them. It sounded like someone bellowing very slowly through a megaphone with a throat full of gravel. Woad jumped almost a foot in the air.

The huge stone face with the oak beard and hair had spoken, its stone eyes glared down at them, rolling in their sockets like dusty medicine balls. The carved leaves came to life as well, writhing and shaking about its face as though blown by the wind. It peered down on them with interest.

"The door … spoke … to us," Robin whispered after a moment.

"**We Have Ears As Well As Mouths, Little Fae,**" the other door boomed in its slow and deafening voice, scowling down at them. "**It Is Rude To Whisper. We Do Not Like Rudeness.**"

Of the three of them, Karya recovered fastest. "They must be enchanted," she said. "Made by whoever made that viaduct."

She turned to the giant stone faces. "Please, we need to pass. We have to get through quickly."

"**Quickly She Says,**" bellowed the ivy-covered face, casting a sidelong glance at its companion. "**Down Here We Are, Since The Fall Of The Great Nethercity. Aeons Of Silence. Nothing To Do, Century After Century, But To Watch The Crystals Grow And Listen To The Earth Above Us Creak. And … Quickly … She Says.**"

The oak face ruffled its great beard of leaves with a sound like a small landslide "**Despicable. Abominable,**" it said. "**The Youth Of Today. Always In Such A Rush.**"

"Please. There are harpies," Robin implored. "They're chasing us."

"**Ugh. Harpies,**" the oak face grumbled. "**Nasty Smelly Little Things.**"

"**Get Stuck In The Teeth,**" the Ivy face agreed.

"We will be stuck in their teeth if we can't get away!" Karya said hotly.

"**Whippersnapper. Being Bad Tempered Will Get You Nowhere Fast,**" the Ivy face said, glaring at her.

"**Being Polite And Patient Will Get You Everywhere Slowly,**" the Oak face agreed.

Karya threw up her hands in exasperation. "We really don't have time for this," she hissed to Robin and Woad.

"**Time?**" the ivy face said grimly and ponderously. "**Time Is All We Have.**"

"**It's Not Much Of A Life, Being A Door, To Be Honest,**" the oak face confided. "**Eye-Spy Is Frankly Rather Depressing When You Have The Same View For Millennia.**"

"We need to get through," Robin insisted.

"**Stay And Chat,**" the Holly Face suggested. "**We Never Have Company.**"

"**Never,**" the oak face agreed sadly.

"**Never Ever.**"

Robin, acutely aware that he and the others were seconds from being torn asunder, nevertheless felt a pang of pity. These enchantments were truly lonely, here deep under the world.

"Look, we can't," he implored. "Not now, anyway. But if you let us through, I swear … I'll come back someday and talk as long as you like."

"**He Promises?**" the oak door said to its companion.

"**Does He Know Stories?**" the Holly door wondered, "**Songs? Riddles?**"

"Hundreds of them. Trust me, I … I'm the Scion of the Arcania. I wouldn't lie to you. I swear I'll return."

Both faces eyed him stonily.

"**I Suppose...**" said the ivy door very grudgingly. "**You May Choose Your Path. Fleshy Ones Are Always Rushing. Only One Of These Doors Will Open For You. Choose Your Path Wisely.**"

"How are we supposed to know which one to choose?" Karya asked, walking over to them. "Where do they lead?"

"**One Way Leads To The Surface, High In The Mountains,**" the oak door said. "**The Other Leads Deep Into The Darkest Burrows Of The Underearth. To The Very Ruins Of The Nethercity Itself.**"

Robin ran his hands through his hair. His mana stone had just jittered briefly against his chest, indicating that the Breezeblock had now run out of power. The creatures, freed from their invisible barrier would be flying up the dark tunnel towards them. They had seconds at best.

Robin looked from door to door. The oak king seemed the more friendly-looking of the two, but if there was one thing Robin had learned since he first came to Erlking, it was not to take anything at face value.

He was suddenly distracted by a vibration at his side. He glanced down, confused. Phorbas' dagger was quivering, tucked into the belt of his jeans. The garnet mana stone flashing.

"What on earth?" he exclaimed, astonished. He pulled the knife out of the belt. It swung around excitedly in his hand as though it had a life of its own.

"Why are you waving your dagger about? It won't do much good against the harpies," Karya said.

"I'm not doing it," Robin said, gripping the dagger by its hilt with both hands. "It's doing it on its own. Like it's possessed or something."

The dagger gave a lurch, and despite Robin's best efforts, slipped out of his grip.

It fell and landed on the rocky floor of the cave, where it bounced around like a jumping bean, then settled on its side and began to spin.

"This is no magic I've ever seen before," Karya said wonderingly, as the three of them gave the spinning blade a wide berth. "What is this, spirit magic?"

"They're coming!" Woad said urgently, staring back at the tunnel.

Robin and Karya did not take their eyes off the dagger, spinning faster and faster, its mana stone shining like an orange beacon, until, as suddenly as it had begun, the dagger stopped suddenly, mid spin. It pointed, blade quivering, straight at the vast holly door. Robin stared up at the carved face, which regarded him shrewdly.

"No time," he said, noticing Karya's questioning look. "We'll figure it out later." He ran towards the door, scooping up the dagger in his hands as he went. Karya and Woad hurried after him.

"Open up!" he yelled at the ivy face. "Hurry! We choose this path!"

The ivy face closed its vast eyes and slowly opened its mouth, wider and wider, until it formed a large opening, a carved archway leading into a gloomy passageway beyond.

Ignoring his natural instinct not to run into the throat of an enchanted stone colossus, Robin plunged inside just as the vast shrieking mass of harpies surged into the glittering cave, smothering the light. The harpies had arrived.

"Close! Close!" he heard Karya yell behind him, and the ivy door clamped its jaws together behind them with a heavy and very final thud.

Muffled noises thudded behind the door, as the harpies threw themselves into it in useless frustration, soon replaced by squeals of harpy panic as the doors apparently decided to retaliate. There were many unpleasant crunching noises and what sounded like a gravelly chuckle.

Robin and the others raced down the passage beyond, not stopping until they reached a small round chamber at the passageway's end. Robin panted to get his breath back, turning Phorbas' dagger over in his hands. It lay quite inert and regular. The tiny carving of a faun's face on the side looked up at him mysteriously.

"I have no idea how that happened," he gasped. "It just … came to life. I didn't have anything to do with it."

"The Oracle did say something about your knife being odd," Karya pointed out.

"It's not 'my' knife," Robin said. "It's like it was helping us choose."

"Let's hope it chose well," Woad said with narrow eyes. "I've never trusted my life to cutlery before."

"Where do we go from here?" Robin said, looking around the small chamber.

Karya pointed. A narrow staircase encircled the wall, spiralling endlessly away. They seemed to be at the bottom of a phenomenally deep shaft.

"Up," she said. "And hopefully out."

Robin raised his eyebrows, looking at the dizzying spiral of steps above him. They were narrow, carved directly from the rock walls. "I suppose a handrail would have been too much to ask for, wouldn't it?"

Woad cackled and scampered up the steps on all fours, springing from one to the next like a cat.

Karya gave Robin an odd look, as though she were weighing something up.

"Good work back there, Scion. There's more to you than meets the eye."

Before Robin could reply to Karya's very unexpected compliment, she set off up the steps. Casting one look back the way they had come, he tucked Phorbas' knife away and made his way up after the others.

Chapter Twenty One – The Pass of the Gorgons

They seemed to climb up the carved steps forever. After a while, they could no longer see the bottom of the shaft, and every step seemed to cause their bodies to lurch toward the central gulf, willing them to fall and be swallowed up by the deep blackness below.

Eventually, legs burning, they reached the top. The light and warmth was the nicest thing Robin had ever felt. He filled his lungs greedily and the three companions practically fought one another to be the first to emerge from the doorway into the open air. Fresh wind met them, whipping about the travellers as they emerged to find themselves in a narrow nook between two large rocks. A sheer cliff lay before them, the landscape below far enough away that Robin wouldn't have been surprised to see clouds pass beneath. Behind them the rocks rose up … and up and up. An almost sheer wall of rugged stone soared for what seemed like miles. All around them rose mountains, massive and craggy. Threading through these jagged peaks, a trail wound precipitously, hugging cliff edges and snaking up and down the rock walls, leading off further into the rocky heights.

"Wow, we're pretty high up," Robin said, peering down at the landscape below them, getting as close to the narrow edge as he dared. In the distance on the shimmering horizon, the ground looking glittering and flat, and Robin guessed it was the edge of the Singing Fens.

"It's hard to believe we've covered so much ground in so short a space of time," Karya said with wonder, looking out over the sweeping vista, a hand shielding her eyes from the sun. "Had we not run into that Fae, we wouldn't have even reached the Singing Fens by now. And then we'd have miles and miles and indeed miles of wet boggy ground still to cover."

"Not to mention having to deal with bog-hags and pyreflies," Woad added, teetering fearlessly on the lip of the cliff with perfect balance. "And willos. You know how I hate willos," he added darkly.

"Well," said Robin. "If we come back this way once we've found Henry and Phorbas, we're taking the long overland route thanks. I don't care how long it takes. I don't fancy meeting up with those harpies ever again."

The others nodded in rueful agreement.

Karya turned to the other two, her hands on her hips impatiently.

"Well, come on, we've been out of the daylight for quite some time, but if I'm any judge of this sky, it's getting on for late afternoon. Night falls faster than a lead balloon in the mountains and we won't be able to travel in the dark."

"Unless the direction you want to go is straight down, and very fast," Woad added happily to Robin with a wink, scampering after the girl.

"Exactly. So we should make as much ground as we can while it's still light." She looked at Robin curiously. "And we'll have a closer look at that strange dagger you're carrying when we make camp for the night, Scion."

Robin followed her and Woad along the pebble-strewn path. He couldn't help thinking from her tone that Karya felt he was keeping secrets from her – although, in truth, he was as mystified by the dagger's strange actions as the rest of them.

* * *

Trekking through the high mountains was difficult and hair-raising. The thin trail hugged the sheer cliffs, dropping away into nothingness all around them. They travelled right until nightfall, before falling into an exhausted sleep. Robin didn't stir at all until Woad woke him at dawn. "Come and see, Pinky," the faun said merrily.

"What is it?" he yawned. "What's so important that we can't even have our cold sausage and dried bread breakfast before we set off?"

The sun was still low and bright, the mountains steaming with morning dew.

Robin realised that back in the human world, it was Christmas day.

Karya pointed ahead. "The Pass of the Gorgons," she announced in a satisfied voice. "We were right on its doorstep and didn't even notice."

A great ravine lay before them, the void filled with clouds and morning mist, shimmering like a liquid gold ocean beneath them. A thin stone bridge arched over the sea of mists to the far side.

"No handrails," Karya murmured.

They made their way carefully onto the bridge, grateful for the churning clouds below which hid the great height from them. Robin risked a look down a few times and once, the mists seemed to eddy and thin, and he thought he saw a glimpse of rocky slopes and trees ridiculously far below. It was like looking out at the countryside from an aeroplane window, and he quickly averted his eyes, keeping them firmly on the thin arch of stone underfoot.

Woad had already reached the far side of the great ravine. He disappeared into the narrow fissure in a blue flash, and returned after several seconds, quite excited, just as Karya and Robin reached the relative safety of the end of the bridge.

"Hurry, you slow marmosets! Come and see, through here."

The fissure formed a thin corridor. After a few twists and turns it spat them out into a wide sloping cliff-top meadow.

There were groves of trees dotted around, leaves whispering softly in the sheltered dell's breeze. Situated near the edge of the cliff was a strange structure, which looked like a cross between an ancient Roman manor house and a makeshift observatory. Even from this distance, they could see it was a ruin. Nothing more than the shell of a once-beautiful house. It was ivy-choked and several of its columns lay toppled in the long. It stood in the sunlight like a peaceful tomb.

"Wow, this is beautiful," Robin said.

They set off towards the ruin. They were sheltered from the winds and it seemed awfully quiet as the long grass brushed against them. Near to the ruined house, on the edge of the cliff, was an odd structure like a small ski jump.

Karya looked around the ruin with interest. The doors were long gone and the dark interior was piled with junk. Karya poked a broken vase on the floor with her toe. "Where would this magical craft be, then?"

"How should I know?" Robin shrugged. "Let's have a look around."

There were a few scattered pieces of furniture, an upturned table against the wall, a broken chair jammed into the leaf-filled fireplace. Most of the interior had been cleared out however. It was silent and gloomy after the bright morning light outside. They split up, rummaging through the debris.

"There's a door over here," Robin called to the others, pulling down a large dust sheet. The noise startled two small birds, which flew out into the sunshine in a flurry of wings and startled complaints.

He leaned against the door with his shoulder and forced it open. The room beyond was jammed with bric-a-brac and junk. Towering piles of yellowing paper stood taller than Robin himself. Models and puppets hung on tangled wires from the rafters. Shelves and boxes were everywhere. They were littered with cogs, brimming with springs, wheels, egg timers, odd glass-blown shapes. Jars and bottles of every size and shape cluttered every surface. Several of the larger shapes were covered with grimy-looking dustsheets. There was barely room to move. It was chaos.

"If it's here, it must be under one of these sheets," Robin said doubtfully. "This whole place is a tip. Everything looks broken, rusted, or useless."

"When Eris' Peacekeepers came here, I imagine they would have smashed the place up," Karya said, making a distasteful face. "If there was nothing they thought they could loot or plunder. No one's lived here in nearly a hundred years, I'd judge."

Robin made his way through the clutter, trying not to topple anything over. He pulled a large dustsheet off what was revealed to be some kind of modified canoe with an adjustable snorkel made of smudged and thumbed brass.

"Well, this isn't it … I hope," he said.

The others followed his lead, unveiling oddity after oddity, raising great clouds of dust as they went. There were all manner of contraptions but nothing which looked like it might fly.

Robin had just uncovered a bamboo chair which seemed to be fitted with mechanical spider legs when he heard an odd noise. It sounded for all the world as though someone were playing the maracas.

"What was that?" Robin said, eyeing the contraptions warily. Woad still gripped a pale papery dustsheet.

"It sounded like…" Karya began, but was cut off as the dust sheet grasped in Woad's hand slipped and rustled loudly to the floor, the end still clutched in the faun's hand.

Woad glanced down, and with a startled shriek, dropped it.

"A face!" he yelped. "It's got a face!"

They stared down at the crumpled, papery mass at his feet. It did indeed have a face, like a crumpled latex mask. The shape of shoulders, arms and a torso was visible before it dissolved further down into a long crinkling mass.

"That's not good," Karya said in a very small voice.

"What is that?" Robin asked in shock.

The hissing rattle came from the dark house again, closer. Something was moving slowly towards the workshop, It sounded like something heavy being dragged along the floor.

"It's a skin," the girl told him. "A shed skin."

Robin stared from the pale mass on the floor to Karya in confusion. "What? As in a snake-skin? It has a head!"

"Not snake," Karya replied, looking to the doorway. "Gorgon."

The hissing came again, and a dark shape, huge and swift, passed in front of the doorway, banging against the door lintel and dislodging a flurry of dust.

"Whatever you do, if it opens its eyes, don't look!" Karya told him urgently.

"Oh there's nothing for you to worry about, my little warmblood," a voice came, deep and full of sibilant malice. "You have nothing to fear from me … not anymore."

A scaly clawed hand, appeared around the doorframe. It was large and long-fingered, much bigger than a normal human hand and much higher up the doorframe than anyone should have been able to reach. The skin was shiny black and banded with bright orange stripes along the fingers, ending in wicked-looking nails.

"We're here peacefully, gorgon," Karya said sternly. "We mean no mischief. Let us be."

A dry raspy cackle escaped from the darkness.

"Mischief-makers," it said resentfully. "All who come here, all who enter into Stheno's garden. Mischief and trickery."

The gorgon pulled itself into the workshop, her flanks brushing both sides of the doorframe.

She was enormous. Twice as large as any full-grown person. Below the waist, her body resolved into a thick, muscular tail, covered in jet black scales, glossy and flexing. Bright orange bands of colour rolled down her torso.

Her face was almost completely covered behind a long tangled mop of stringy black hair, so that only her mouth and chin was visible. Her lips curled into a cruel smile. The hair itself waved slightly to and fro, and it took Robin a moment to realise that it was composed of thousands of tiny snakes, hanging placidly. They stirred against one another slowly, making the great creature appear as though her head were underwater, swayed by unseen currents.

"We don't know who you mean," Karya said, her eyes firmly on the floor. "We travel alone."

The gorgon glided forward slowly with hypnotic, sinuous grace. She loomed over them. The gorgon couldn't possibly have seen Karya stepping backwards with her face hidden behind her long veil of hair, but she snapped her head around nevertheless, as fast as a striking cobra.

"Liars," she snapped. "Warmbloods are all the same. Stealing, tricking, maiming." She hissed, a long forked tongue flicking out from her lips. "Should have turned them both to stone, made pretty statues for my garden." Her mouth turned down in an ugly grimace. "But they were quick, Tricked old Stheno with illusions, lies of the…" She gave a grim, sad laugh, "… eyes."

"We really have no idea what you're talking about," Karya insisted. "Honestly. There's just the three of us. We came here looking for something, that's all. No tricks, certainly not to bother any gorgons."

"They stole from old Stheno, little trespassers." The gorgon turned her head this way and that, her snake hair shivering. "No more stone-making. No. They took my power!"

She reached up with scaly arms and parted her hair. Karya and Woad both squeezed their eyes shut. Robin didn't react fast enough. He felt panic thud in his chest, expecting at any moment to meet the gorgon's stare. But the upper half of the creature's face was hidden by a stained blindfold.

"They took my eyes!" the gorgon hissed.

It laughed miserably at the three surprised children and let its hair fall back into place slowly. "Scary sight, isn't it?" she growled poisonously, her lips curled with loathing. "Like a dog with no bark, a scorpion without a tail."

Karya opened her eyes, staring at the blinded creature in amazement. Woad on the other hand, not only still had his eyes closed, but his hands clamped over them as well, just in case.

"They took your eyes?" Karya asked, her voice full of shock. Clearly not something easily done, Robin thought.

"Mischief makers. Tall and pale. Full of tricks. Put old Stheno to sleep they did. When I awoke…" She pointed towards her head with her great arms, gesturing to her disfigurement. "And now you are here. What have you come to steal?"

"Nothing, I promise!" Robin said, holding his hands up innocently. He considered this a moment. "Well … nothing of yours anyway. We … we've come looking for something that belonged to the Fae who lived here."

The gorgon's fangs glistened with venom. "No one has lived here for a long, long time. No one but Stheno and her sisters. But they are both gone now." A wistful look came over her face, contorting her dark features. "Youngest little snakeling, lost her head over a mortal boy. Long ago … far away … shame."

"And the other?" Karya prompted, clearly wondering if there was more than one gorgon hanging around the place.

"Euryale?" the gorgon said with a sneer. "Eldest was a foolish girl. Found a pool of water. Decided to admire her own beauty." She sighed in a rattling hiss. "Now she's a lawn ornament, out by the cliff edge. Birds roost in her frozen stone coils."

She cackled darkly at this. Robin couldn't help but think that losing her eyes had unbalanced her mind somewhat. But then he had never met a gorgon before. Perhaps they were all like this.

"What are you looking for then? Did the fae have treasure here? I like treasure." She leaned in closer. "You smell like fae as well. Not many of your kind left in the world," she added with relish.

"Eris has seen to that," Robin replied darkly. "Are you loyal to her?"

The gorgon spat on the floor, her venomous spit sizzling in a pool. "We gorgons owe our allegiance to no one. Least of all that dark apple. Never has Stheno known a blacker heart. If ever Eris met a gorgon's stare, I would not be shocked to find her eyes hard as diamond."

"It's not treasure," he said. "It's a machine, I think. I don't suppose you know if there's anything around here called the Auroracraft?"

The gorgon looked disinterested. "Asking questions of old Stheno," she muttered. "Was a time when men were frozen with terror … unable to draw a breath to speak when faced with the majesty of gorgons. Now see … a child asking questions." She raised her claws as though to look at them in wonder.

"Have you become so old?" she muttered moodily to herself. "A blind gorgon." She grimaced dangerously at them all. "Who ever heard of such a thing?"

"You're still very … um … impressive," Robin said. His words hung for several seconds in the dim light and dusty silence. "Scary, I mean."

Stheno turned her blindfolded face to him doubtfully. "Scary? A gorgon who can't turn anyone to stone?" she snapped. "Can't even give you stiff joints?"

"Yes," Robin insisted. "Absolutely terrifying. I mean, okay, fair enough, maybe you can't turn us to stone anymore, but you could easily squeeze us to death, couldn't you?" Robin continued encouragingly. "Or tear us to ribbons with those claws? They're massive."

The gorgon seemed to muse on this. "Yes, I suppose … I hadn't really thought…"

"There are plenty of ways to strike fear into the hearts of your victims, aren't there?" Robin assured her enthusiastically. "It's better than just glaring at everyone all the time."

The gorgon sounded slightly less moody and depressed. "You get stuck in a rut don't you … after so long." She looked slightly uncertain of itself. Marginally less terrifying.

"I'm sure whoever did this to you must have been very powerful, in order to overcome you," Robin said.

The gorgon scowled at him. "More powerful than Stheno?" Her lip curled.

"Oh no! No of course not," Robin back-pedalled. "I meant devious … not powerful. Devious and … cowardly."

This seemed to mollify her slightly.

"There were two of them, you said?" Robin asked. "What did they want your eyes for?"

It was Karya who answered. "Gorgons' eyes are highly prized, Scion. Very powerful magic. The lore goes that the fresher they are, the more powerful the magic."

She looked to Stheno. "Somebody wanted to use your eyes against someone very, very powerful indeed if they needed gorgon eyes so fresh."

"Strife," Robin said thickly.

He pictured his aunt and Mr Drover, standing in the hallway of Erlking. Frozen statues. His aunt may appear to be a fragile old lady, but she was steward of Erlking, the last bastion of fae power. She must be very powerful.

He looked back to the gorgon. "When did this happen? When did the pale men come?" he pressed.

"At the time when the walls between the worlds are thin," the gorgon replied hissing, lowering herself a little. She looked less inclined to strike out at them now.

"Halloween," Karya translated to Robin.

"That was when Strife came to Erlking," he fumed. "They've been planning this for ages then."

The creature rattled her tail. "This is your fault?" she growled. "This is what you say? This happened to old Stheno because of you children?" She was flexing her great hands, clearly now considering the rending and tearing.

"No," Robin told her firmly. "These men, the ones who tricked and stole from you. They're our enemies as well."

"They stole from us too," Woad chimed in, still with his hands clamped over his eyes. "Only they didn't just take eyes, they took whole people. Two of them. Well, nearly two whole ones. They left a bit of broken horn behind."

The gorgon flicked her great tongue, her thick black hair writhing with agitation as her temper soared. "They should be punished! They took what was not theirs!"

"We have a common enemy. You could help us." Robin said.

"Warmbloods?" Stheno wrinkled her scaly nose in distaste. "Why would a gorgon help your kind? What business of yours could Stheno care about? Stheno, who is immortal."

"Because it would ruin the plans of the mischief-makers," Karya said.

Robin nodded. "Wouldn't that be more satisfying than eating us?"

She considered this for a long time. It was clearly not a simple choice.

"Hmm," she grunted eventually, after a long tense silence. She beckoned with a claw. "Follow me, little morsels."

In one fluid movement she doubled back on herself into the ruined darkness of the house. When the end of her huge tail disappeared, Karya looked at Robin.

"What in all the world are you trying to do, giving her ideas about crushing us or ripping us to bits?!"

Robin shrugged. "She seemed depressed. I thought if I tried to cheer her up a bit, she might be in a better mood."

He followed the gorgon out of the workshop, leaving the others to follow him.

Stheno led them back into the bright sunlight. The gorgon swished through the long grass like a sidewinder, throwing up clouds of pollen in her wake. She led them away from the house toward the cliff, and they had to jog to keep up.

As they approached the makeshift ramp which projected out over the edge of the dizzying cliff, they noticed a large irregular shape positioned at its apex, covered with a hefty tarpaulin.

"This is what you seek, little warmbloods," the gorgon said. "Pale men didn't go near. They flew on winged beasts. Dark magic from Eris."

"They flew here?" Robin asked, catching up.

The gorgon raised a glossy claw and pointed out over the horizon. From the cliff's edge there were no further mountains. It was an awfully long way down to the countryside below. There were clouds scudding below them.

"To the Isle of Winds," Karya said, scanning the horizon, although there was nothing in the sky but birds. She clambered onto the wooden ramp and ran across to the large shape at its end, grabbing the tarpaulin and pulling it free.

Beneath was a large construction, which looked very much like an oversized rowing boat. It was large enough to hold at least ten people, and attached to its sides, unfurling slowly as it was freed from its covering, were long wings. They seemed to be constructed from paper, wax and cloth, haphazardly covered with feathers every colour of the rainbow. A riot of magnificent carnival colours, each hue fighting for dominance.

The boat itself was painted sky blue, and along its prow, in curling white letters, lovingly painted, was the name 'Aurora'.

"Look to the goddess of dawn to find your path," Woad grinned.

"Well, Scion," Karya said with great satisfaction. "Merry Christmas."

* * *

They examined the Auroracraft inside and out. There were no oars and no visible controls which made any sense. At the prow was a complicated-looking console of brass and leather. Odd gauges, dials and clocks were dotted everywhere, but none of the companions had the faintest clue what any of these indicators might mean. The vast, multi-coloured wings, as far as they could see, were not connected to anything other than the hull of the boat. There were no levers or pulleys to operate them. They simply hung limply down either side of the steep ramp.

"It's all very pretty," Karya said after inspecting it. "But how in the world do we operate it?" She flicked a finger on some thick copper piping which ran in wavy lines along the base of the boat.

"If it even works after all this time," Woad said, sniffing what appeared to be a large pair of oversized bellows where a rudder would usually be. "Plenty of time for springs to rust and cogs to snap, boss."

"No clue," Robin said, tapping a couple of the dials on the large console experimentally. "But it's our only hope of getting to the Isle of Winds isn't it, so I suppose we'll just take our time and have a few dry runs before…"

"Before we hurl ourselves off a very high mountain cliff in a rusty old boat?" Karya supplied helpfully. "Yes, I think that would be wise."

Robin reached under a seat, glowering at her, "Maybe there's a user's manual somewhere?"

"Old Stheno knows how it flies," the gorgon said. The three children had been so engrossed that they had actually forgotten she was there.

"Fae hid life inside the ship," Stheno explained, which didn't really help.

"But we don't know how to make the wings flap," Robin replied, pulling a lever he had found at the front. It let out a loud rusted squeak, but nothing happened.

The gorgon moved sinuously around the boat towards the rear, where the entire craft was tethered to the top of the ramp by a thick, sturdy rope – the only thing, presumably, that stopped it rolling down the wooden boards and off the cliff edge.

"Idiot children," Stheno grumbled, feeling around with her blind hands until her black claws gripped the rope itself. "How do baby birds learn to flap their wings?"

"Hey! Wait!" Robin said, noticing her grip tighten. "What are you doing? Be careful back there, don't…"

"You throw them from the nest," Stheno said decisively, her lips splitting into a wicked grin.

Long claws shredded the rope in a swift movement.

There was one horrible floating moment, when nothing seemed to move. Time itself seemed to stop, and the children all stared mutely at the severed rope. Then the boat lurched and began to roll down the long slope with a grumble of wheels. The papery wings dragged alongside it uselessly on either side, shedding feathers like a multi-coloured chicken as it went.

Robin looked back in horror and saw the gorgon standing at the tip of the ramp, looking very pleased with herself, framed against the rocky mountains beyond the beauty of the hidden glen. Then his attention was dragged inexorably forward as the boat barrelled onwards. They were running out of ramp, and fast.

"Grab on to something!" Karya yelled. She had thrown herself between the padded leather bench and the wooden walls as the wind tore through her wild hair. Woad was clinging to the large bellows at the back of the boat, like a drowning man grasping flotsam. His face was nothing but a pair of huge, startled eyes. "Scion," Karya yelled again, dragging Robin's startled attention back to her. "We're going over the edge! Hold on or you'll be making a trip on your own!"

Robin's eyes flew desperately around the boat. As he searched in a panic for a handhold, the boat lurched off the edge of the cliff, shooting giddily into thin air.

There was a surreal moment of weightlessness. A sudden silence as the wheels left the wooden ramp. Robin felt his feet begin to lift from the boards as the craft fell.

The odd squeaking lever he had tried earlier caught his eye, and he grasped for it desperately.

The Auroracraft fell out of the sky.

Karya, usually stoic and calm, let out a long piercing scream. It lasted for several seconds as they fell, spinning wildly like a falling leaf. The wind whipped past them, howling. Robin's stomach seemed to be in his throat. Mountainside and cliff face flashed past them. It was all he could do to hold on for dear life.

Woad had his eyes screwed shut, his knuckles a very pale blue as he gripped the bellows doggedly. They passed in and out of sudden patches of thick mist as the boat fell through the clouds. The long useless wings of the old boat were whipping around, the passing air slapping them rapidly in every direction.

After a short while, Karya stopped screaming. It was a very long way down and you can only keep a scream up for so long. The ground may indeed be rushing up to greet them, but it was still a long way off, features hazy and indistinct as they plummeted towards it.

"We're … going … to … die!" Karya yelled to Robin, her voice almost entirely whipped away by the wind. She sounded more angry than afraid. The boat lurched, spun in an eddy, throwing Robin clear of the lever. Luckily he rolled along the floor and managed to grab the edge of the leather seating, keeping his body pressed flat to the boards.

"I know!" he yelled back.

"I don't want to die!" Woad bellowed, opening his eyes wide.

"None of us want to bloody well die!" Robin screamed. "Bloody … insane … gorgon!" He stared at Karya, still wedged in her spot, gripping the sides of the craft for dear life. "Can't you do something?!" he yelled, bellowing to be heard over the rush of the wind.

"Well," she seemed to consider this for a moment. "I'm pretty sure I can cover about half a square mile like jam when we hit the ground!" she shouted back. "Don't see how helpful that will be though!"

She forced herself into a standing position and peered over the edge of the boat. The wind whipped her hair straight up from her head so that for a moment she looked like the bride of Frankenstein.

"About a minute before we meet the ground!" she screamed to the others.

The boat lurched and pitched again as it plunged through the alarmingly empty air. A minute is a long time when you're falling to your death.

Robin dragging himself along the side of the boat until he reached the helm. He gripped the console with steely determination, his eyes streaming from the wind, roving over the countless dials, lever and buttons. He began to pull them and push them indiscriminately.

"What are you doing?" Karya yelled in panic. "Don't just pull things at random! You'll make things worse!"

Robin stared at her over his shoulder in amazement. "How?!" he bellowed.

She stared back at him blankly for a moment in silence. He had a point.

"Hurry!" Woad gibbered.

Robin turned back to the console, trying various levers once more. Many seemed rusted beyond use, refusing to budge even the slightest inch under his sweaty grasp. Others pinged and twanged as he pulled them, to no clear effect. He jabbed buttons and dials urgently, but nothing happened. The little clock hands in the displays were spinning wildly, as though they were panicking as well.

"Nothing's working!" he shouted back to the others. Karya looked almost as pale as Mr Strife.

He tried to turn, wondering if there was maybe something at the rear of the boat they had overlooked, anything that might help, but his belt snagged on something and he found himself stuck fast.

Looking down, he was surprised to see that Phorbas' dagger had jammed between two cogs under the main console. Gripping the hilt, Robin tugged, trying to free it. Nothing happened. Cursing under his breath with some very inventive words which would almost certainly have had Aunt Irene chasing him with a fireside poker, he wriggled it to and fro violently, trying to loosen it. It was no good, the rusted teeth of the cogs held it fast in their jaws.

"It's jammed! Bloody thing!" He pulled with all his might and for a moment, it felt as though the blade shuddered under his fingertips. For one horrible moment he thought it was going to snap, but then the garnet mana stone in the pommel flashed once, whether with inner power or simply because it caught the sun he wasn't sure.

The dagger sprang free, knocking Robin backwards off his feet. He fell heavily, scooting along the tilting floor. The two cogs shook furiously, and then, remarkably, began to turn, slowly at first but then faster and faster until they were whizzing round at lose-your-finger speeds.

There was a lurch and a creak. The copper pipes which lined the bottom of the craft rattled and clanked against one another with alarming vigour, making Robin leap up off them quickly. They had gotten very hot in seconds.

"What's happening?" Karya yelled, grabbing his arm before he was unbalanced and pitched over the side. Dials everywhere on the console began to whir. There was a series of clicks, and with a loud bang, like a car backfiring, a huge belch of steam erupted from the bellows at the back of the boat, causing Woad to let go with a shriek. They began pumping of their own accord, emitting a ludicrous wheeze and creak, throwing out great puffs of steam. With a deafening whir, the uselessly fluttering wings flexed and straightened themselves, unfurling in resistance to the wind. They levelled out with a resounding and triumphant whoosh and began to flap, in slow, sweeping movements, cutting through the air like oars through water. The boat was no longer in freefall, Robin's stomach no longer felt as though it were trying to work its way up through his ribcage. They had begun, against all odds and reason, to slow down.

"It's working!" Robin whooped, hardly daring to believe it.

"We've … we've stopped falling?" Woad said, staring at the wings as they beat rhythmically at the air.

"It's true," Karya said in wonder, looking over the side. The distant landscape below stayed reassuringly distant. In fact, as she watched, it seemed to be receding. An uncharacteristic laugh escaped her, sounding just this side of hysterical. She turned it into a hasty clearing of her throat. "We're climbing. You did it, Scion!"

Robin was too breathless to speak. He half-sat, half-lay on the leather bench, gripping the side of the boat and waiting for his heart to stop hammering, simply enjoying the sensation of not plummeting towards his death.

"Bloody hell," he said eventually.

They were soaring away from the mountains now, leaving them far behind. Rivers and lakes passed below them, tiny and twinkling far below. Broken hills studded with menhirs stretched out to the horizon. Small forests and woods dotted the valleys below. The shadows of the clouds sailed over the landscape like enormous sweeping ghosts.

"I can't believe this thing is actually flying!" Robin said. "We're making good distance as well. It must be going pretty fast." He moved back to the front of the craft, his legs still a little shaky, and examined the dials spinning wildly on the console. "I haven't got a clue what any of this means, though," he admitted, after frowning at it for a moment or two.

Karya stood up and made her way over to him, also wobbling slightly. "Do we have any method of steering this thing?" she asked. "I've never been in a boat before, let alone a boat that flies."

Woad was poking the wheezing bellows at the back of the craft. "This thing moves around," he announced, pulling the bellows to the left. The angle of the long feathered wings suddenly changed and the boat swung alarmingly to the left, banking steeply and almost throwing Robin and Karya off their feet. Amidst their yells, Woad righted the craft with a sheepish grin. "Sorry," he said.

"Well, we know how to steer it then," Karya said. She looked out over the wide horizon ahead of them. "Now all we need to know is where to steer it to."

They were still rising sharply like a balloon, the clouds above them getting closer.

"Up, I imagine," Robin said. "This island's supposed to be an uprooted mountain after all. If you're going to hide a whole mountain in the air where no one's going to see it, it would have to be pretty high up."

"Hold on to your hamstrings then," Woad grinned, and twisted the bellows. They belched puffs of noisy steam downwards, the wings soared and rustled in the breeze, and with a giggling shout of glee from the faun, the Auroracraft soared like a rocket towards the clouds.

Chapter Twenty Two – Dawn Sailing

Soon they were sailing majestically high above the clouds, the craft clanking like an old boiler, belching copious amounts of hissing steam.

It was a strange, serene landscape full of slow-moving grace, the ground hidden by a fluffy white sea. The rolling waves of snowy cloud were broken here and there through which they occasionally glimpsed the world below. The terrain was becoming less mountainous and after a few hours of peaceful cruising, the cloud gaps revealed moorland and plains. When next they passed out of a cloud bank, a vast forest spread out far below them, stretching in every direction like a green spiky carpet. Robin wondered what the sprawling forest was called, but neither Karya nor Woad had any idea.

After enjoying the views for a while, and revelling in the novelty and luxury of travelling while sitting comfortably, they settled down and divided up the remaining food they carried.

The day wore on and for want of a better plan, they held a straight course, on the lookout for any vast flying lumps of mountainous rock.

Woad settled down in the stern of their craft and was soon asleep, leaving Robin and Karya alone in the clouds.

"So…" Robin said after a while. She had joined him at the helm and they had both watched the landscape far below slide by for some time.

She looked at him sidelong. "What?"

"What's your deal, then?" he asked. "Are you going to tell me who you are? Why you're on the run from Eris? Or are you planning on being stubborn and mysterious forever?"

"The less you know the better. You have your own problems right now, Scion. Enough to say, I have my own reasons for helping you. And plenty of reasons to hate Eris."

Robin rolled his eyes. "Whatever." Little else made sense in the Netherworlde. Why should she? "Just one thing. You said you ran away from home, right?"

Karya didn't answer. She was snuggled in her furs against the cold, hair whipping in the breeze.

"Mr Strife's been chasing you. I'm guessing to bring you … home."

"I've never had a home." Karya replied flatly. "Home is where the heart is. I wouldn't know anything about that."

Robin glanced at her, but her face was inscrutable. He didn't know what else to say.

"Get some sleep, Scion," she said, nudging him with her shoulder playfully. "I'll wake you up the next time we're about to die."

* * *

The light of sunrise hit Robin's face, waking him from deep sleep. He was curled on the floor, and was surprised to find himself beneath what felt like a large, shaggy brown blanket. He sat up, even more surprised to find that it was Karya's huge coat covering him. She was standing at the rear of the boat, steering with the bellows. Without the bulky coat, she looked tiny.

"What?" she said defensively, noting his expression, as he dug himself out from under the warm coat. "It got cold in the night. You were shivering in your sleep." She sniffed. "It was quite irritating to listen to."

Robin sat up stiffly, looking around at the rising dawn.

"Thanks … I think," he said. "Any sign of the Isle of Winds?"

Karya shook her head, walking over and taking the coat from him. She shrugged her way back into it, looking instantly less small and vulnerable, and more like a bad-tempered bear cub. She nodded ahead. "Nothing as far as I can see," she said. "Nothing island or mountain-shaped, anyway, although it's good that you're awake. There is something I think we should be concerned about."

Robin stared ahead. They had cleared the immense forest sometime in the night while he had slept. The ground below them now was grassy and calm. Up ahead, on the very edge of the horizon, the land stopped in a jagged tear. Beyond, there was nothing but a blueish haze.

"I suspect it may be the edge of the world," Karya said, in rather unconcerned tones. "I wonder if we'll fall off?"

Robin grinned at her.

"That's not the end of the world," he said. "Just the end of the land. You better go and wake up Woad. He'll want to see this. It's the ocean."

With some difficulty, Woad was roused, and they huddled at the front of the Auroracraft as it made its way towards the coastline. The sea became clearer as they approached. Rolling and swelling before them endlessly in great dark waves.

"That's an ocean?" Woad blearily rubbed sleep from his eyes. "It looks very big … and wet."

"Poetic, Woad," Karya said drolly, though she was staring at it too, her eyes wide. "I've never seen anything so big. The Silver Sea."

Seagulls wheeled around below them, caught in the updrafts.

"We appear to be heading over it," Karya said pointedly. "Are we certain that's wise? I mean, there's no land out there. What happens if we run out of fuel? We would fall right into the water."

Robin raised an eyebrow at her. "Karya," he said. "We're in a boat."

"Ah, yes," she conceded after a moment. "Boats. They are good at water, aren't they?"

"Traditionally, yeah," Robin assured her. "Better at water than say, crashing from a height onto dry land at least. Come to think of it, it seems a likely place to keep an island hidden, offshore where there's no one around."

The Auroracraft slipped effortlessly over the cliff edge, passing across dry land to open water without any trouble. The wings continued to beat; the bellows punched commas of steam into the air behind them. Robin was quietly relieved.

"We could get lost out here," Woad pointed out. "There aren't any landmarks. It's all just big and wet."

"We're already lost though, aren't we?" Robin pointed out. "Maybe we can keep the cliffs in sight. I wish this thing had a compass or something. I don't even know what direction we're travelling in."

Woad snorted with derision. "Forward, you numbskull. Anyone could tell you that."

"There's a Janus station down there," Karya said, ignoring the others and looking back at the cliffs. The others followed her gaze. There was indeed a small sandy cove at the base of the cliffs. They could just make out a circle of tall stones planted in the sand.

"What?" Robin said aghast. "Are you telling me we could have just flipped right here from Knowl Hill?"

"No, Scion," Karya said patiently. "It doesn't work that way. We didn't know this particular Janus station existed, did we?"

"You need to know where you're going when you use a Janus station," Woad explained. "Or you could end up anywhere."

"So you can't use Janus to get to a station you don't know is there?" Robin asked.

Karya nodded.

"I'll never get used to the Netherworlde," Robin said.

They sailed on for a few hours, until the sun was high in the sky. The water below was vast and seemingly endless. They began to feel as though they were lodged between two vast blue bowls, paler above and darker below. The occasional high white streamer of cloud reflected below as in a rippling mirror.

Karya and Robin were hanging over the side of the boat, idly watching the shadow of the Auroracraft below them, when suddenly Woad gasped.

"Wow, that's some cloud," the faun said. Ahead of them, filling the sky was a towering cloud of goliath proportions. It stretched massively high, up perhaps to the edge of space, so that it seemed to be flattened on top.

Robin stared. It was hard to take the whole thing in with one look. He had heard in school about towering clouds like these. They were usually storms, great bruise-black thunderheads filling the sky. But in contrast, this titan was as white as a marshmallow. It was beautiful. It looked as large as a…

"Mountain," he finished aloud, in awe, as they sailed towards the towering mass. "It's as big as a mountain."

He rushed to the front of the boat and grabbed Woad's arm with excitement. "This is it! The Isle of Winds!"

Karya shaded her eyes against the sun, peering at the momentous cloud. "I just see a cloud," she said flatly. "A big one, granted, but…"

"Camouflage," Robin said. "It's hiding the island." He peered around. There were only a few other clouds, thin and wispy. "See? See? They're moving in the wind, all the others. This one isn't. It's hiding the island. We've found it." He was grinning from ear to ear.

"We need to fly into the cloud," he said decisively, looking at Karya.

"Is that the cleverest plan, I wonder?" the girl replied, looking quizzical. "Flying blind into what is effectively a heck of a lot of fog, when we suspect, indeed hope, there is a very large mountain inside?"

"Boss has a point," Woad said, scratching his head. "That way lies splintered wood and bones."

"We'll be fine," Robin said dismissively.

Karya gave him a rueful look and opened her mouth to reply, but before she could speak, she was knocked to the floor.

Something large and dark hammered into the side of the boat with a tearing crash. Woad shouted something unintelligible, his voice high and filled with panic as he struggled to stay on his feet. He had seen more than the others.

A second dark shape appeared, as large as the first. It swooped from above, raking the deck with a splintering of wood and smashing off through one of the rainbow-feathered wings. It was gone as swiftly as it came, speeding beneath the craft and away out of sight, an alarming flurry of feathers trailing in its wake.

Robin, with Woad's help, scrambled to his feet, staring in shock and disbelief at the wreckage of the floor. A noise came through the fresh ocean air from behind them. A long low mournful howl which sent shivers of dread through Robin's spine. His nose was filled with the smell of musky fur.

"Skrikers!" he yelled, staring at Karya and Woad. "... How?!? How are they flying? Why did no one tell me skrikers can fly?!"

Some distance behind them, gaining fast, were three dark masses. They were only barely clinging to the idea of a dog-shape. From their huge, matted shoulders, each skriker sprouted a pair of long and ragged wings, great in span and as hazy and smoky as the rest of them. Worst of all, Robin saw, the central nightmare held a rider.

Even from some distance, there was no mistaking the long-limbed skeletal silhouette and the glint of luminous green hair.

"Strife!" Karya cried.

The Auroracraft tilted sharply. The ravaged wing had been badly damaged and the craft was listing wildly. Woad, with surprising self-control, had gripped the bellows and was attempting to keep them level.

"How is Strife here?" Robin yelled.

"The important question is, how did he track us so quickly?" Karya said, staring wide-eyed at their pursuers.

There was no time to answer. The struggling craft was getting closer to the immense cloud, and the skrikers banked, as though in formation, coming around for another pass.

"They're coming back!" Robin said. "They're trying to take us down."

He ran to the front, skipping over the broken floor, and all but throwing himself on the console.

"Can't we make this thing go any faster?" he shouted, staring at the incomprehensible dials and levers.

One of the dark beasts swooped over them again. Robin ducked instinctively, but it was gone, long claws raking the broken wing again and sending up a riot of feathers.

"They're tearing the boat apart!" Robin cried.

"The boat is made of wood," Karya yelled from the rear. "I could tear us through – to the human world, I mean."

"Bad idea, boss," Woad said. He was still straining with the boat's bellow-rudder. "We're very high up."

Karya ground her teeth. "Damn! You're right. No good turning up in the human world half a mile above the ground. We'd be just as dead as if we stay here!"

Another of the skrikers had drawn level. It growled and took a swipe at Woad, trying to snatch him away from the bellows. The faun ducked nimbly beyond the creature's reach, hissing at it like an angry cat and rolling to the other end of the boat to land at Robin's feet.

With a frustrated roar, the skriker swooped off, slashing at the side of the boat as it banked away, tearing a great splintering chunk out of the lovingly-made craft.

"Help me, Woad," Robin said, staring at the dials. "There must be something…"

Before Woad could reply, a voice like a cold knife cut through the air behind them.

"Thus ends the chase, young ones," Mr Strife said, eyes wide in their sunken sockets, his usually neat hair whipping about his head in the wind. "All this fuss. You merely delayed the inevitable. You should have come quietly, boy. No harm would have come to you."

"Yeah right!" Robin yelled back, struggling to keep his footing on the wobbling boat. "What was the big knife for, eh? A present?"

"Not for you," Mr Strife insisted, smiling like a shark, his dead eyes roving over the ship as his skriker flew alongside. "Just them," he indicated offhand, as though Karya and Woad were of no consequence to him.

"Tell me, Scion. How many more people will you allow to die for you? Your Grandmother, your poor demented aunt and her bumbling servant. Then your human friend, and the satyr." Strife's face contorting into distaste. "And now these two…" His eyes narrowed with malice. "How many more innocent bystanders will you sacrifice to save your own skin?"

"Henry and Phorbas are alive!" Robin cried, fear surging in him. "You're lying! You wouldn't dare!"

"Do not be so unwise as to dare me, boy," he sneered, raising his hands. "You will find there is very little I would not dare, very little indeed."

The skriker banked away, and as it did so, Mr Strife raised a strange dark tube, which for a mad second Robin thought was a gun. "A parting gift. I will educate you as to what happens to those who defy my Lady Eris. Allow me give to you the gift of grief."

He put the tube to his lips, and turning toward Karya, he blew.

With a yell and a wince of pain, the small girl's hand flew to her neck.

"Karya!" Robin yelled in alarm.

Mr Strife wheeled away. "Finish them," he barked to the creatures. "Spitak! Siaw! Take them down."

"Boss!" Woad wailed, ignoring the creatures wheeling around them. Karya had collapsed, her hand still clutched to her neck. Her eyes rolled backwards in her head until only the white showed. Robin stared in shock, rooted to the spot with horror as the scarecrow figure of Mr Strife wheeled away into the air. A large vicious-looking black barb was sticking from Karya's neck. Oily with some dark fluid.

A blowdart, Robin thought in panic. *Poison.*

Before he could convince his legs to move, a skriker barrelled into him from behind, clawing through his shirt and sending him flying to the ground. The creature didn't close in for the kill, however. It turned and leapt out over the side, reaching out with dark claws, and tore the one good wing clean off.

The Auroracraft lurched immediately into a swift nose dive. Robin forced himself onto his knees, ignoring the pain in his back, gripping the side of the boat for balance.

Cool thick fog suddenly enveloped them, damp and cold and instantly blinding. Their falling craft had pierced the vast cloud.

"Karya!" he shouted, barely able to make out the shadowy figure of Woad cradling the girl only a few feet away.

"Pinky! The boat! We're going to crash!"

Robin turned, fog and wind whipping furiously against his face. The massive clouds parted suddenly as they broke through the veil. What Robin saw took his breath away. Inside the cloud was a mountain. A monumental craggy shark's tooth of grey-green rock. It hung suspended before them – unreal, impossible and weightless.

The floating mountain was scattered with patches of scree and heather, clumps of trees growing from damp crevices and gullies dotting its surface. Moss and barnacles smothered its lower slopes, as though from time to time the immense rock dipped into the ocean.

"The Isle of Winds," Robin said in awe. He had a brief moment to glance toward the peak and glimpsed a city, hidden behind a tall golden wall. There was no time to see anything else. No time to think or move. They hit the mountainside with a shattering crunch of splintering wood. The noise and impact were deafening, and then, mercifully, there was only blackness.

Chapter Twenty Three –The Isle of Winds

Robin's eyes snapped open.

He was lying flat on his back in a patch of incredibly thick damp moss. Woad was leaning over him, shaking him by the shoulders.

"You're alive!" the faun yelped. "I thought you were gone for good there!"

"You can stop shaking me now," Robin said groggily.

He tried to sit up as Woad released him, and his head swam alarmingly. "Ouch," he said, with feeling. "I must have hit my head." His entire body ached. He looked around at the silent rocky landscape. After a moment he added. "We crashed?"

"Yep, right into the mountain," Woad affirmed. "The only solid part of the entire sky and we bash right into it."

Robin noticed that Woad's jaw looked angrily bruised. "There's this moss growing everywhere. It could have been worse, we could have hit the rocks," Woad continued. "A tree slowed us down, we took off most of its branches."

"Karya…" Robin shook his head to clear it. He struggled to his knees. His left arm didn't seem to do as he wanted.

The ruins of the Auroracraft lay all around them. The hull was mostly still intact, on its side and wingless.

Karya lay sheltered in this shell, laid out on the bed of moss. She looked terrible, her skin white against the green carpet of lichen.

"Is she…?" Robin couldn't finish the sentence. The word stuck in his throat.

"She's alive, but I can't wake her, Pinky," Woad said, stumbling over to the fallen girl. The moss was slippy and springy underfoot. "Strife's dart was full of poison. Blackwort, if I'm any judge. Really bad stuff." He wrinkled his nose in disgust.

"Can't you help her?" Robin said, limping slightly as he looked around the steep and rocky mountain slope. "I don't know anything about poison. Aren't you supposed to make the person be sick? Or is it that you're supposed to make sure they're not sick? I can't remember." He pushed his wet hair off his forehead, wincing as his back complained.

"Wouldn't do any good. Only cure is the antidote." Woad knelt beside Karya, his hand on her forehead. "Boss is cold," he announced.

"But she's alive, right?"

"Not for long," Woad said sadly, brushing the hair from Karya's temples. "Boss is strong, much stronger than she looks, but even she can't withstand blackwort."

Robin glanced around at the bare mountainside. They appeared to be close to the summit. Here and there scraggly trees had managed to find purchase and gripped the steep slopes for dear life. It would be easy enough to climb up.

"There's a town up there," he said, "I saw it when we broke through the cloud. There might be people, someone who can help."

"You lead the way, I'll bring boss," Woad said.

"We should be able to carry her between us," Robin said. "As long as..." Woad, however, had already picked Karya up and slung her effortlessly over his thin shoulders.

"Never mind," he finished, picking up his backpack with his good arm. "Come on then."

* * *

Eventually, they reached the large flattened summit. A smooth wall loomed over them, stretching away on either side. It was made of beaten bronze, shining in the misty sun like dulled fire.

Before them, directly at eye level, a single word was carved into the metal in bas-relief.

AEOLUS

"Well, at least we know we're at the right flying mystical mountain then," Woad said breathlessly. They passed through the shining archway and into the city.

The streets within, they soon discovered, were utterly deserted. They found themselves in an empty square with a raised stone platform at the centre. Large buildings rose up on all sides, carved from great blocks of grey blue stone.

There was not a soul in sight – no sign of a single living being. Only silence and soft rustling wind. Everywhere streets branched off, some winding away into shadows between the buildings, some of them little more than cobbled alleys. Across the square, the main thoroughfare led deeper into the silent town.

"Where is everybody?" Woad said, looking around. His voice sounded unnaturally loud.

As they made their way across the wide square, Robin saw that the buildings were mostly derelict, windows dark and doors long rotted away.

Many were crumbling, the roofs fallen in or choked with ivy. They were just empty shells. The Isle of Aeolus was dead. Abandoned and empty.

"This is a ghost town," he said. "There's no one here, Woad. Look at the state of the place."

"Whoever lifted this place into the sky didn't hang around for long," Woad said. "I can't smell any life at all, nothing apart from birds and worms." Woad scratched his nose. "Could be worse, I suppose. At least I can't smell revenants."

"What are revenants?" Robin asked, peering down the desolate, haunted streets. The mountaintop town must have been beautiful once. Now it was just unsettling in its emptiness.

"Bad things," Woad said, not very helpfully. "Revenants like abandoned places. Ruins and places gone bad. You don't want to meet any of them, trust me. Don't worry though," he said with a reassuring grin. "I'd know if there were any here. They stink."

He took a deep breath through his nose to prove the point and stopped, wide-eyed.

"What is it?" Robin asked.

"I just got a whiff of … I smelled…" Woad sniffed the air again and peered up the long wide thoroughfare. "Human!"

He sniffed again. "Definitely, Pinky!" he said. "I know this smell! This is Henryboy! Henryboy is nearby!"

"You're sure?!" Robin asked. He grabbed Woad by the shoulders, almost causing the excited faun to drop Karya's lolling body.

Woad nodded, grinning. "This way!" he said, setting off at an impressive trot considering his burden. Robin followed eagerly as the faun disappeared down a dark alleyway.

Robin had to admit, this was the perfect place to hide something you didn't want anyone to find.

They eventually emerged from a dusty side street into a large open space. An agora, according to Woad, with a derelict temple on the far side. It had a sloping triangular roof, densely carved with figures, all supported by a row of tall columns.

"In there," Woad said breathlessly, shrugging Karya's limp form on his shoulder.

Robin raced across the empty square.

"What is this place?" he asked Woad, as the blue boy caught up.

"A temple to the winds, I think," Woad hazarded. "An air shrine."

They scanned the statues and carvings, but time and wind itself had worn them down, eroding them into faceless ghosts.

"If Henry and Phorbas are here, we have to get them before Strife catches up with us," Robin said. He ran up the steps and stopped abruptly at the top, looking to Woad, confused. "I thought this was a way in," he said. "It's just a recess in the stone."

Robin was correct. There was no entrance, just a hollowed out cube of stone which looked like a doorway from afar. It had probably been used to house some great statue at one time.

"There has to be a way in! Who would build a temple without a door?"

Woad eyed the stone before them in the flickering light.

"Look here," he said. "This isn't real." He nodded towards one of the stone slabs which made up the wall in front of them. Someone had carved a tiny rudimentary eye into the stone, small enough to miss if you weren't looking for it.

"What is that?" he asked.

"This is a glamour," Woad said. "A pretty powerful one at that."

Robin frowned, unconvinced. He rapped the stone with his knuckles. "Feels pretty real to me."

"This symbol was always carved wherever a permanent glamour was set," Woad insisted. "They aren't tricks or sleights of hand like one of your human world card tricks. They're powerful magic. Once a person succumbs to a glamour, it may as well be real. There's no wall in front of us, but that doesn't make any real difference. We're trapped in the glamour, the only way to move forward would be to dispel it."

"I've seen glamours before," Robin remembered. "Aunt Irene cast one on Erlking Hall for me at Halloween. It was pretty convincing, but just a trick, right?"

Woad nodded. "If you like, but if you'd touched a broken window, you probably would have cut your finger."

Robin considered this. "That's mental," he said after a moment.

Woad smirked. "The only way for you to have broken that glamour would have been if you'd touched the old lady's mana stone," he explained. "Direct contact with the mana of the caster will always break the spell."

"There has to be some other way," Robin insisted. "Whoever cast this is long gone."

"Well, there are certain glamour-dispelling herbs and potions," Woad said thoughtfully. "Trusight is a concoction which some apothecaries stock, but it's hard to come by. Other than that, we would need glam roots. But they have to be steeped in moonlit water for thirteen nights before we could grind them up and…"

"Wait a minute," Robin said. "Glam roots? Are they from a plant?"

Woad looked at him curiously. "Well, a fruit actually, but I don't think this is the best time to give you a lesson on Netherworlde botany, Pinky."

Robin ignored the sarcasm, dropping to one knee and rooting through his backpack on the floor.

"What are you looking for?" Woad asked.

Robin pulled out a large jar from his bag. "This," he said triumphantly. "Hestia's supplies. It's the last of our food."

"Is that … a pot of jam?" the faun asked carefully, in tones which suggested Robin had lost it completely.

"Glam-glam jam!" Robin said.

Woad grinned, snatching the jar. "Pinky, you may just turn out to be a genius," he declared, unscrewing the top.

He sniffed the contents delicately. "Yes, there's definitely glam fruit in there somewhere … and orange peel and crushed strawberries, I think, but it might still work."

"So what do we do? Eat it?" Robin asked. Woad shook his head.

"Close your eyes," he said. "We smear it on our eyelids. It should clear the glamour from our vision."

Robin dutifully held still as Woad smeared the clear jam gloopily onto his eyelids. It was an odd sensation, swift and light, and strangely familiar.

"Right," the faun announced a moment later. "Open up."

Robin opened his eyes. He looked at the flat wall in the shadowy recess in front of him expectantly. To his amazement, it wasn't there anymore.

Robin stumbled inside, blinking rapidly. Once inside he wiped the jam from his eyes with his tattered sleeve.

"Ugh, this stuff is horrible," he said.

"It doesn't bother me," Woad said, trailing behind with wet eyes. "Stop complaining."

They found themselves in a ruin, gloomy after the brightness outside. There was rubble everywhere, toppled columns lying in wedges. A portion of the high roof had caved in at the far end. Slanted sunbeams poked through the shattered roof, falling on a raised dais thick with creeping vegetation and opportunistic flowers. Atop this, the centrepiece of the temple, there was a statue of a woman, carved from translucent alabaster. She had long flowing hair, frozen forever in stone. Her billowing robe flowed around her in artful curves so that her solid dress seemed always on the verge of motion. In one hand she held a carved spear, and the other a shield decorated with an emblem of a bird.

From her back sprouted four enormous wings, two spread wide and two seemingly caught in a downbeat.

"Who is that?" Robin asked in a hushed whisper.

"That's Aeolia, daughter of Aeolus," Woad said as they made their way carefully through the huge room.

He stopped suddenly. "Look!"

At the base of the statue lay a slumped figure on the floor, half-hidden by creeping vines. His clothes were ragged and dirty, his head bowed, unconscious. There was a manacle around his bare ankle fixed to the dais. The shackle looked like a very recent addition to the shrine.

Robin took in all these details in a single heartbeat.

"Henry!" Robin cried out, almost bursting with relief. The boy did not respond. He lay as limp and insensible as Karya, who Woad had laid carefully against one of the ivy tangled pillars.

"Master Robin?" A weak voice came from the darkness. "It cannot be … Who is that? Who's there?"

"Phorbas!" Robin cried out. "It's me, it's Robin. We've come to rescue you. Are you hurt? It's so dark in here."

"Only my pride is wounded, Master Robin," Phorbas' voice came again. He coughed dryly. "My body remains intact, I assure you." He sounded wheezy and tired. "I cannot believe you are really here. I never imagined we would meet again."

"Hang on. I'm coming over."

"We've no time to lose!" Phorbas said urgently, coughing again. "Listen to me, Master Robin. They have been looking for something here I think. Something hidden. They have turned the place inside out. Whatever it is, we have to find it before they do. You have to find it, Master Robin. Perhaps only you can."

Robin dimly made out the horned outline of Phorbas supporting himself with one hand on the column's rough surface.

"That doesn't matter," he replied dismissively. "We have to get out of here. Are you chained up like Henry?"

"An old goat on a short leash," the satyr laughed humourlessly. "But listen to me, Robin. This is the Shrine of Winds. A legendary place. There is something of great power here. Something Eris wants as a weapon. If we can find it first … you must use your gift."

"Robin…" Woad said behind him. In his relief at finding Phorbas and Henry, Robin had almost forgotten his companions.

"We have a girl here," he said to Phorbas, cutting Woad off. "Strife has poisoned her. Can you help?"

"Yes of course," Phorbas said. "But first we must find…"

"No, first we have to help her," Robin interrupted. "I don't care about the other stuff. I'm going to find something to get you and Henry out of those chains and then we have to see to Karya right away."

"Robin…" Woad began hesitantly. "Something's not…"

Phorbas cut him off, stepping forward out of the shadows. "I will not ask again!" he said sharply. "Unlock the magic, Robin! I am your tutor and you will do as I say. There are great things at stake here. The girl is not important!"

Robin stared, shocked. Phorbas' face, shadowy across the large room, was hard and grim. He looked so cold-hearted, utterly unlike his normal jovial self.

"Robin," Woad insisted, tugging the boy's arm to get his attention. "That's not…"

Before the faun could finish his sentence, something large and dark barrelled into him, knocking him to the ground and sending Robin stumbling away.

A skriker had bounded into the chamber and floored Woad, knocking him unconscious. Its great hulking shape stood over the fallen boy threateningly.

Robin wheeled around in shock. Four other skrikers slunk into the temple behind him. Wicked yellow eyes glowed at Robin in the darkness as they circled by the doorway, blocking any escape.

Beyond them, Robin saw the unmistakable form of Mr Strife, leaning nonchalantly against the wall with his long legs crossed at the ankles and his arms folded, as though he had all the time in the world. He had followed them after all.

"Phorbas! Strife is here! We have to…"

His words faded away as he looked back to his tutor.

The satyr has stepped forward into the falling sunbeams, standing between him and Henry. He no longer looked injured. His face was a strange mixture of cruelty and mockery.

"Yes, yes, he certainly is here, isn't he, Master Robin? How terrible for all concerned. And look…" he gestured around the room, "… all of your little friends are either dead or dying. It would appear that you are very much on your own."

The satyr turned and crossed to the slumped form of Henry, roughly grabbing a fistful of his hair and pulling his head up. "Now then," he said to Robin. "Charm and persuasion seem not to have worked, and frankly, I am weary of this entire charade. For the last time of asking, Young Master Robin, use … your … gift."

Robin stared at his tutor. "Why are you …? You never would …? … You're not Phorbas! You're using some kind of glamour. Woad could see through it, couldn't he? He didn't wipe the jam off his eyes. That's what he was trying to tell me! You're not Phorbas. Phorbas wouldn't help Strife."

"You have no idea what Phorbas would or would not do, boy. You have never met him," Mr Strife said behind him. "Enough of these illusions," he said to the satyr. "They have served their purpose. I find your games tiresome at best."

As Robin watched, the image of his trusted tutor dissolved entirely before his eyes, drifting away into nothingness like multi-coloured smoke. It left behind a tall, impossibly thin man, wearing an identical dusty old suit to that of Mr Strife. His white face was grinning and atop his bright green eyes sat a wild shock of orange hair.

Robin had met him once before.

"Moros!" he said, as the glamour faded utterly.

"*Mr* Moros, if you please, young Master Robin," the pale man replied, his eyes twinkling brightly. "One must respect formalities, even in the direst of situations. It is indeed the mark of a true gentleman."

"What did you mean when you said I've never met Phorbas?" he said, taking hold of Phorbas' knife. Strife sighed behind him in a bored way. Robin turned, trying to keep the two brothers in sight.

Mr Moros waved a finger admonishingly. "Now, now, Scion," he said. "Your tutor never made it to your first meeting, it's that simple. Our aim has always been to get you to the Netherworlde, to bring you here." He sighed theatrically. "We had hoped to intercept you as soon as the wards broke at your grandmother's house, but things were … complicated for a time."

"Your grandmother was a wonderful dancer," Mr Strife said darkly. "I have no taste for dancing myself, but one does what one must in the line of duty." There was an unspoken laugh beneath his words.

Robin turned to him, waving the knife in front of him. "What do you mean?" he said, staring at the cool, shark-like expression on the old man's face, but it was Moros who spoke.

"And then, of course, that interfering old traitor got involved!" he continued. "Whisking you off to the safety of Erlking, where she could keep you out of everyone's reach. That posed a problem, let me tell you." He steepled his fingers under his chin. "But we needed you here, you see. There were prophecies. The seers had discovered your existence. They spoke of *such* things. Of great secrets hidden in the Netherworlde, and of one who was born to find them."

"I doubt they understood that this 'great one' would be a snivelling child," Mr Strife sneered offhand.

"Indeed," Mr Moros confirmed brightly. Robin turned back to him, his heart beating so loud he wondered that they couldn't hear it. Perhaps they could.

"Imagine my surprise at the train station," Moros continued. "There I was, lurking in wait for the foolish goat man, when I stumbled upon the Scion himself, witless *and* clueless!" He sighed. "So close…"

"You've never been missing…" Robin said.

"Quite," Moros continued. "I ambushed Phorbas and took his place. However, casting a glamour to make a person look like another is very, very advanced. The person you are impersonating needs to be incapacitated utterly, which is a difficult thing to do to a panthea."

"It involves the separation of body and spirit," Mr Strife explained with sharp satisfaction. "And the disposal of both."

"What did you do to Phorbas?" Robin said through gritted teeth.

"Disposed of him. Aren't you listening?" Moros said. "His soul, however? Well, that I needed to keep close by, to keep the glamour working, you see?"

Robin stared in disbelief down at the dagger he carried.

"You put Phorbas' soul … in his knife?"

Moros laughed.

"Your poor tutor's spirit was rather angry with me, I think." He tittered briefly. "He can be quite lively, trapped in there, can he not?"

The Oracle had known. The knife had saved their lives twice along the way. Phorbas … the real Phorbas … all along helping them find their way.

The knife twisted now in his grip, like a struggling fish. "He wants to kill you," Robin said grimly to Moros.

Moros smirked. "Lucky I got there first then."

"Enough," Strife snapped, humourless as ever. Moros rolled his eyes at his dour brother. "You will do what we have brought you here to do, boy," he continued. "Or your little friends will all die for you, and have died for nothing."

Chapter Twenty Four – Unleashed

Robin looked about the chamber desperately. "I don't know what you expect me to do! I don't know anything. I'm rubbish at magic, I can barely throw a Galestrike."

"But the seers have spoken," Mr Strife said. He took another step towards Robin. The skrikers wove restlessly in and out of the shadows between the ancient pillars. "You are the key, Scion. Lady Eris believes it. It is your purpose."

"Do you remember what I told you – about the Arcania?" Moros said.

"I know what you told me. That the fae destroyed it so that Eris couldn't get her hands on it," Robin said.

"The pieces were not destroyed," Moros said. "They were scattered, hidden away."

"The Arcania can be made whole once more, Scion," Mr Strife said, his face filled with uncharacteristic zeal. "The ultimate power. Waiting to be reunited."

Robin looked from one pale, eager face to the other.

"You think there's something here? A shard of the Arcania? That's what this has all been about?" he demanded.

"We do not think," Strife said. "We know."

"We even know where it is hidden," Moros said, gesturing grandly at the tall winged statue behind him.

"Then what do you need me for?" Robin said. "Why haven't you just smashed the statue to pieces and taken your prize yourself?"

Moros tittered a little. Strife's face darkened with anger. "No force, no strength, no dark magic can extract the shard. Only the Scion can call to it."

Moros clapped his hands. "Sheath your little knife, Master Robin, and come forward."

Reluctantly, Robin forced Phorbas' knife back into his belt, where it lay still. His legs felt heavy as he crossed to the statue, glancing around him at his fallen friends as he walked to the base of the plinth. Moros gripped the fallen Henry possessively by the shoulder as Robin passed him.

"No tricks now, Scion," he said. "I'm not sure young Henry here would survive any surprises."

Robin climbed the dais and stood before the statue. He wondered distantly what he was supposed to do. He didn't feel any tingle or vibration of nearby power, no sudden inspiration or revelation. The statue was silent and enigmatic.

He brushed his hand over her shield, searching for inspiration. The pale alabaster was light and warm to the touch.

His mind raced. What was he supposed to do? He didn't understand anything about his so-called powers. Aunt Irene may have said that he had more mana than anyone else she had ever met, but that meant nothing if he couldn't use it.

Robin cursed himself inwardly. He had been relying so much on Karya and Woad, dragged along for the ride into the Netherworlde like a clueless tourist. But they couldn't help him now.

Robin was utterly alone, here with his enemies. He had never felt more useless.

His eves roved over the statue. Her blind white eyes offered no clue or comfort. His hand went to his mana stone, hoping for some kind of inspiration, but it lay inert against his chest, nothing more than a pretty lump of stone.

"Is there a problem?" Mr Moros asked politely from behind him.

Robin scowled. It was just possible he hated Moros more than he hated Strife.

"Perhaps the Scion is stalling," Strife suggested wanly. "Perhaps the Scion needs reminding that the poison currently coursing its way through his little companion's body is getting stronger by the moment, and that neither she nor he have the luxury of time."

"I'm thinking!" Robin snapped.

"It would be a terrible waste, Master Robin," Moros said lightly, "were it to be discovered that you were of no further use. Our Lady Eris deplores useless things."

Robin ignored them and looked back to the statue, at the carved tousled locks of hair, the pale feathered wings reaching out behind, the tall spear and stone shield with its carving of a stylised bird and the swirling decorations. The swirls looked oddly familiar to Robin. He traced the lines with his fingers. His lips moved silently as his fingers followed the shape. "This is…" he began haltingly, unsure of himself. "I think … this is script."

"Nonsense?" Strife snapped. "We have examined every inch of that statue. There is no script."

"No. There's writing around the shield," Robin said, wondering how he knew that. It certainly wasn't in English. "All around the Halcyon bird."

Come to think of it, how did he know what type of bird it was?

"What does it say?" Strife asked impatiently. Robin opened his mouth to reply that he didn't have a clue, but found oddly that that he did. He could read it just fine. He traced around the edge of the shield with a shaking finger, deeply confused and a little unsettled.

"'The gift which does not exist until given'," he said. "'The giver has no use for it but wishes to give; the receiver cannot keep it but yearns to receive'."

"A riddle," Moros said merrily. "There is a riddle upon the Shrine of Winds, my brother. Why is it that we did not find this?"

"Because … clearly…" Strife said, speaking each word with great weight, "… we are not the Scion."

"What is the answer?" said Moros to Robin eagerly.

"I don't bloody well know, do I?" Robin replied angrily. "I can barely understand it. I haven't got a clue!"

Moros' face fell immediately, and he grabbed Henry by the neck, quick as a snake. He shook the boy roughly like a limp rag doll. "Well, perhaps, Master Robin, you should bend your mind toward it wholeheartedly. We are not famed for our patience, after all."

"Kill the human boy," Strife said in a business-like tone. He looked quite bored. He had taken out an old pocket watch and was peering at it with heavy lidded eyes. "We don't need all three of them after all. It may motivate him."

"No!" Robin said desperately as Moros grinned, revealing a mouth full of very white teeth. "I'll solve it, don't kill anybody! Just … just give me a minute." He read the riddle aloud again.

Silence descended in the shrine. His mind was a total blank. Gran had loved puzzles. She would have solved this in a minute. He could still remember her poring over her puzzle books when he had been young enough to sit on her knee, trying to help with the crosswords and word searches. She had been so good at cryptic clues. Whenever Robin had managed to get something right, she had always been so delighted, and had cackled and given him a smack of a kiss on the forehead.

Robin's finger paused tracing the lines.

"I think … I know the answer," he said quietly.

Robin looked up at the statue's white face. Its unseeing eyes, the line of its delicate nose. Its carefully carved and slightly parted lips.

"A kiss," Robin said.

The statue is hollow, the small voice in his head said. The Statue of Winds.

"Air unlocks the Shrine of Air," he said wonderingly, as realisation dawned.

"What?" Strife snapped, but Robin ignored him.

"Breath," he said in response to Strife. He placed his lips against those of the alabaster statue, feeling the same calm sensation as when he had played the flute back at Erlking. The same feeling of knowing exactly what he was doing.

He took a deep breath and, very softly, breathed into the hollow statue, putting all of his mana behind the breath.

Pure energy pulsed from the statue like a shockwave, the force of it hitting Robin like a fist in the chest, throwing him backwards through the air. He soared over Strife and Moros, landing painfully on his back amongst the rubble.

Air was roaring deafeningly through the temple, shaking aeons of dust from the high ceiling. Robin's ears popped. The grim brothers were staring at the statue. Its four wings were aligning with a great crunching of stone. The stone hair writhed and the carved folds on the dress rippled. Robin saw the newly animated woman lower her spear and shield, her head inclined, taking in each member of the gathered assembly. He felt those blank eyes pierce him from across the large room. His hair stood on end. And then, the statue raised its white glowing arms above its head and with a final deafening thrash of its great stone wings, it exploded blindingly, disintegrating into a cloud of dust.

Robin, Moros and Strife blinked in the aftermath of the roaring explosion. Robin rubbed his eyes with the heels of his hands.

Where the statue had stood only moments ago, there was now a shape, no bigger than an egg, hanging impossibly in mid-air. It looked like a jewel, spinning slowly in place, throwing out light and painting the shadows and walls with rippling rainbow colours. It kept changing shape before his eyes, elongating, then turning, revealing more planes and facets, as though it were continually folding in on itself without getting smaller – a tiny stable supernova. After the roar of the wind, it was utterly silent, and power emanated from the object in humbling waves, which made Robin's teeth ache. Robin forgot about Mr Moros and Mr Strife. He even forgot about Henry and Karya and Woad. The ever-moving object demanded his full attention.

"The Shard of Air," Moros breathed, his voice hushed and reverent.

Strife, ignoring Moros, took a step forward, his eyes wide and rapt. He pushed his brother roughly aside and approached the dais, reaching out before him.

"I claim this prize," he whispered. "And with its power shall bring down the furies upon the heads of all enemies."

It's over, Robin thought. He couldn't think of anything to do. He tasted blood on his lip absently. His whole body ached. He hadn't realised how much it had hurt being thrown the full length of the chamber. Now he felt weary, and Strife and Moros had won.

Not what I expect from a grandson of mine, Gran's voice spoke in his mind. *You're not dead yet, so don't lie down.*

Robin steeled himself. With shaking fingers, in the flickering shifting light, he reached for Phorbas' dagger. He wasn't going to make it easy for the brothers. He would defend his friends to his last breath.

Strife climbed the dais, his figure burned into nothing but a skeletal silhouette. The object flashed, slowing to a halt. For a moment, it hung glittering in mid-air, inches from Strife's outstretched fingers. It had solidified into a slim, multi-faceted icicle.

With a whoosh, it suddenly flew through the air like a thrown spear, a visible Galestrike, away from Strife, swift as an arrow shot from an invisible bow.

The shard flew over Moros' upturned face, piercing the shadows and dust, straight towards Robin.

He had no time to dodge. No time to react.

It hit him in the chest like a knife, throwing him off his feet again.

Robin hit the floor. It didn't hurt this time. Nothing hurt anymore. All pain was gone.

"No!" Strife screamed, his high voice like rasping knives.

Robin sensed the shard of the Arcania inside him. He felt its raw, uncontrollable power flood through him, intoxicating, overpowering. Robin felt something deep within his mind awaken, a long-forgotten door thrown open. An unfamiliar smile passed over his face.

"What's happening?" wailed Moros. "The shard? What has he done? The horrible boy!"

"Kill him!" Strife seethed through clenched teeth. "Now, before…"

"**Enough,**" Robin said.

The Tower of Air … The wind was his, the air. He knew how to control it. All of it.

The brothers stared in horror as he rose smoothly from the ground, the air supporting him effortlessly. It's so simple, Robin thought distantly.

He lifted himself into a standing position, his feet hovering above the flagstones.

"What has happened to the boy?" Moros gibbered. "Why does he look like that?"

Robin's pale blue eyes were now brightest green, sharp, clear and full of fury. His blonde hair had turned pure white, whipping upwards from his head in the self-contained gale he had created. Barely visible on either side of his head were ghostly horns, only their outlines shimmering, as though someone had sketched them in the air with glowing chalk.

When he spoke, his voice was not his own. His strange inner voice spoke for him. The part of him which knew what a halcyon bird looked like, which knew how to play a flute; the part which could read ancient languages. It was no longer a small voice in the back of his consciousness.

"**I am the Scion.**"

"I will kill you!" Strife cried, pulling out his knife, fuelled by rage at being cheated of his prize.

"**No,**" Robin raised an arm. "**You will not.**"

He threw a Galestrike across the room. It left his hand with a loud crack, the air moving fast enough to tear the sound around him.

The force hit Strife like a juggernaut, throwing him backwards. He toppled head over heels, over and over, the dark knife thrown far from his grasp. He came to a halt in a spinning crunch, smashing into the dais.

Robin lifted himself higher into the air, the wind roaring about him.

Mr Strife struggled to his feet, his face filled with shock and fury, his lip bloodied.

"Filthy fae scum!" he screamed. "Human world half-breed! How dare you raise your hand to me?!"

"**Silence,**" Robin said firmly.

He blinked at Mr Strife. With Featherbreath, he effortlessly lifted the ghoulish man into the air, none too gently. Strife howled and struggled, his long limbs thrashing out uselessly. He rose higher, where Robin, his mana stone blazing on his chest like flickering lightning, held him fast.

"**I could end this now,**" Robin said. "**You have harmed my family and friends. You invaded my home. You have kidnapped, lied and deceived. You have hounded, pursued and poisoned. With no more than a single thought, I could pull the air from your lungs and watch you drown on nothing.**"

Strife stared at Robin, his usually slicked and oiled appearance in disarray, his eyes bulging from his face in fear and loathing.

"**But I will not,**" Robin said. "**Because I am not you, Mr Strife.**"

Robin lowered his horned head, seeking out the other grim brother.

Moros, cowering in the rubble below like a frozen rat, stared up at him fearfully. There was no glee or enjoyment in his wicked face now.

"**You,**" Robin demanded. "**Give me the gorgon's eyes.**"

Moros reached in to his jacket, staring in disbelief at Robin, the fury of the fae incarnate. He took out the vial containing the gorgon's eyes and held up it in his shaking hand. His face darkened with resentment.

"Filthy fae-child," he spat, his high voice quivering. "You presume to give orders to Moros? You think I am afraid of your horns? I carved my belt buckle from the horn of one of your people. You are nothing! I will never give you what you ask!"

He threw the vial to the floor, his face full of defiant spite. Robin merely reached out a hand and caught it with a Featherbreath. The vial flew upward through the air where it landed in his hand effortlessly.

"**Go back to your mistress,**" Robin said. "**Tell her how you have failed here. That, I imagine, will be a fitting punishment.**"

Robin breathed deeply, drawing on the power of the Arcania. He sent out his mana in a vast wave of air, lifting rocks and rubble from all over the temple. They hung in the air around him, deadly missiles, dozens of them suspended throughout the chamber, a silent hovering threat.

Mr Moros crawled over to Mr Strife. Both of them looked around the chamber, at the hail of suspended fury above. They stared up at the centre of the silent maelstrom, at the boy regarding them. The world's last changeling looked down like the spirit of judgement. The Scion of the Arcania.

"When next we meet, Robin Fellows," Strife said shakily, his brother trying desperately to pull him toward the doorway, "you will not find me so unprepared. I promise you that!"

Robin replied by letting one of the large masonry blocks fall from mid-air. It crashed into the floor at their feet, shattering into pieces and smashing the flagstones.

"**You speak empty threats to the Arcania itself. I am the Puck. The next stone will not miss.**"

Moros and Strife picked themselves up of the floor and fled the chamber without another word. Their footfalls echoed on the rocks as they made good their escape to the city outside.

When he was sure they were truly gone, Robin closed his eyes and slowly lowered himself and all of the rocks gently back to the floor.

"Robin?"

His eyes snapped open. Amidst the rubble, Henry was sitting up. The manacle around his ankle was still attached, but it had been freed from its moorings when Strife hit the dais.

"Bloody hell!" he said after a moment, his voice dry and papery. "What in the world happened to you?"

Robin stared. In the corner of his mind, his heart leapt. Henry was okay. He wasn't in a coma or any of the other things he had feared when he had first seen him. The Puck, the part which held the reins at the moment, merely regarded the human boy distantly with detached interest.

"**Are you injured?**" he asked.

Henry shook his head, looking dazed. "Feel as though I've gone six rounds with a heavyweight, but I reckon I'll live.

"Where are we, Rob? I feel like I've been asleep forever. There was a fight at the house, then Phorbas grabbed me. It was all so confused..."

He glanced back up at his friend. "Robin, hate to be rude pointing this out and all, but you've got bloody great big horns!"

"**We are in the Netherworlde,**" Robin told him. He half-walked, half-floated over to Woad, who was groaning on the floor as he slowly regained consciousness. Boulders moved obediently out of his way as he went, clearing his path. "**I will explain everything later. There are things we need to do first.**"

Woad sat up as Robin approached. "What happened, Pinky?" he asked in a groggy, wheezy voice. He looked up at Robin and blinked. "Wow, something big, I'd say! Are you possessed? Where's the skrikers gone?"

Robin shook his head. "**I am myself, Woad. Only … more so. The skrikers, and the servants of Eris, are gone. Are you injured?**"

Woad looked embarrassed. "Nah. No one gets knocked out better than me. Where are the bad guys again?"

"**They left,**" Robin said simply as Woad got up. Robin turned away and walked to Karya.

Woad watched him go, then turned to Henry, who was stumbling through the chamber, dazed and limping.

"Henryboy!" the faun cried jubilantly. "You haven't even been a little bit killed!"

"Woad. Sight for sore eyes you are, you insane blue nutter. Where's Phorbas?" Henry asked. "And why is Robin like that? What the bloody hell is going on here anyway?"

"That's a lot of questions," Woad said, looking around at the devastation of the air shrine. "Long story, explain later. We have to help boss though."

"Boss?" Henry asked clearly confused. They joined Robin, who had knelt on the floor beside Karya's body. Henry looked down. "Who's the girl?" he asked.

"What did I just say about questions?" Woad said impatiently. "Pinky, is she…"

"**She is not dead, not yet,**" Robin replied.

He placed the palm of his hand over Karya's white lips. Her skin was waxy pale and clammy. Robin closed his eyes. The Whitewind cantrip rushed out of his palm. He felt for the poison with his mind, wrapped his mana around it, and pulled his hand away.

Henry and Woad watched as a plume of black and purple smoke erupted from Karya's mouth, thick and viscous. It dissipated instantly and harmlessly in a small gust conjured up by Robin.

The three boys, human, fae and panthea, crowded round the girl, peering down. Her eyelids fluttered, and then with a great hacking cough she opened her eyes. Woad, with overwhelming relief, helped her into a sitting position.

"What…?" She looked around, blinking rapidly, squinting in the gloom. "Where is this? Ugh … I feel like a skriker chewed me up and spat me out."

"Boss, you're okay!" Woad grinned. "I knew you would be. I carried you, you know. You're really heavy for a girl."

"This is the human boy?" Karya asked Woad blearily, peering at Henry. "Oh good … and the satyr?"

Woad shook his head. "He was evil," he explained.

"**The satyr was not evil; he was not himself. It was Moros all along,**" Robin said. "**Phorbas, the real one, is trapped within his knife. All will be explained, but later.**"

Karya looked at him impatiently. "I want a full report here. What do you mean? What's been…" She trailed off, finally looking at Robin properly.

"Scion…" she whispered. "Just as in my vision…"

"**We must hurry,**" Robin said to the three of them. For the first time since being hit with the shard, he felt a flicker of uncertainty. "**I don't fully understand what has happened, but I don't think this…**" He held up his pale hands, staring at them as though he hadn't seen them before. Eddies of wind flickered between his fingers. "**… I don't think this will last.**"

"Our ship crashed, remember," Woad said. "It won't fly without wings, Pinky."

Robin peered up from his hands, his emerald eyes glittering at Woad.

"**Oh, it will fly for me.**"

* * *

Henry remembered nothing of his journey to the Isle of Winds. So his first real experience of the Netherworlde, the place he and Robin had schemed all winter to get to, did not ultimately disappoint.

Emerging from the temple and making their way through the abandoned city to find themselves on a flying mountain wreathed in an eternal golden cloud was one thing. Watching his best friend stalk down the mountainside looking like a young pagan god, and seeing him reassembling the shattered pieces of the blasted Auroracraft in a controlled whirlwind of wood and feathers was quite another.

Neither Woad nor the strange girl seemed to have the slightest compunction about climbing aboard the broken boat. Robin stood silently at the prow, looking like the most disturbing figurehead Henry had ever seen. He climbed aboard also, albeit gingerly. Robin lifted the splintered wingless craft into the sky and they soared away from the mountain. Henry leaned over the broken side of the boat, peering at the impossible sight of the floating island.

"So, this mountain, it just kind of floats above the ocean, then? Just like that?" he asked weakly as they passed into the vast golden cloud, the magnificent vision of the Isle of Winds disappearing into the mist.

"Yup, that's right," said Woad. He was sitting at Karya's feet in the bottom of the boat, happily grinning while she absently scratched behind his ears. Karya herself had barely spoken since they had left the air shrine. She was still weak and pale, and she watched Robin's back thoughtfully as he steered their craft through the air.

"That must be a pretty difficult piece of magic to pull off," Henry said, as they passed out of the far side of the cloud and into the clear ocean air beyond. "To float a whole mountain like that."

"**Not really,**" Robin's strange wind-borne voice came back. "**No more difficult than floating a squirrel.**"

His friend may have undergone a strange and powerful transformation, but Henry knew him well enough to know that Robin was smirking.

* * *

None of them spoke much as they made their way under the night sky. Robin barely acknowledged his friends around him. He needed all his concentration to keep them flying, and the Puck, this odd other self, wasn't very interested in them. Robin still felt like a passenger in his own body. He was just along for the ride, not driving … but maybe helping with the directions and choosing the radio stations. He smiled to himself.

The others slept as the ocean flew swiftly by below.

* * *

As dawn broke, the cliffs came into sight. Robin was feeling weaker, burning through his resources and with every passing moment he felt closer to collapse.

"Take us in down there, Robin," Karya said, appearing at his shoulder and pointing down to a sandy inlet of beach with a rough circle of stones standing half hidden in the mist. "It's the Janus station we saw, remember? If you can get us there, I can get us all back to Erlking."

Robin nodded, moulding the air around them and swooping the suspended Auroracraft gracefully out of the sky.

"Are you okay?" Karya asked. "You're looking a little less … well … spooky than you did before."

"**I'll be fine,**" he replied. "**Just let me get us there.**"

The Auroracraft made a reasonably graceful landing in the soft white sand. It ground to a halt not far from the circle of weathered stones marking the Janus station.

Robin gratefully dispelled the Featherbreath once they had clambered out of the boat. The Auroracraft, released from the cantrip, collapsed into a pile of clattering and useless lumber. The greatest creation of the fae's most celebrated inventor, destined to become nothing more than anonymous driftwood.

Robin's eyes blurred, and a wave of dizziness stole over him. Karya grabbed his arm, steadying him as best she could.

"What's wrong with Superboy?" Henry asked, his face worried. "Rob, your horns, they're kind of fading away."

"The power is leaving him," Karya explained, as Henry shouldered Robin's weight from the other side. Together they carried him with difficulty through the loose sand toward the stones in the cliff's shadow.

Woad had scampered on ahead and was running from rock to rock, slapping the stones and bringing the Janus station into operation.

"Not bad really," Karya said, grunting under Robin's weight. His head was lolling on her shoulder, utterly spent, almost unconscious. "For a hornless wonder, at least."

Robin heard their voices, far off and muffled. The sunlight around him seemed too bright, bouncing up off the sand. *I'm going to pass out*, he thought to himself. *So very, very tired.* The godlike feeling was gone. His vision blurred and he just had time to think about how un-heroic it would be if he threw up all over himself.

"There's a light coming out of his chest," he heard Henry say, worry in his voice. "I'm pretty sure that's not normal. What's happening to him?"

If Karya replied, Robin didn't hear her.

Chapter Twenty Five – The Beginnings

The room was huge and pitch black. Robin couldn't see a thing around him.

"You did well, Robin," a voice came softly from somewhere in the darkness.

"Who are you?" he asked. "Where am I?"

"Hidden," came the reply. "For now at least. You need to rest, Robin. You have taken on a great deal of late."

"I feel fine," Robin replied, blinking uselessly in the utter blackness. It was true.

"Of course you do," said a second voice. "But then you are dreaming after all."

"I like it here," Robin decided. "It's peaceful. Can I stay with you?"

"Of course not," said the first voice, not unkindly. "You're not really here anyway. You have places to go and much to do."

"Sorry about that," the second voice added, not sounding very sorry at all. "There is so much to do."

"And less time than once we had," the first voice agreed.

A third voice suddenly came out of the darkness.

"Snakes and ashes, Robin! Are you going to sleep the day away? You'll be late for school, you know."

"Gran?" Robin turned, confused in the darkness, or at least he thought he did. It was hard to tell. "Now I know I'm dreaming."

"Not quite, my boy. You are here because what you have done has left ripples throughout the Netherworlde. *They* are dreaming of *you*."

"They?"

"Time to wake up," Gran's voice cackled. "Stop bothering the good folk. Let them rest … for now."

* * *

Robin opened his eyes slowly. He felt groggy and stiff, as though he had been in a deep sleep for a long time – which as he would later discover, he had. He was lying on his back staring up at a peaked white plaster ceiling, criss-crossed with dark wooden rafters. It was very quiet.

The ceiling above looked oddly familiar, but he had been through so many strange experiences recently that it took him a moment to realise that he was actually lying in a soft bed, and that he was staring up at his own bedroom ceiling. He was in his tower at Erlking Hall.

Robin sat up in bed far too suddenly, causing his vision to swim. He blinked rapidly, looking around. It was true. He was in his own bed. The room looked as it always did, if considerably tidier than usual. The diamond paned window was slightly open, letting in a cool breeze and the bright crisp sunlight. The only noise in the room was a soft and peaceful snoring next to him. Henry was sitting in a chair next to his bed, a book slumped on his chest. He was fast asleep, sprawled in an ungainly manner. The boy looked better now; healthy, peaceful and back to normal.

Careful not to wake his sleeping friend, Robin slipped out of bed, and crossed on watery legs to his wardrobe, opening the squeaking door. He looked at himself critically in the dark-spotted mirror inside.

He also looked perfectly normal. His hair was blonde, eyes blue. There were no horns sprouting from his head, ghostly or otherwise. He felt carefully in his hair with his fingertips to be sure.

He was his own, usual, unremarkable self again. No sign of Puck.

Also, no sign of pain either. His left arm felt fine and there wasn't the slightest twinge from his back. Turning around, he hiked his shirt up and looked back over his own shoulder, staring at the marks left by the skriker. There were four long thin white lines, pale silvery scars stretching from his right hip to his left shoulder. It could have been a lot worse, he reasoned. It should have been. Perhaps fae heal better than humans?

Noticing for the first time that he wasn't wearing his mana stone, he glanced about the room. The seraphinite stone lay in a small silver dish atop his chest of drawers. Robin shrugged his t-shirt back on and crossed the room. As soon as he slipped his mana stone on, he felt better. More himself.

The small voice in his head, the force that had taken him over back at the Isle of Winds, seemed also to be gone. No, he corrected himself. Not gone. But it had receded to where it had always been.

"You're awake!" Henry suddenly yelled, leaping up from the chair, making Robin jump with surprise.

"I didn't think you were ever going to wake up!" Henry grinned. "We all thought you were done for back when you passed out on the beach. To tell the truth Rob, you looked bloody awful!"

"Thanks a bunch," Robin said.

"No, really," Henry insisted, staring earnestly. "*Really* awful."

"Yeah, I got that part," Robin said wryly. "How did we get back here? Where is everyone? And what day is it anyway?"

The door to the bedroom opened and Woad and Karya burst in the room.

"Pinky!" Woad cried. "Told you I heard him talking," he said to Karya. "No one has sharper ears than this faun."

"Welcome back, Scion," Karya said. "Are you…" she began hesitantly. "Is everything…?"

"I'm just me, if that's what you're asking," Robin said.

Karya gave one of her odd half smiles. "Happy New Year by the way," she said. "Henry and Woad have been taking shifts sitting with you since we got back."

"You haven't?" Robin teased.

Karya rolled her eyes. "Don't be impractical," she said. "I didn't see how it would help. You'd either heal and wake up or you wouldn't. My being here would hardly make a difference." She flicked a thumb at Woad and Henry. "These two are sentimental-old-lady-types, though."

"You're as heartwarming as ever, I see," Robin said, laughing. Then he frowned. "What do you mean, Happy New Year?"

"It's the tenth of January, mate," Henry told him. "Like I said, you've been out for a while now."

"The tenth of January?" Robin cried, staggered. "But…"

"No more questions," Karya said bossily. "First things first, put on some proper trousers. Those silly pyjamas are unsuitable for a serious conversation. I can't abide polka dots. And then second things second, come downstairs. There's a lot you need to talk about."

Karya would not be pressed further, and she ushered Woad and Henry out of the room as well.

Robin dressed as quickly as he could and made his way downstairs. Irene was waiting for him in the hall, her hands clasped patiently before her.

"Aunt Irene!" Robin almost ran down the steps. "You're alright? I mean, you're not stone anymore!"

"Indeed, my nephew," Irene smiled tightly, looking at him over the top of her half-moon glasses. She gestured to her study door as Robin reached the foot of the stairs. "I understand that you have only recently awoken and are probably still convalescing, but if you would feel up to it, there is much we need to discuss, my young ward."

Robin nodded, following his aunt into her rooms. She sat by the fire. Robin took a seat opposite her.

"Before we discuss recent events, Robin, there is something I must first do," the old woman looked very grim. She looked directly into his eyes.

"I need to apologise to you," she said.

Robin raised his eyebrows in surprise.

"I am truly sorry, Robin," Irene continued. "I am your guardian. My job, as the title implies, is to guard you. To offer you sanctuary and protection from those who mean you harm. I am ashamed to say it, but I have failed rather spectacularly in this duty."

Robin opened his mouth to protest but she silenced him with a raised hand.

"Indeed, were it not for your own ingenuity and resourcefulness, both myself and Mr Drover would still be a pair of rather unattractive statues gracing the main hallway. Although, I should add that at least we would be polished and cobweb free. Poor Hestia took very good care of our upkeep in your absence, after her own fashion. I'm not sure she knew what else to do with us." She smiled briefly. "Indeed, I can still taste beeswax polish every time I lick my lips."

"It wasn't your fault," Robin insisted. "Moros fooled all of us the same. No one knew that he wasn't really Phorbas."

Irene sighed, looking sad.

"I wouldn't have gotten anywhere without Woad and Karya," Robin confessed.

Irene looked at him for a long time, her face inscrutable. "Very well," she said at length. "You are a remarkable person, Robin Fellows."

She sat back in her chair, folding her hands in her lap neatly. "Now, I suppose you would like bringing up to date, as there is much that has happened since you took to your bed…"

Irene explained the events of the past few days, occasionally jabbing at the fire with a silver poker as she recounted everything that Robin had missed.

"Hestia was ... rather inconsolable when your friends explained the reason why Mr Phorbas was not with you," Irene said, frowning into the fire. "I feel rather terrible for her you know. She can be difficult, but she did not deserve to be used by someone like Moros."

Hestia had tended Robin's wounds. "She is a skilled herbalist," Irene said. "You were in good hands." She looked up from the crackling fire. "I am afraid you will carry the scars on your back for the rest of your life, Robin. But that is not always a bad thing. Better to have them to remind you, than not and to forget," she said. "Your friends were all most concerned for your wellbeing. And also, I think, a little in awe of you." She paused for a moment. "They told me what happened to you on the Isle of Winds."

She reached into a drawer in the table behind her and took out a small orb.

"The shard which had possessed you." It was round now and seemed to be made from deep blue glass flecked with streaks and whorls of white and silver. It looked for all the world like an expensive paperweight. Irene handed it gently to Robin.

"It appears to be quite inert ... for now," she said, and Robin handled it gently. No waves of power flowed from it. It felt slightly warmer than it should, but was otherwise utterly unremarkable.

"This is a shard of the Arcania, Robin," Irene said. "One of seven, which came into being when the Arcania itself was shattered. No one knows where the other six lie. It is one of the most powerful and dangerous objects in this world or the Netherworlde. And it is yours."

Robin stared at the globe. In its depths, the tiny flecks of white seemed to move.

He held it out to his aunt. "I'd like you to have it," he said.

She raised her eyebrows. The fire crackled in the hearth between them in the cosy study.

"I would be honoured to take stewardship of it for you, Robin," she said eventually, taking it back. "I shall keep it safe, until such time as you may need it."

Robin smiled. He felt oddly relieved. “Sounds good to me. I’m not ready for that kind of power.” He breathed out. “I’m not sure I ever will be.”

“All things in time, my young ward,” she replied. “Your temporarily amplified powers may have gone, but I expect you will find that your inherent skills in the Tower of Air will be somewhat stronger than they were previously.”

“Really?” Robin brightened up. His aunt nodded.

“I imagine your Galestrikes will carry more weight from now on.”

“I can’t wait to practise with—” Robin began, but stopped himself. He was about to say Phorbas. But, of course, Phorbas wasn’t there anymore. Phorbas had never been there.

Aunt Irene seemed to know exactly what Robin was thinking.

“I’m truly sorry about your tutor, Robin,” she said. “I knew Phorbas, the real Phorbas, for many years. I can attest that Moros’ impersonation was spot on. Phorbas was a remarkable satyr and a good friend.”

Robin glanced at the large writing desk behind Irene. Phorbas’ dagger lay there on the table’s surface, polished and gleaming.

“If Moros and Strife separated him, body and soul, he is not truly dead,” Irene said. “I know that it not much comfort to us. If only his body had not been lost, we could reunite them. But this way, at least his soul lives on within the dagger itself. It is yours now. He is still with us.”

Robin nodded, though he felt like a bowling ball had settled in his stomach.

“So what happens now?” he asked after a moment. After everything that had happened, his whole adventure in the Netherworlde, defeating Strife and Moros and gaining a shard of the Arcania, he was at a loss.

“Now?” his aunt cocked her head to one side. “Now we continue. We go on as before. You still have a lot to learn about the Netherworlde and the Towers of Magic. And you will need a new tutor of course. I shall look into the matter promptly. We shall continue your education. You have awakened a shard. The others will call out to you, and each other.” She stood up briskly. “I can, with some certainty, say that you are by far the most interesting nephew I have ever had.”

Robin stopped at the door on his way out of the room and turned. “Aunt Irene?” he said.

She looked up. “Yes, Robin?”

"There was one other thing I wanted to talk to you about," Robin said hesitantly. "The girl who brought me home, along with Woad and Henry…"

"Yes. The little wild-looking thing. She is a strange one, isn't she?" Irene said. "And more than she seems, that's for sure." She shook her head, clearing her thoughts. "But they are questions for me, not for you. What of her?"

"I think … I think she used to work for Eris," Robin said. "She told me, kind of. To be honest, it's hard to get a straight answer out of her at the best of times. But she ran away. She's been on the run for a long time and Eris has been trying really hard to get her back."

"I imagine so," his aunt said levelly. She was wearing what Robin had come to think of as her 'poker' expression.

"Well, it's just…" Robin pressed. "I was wondering if, I mean, I don't even know if she'd want to, but, maybe she could stay here with us … for a while?"

Irene looked at him silently for a moment. "Do you know what she is, Robin?" she asked.

"Not really," Robin said. "She's not fae or panthea, is she?"

"No … no she isn't," Irene replied.

"But I know she's a friend," Robin said firmly.

Irene nodded smiling. "And there," she said lightly as she closed the door. "You have your answer."

James lives in the North of England, close to wild moors and adjacent to a haunted wind farm, with his extremely patient and long-suffering family and a very old cat named Gargoyle. When the cat dies, James plans to buy a raven and name it Quoth. He is the author of the Changeling fantasy series, following the adventures of Robin, a seemingly unremarkable boy who is swept up into a war between our world, and the Netherworlde, a shadowy realm which lies beyond our own. In addition to fantasy, James also writes Science Fiction, Urban Gothic and Steampunk, for people old enough to know better.

35245672R00143

Made in the USA
San Bernardino, CA
18 June 2016